The Sugar Camp Quilt

An Elm Creek Quilts Novel

Jennifer Chiaverini

Simon & Schuster
New York · London · Toronto · Sydney

SIMON & SCHUSTER
Rockefeller Center
1230 Avenue of the Americas
New York, NY 10020

For information regarding special discounts for bulk purchases, please contact Simon & Schuster Special Sales at 1-800-456-6798 or business@simonandschuster.com

BOOK DESIGNED BY LAUREN SIMONETTI

ENDPAPER ILLUSTRATIONS BY MELANIE MARDER PARKS

Manufactured in the United States of America

10 9 8 7 6 5 4 3 2 1

Library of Congress Cataloging-in-Publication Data
Chiaverini, Jennifer.
The sugar camp quilt : an Elm Creek quilts novel / Jennifer Chiaverini.
p. cm.
1. Maple sugar industry—Fiction. 2.Women pioneers—Fiction. 3. Quiltmakers—Fiction. 5. Historical fiction. I. Title.
PS3553.H473S84 2005
813'.54—dc22   2004059043

ISBN 0-7432-6017-1

In memory of my father,
Nicholas Robert Neidenbach,
who left us too soon to read any of my books
but knew I would write them someday.

Acknowledgments

I am deeply grateful to Simon & Schuster and Witherspoon Associates for their ongoing support and for their tireless efforts on my behalf. I especially wish to thank Denise Roy, Maria Massie, and Rebecca Davis for their countless contributions to the Elm Creek Quilts novels through the years.

Many thanks to Lisa Cass and Jody Gomez, for caring for my boys so I could write, and to my dear friend Anne Spurgeon, for her careful reading of the manuscript, insightful suggestions, and historian's eye for detail.

I also wish to thank Tom McCrumm, Executive Director of the Massachusetts Maple Producers Association, for his gracious and informed responses to my questions about maple sugaring in the early 1800s.

Thank you to the friends and family who continue to support and encourage me, especially Geraldine Neidenbach, Heather Neidenbach, Nic Neidenbach, Virginia and Edward Riechman, and Leonard and Marlene Chiaverini.

Most of all, I am grateful to my husband, Marty, and my sons, Nicholas and Michael—and they know why.

The
Sugar Camp
Quilt

Chapter One
1849

"ABEL WRIGHT INTENDS to purchase his wife's freedom before the month is out," Dorothea's father said to Uncle Jacob.

"At long last," Dorothea's mother declared. "If Abel has raised the money he must do it quickly, before her owner can change his mind again. You will go with him, of course?"

Robert Granger nodded. They had spoken of this occasion often and had agreed that Robert ought to accompany Mr. Wright south to Virginia, both to share the work of driving the horses and to discourage unscrupulous interlopers. The abolitionist newspapers told of proslavery men who became so incensed at the sight of a newly freed slave that they would seize him and sell him back into slavery. Not even Mr. Wright was safe from their ilk, for all that he had never been a slave. If anything, enslaving him would bring them even greater pleasure.

Uncle Jacob's face bore the grim expression that Dorothea likened to a block of limestone. "You can't think of leaving in the middle of harvest."

"Abel needs to leave at sunup," Robert explained apologetically, as if humility would protect him from Uncle Jacob's wrath.

"Surely he can wait a few weeks until the crops are in."

"He said he can't. He'll go alone rather than wait for me."

"Then let him go alone," glowered Uncle Jacob. "Hasn't he done so often enough to sell that cheese of his?"

"This time is different," said Robert. "He will be exchanging a considerable amount of money for the person of his wife."

"Wright raises goats. He likely has more goats than corn on his place. He can afford to leave his farm during the harvest. We can't."

Dorothea waited for her uncle to announce yet another visit to his lawyer. The implication was, of course, that he intended to change his will, and not in favor of his only living relatives. Dorothea waited, but Uncle Jacob said nothing more until mealtime gave way to evening chores. As they cleared the table, Dorothea's mother remarked that Uncle Jacob had not expressly forbidden Robert to go, which in his case was almost the same as giving his blessing.

"According to that logic," Dorothea replied, "if I tell my pupils not to put a bent pin on my chair, what I really mean is that I would prefer a nail."

"Your pupils have far too much affection for you to do either," said Lorena, deliberately missing the point. They both knew she was putting her brother's obvious disapproval in a better light than it deserved. Dorothea knew her uncle would have expressly forbidden the journey for anyone but Abel Wright. Uncle Jacob had no friends, but he respected Mr. Wright for his independence, thrift, and industriousness, qualities he would have admired in himself if doing so would not have occasioned the sin of vanity.

Uncle Jacob had never declared whether he was for or against slavery, at least not in Dorothea's presence. According to Lorena, Uncle Jacob's long-deceased wife had been a Quaker and a passionate abolitionist, but he never spoke of her and Dorothea had no idea whether he shared her views. Still, she suspected her uncle's objections to the journey had nothing to do with his moral position on the subject of slavery and everything to do with the pragmatics of farming. Despite Mr. Wright's reasonable urgency to free his wife from bondage, Uncle Jacob likely could not comprehend how a sensible farmer could take off on any errand when the most important work of the year needed to be done. Of course, Uncle Jacob knew all too well that his sister's husband was *not* a sensible farmer. If he had been, Uncle Jacob would not have been obligated by the ties of family and Christian charity to take in his sister's family after they lost their own farm.

Later that night, Dorothea asked her father if she might accompany them, but her father said this particular errand was too dangerous for a girl of nineteen.

"But Mr. Wright has made the trip so many times," protested Dorothea.

"You are needed at home," said Uncle Jacob. "Already I will have to hire hands to make up for your father's absence. I will not hire kitchen help, too."

Even without Lorena's look of warning, Dorothea knew better than to protest. Her uncle had not even looked up from his Bible as he spoke, but any interruption of his nightly devotion was unusual enough to reveal the strength of his feeling on the subject.

Robert left for the Wright farm as soon as the sky had lightened enough for safe travel. Though the sun had not yet risen, Uncle Jacob was already at work in the barn, but he did not break away from his chores to wish his brother-in-law a safe journey. Lorena had packed the horse's rucksacks with so much food that they strained at the seams, and Robert thanked his wife for providing enough to eat for a month of sightseeing. Mother and daughter smiled at his joke, for they knew he intended to make the journey as swiftly as possible. They kissed him and made him promise to take care, then followed him down to the Creek's Crossing road, where they stood and watched until horse and rider disappeared into the cool, graying mists that clung to the hills south of the farm.

When they could no longer see him, Lorena glared at the barn and said, "See how little he cares for us. He might never see my husband again, and yet he cannot even stir from the barn to bid him farewell."

Dorothea's heart quaked at her mother's ominous words, but said, "Likely Uncle Jacob knows how little we care for him and feels no need to make any pretense of fondness. Likely, too, he knows Father will certainly return."

Immediately Lorena was all reassurance. "Of course, my dear. Of course your father will return. Perhaps earlier than we expect him. Mr. Wright will not want to linger in the hostile South." She frowned at the barn. "If I would not miss him so, I would ask your father to take his time just to spite your uncle."

Dorothea smiled, knowing her mother would never wish for anything that would part her from her husband. Dorothea knew, too, that her mother often spoke wistfully of small acts of disobedience none of them dared commit. They were beholden to Uncle Jacob and must not commit any transgression that might tempt him to send them away. Uncle Jacob had no wife and no children, and therefore, no heir save his nephew, Dorothea's younger brother. If they served Uncle Jacob well and bided their time, one day Uncle Jacob's 120 acres, house, and worldly goods would belong to Jonathan.

For five years her parents had clung to these hopes with almost as much fervor as they pursued the abolition of slavery. They rarely seemed troubled by the doubts that plagued Dorothea. Uncle Jacob might marry again. He was older than her mother but even older men had taken young brides, although Dorothea could name no young woman of Creek's Crossing whose prospects were so poor she should settle on a stern, gray-haired, humorless man who had ample property but eschewed anything that hinted of romance. If he had once had a heart, he had buried it in the maple grove with his young bride and twin sons long before Dorothea was born.

Sometimes Dorothea suspected her parents were not entirely certain Jonathan would succeed in inheriting his uncle's farm. From an early age they had fostered his interest in medicine, and for the past two years he had served as an apprentice to an old family friend, a physician in far-off Baltimore. Jonathan had learned enough about farming to earn Uncle Jacob's grudging acceptance during his infrequent visits home, but he made no overt attempts to win his potential benefactor's affection. Dorothea wondered if his assured success in the vocation of his choosing had made him indifferent to the inheritance the rest of his family relied upon.

Either way, Jonathan surely would have been permitted to accompany their father and Mr. Wright south to Virginia. Though he was three years younger than Dorothea, he was a boy. Dorothea felt herself restricted and confined every minute she spent beneath Uncle Jacob's roof, even when he himself was not in the house. Her only moments of ease came as she walked to and from the schoolhouse on Third Street where she taught twenty youngsters reading, arithmetic, natural sciences, and history. When she felt the wind against her face as she crossed Elm Creek on the ferry, she feared that this was as close as she would ever come to knowing the freedom Jonathan took for granted.

At noon, Uncle Jacob and the hired hands came inside to eat. There was little conversation as Dorothea and her mother served; the men, whom Dorothea knew to be lively enough in other company, were uncomfortably subdued under Uncle Jacob's critical eye. It was well known in Creek's Crossing that he had once fired a man for taking the Lord's name in vain when a horse kicked him, breaking his jaw. Dorothea did not care for rough language, either, but even she could concede the injured man had had cause.

The men had seconds and thirds, clearing the platters of corn, baked squash, and shoofly pie as quickly as Dorothea and her mother could place them on the table. The other men quietly praised

Lorena's cooking, but Uncle Jacob did not address her until after he finished his meal, and only to state that Robert's absence had hurt them badly. As they did every year, the Creek's Crossing Agricultural Society had arranged for a team from Harrisburg to bring a horse-powered thresher into the Elm Creek Valley. Every farmer of sufficient means paid for a share of days with the machine, and Uncle Jacob's turn was fast approaching. Robert had left before the oats and wheat could be cut and stacked, and if Uncle Jacob did not finish in time, the threshers could not wait for him. He had no choice but to go into Creek's Crossing and hire more men.

Dorothea and her mother exchanged a hopeful look. "May we accompany you?" Lorena asked. "Dorothea and I have many errands we were saving for a ride into town."

"I have no time to waste on your errands," said Uncle Jacob, pushing back his chair, "and your time is better spent on your chores."

The hired men recognized the signal to leave and bolted the rest of their food. One man quickly pocketed the heel of the bread loaf, while another hastily downed a generous slice of pie in two bites.

"What errands?" asked Dorothea as the men returned to the fields.

"I would have invented some for the chance to go into Creek's Crossing." Lorena sighed and began fixing a plate for herself, motioning for her daughter to do the same. "It has been three weeks. We might as well live a hundred miles from the nearest village."

"If Uncle Jacob goes on horseback, we could take the wagon."

Lorena shook her head. "Chances are we would run into him in town if not on the ferry. Even if we managed to avoid him, he would discover our incomplete chores upon his return."

"No two mere mortal women could finish all he has assigned us." Briskly Dorothea scraped the remnants of her uncle's meal into the slop bucket for the pigs. "He cannot be satisfied. He knows you and Father are merely waiting for him to die so that Jonathan may have the farm, and he is determined to thwart our every attempt at happiness until then."

"Dorothea." Lorena laid her hand on her daughter's arm. "Clearing can wait. Eat something. We have a long day yet ahead of us."

Rather than argue, Dorothea complied, although the ravenous men had left little for the women to share. She resented her uncle for his power over them, but her parents' morbid anticipation shamed her. She remembered a time when they would not have been content to live at the whim of another. Perhaps they had been too idealistic in those days, but at least they had insisted upon setting the course of their own lives.

DOROTHEA AND HER MOTHER could not have stolen into town in the wagon after all, because Uncle Jacob took it. Three hours after his departure, Dorothea heard the wagon coming up the road. She stopped scattering chicken feed and straightened, shading her eyes with one hand. What she saw made her want to duck behind the hen house and hide.

Her mother had also paused at the sound of the wagon. "It couldn't be," said her mother, with a soft moan of dismay. "Not Amos Liggett."

"I wish it were anyone else." Dorothea watched as the wagon brought the gangly, round-shouldered man closer. His red face was beaming with jovial pride behind greasy, unkempt whiskers. Uncle Jacob drove the horses stoically, apparently oblivious to his companion's chatter. "I can almost smell the liquor on him from here."

"Dorothea," her mother said reprovingly.

"You don't like him any more than I do." For that matter, Uncle Jacob despised him. Every winter Mr. Liggett asked Uncle Jacob to exchange work with him at sugaring time, a request Uncle Jacob always refused. "I don't want that blasted fool to set one foot inside my sugar camp," he had grumbled the previous winter, after Mr. Liggett had cornered him in church before Christmas services to plead his case yet again. "He's more likely to overturn the kettle and tap an oak than to give me a penny's worth of real help." There must have been no one else in all of Creek's Crossing to hire, or her uncle never would have brought Amos Liggett home.

Mr. Liggett offered the women a gap-toothed grin as the wagon rumbled past. Dorothea and her mother nodded politely, but quickly averted their eyes. "Stay clear of him," her mother cautioned, as if Dorothea needed the warning.

Mr. Liggett had brought his own scythe, an implement Dorothea surmised must be as sharp as the day he purchased it, given his inattention to his own fields. Uncle Jacob put him to work cutting oats with the others. Throughout the afternoon, as Dorothea passed from the garden to the kitchen where she and her mother were pickling cabbage and beets, she glimpsed him at work, swinging his blade with awkward eagerness, with none of the practiced, muscular grace of the other men. More often than not, he was at rest, his scythe nowhere to be seen, probably lying on the ground. The blade would not keep its shine for long.

At sundown, the men washed at the pump and trooped wearily inside for supper, smelling of sweat and grass and fatigue. Uncle Jacob offered Mr. Liggett the loan of a horse so that he might return to his own home for the night—an uncharacteristic display of trust and generosity that astonished the women—but Mr. Liggett declined, saying he would spend the night in the hayloft quarters with the others. Then he said, "Before we retire, I surely would like to get a look at that sugar camp of yours."

Uncle Jacob frowned. "For what reason?"

"Because everyone knows you make the best maple sugar in the county." Mr. Liggett let out a cackle. "And you never let anyone near your sugar camp. I know folks who'd pay good money to know your secret."

"I have no sugar-making secrets to share," replied Uncle Jacob.

Mr. Liggett chuckled and waited for him to continue, but when Uncle Jacob said nothing, his grin faded. He had thought Uncle Jacob spoke in jest, which, of course, he never did. Dorothea doubted Mr. Liggett had noted her uncle's careful choice of words. He did indeed have sugar-making secrets, but he had no intention of sharing them with Mr. Liggett.

"Perhaps you burn the syrup," suggested Lorena as she offered Mr. Liggett more mashed turnips. "It must be watched and stirred constantly or it will be ruined."

"I can't stand in front of a kettle all day," said Mr. Liggett, scowling. Then he brightened. "Say, Jacob, how about we trade work this winter? I'll help you with your sugaring, and you can help me."

"Thank you, but my family will provide all the help I need."

With that, Uncle Jacob excused himself and retired to the parlor. Mr. Liggett resumed eating, glancing hopefully at the doorway now and again as if expecting Uncle Jacob to appear and beckon him within. But Dorothea knew her uncle was by now well engrossed in his Bible, and he would not have invited Mr. Liggett to join him in the house's best room in any event.

AT BREAKFAST, MR. LIGGETT spoke to the merits of various woods for producing steady flame, as well as the skill of local blacksmiths in producing cast-iron kettles of size and durability. When his hints about visiting the sugar camp became too obvious to ignore, Uncle Jacob said that too much work remained for them to consider indulging in idleness.

Dorothea was relieved when the men left the breakfast table for the fields, and in the two days that followed, she learned to dread mealtimes. When Mr. Liggett was not querying her uncle he was grinning at her, casting his gaze up and down her person with shameless appreciation, as if his sour smell alone were not enough to turn her stomach. Lorena kept her out of his sight as much as she could and never left them alone together, but once he came upon her unaccompanied in the washhouse. He complimented her dress and had just asked if she might like to go riding some Sunday after he had his horse breeding business going when Uncle Jacob rounded the corner and fixed them with an icy glare. Mr. Liggett muttered excuses and slunk away, while Dorothea stood rooted to the spot until her uncle ordered her back to the house. She left the laundry in the washtub and obeyed, shaking with anger, her cheeks ablaze as if she had earned the accusation in her uncle's eyes. She wished her father would hurry home so that Mr. Liggett would no longer be needed.

Her father had been gone one week on the morning Mr. Liggett did not come to breakfast. Uncle Jacob ordered one of the hired hands back to the barn to rouse him from his sleep, only to learn that Mr. Liggett had been gone all night. "He left right after sundown," the hired man said. "He told us he desired to slake his thirst."

"Perhaps he fell into the well," said Lorena. Uncle Jacob sent a man to check, but when he found no sign of any mishap, Uncle Jacob told Lorena to serve the meal. His expression grew more stern as they ate in silence, listening for Mr. Liggett's approach.

He did not come. The other men went to the fields to cut the last two acres of wheat, looking to the sky as a low rumble of thunder sounded in the far distance. There were few clouds overhead, but the air was heavy and damp, and Dorothea knew they must hasten before rain pelted the heavy shafts of ripe wheat, dashing the grains to the earth, ruining the crop.

She was gathering carrots in the garden when Mr. Liggett returned, shuffling his feet in the dirt on his way to the barn. "Pray tell, Miss," he addressed her, with slurred, exaggerated formality. "Where might I find the master of this establishment?"

"My uncle is cutting wheat with the others."

He made a mocking bow and headed for the fields. Dorothea watched him as she worked. When Mr. Liggett reached the men, Uncle Jacob rested on his scythe, mopped his brow, and said something low and abrupt to the latecomer before raising his scythe again. Mr. Liggett took his hat from his head and fidgeted as he tried to explain, but Uncle Jacob did not appear to respond. After a moment, Mr. Liggett slammed his hat back on his head and hurried to the barn for his scythe, muttering angrily to himself. Dorothea had never seen him move so quickly, though he stumbled and once nearly fell sprawling to the ground.

At midday, through the kitchen window, Dorothea overheard the hired hands talking as they washed up at the pump. "Have to run home to care for your livestock, Liggett?"

Dorothea recognized the teasing drawl of the youngest of the men, a former classmate named Charley Stokey.

"Never you mind," snapped Mr. Liggett as the other men guffawed. It was well known that Mr. Liggett owned only one scrawny mare and a few chickens, for all that he boasted of one day raising prize racehorses.

"No, he was tending to his vast acreage," said another, evoking more laughter. Mr. Liggett was forever bragging about the improvements he planned for his farm, though he rarely would lay hand to plow or hammer. Though he owned forty of the valley's finest acres, he had let all but a few run wild.

"I know more about running a farm than you fools ever will," said Mr. Liggett. "My people own one of the richest plantations in Georgia."

"Then why aren't you down there helping them tend it?" Charley inquired.

Another man answered before Mr. Liggett could. "His people don't care for him any more than anyone else."

Over the laughter, Mr. Liggett said, "I'm telling you, it's one of the richest and the biggest. When I was a boy I could climb on my horse at sunup at the eastern edge of the plantation, ride west all day, and still be on my grandfather's property at sundown."

"I had a horse like that once," remarked Charley. "We named him Snail."

The men burst out laughing, and a moment later, Mr. Liggett swung open the kitchen door with a bang and stormed over to the table. "Are you going to feed us or let us starve?" he barked at Lorena.

She regarded him evenly. "We're waiting for my brother. He will be in shortly."

Uncle Jacob had come in from the fields ahead of the others in order to work on his ledgers. He entered the kitchen just as Lorena finished speaking and took his seat at the head of the table with a stern look for Mr. Liggett. Mr. Liggett dropped his gaze and tore a chunk from the loaf of bread.

The men ate swiftly, mindful of the threatening rain. The wind had picked up; the low growls of thunder in the distance had grown louder and more frequent. Dorothea wondered where her father was and hoped he was well out of the storm's path.

Not long after Uncle Jacob and the men returned outside, Dorothea heard a furious shout from the direction of the wheat field, followed by a string of curses.

"What on earth?" gasped Lorena as she and Dorothea hurried outside. Two of the hired men were heading for the house support-ing Charley between them, his face covered in blood. Behind them, Uncle Jacob stood before Mr. Liggett, palms raised in a calming gesture. Mr. Liggett quivered and tightened his grip on his scythe. The blade was stained red.

"Put it down, Liggett," commanded Uncle Jacob.

"I didn't mean to," shrilled Mr. Liggett as the women ran to help Charley. "He got in the way. He came up behind me."

Uncle Jacob again ordered him to put down his scythe, but whether he obeyed, Dorothea could no longer watch to see. Charley was moaning and scrubbing blood from his eyes as Lorena and Dorothea lowered him to the ground. Lorena tore off her apron and sopped up the blood. "I cannot tell where he was struck," she murmured to her daughter. "There is too much blood."

Dorothea, Charley's head resting on her lap, snatched off her own apron and dabbed at his face. Distantly, she heard the voices of Uncle Jacob and Mr. Liggett coming nearer. "Here," she said, pointing, as blood seeped from a long gash along Charley's hairline.

"Is it bad?" one of the men asked.

"It is not as bad as it could have been," said Lorena, a tremble in her voice as she pressed the cloth to the wound. Charley flinched, but Dorothea held him firmly. "Nor as bad as it seems. It is not deep, but cuts on the scalp bleed profusely. Dorothea, run inside and fetch my herbs and plasters."

Charley let out a yelp, and as Dorothea set him down gently and ran for the house, she heard one of the hired hands ask Lorena if they ought to give Charley a strong drink to ease the shock and the pain. He might not know that Uncle Jacob permitted no liquor on his farm.

"Squeeze Liggett, and you'll get a pint," the other hired man said darkly.

Dorothea returned minutes later in time to see Uncle Jacob, the bloody scythe in his hand, order Mr. Liggett off his property. "It's bad enough that you were too drunk to find your way back last night," said Uncle Jacob. "It's far worse that your drunkenness could have killed a man today."

He waved Mr. Liggett off, gesturing toward the road. When Mr. Liggett realized that Uncle Jacob meant for him to walk home, he said, "What about my scythe? And my pay?"

"I'll deliver your scythe to you tomorrow. As for your pay, consider it forfeit."

Mr. Liggett flushed. "But I worked six full days for you. You owe me for six days."

"You worked five and a half days. Bearing in mind what has happened here today, considering that the work is not finished, and that you have cost me Mr. Stokey's labor as well as your own, you are fortunate I am willing to let you go without calling in the law."

"I want what's owed me."

"I'll give him what's owed him," said Charley weakly, lying on the ground as Lorena threaded a needle beside him.

"You," jeered Mr. Liggett, but he took a step backward, then turned and broke into a trot.

"It was only a glancing blow," said Lorena when Mr. Liggett was out of earshot, with an inscrutable look for her brother, which turned into a glance to the sky as thunder pealed overhead. "Help me get him up. This is better finished inside."

The cloudburst soaked them before they could reach shelter indoors. As the furious rain battered the ground, Uncle Jacob glowered out the window in the direction of the wheat fields.

The threshers would not arrive for two more days, but they had done all they could. They had lost the last acre of wheat to the storm.

THE NEXT MORNING, UNCLE Jacob paid the hired hands and agreed that Lorena could drive them back into town, and that Dorothea could assist her with her errands. When Lorena suggested they deliver Mr. Liggett's scythe to him, Uncle Jacob snorted and told them to spare the horse a few miles and leave it at the tavern. Dorothea had her doubts, but when Mr. Schultz readily agreed to hold the scythe for Mr. Liggett, she acknowledged that perhaps Mr. Liggett did indeed spend more time at the tavern than within the crude log walls of his cabin home.

Afterward, Lorena stopped the wagon in front of the general store, and as she shopped for coffee and sugar, Dorothea fingered the yard goods and thought wistfully of the dressmaker's shop across the street.

"Dorothea," a woman called from behind her. "Dorothea, dear, did you hear the news?"

Dorothea turned to her greeter, the mistress of the farm directly to the north of Uncle Jacob's property. One stout arm was linked with that of her young daughter, a beautiful dark-haired girl not yet fourteen years old. Their simple calico dresses belied the prosperity of their farm.

"Good afternoon, Mrs. Claverton," said Dorothea, and smiled at the girl. "Hello, Charlotte."

Charlotte returned her greeting softly, smiling but with eyes cast down shyly.

"Did you hear the news, dear?" repeated Mrs. Claverton eagerly. "Creek's Crossing has acquired a prominent new resident."

"Yes, I know," said Dorothea. "My father is traveling with Mr. Wright to bring her home."

"What?" For a moment confusion clouded Mrs. Claverton's face. "No, no, dear. Good heavens. Not the Wright girl. Mr. Nelson. The young Mr. Nelson is coming to take possession of Two Bears Farm."

"I had no idea the Carters intended to leave." They had been the Nelson family's tenants so long that few people in town remembered the farm's true owners. Dorothea herself had never met them.

"As I hear it, they had no such intentions." Mrs. Claverton lowered her voice in confidence. "The young Mr. Nelson forced them out."

"Forced them?" Dorothea echoed. "He sounds very unlike his father. The Carters always referred to him as a generous man."

"He was. And still would be, I suspect, if his son had not driven him to such ends."

Intrigued, Dorothea glanced at her mother, safely out of earshot on the other side of the store. Lorena disapproved of gossip. "What ends? This sounds dire."

"By all accounts Thomas Nelson did not inherit his father's strength of character. I have it on very good authority that he comes to Creek's Crossing almost directly by way of prison."

"Prison," exclaimed Dorothea.

Mrs. Claverton shushed her and lowered her voice to a whisper. "He says that he has been suffering ill health, and that his father sent him out here to manage Two Bears Farm while regaining his strength in our milder climate. What he does not say is that the depravities of prison caused his illness, and that his father banished him here, where his shame is unknown."

"It will not be unknown for long," said Dorothea, amused.

"I don't doubt it, although if he wanted to avoid being the subject of gossip, he should have lived more virtuously. Unfortunately, many members of society will welcome him for his father's sake, regardless of his past, and we can hardly shun him after that." She shook her head. "I confess I have some misgivings about exposing my daughter to such an influence, but as he will be charged with the education of our youth—"

"What?"

"Mama," warned Charlotte, too late.

"Oh, my dear," said Mrs. Claverton, dismayed. "I certainly did not mean for you to find out this way. The school board has written you a letter."

"Mr. Nelson is to be the new schoolmaster?"

Mrs. Claverton nodded. "After all, his father did donate the land and the funds to build the school. When he wrote to request a position for his son, well, the school board couldn't refuse him, could they?"

"Apparently they could not, since it would seem the decision has already been made."

"Now, Dorothea." Mrs. Claverton patted her hand. "Don't be angry. You do remember you were hired as the interim schoolteacher only. You may have been the brightest pupil in the Creek's Crossing school, but before his more recent troubles, Mr. Nelson attended university."

"Did he? Then if he is a felon, at least he is an educated felon."

"Mr. Nelson's minister assures us he has repented his crimes and that he has been entirely rehabilitated," said Mrs. Claverton. "If we withhold from him the opportunity to contribute to society, he may never be able to atone for his misdeeds. You are a properly brought-up girl; you shouldn't need me to remind you of these things. You must drive your poor mother to distraction. You should look beyond your own apparent misfortune and find the opportunity."

"I completed the Creek's Crossing school years ago," Dorothea reminded her. "Even if Mr. Nelson were qualified to teach at a secondary academy, I cannot imagine what education I should care to receive from him."

"I was not speaking of your education. Did I mention that Mr. Nelson is unmarried?"

Dorothea could not help laughing. "Mrs. Claverton, did you not just inform me that Mr. Nelson is a former convict?"

"But a repentant one from a good family," she retorted. "And, I might remind you, he is an educated man with a prosperous farm. Why, if my Charlotte was not already promised to your brother, I might consider Mr. Nelson for her."

The girl started, setting her two ribbon-tied braids swinging down her back.

"She didn't mean it," Dorothea assured Charlotte.

"No, indeed, I did not." Mrs. Claverton gave her daughter a quick hug. "Well. It is plain to see young Mr. Nelson has already upset us. I cannot imagine what will happen when we are finally forced to meet him."

ON THE WAY HOME, Dorothea told her mother about the arrival of Mr. Nelson only to discover that she already knew. She had learned from the shopkeeper, who was also the mayor, that there would be a party in Mr. Nelson's honor on Sunday afternoon at the home of the school board president.

Dorothea wondered if the shopkeeper had mentioned the rumors circling the guest of honor. "I would rather not attend."

Mother regarded her, eyebrows raised. "You would prefer to stay home with your Uncle Jacob?"

Dorothea said nothing.

"It is a pity you lost your position so close to the start of the new term, and after you spent all summer preparing your lessons," said her mother. "But you mustn't sulk. You did a fine job and will receive a good reference from the school board. You will find something else."

"Perhaps it is Mr. Nelson who ought to find something else."

Her mother said nothing, the silence broken only by the sound of the horse's hooves striking the hard-packed dirt road. "Your father and I wish we could afford to further your education, but since we cannot, you must make the best of it. You need not set your heart on the women's academy in Philadelphia when you have a library full of books at home. Look to books and nature for your teachers. You shall learn more from them than in any classroom."

Dorothea nodded, although she did not entirely agree. She had read all of the books in her parents' modest library at least twice, even the dullest collection of essays. As for learning from nature, for most of her first twelve years she had explored the forest and fields of the Elm Creek Valley until she had learned them by heart. She knew every bend of Elm Creek, every type of tree that grew along its banks. A woman of Shawnee heritage who had lived at Thrift Farm for a time had taught her the lore of local herbs and roots. She knew which leaves to brew into a tea to ease the pain of toothache and where to scrape the bark of a tree for a poultice to reduce the inflammation of wounds. Jonathan had abandoned this knowledge as soon as he left to study real medicine, but it was all Dorothea had and she cherished it.

When Uncle Jacob declared that it was unseemly for a girl her age to wander about in the wilderness without an escort, her heart constricted in grief, but she resolved to learn as much as she could within the confines of her uncle's farm. Indeed, she did learn much from her uncle about the raising of crops and the husbandry of animals, but she mourned the loss of everything she would never learn. She tried not to envy her brother and told herself the people of Creek's Crossing were fortunate that books and nature alone were not considered adequate teachers for a future physician.

When she was the schoolteacher, Uncle Jacob had claimed half her wages, but Dorothea had saved every penny of what remained. Even that was not enough for one semester's tuition at the women's academy. Dorothea shook her head and told her mother, "If I do not have enough education to teach the pupils of Creek's Crossing, where people know me and have confidence in me, I cannot see how any other school would have me."

"Then you cannot see far enough."

Dorothea frowned at her quizzically, but her mother looked

beyond her. "Look," she said, nodding to the pasture. "Father is home."

Dorothea heard the clanging of a cowbell and quickly spotted her father driving in the two Guernseys and the calf. He waved his hat and shouted something, but the breeze carried his voice away.

"He's home a day early," exclaimed Dorothea.

"Yes, and already your uncle has him working. We lingered in town longer than we should have if he has had time to begin your chores as well as his own." Dorothea's mother chirruped to the horse and shook the reins to quicken his pace. "Your uncle will be stomping around the fields like an old bear, wondering why I have not started his supper."

"If we hurry, perhaps he won't see us. He won't know when we arrived."

"Deception by an omission of the truth is as bad as a lie," her mother chided, but mildly. Dorothea was expected to speak respectfully of her elders, but her parents often made an exception for Uncle Jacob if no one but themselves were around to hear.

It was not for Uncle Jacob that her mother hurried to the barn, Dorothea knew. Her father met them there, and her parents greeted each other with a warm embrace and a discreet kiss Dorothea pretended not to observe. When her father removed his hat, she saw he was sunburned beneath his thinning blond hair. He was slender, although years of farm labor had added muscle to his frame, and he was scarcely as tall as his wife.

"Tell us about your trip, Father. Please," she remembered to add, hungry for news of the world beyond the valley. "Did Constance's master change his mind again? Did you have to elude slavecatchers?"

Father smiled, but his eyes showed the strain of hard travel and little sleep. "No, Dorothea. You would have found our journey dull. We reached Virginia, paid the plantation owner the ransom he demanded, and were on our way. It was all very civilized, like any business transaction." His voice was so mild no one but Dorothea and her mother would have detected his disgust. "Mrs. Wright carried all she possessed wrapped in one small quilt, so it took us only minutes to load the wagon. We left as soon as the horses were rested and stayed one night at the home of a sympathetic friend an hour's ride north."

"How is Mrs. Wright settling in?" asked Mother. "What a poor wedding party awaited the bride and groom. I wish we could have prepared a meal for them, but I was not certain when you would return."

"They're happy just to be north and home. They weren't expecting a party. On our way south, we pushed the horses as hard as we could without ruining them." He glanced at Mother and unhitched the horse. "We arrived a day earlier, but none too soon. A few days more . . ." He shrugged and led the horse away.

Mother turned toward the house and Dorothea fell in step beside her. "What did he mean, a few days more?" she asked.

Mother was silent for a moment, as if considering how much to say. "The last time Mr. Wright visited Constance, other slaves warned him of rumors that Constance's master wished to increase his number of slaves."

"He intends to buy more?"

"No," said her mother carefully as they entered the house through the kitchen door. "He does not mean to buy them."

A moment passed before Dorothea understood. "I see."

"The indignity of having his wife taken by another man—that, Mr. Wright could bear. If Constance could endure it, he certainly could, and they have had to throughout the two years of their marriage. Her owner is a greedy, spiteful man. He only turned his attentions to Constance after she married Mr. Wright, to punish her for marrying and, I suppose, to punish Mr. Wright for being born free in the north. Mr. Wright had to obtain Constance's freedom before she became pregnant. Her owner would not have allowed her to leave until after her child was born and weaned, if he did not change his mind entirely. There was also no guarantee he would have parted with the child, or sold him to the Wrights rather than another slave owner."

"Even if the child had been Mr. Wright's?"

"Even then. And I'm sure I don't need to remind you never to mention this to the Wrights, or anyone else, for that matter. They have enough to bear without adding the embarrassment of gossip regarding how Mrs. Wright has been violated."

Dorothea nodded, her heart going out to the Wrights as she imagined what they had suffered, and the certain anguish they had narrowly escaped.

With Dorothea's help, her mother finished cooking supper with moments to spare. Dorothea was setting the table when they heard Uncle Jacob working the pump handle outside as he washed up for the meal. Dorothea did not look up at the sound of two heavy footsteps on the wooden floor, the sound of the kitchen door closing behind him, and a pause while he removed his boots. She greeted him in a murmur as he pulled back his chair and seated himself; he replied with a nod. Like his sister, Uncle Jacob was thin and tall, but where Lorena was dark he was gray-haired, down to the scruff of beard he shaved off every Saturday night. The hollows in his cheeks were a darker gray; they might have been dimples except he never smiled.

He had not always been so grim, Lorena had confided to Dorothea not long after they came to live with him. As a boy he had been proud and pious, but lighthearted. He had won the affection of the most beautiful girl in the valley and had been the envy of all his friends. His farm had prospered; his wife bore him two fine, strong sons. Then scarlet fever swept through Creek's Crossing. Uncle

Jacob thought they would be safe, isolated on their farm, away from the contagion of the town, but his wife insisted on returning to nurse her stricken parents. She fell ill soon after her parents died, and against his better judgment, Uncle Jacob brought her home to care for her. Lorena offered to take the children to Thrift Farm, but Uncle Jacob thought the sight of her children would encourage his wife to fight off the illness.

Uncle Jacob did not tell his wife when her precious babies died, and to the end, he soothed her with lies about how they grew stronger every day, how they were playing outside or sleeping when she begged to see them. When she died, Uncle Jacob nearly went mad with grief. He would let no one into the house to attend to the bodies. He chased the minister off with his rifle. Only Lorena was permitted to enter, and he sat in his chair by the window, face buried in his hands, responding numbly when Lorena asked him what his wife and children should wear, where he would like them to be laid to rest. He picked a clearing in the maple grove and dug the graves alone, rebuffing Robert's offers of help.

After a time he regained himself and resumed the work of the farm. He rid the house of all relics of the woman and children he had loved. At first Lorena assumed he would marry again, but his heart had scarred over and would permit no more joy within it. He never again smiled, or laughed, or showed any sign that life was anything more than a burden to be endured. His Bible was his only consolation. The two decisions he had made with his heart rather than his head had cost him all that he held dear in this life, and he would not make that mistake again.

Outside the pump clanged and gushed as Dorothea's father raced through his washing. He joined them, breathless, just as Lorena began to place serving dishes on the table—boiled turnips, sweet corn, stewed greens, bread from the previous day's baking. Uncle Jacob waited for them to be seated before leading them in prayer. Wordlessly, he served himself a heaping spoonful of turnips and passed the dish to Robert on his left, repeating with each of Lorena's dishes in turn. He spoke only to ask for butter for his bread; at a glance from her mother, Dorothea hurried to fetch it from the cool of the cellar.

By the time she returned, Uncle Jacob had sated his hunger enough to engage her father in a discussion about the crops. The threshers had sent a man over early that day to report that they would arrive the next morning, as scheduled. "We lost an acre of wheat because of you," said Uncle Jacob. "Why you could not have waited another week for your trip down South is beyond me. We'll need to work day and night to make up for the time you wasted."

"Except for Sunday afternoon," said Dorothea's mother. "There is a social in town to welcome Mr. Thomas Nelson, and we are expected."

"A social?" Uncle Jacob shook his head. "What fool planned a social for the middle of harvest?"

"The mayor, I believe. And the school board."

"What nonsense. No one will attend, not at this time of year. Likely not even Thomas Nelson would care to interrupt his harvest chores for a silly party. If we want to be good neighbors, we should leave him in peace to finish his work."

"We must have some representative of the family present," said Robert. "Dorothea, at least, ought to meet with Mr. Nelson, as he is to take over as schoolmaster."

Uncle Jacob looked Dorothea squarely in the eye. "You said nothing of being replaced."

"I learned of it only today."

"Your wages will be sorely missed." Uncle Jacob took a bite of greens and chewed slowly, thinking. "Very well. Dorothea must go, and since she cannot go unescorted, you two must accompany her. Fortunately, I see nothing requiring my presence." He regarded

Dorothea again. "Do you think you can be gracious to this man who is taking your situation when he likely has no real need of it?"

Surprised, Dorothea said, "I believe I can manage to be civil."

"Then it's settled. I'm sure you won't do anything to shame this family." Uncle Jacob wiped his lips, set his fork and knife neatly on the edge of his plate, and pushed back his chair. "You worked hard as you always do, Dorothea, but they made their choice and it can't be helped. Robert, join me in the barn when you're through."

With that, he left.

As soon as the kitchen door swung shut behind him, Robert quietly said, "If I didn't know better, I'd say that was an expression of sympathy."

"He regrets only the loss of her wages." Lorena began clearing the table. Dorothea quickly shook off her astonishment and rose to help.

TWO DAYS LATER, DOROTHEA put on her best dress and rode with her parents to the home of Mr. and Mrs. Hiram Engle. None of the Grangers had called upon the couple since their marriage six months before, a slight somewhat excused by the fact that they had not been invited. Mr. Engle owned the livery stable and the only hotel in town. Until the former Mrs. Violet Pearson had ensnared his affection a year after her first husband died, Mr. Engle's prosperity had rendered him a highly desirable bachelor despite his facial tic and ample waistline. Uncle Jacob spoke approvingly of Mr. Engle's business acumen, but Dorothea's parents did not care for his politics and avoided spending too much time in his company.

Mr. Engle had offered his livery stable for guests traveling from outlying farms, and from there it was a short walk from the riverfront to the more fashionable street in the center of town. It was not the oldest block; the more modest, wood-frame buildings along Elm Creek were the first to be built when the village that became Creek's Crossing was settled, but as their owners prospered, they moved their families to more spacious limestone dwellings farther away.

The Engles had hired several servants and a quartet of musicians for the occasion, and as one servant took their wraps, Dorothea glanced through an open doorway and saw that what was presumably the parlor had been all but emptied of furniture to make room for dancing. Several couples danced merrily to a popular schottische, but when Dorothea's father headed in that direction, her mother took his elbow and steered him toward the publisher of the local newspaper, no doubt to prevail upon him to write another editorial denouncing slavery or supporting woman's suffrage. On her own, Dorothea decided to stroll through the house in search of her friends before seeking out the hostess and an introduction to the guest of honor.

She found a small group of young men and women laughing and chatting near the punch bowl, friends since her first days as a student at the Creek's Crossing school. The young men were tanned from long hours in the fields, but the women had endeavored, as Dorothea herself did, to protect their skin from the harsh sun. The condition of their hands revealed their station in life; town girls had smooth, pale hands, while the hands of farm girls were as sunbrowned as the men's faces. Since Uncle Jacob did not permit trips into town for mere social calls, Dorothea had not seen them all together in months, and she eagerly caught up on their news. Apparently her own news had not circulated as rapidly as she had expected; one young man, who had always teased Dorothea for knowing all the answers in class, grinned as he asked her if she planned to send her pupils crawling along the creek banks looking for curious rocks as she had the previous year, or if she had moved on to studying pictures in the clouds. Dorothea strained to betray no emotion as another young woman murmured in his ear, and struggled to smile graciously as he apologized. "Nelson might be a good teacher but he can't be as clever as you," he said, and as the others added their assent, Dorothea's smile threatened to collapse, forcing her to pretend to look around for her parents rather than let them see how much the loss of her position grieved her.

As some of her friends left to join the dancing, Dorothea heard a polite cough and turned around. "Why, Miss Granger," said Cyrus Pearson, giving her a slight bow and a mischievous grin. "I'm honored by your presence at my party. If I had known your uncle would allow you to have a bit of fun on a Sunday, I would have delivered your invitation myself."

Dorothea smiled back. "It's your mother's party and her invitation to give, but thank you just the same."

"Quite right," replied Cyrus, rueful. "It's not even truly my home, however welcome my stepfather has made me feel beneath his roof."

"So welcome that you have spent most of the past six months abroad."

He raised a finger in playful warning. "No more questions, Miss Granger. I am not a plant or insect for you to study." He offered her his arm. "I see I must ask you to dance before you have me entirely figured out."

Uncle Jacob would have been offended to see his niece dancing on a Sabbath afternoon, but despite this—or perhaps because of it—Dorothea accepted. It was, as Cyrus had promised, difficult to talk during the lively country dance, and whenever they did have an opportunity, Cyrus kept her laughing with amusing observations about the party. She learned nothing more about his stepfather. If only she could dispense with her obligation to the guest of honor as easily.

After a second dance, Cyrus escorted her from the floor, explaining that his mother had made him promise to see to it that no young lady was allowed to remain a wallflower at one of her parties.

Dorothea regarded him, eyebrows raised. "Is that why you danced with me?"

"Miss Granger, I believe you know the answer to that." He gave her a wicked grin as he bowed over her hand, then he moved off into the crowd.

"He is full of fancy manners, that one," said Dorothea's best friend, Mary, appearing at her side, her light brown hair braided into a knot at the nape of her slender neck. "I suppose he thinks he's charming."

Dorothea watched him depart, his golden curls visible above most of the other men in the crowd. "I'm sure he is not alone in that opinion."

Mary sniffed. "I hope you do not share it."

Dorothea hid a smile. From the time they were children, Mary had secretly admired Cyrus—so secretly that no one else but Dorothea knew of it—but Cyrus had never noticed her. Mary had never spared a kind word for any girl who did attract his attention, and after she fell in love with a more receptive young man, she had nothing good to say about Cyrus, either.

"Cyrus is neither as fine as you once thought nor as terrible as you think now," teased Dorothea.

"I do not believe your parents would approve," warned Mary. "It is no secret where his mother stands on the slavery issue. I confess I do not always share your parents' fervor, but unlike Violet Pearson Engle, at least my heart is in the right place."

"Cyrus Pearson is not his mother," said Dorothea. "I would no more condemn him for his mother's sins than I would have anyone condemn me for the wrongs my parents have committed."

She smiled to soften her words, but slipped away before Mary asked her which wrongs she meant.

By that time the newlyweds' home had filled almost to bursting with what appeared to be nearly every resident of Creek's Crossing within the range of Mrs. Engle's condescension. Dorothea found her father engrossed in conversation with the mayor, but merely waved to him on her way to the kitchen, where she found her mother chatting with the colored cook about abolition and woman's suffrage. The cook regarded Dorothea's mother curiously and with some wariness, as if she did not know what to make of this white woman who spoke so passionately about impossibilities in the heat of the kitchen, rather than enjoy the laughter and music of the party. Dorothea was so accustomed to her mother that she sometimes forgot that others often found her inscrutable.

Dorothea's mother greeted her affectionately and introduced her to the cook, who nodded a greeting as she removed a pan from the oven and looked Dorothea over with renewed cautious curiosity.

"So, Dorothea," her mother said. "How was your conversation with Mr. Nelson?"

"I have not met him yet. I had hoped someone would offer a toast to him so that I might be able to pick him out of the crowd."

"You must have gone out of your way to avoid him." Mother described him—a bespectacled, brown-haired man, slender, somewhat pale—and pointed out that he would be one of the very few people in the familiar crowd Dorothea did not already know. "Swallow your pride and meet him soon," she added. "We must leave before long or all the evening chores will be left to your uncle."

With a sigh of resignation, Dorothea left the kitchen and made her way to the parlor, where she spied a man chatting with Cyrus Pearson who fit her mother's description. He was not quite as tall as Cyrus, but he wore a finer suit with an overlarge but not unattractive boutonniere on his lapel. Dorothea made her way to an unoccupied spot nearby, where she could await a suitable moment to introduce herself, if Cyrus did not see her there first and take care of the formalities.

She fixed a pleasant smile in place and observed the dancing. Abner whirled Mary about; Mrs. Claverton waggled her fingers and called out a greeting as she and her husband passed. Dorothea returned the greeting with a smile and looked around the room for Charlotte, hoping for the girl's sake that her parents had possessed the sense to allow her to remain home, as befitting her age.

"You have not danced one single set all afternoon," Dorothea overheard Cyrus chide the young Mr. Nelson, if that was, in fact, who he was. "Surely your health cannot be as bad as all that."

"It is not for my health that I refrain," came the reply, in a voice both deeper and more disdainful than Dorothea expected.

"What is it, then? Come, now, my mother made me promise that there would be no young ladies unattended at her party, and I insist you help me."

"While I regret disappointing the woman who so kindly organized this gathering for me," said Mr. Nelson, "you will have to satisfy your obligations to your mother yourself. I dance when I am inclined to do so, and at this moment, I am not so inclined."

"Why not? Look—there are three, four, no, five ladies not engaged at present. Your legs are obviously not broken whatever else might ail you. You will not do yourself an injury if you take one turn about the floor."

"Nevertheless, I decline." He paused and gave Cyrus a slight bow. "With my apologies."

"I cannot understand you, Nelson. You are newly arrived in Creek's Crossing, and apparently you mean to stay. Surely you wish to make the acquaintance of our charming local beauties."

Mr. Nelson frowned and indicated his boutonniere. "If their

taste in conversation resembles their taste in flowers, we will have very little to say to each other."

Cyrus laughed, incredulous. "You cannot mean it. I am as well traveled as you, sir, and I defy you to say the ladies of Creek's Crossing are not as pretty or as charming as those of New York, Paris, or London, without all their artificial graces."

"Pretty?" Mr. Nelson paused. "Yes, perhaps one or two of them are somewhat pretty, but I do not find ignorant country girls amusing. It is far better for me to avoid them than to subject us both to an excruciating attempt at conversation."

"I cannot believe you seriously mean this. What about her?"

Dorothea closed her eyes, hoping fervently that Cyrus was directing Mr. Nelson's attention toward the other side of the room.

"That young lady is Dorothea Granger," said Cyrus, with a suggestion of pride. "Surely you can see how lovely she is. She is not yet twenty, and yet she is so clever she was appointed interim schoolteacher after your predecessor stepped down."

"That says more about your school board's standards than her cleverness. In any event, the manner in which she gazes so longingly at the dance floor suggests that she has not set foot on one in quite some time. I assure you, I have no intention of directing my attention to any woman ignored by other men, especially those here, who know her character."

"Don't be ridiculous," said Cyrus. "Some may say she is too clever for her own good, but no one would ever question her strength of character. Let me introduce you. Miss Granger?"

When he called to her, Dorothea took a quick, steadying breath before turning around to face them. "Yes, Mr. Pearson?"

"Allow me to introduce you to Mr. Thomas Nelson, our guest of honor. He just finished telling me how very much he wishes to make your acquaintance."

Mr. Nelson masked his annoyance poorly as he bowed to her.

"Welcome to Creek's Crossing," said Dorothea. "I regret that so far you have found very little to like about it."

Mr. Nelson gave not a flicker of acknowledgment, but Cyrus had the decency to appear mortified. "Miss Granger, please accept my apologies for my companion's boorish remarks. You were not meant to overhear them."

"You are not the one who should apologize."

Mr. Nelson gestured impatiently to his boutonniere. "If you refer to my criticism of this collection of twigs and vegetable matter—"

"I do not refer to it, but since you mention it, I must speak in its defense." Dorothea gave the boutonniere a quick survey. "It is an unusual arrangement, but its maker's intention is evident. Those twigs, as you call them, are maple seeds, and maple sugar is a significant part of our local economy. These are the leaves of the elm, which grow in abundance throughout the valley and whose beauty is a particular source of pride for us. The leaves of the rose, here and here, represent hope, while the water lily symbolizes purity of heart. The ribbon I recognize—the mayor's wife wears a similar trim on her spring bonnet. To speak plainly, this nosegay that you disparage welcomes you to enjoy the beauty and prosperity of the Elm Creek Valley, with hopes that you will remain honest and true to your calling as the educator of our youth."

"You could hardly ask for a better welcome than that," remarked Cyrus.

"What I would ask for," said Mr. Nelson, "is to be permitted to wear the flower of my choosing."

Dorothea glanced at his hands. "Would that have been a blossom plucked from a round cluster of small white flowers growing on a rather tall stem?"

He almost managed to hide his surprise. "Yes, that's right. Queen Anne's lace. You must have seen me discard it."

Dorothea let out a small laugh. "No, I assure you, I was not paying you that much attention. Nor was your flower Queen Anne's lace. We call it cow parsnip, although it is actually a member of the carrot family. Curiously enough, while it is edible, it is a particularly noxious weed to the touch. The rash on the back of your hands will pass in two or three weeks, longer if you scratch it. I would offer you a healing salve, but as I am merely an ignorant country girl, I am sure my humble medicines are beneath your regard. Next time, if you wish to choose an appropriate flower, I would recommend a narcissus." She turned a blistering smile on Cyrus and ignored his companion. "Good afternoon, Mr. Pearson."

She quickly departed, nearly bumping into Mary as she and Abner left the dance floor. "Goodness, Dorothea, what's wrong?" asked Mary. "Your face is so flushed! Are you ill?"

"I am not ill." Dorothea refused to allow Mr. Nelson and Cyrus to see how angry she was. "Abner, will you excuse us, please?" She linked her arm through Mary's and drew her toward the far end of the room, where she asked, "Have you had an opportunity to meet our new schoolmaster?"

Mary nodded. "Mrs. Engle introduced us. He's handsome in a bookish way, but I suppose that suits his profession. He certainly doesn't look much like a farmer. Would you like to meet him?"

"No! No, thank you. I know him as well as I care to." She told Mary about the encounter.

Mary glanced at the ill-humored schoolmaster and turned away quickly, unable to contain her amusement. "Honestly, Dorothea! Mrs. Deakins may have little talent for flowers, but she meant well, and he had no call to be so unkind. In your place, I would have been tempted to slap him."

"I did not say I wasn't tempted."

"I considered him somewhat aloof when we were introduced, but I had no idea he was so rude." Mary's eyes widened and she grasped Dorothea's arm. "Oh, he's looking this way. He surely knows we're talking about him. But I suppose he doesn't care about the opinion of a couple of ignorant country girls."

"I suppose not," said Dorothea, laughing. "Ignore him. We cannot let him think he is important enough to be the subject of our conversation."

At that moment, she felt a hand on her elbow. "I'm afraid you must bid your friend good-bye," said her father, her mother at his side. "We have chores to attend to at home."

Dorothea let out an exaggerated sigh. "That's fine, Father. I was merely gazing longingly at the dance floor, wondering if I shall ever set foot on one again."

Mary giggled as Dorothea's parents exchanged a puzzled look. Then Dorothea's mother said, "You did find an opportunity to speak to Mr. Nelson?"

"Yes, I spoke to him, the odious man."

Lorena's eyebrows shot up, but before she could inquire, Dorothea hugged Mary good-bye and promised to call on her soon. After giving their regards to the hostess, the Grangers left the party.

"I gather," said Robert carefully as they walked to the livery stable, "that Mr. Nelson did not make a favorable impression upon you?"

"Entirely the opposite," said Dorothea, and she told them what had happened.

"What a rude young man," said Lorena, but she smiled. "Of course, he assumed he was speaking in confidence, unaware of your eavesdropping."

"I was not eavesdropping. I was merely waiting for an appropriate moment to introduce myself," said Dorothea. "Besides, you have often told me one should not do in secret what one would be unwilling to have known in public."

"Not all deeds fall into that neat category, dear. Nor all words."

Her father shook his head. "Are you sure you did not misunderstand him, Dorothea? His father is such a reasonable, just man. I considered him a friend and was disappointed when he returned to the East. It is difficult to believe his son could be so unlike him."

"I understood every word with perfect clarity." Dorothea threw up her hands and quickened her step. "I cannot bear for you two to defend him! Whatever fine qualities his father may possess, Mr. Nelson the younger does not share them."

"Still, it was a fine party," offered her father.

"He seemed as oblivious to its charms as to those of everything else in Creek's Crossing," retorted Dorothea, quickly outpacing her parents.

"Cheer up," called her mother. "He has only just met us. Perhaps once he knows us better, he will decide to move on to some other town, where the women have greater skill with flowers."

Dorothea tried to stay angry, but she could not help it; she burst out laughing. "One can hope," she said. She paused and allowed her parents to catch up to her. She thought, but did not say aloud, that if Mr. Nelson did leave, Creek's Crossing would need another schoolteacher.

Her father was right. It had been a fine party, but it was wasted on Mr. Nelson. Dorothea's thoughts went to the small farmhouse to the southwest where Abel and Constance Wright were finally enjoying the comforts of freedom. No wedding supper, no bridal quilt, no wedding party had marked their homecoming. How much more appropriate it would have been for the people of Creek's Crossing to welcome Constance with music and celebration, and to allow Mr. Nelson, the convict-turned-schoolmaster, to eat a cold supper alone.

Chapter Two

DOROTHEA'S FATHER AND uncle finished the harvest, aided by the threshers and a spell of temperate weather that made Dorothea wistful for the long-ago days that she and Jonathan spent exploring the shores of Elm Creek barefoot and happy. Once they wandered so far they scaled the peak of Dutch Mountain, unaware of the distance they had conquered until the entire Elm Creek Valley lay spread out before them. They returned home to Thrift Farm late for their chores, but it never would have occurred to their parents or the other adults who occupied the cabins scattered about the main residence to scold. They were a community of Christians with strong Transcendentalist inclinations, and they believed children had to be allowed to pursue their own hearts' desires without adult interference. If they had not also believed human beings were obligated to treat the animals in their care with respect and kindness, the Granger children might never have learned any part of what it meant to run a farm.

Dorothea wondered what had become of those optimistic men and women who had tried to build a utopia in the Pennsylvania wilderness. None had perished in the flood, but after Thrift Farm lay underwater, the group was forced to disperse. There was some talk, at first, of moving out west to start again, but the money for the journey and the perfect plot of land could never be found. Singly or in pairs, the former residents of Thrift Farm drifted away from the Elm Creek Valley like cottonwood seeds on the wind. Dorothea's parents occasionally received letters from friends who had gone to Kansas or California; Lorena would linger over them, caressing the precious words with her fingertips.

Uncle Jacob had taught the Granger children how to run a farm properly and a child's proper place within the household. Their education was swift and jarring, but they learned. Dorothea's parents caught on more slowly, but Uncle Jacob eventually made able farmers out of them. Dorothea learned, too, that as hard as Uncle Jacob worked them, there were advantages to his methods: Her days were no longer hers to fill as she chose, but the forest did not reclaim the fields and the crops did not fail. Jonathan no longer complained of hunger in the middle of the night and his persistent headaches disappeared. Dorothea grew three inches the first summer after Uncle Jacob took them in, after which he ordered Dorothea's mother to put her in long skirts rather than dungarees and forbade her to wander the valley as if she were, as he put it, a wild Indian or Irish.

If nothing else, Uncle Jacob's restrictions on the children's carefree wanderings allowed them more time for books. Jonathan's aptitude for the scholarly life was apparent even to his uncle, who generally mistrusted such inclinations. It was Uncle Jacob who first introduced his nephew to the local physician, who, after a year as his tutor, recommended that the boy broaden his experience in a larger city. For two years Jonathan had lived in Baltimore, and as proud as Dorothea was of his accomplishments, she could not deny feeling an occasional stab of envy.

In the past Jonathan had returned for at least part of the harvest, but that year he did not, citing important ongoing cases that his mentor insisted he observe to the end. Uncle Jacob grumbled but did not order him home, and instead kept on the hired hands and agreed to exchange work with Abel Wright. He had done so every year as far back as Dorothea could remember, even though the Wright farm was nearly eight miles away, southwest of Creek's Crossing.

This season Abel Wright came to their farm first, but despite Lorena's repeated entreaties, he did not bring his wife with him, saying that she sent her apologies but had so much work to do in her new home that she could not spare even a day away. The next week, when Uncle Jacob and Robert were to help at the Wright farm, Dorothea was pleased when Uncle Jacob told her she and Lorena must come, too, to assist Mrs. Wright however she needed.

"At last we can give her a proper welcome," said Lorena. "We should take a gift. Something useful for the home."

"And something to eat," said Dorothea. "A wedding cake."

"Yes. That's a fine idea." Lorena instructed her to begin beating eggs for the cake while she searched the house for an appropriate gift.

Dorothea went to the hen house, gathered eggs in her apron, and hurried back to mix the cake batter. She cracked the eggs in her mother's large mixing bowl and beat them until her arm ached, pausing only to build a fire in the oven. The eggs were stiff and the oven hot by the time her mother returned, hesitating in the doorway, hands behind her back.

"Did you find something?" asked Dorothea, mixing sugar into the bowl.

Lorena nodded and revealed what she carried.

Dorothea recognized the quilt top before her mother unfolded it. The appliqué sampler quilt top was the first she had begun after coming to live with Uncle Jacob, and it had taken her nearly two years to complete. At that time she had still believed she might complete the customary thirteen tops for her hope chest, but was practical enough to realize that just in case she could not, she ought to make at least one very fine top that could serve as her bridal quilt. Knowing she was hungry for details of city life, Jonathan had written of a new style of appliqué quilt the fashionable ladies of Baltimore were making. Their intricate designs created still life portraits in fabric—floral bouquets, nestling birds, wreaths, beribboned baskets, urns of greenery. Inspired by her brother's descriptions, Dorothea sketched images from her own life, capturing her memories of Thrift Farm and the Elm Creek Valley with every stitch into the fourteen-inch squares. She had drawn each appliqué template by hand on old newspapers and had spent a good portion of her modest savings on the soft muslin background, bleached to a snowy white by the sun, to which she had sewn the calico flowers, leaves, and figures. She arranged the sixteen blocks in four rows of four, then fashioned an appliqué border of elegant swags gathered by roses. Once she had succumbed to a local superstition and had slept beneath the unquilted top so that she might dream of her future husband. She woke the next morning with no memory of her dreams, a worrisome omen that now made perfect sense.

"You want to give this to the Wrights?" she managed to say. "But—but it is not finished yet. It is not quilted."

"Yes, and the fact that you never bothered to do so tells me it is not very close to your heart. Not so dear that you cannot bear to part with it. Mrs. Wright can quilt it herself, or she can leave it as it is for a summer quilt."

Dorothea thought quickly. "A quilt is a fine idea, but perhaps Mr. Wright would prefer a Rail Fence quilt. I have enough blocks finished. Do you remember how he admired them?"

"We don't have time to stitch your blocks together. Besides, this is a gift for the bride. The flowers will suit the occasion."

Dorothea said nothing.

"Constance Wright came north with little more than the clothes on her back," said Lorena. "Wouldn't she treasure this beautiful quilt? Wouldn't it be a wonderful expression of the friendship we hope will grow between us?"

"It would," said Dorothea. Her mother watched her so expectantly that Dorothea could not bring herself to explain that she had not quilted the top because she was saving it for her engagement party. Everyone in the Elm Creek Valley expected the bride-to-be's best friend or sister to host a special quilting bee where the bride's thirteen tops would be unveiled and all the women would help quilt them. Telling her mother this would be no use. Lorena did not believe that people should allow custom to dictate their behavior, especially if it steered them away from finer impulses such as kindness and generosity.

Dorothea was not betrothed. Even if she became engaged that afternoon, a highly unlikely occurrence, she might still have time to make another bridal quilt before the wedding. She had saved her sketches and most of her templates. She could make another.

"I suppose it would make a fine gift," she said. Her mother smiled and hurried off to find some clean muslin to wrap it in. Dorothea turned her attention to the cake, a hollow sensation growing in her heart. Back at Thrift Farm, she had been taught not to value earthly possessions. She felt ashamed that her instinct was to snatch the quilt top from her mother's arms, race off to the attic, and stash it away in some secret place.

She tried to think only of Constance Wright's happiness as the cake baked and she and her mother packed a basket with jars of preserves, a new ball of butter, and other things Mrs. Wright might need. As Dorothea's father helped them into the wagon, her mother told her that, as the maker, she ought to be the one to present the quilt to the bride.

"What quilt?" said Uncle Jacob as he shook the reins to get the horses underway. When Dorothea's mother explained about the gift, Uncle Jacob said, "Whose idea was this?"

"I suppose it was my idea," said Lorena. "But it is Dorothea's generosity that makes it possible."

Uncle Jacob shook his head. "Lorena, let the girl keep her quilt. Look at her. She's holding it so tight she might squeeze it in two. Mrs. Wright doesn't expect any fool wedding present from people she doesn't even know."

"It's fine, Uncle," said Dorothea. "I can make another."

"It took you all winter to make that one."

Longer, actually, Dorothea was tempted to reply, but instead she said, "It's just as well. I will need something to keep myself occupied in the evenings, since I will no longer have lessons to prepare."

Uncle Jacob snorted. "If you need something to do, I will find work for you."

Dorothea glanced at her mother, who shot her a look of warning. "Thank you, Uncle," she said. "Anything to be useful."

He peered over his shoulder at her, perhaps sensing something less than sincere in her tone, but she looked away, gazing at the passing scenery as if she had not seen those hills and trees a hundred times before.

They followed the road south for a mile, past lakes and marshland until they reached the ford over Elm Creek. They climbed down from the wagon as they crossed the waterway on the ferry, Uncle Jacob and Dorothea's father holding tightly to the reins of the horses. Dorothea withdrew to the railing and watched the town on the distant riverbank. At the ford, the creek was merely an eighth of a mile across, the waters calm unless a storm stirred them. Among the young men of the valley, it was considered a test of courage to swim across Elm Creek three miles upstream at a point called Widow's Pining, where it was nearly twice as wide and far more treacherous, with dangerous currents, sharp rocks, and unexpected undertows. Dorothea considered it a test of great foolishness. It was difficult enough for someone who knew Elm Creek well to manage a boat that far east of the ford, much less swim.

She and her brother had discovered that for themselves not long after the waters had claimed Thrift Farm. It had been Dorothea's idea to take the rowboat to see if they could find the place where their house had once stood. They thought they spied the foundation through the cloudy waters, but the swift current overturned their boat. They clung to it as they were swept downstream, and only providence in the form of a log that snagged the boat before they lost their grasp spared their lives. Uncle Jacob had wanted to switch them when they returned home, exhausted, cold, and bedraggled, but their mother had intervened. She said they had learned their lesson and that the river had already beaten them harder than any man could. Lorena was right. Jonathan had feared the water ever since that day, and he would only wade in the creek, up to his ankles. If obliged to cross on the ferry, he lay down in the back of the wagon, feigning lazy indifference as he fixed his gaze on the sky rather than look at the water, clinging to a book or his hat with white-knuckled hands.

Dorothea, who had not acquired his wariness, never shamed her brother by trying to cajole him out of his fears. She had decided, after their adventure was over, that the river had twice endangered them and had twice left them unscathed. If Elm Creek intended to claim their lives, it would have done so already. Knowing her conclusion was irrational, she confided it to no one, but wished her brother shared her quiet certainty that the creek would not harm them.

The ferry reached the opposite bank, and before long the travelers were back on dry land aboard the wagon. Dorothea hoped Uncle Jacob would drive through town on the chance she might encounter some of her friends, but as she expected he took the longer route south past the wood and limestone buildings, then turned west to rejoin the road along Elm Creek. Uncle Jacob usually preferred direct routes, but he would go out of his way to avoid unwanted conversation.

Not far south of town, Elm Creek diverted from the roadside as it curved around an oxbow to the west, and the road continued past several well-tended farms. Dorothea knew the families—the Shropshires, the Craigmiles—and waved to acquaintances as they rode past. The third and largest farm was Two Bears Farm, which until recently Dorothea had always thought of as the Carter farm. She recalled the two youngest children, girls she had taught at the Creek's Crossing school, and wondered how the family had received the news that they were to be evicted. It was not uncommon for an eastern family to own land in the region and to allow others to live upon it in exchange for improving the land and raising crops, but in the Elm Creek Valley, most tenants eventually bought out their distant landlords. The Carters probably had assumed they would one day, too. Perhaps, with that possibility in mind, they had saved enough money to give them a good start somewhere else. Dorothea hoped so.

She saw several figures working in the fields with horse and plow, but did not wave in case Mr. Nelson was among them. Far likelier he was sitting inside an oak-paneled study in the white house on the hill, reading a book or writing a letter home, begging to be released from his exile to the hinterlands.

"Mr. Nelson has one hundred sixty acres," remarked Lorena. "He does not look to have even half of them harvested yet. Does he expect the oats and rye to wait until he has time to attend to them?"

"He started late," said Uncle Jacob. "A better question would be why the Carters did not finish the harvest before he arrived. *If* one felt obliged to ask such questions, and stick his nose into his neighbors' business."

Lorena said no more, but Dorothea wondered. Perhaps the

Carters had known or suspected that they would soon be evicted and decided not to complete the harvest any more swiftly than necessary. She could not blame them for begrudging Mr. Nelson the benefit of their labor under such circumstances. At any rate, Mr. Nelson would not have to complete the work himself, or even share in it. According to Mary, who lived in town and heard every rumor, he had advertised in the *Creek's Crossing Informer* looking for hired hands. Many had responded, some from as far east as Grangerville, the town of Dorothea's birth, the town founded by her great-grandparents.

They passed the well-tended fields of Two Bears Farm and approached a thickening forest, where a rough dirt road barely wide enough for a wagon disappeared into the trees. Dorothea had never had occasion to venture down it, but she knew it led to the small clearing Mr. Liggett called Elm Creek Farm. She and Jonathan had explored his land as children—uninvited—as they followed the creek through the valley and discovered the places where local legend claimed the waters were narrow enough to be crossed by a bridge. When Dorothea asked her parents why the region's first residents had not built a bridge there instead of the ferry north of town, her mother had suggested that perhaps no one had known of the easier crossing because of the thick trees, or that perhaps once the narrows had been discovered, the owners of the ferry and the town founders had not wanted another ford built lest they lose the prestige and commerce their passage over the waters brought. Dorothea's father had chuckled and remarked that it was fortunate the narrower places had not been discovered earlier, or Creek's Crossing would have been built on Elm Creek Farm, and Mr. Liggett would own most of the town. Then both parents warned the children to avoid Mr. Liggett and his land, because he was reputed to be a drunkard and violent.

Dorothea and Jonathan would have stayed away, except the

creek was so pleasant there, and it would have been a shame to waste so many wild blueberries on the birds, especially since they were the sweetest either child had ever tasted and Mr. Liggett apparently never picked them. It was not only the blueberries he ignored. He had built only one bridge that the Granger children could find, and they had never seen more than a tiny patch of tilled land and one rough log cabin on his forty acres.

Uncle Jacob despised drunkenness, and he held little regard for Mr. Liggett after learning that soon after buying his land, Mr. Liggett felled and burned a half-acre of maple to plant corn. A half-acre of corn would be barely enough to support one man and his livestock, so Mr. Liggett would find no profit in it. In Uncle Jacob's opinion, Mr. Liggett should have cut an acre or two of oak instead, sold the wood to the new lumber mill in Grangerville, and saved the maple from the flames. More recently he had embarked upon a harebrained scheme to raise racehorses—racehorses, when draft animals and the occasional fancy mare to pull a lady's carriage were all anyone ever saw need for in the Elm Creek Valley. Uncle Jacob could not abide the man.

As only infrequently happened, Dorothea's parents shared his opinion, though for Mr. Liggett's poor moral character rather than his questionable business acumen. Seven years earlier, when Thrift Farm still stood above water, Mr. Liggett had secretly purchased a slave woman in Virginia and set her to work in his fields and his grim little cabin. After too many drunken confidences in the tavern, his secret became widely known, and a committee of citizens of the Elm Creek Valley, led by the residents of Thrift Farm, called the law upon him. They demanded that he release the woman, since by law, once in the North, she was immediately free. Mr. Liggett then insisted that the unfortunate woman was not his prisoner but his bride, a claim that outraged an entirely different segment of the local citizenry and one that the woman vehemently denied.

With the entire valley against him, Mr. Liggett had no choice but to acquiesce. When the sheriff visited to be sure he had complied, the woman was gone. Mr. Liggett claimed to have freed her, but months later other rumors surfaced: He had not, in fact, given her the necessary papers, fifty dollars, and passage to Canada as he had claimed, but had taken her south and sold her. Outraged, Abel Wright and others sent word to an organization for freedmen in the city to which Mr. Liggett said she had gone, but as best they could determine, she never arrived.

This alone was not sufficient evidence to convict Mr. Liggett of any crime, and the local law enforcement seemed reluctant to pursue the matter after so much time had passed. Still, it was enough to condemn him in the opinion of many residents of Creek's Crossing. Isolated and shunned, he became even more of a recluse than Uncle Jacob, which was perhaps why Mr. Liggett had thought he spied a kindred spirit in him and had persisted in the misunderstanding that they were friends. Dorothea surmised that recent events had disabused him of that notion.

Not long after they passed the road to Elm Creek Farm, Dorothea heard horse's hooves on the road behind them. Uncle Jacob stiffened, but he did not turn. Expecting to find Mr. Liggett, Dorothea peered over her shoulder to see who followed them and was surprised to discover Cyrus Pearson urging his horse into a trot.

As he caught up to them, Cyrus slowed to match their pace. He greeted Uncle Jacob and Dorothea's parents before turning his smile to Dorothea alone. "Good morning, Miss Granger," he said. "It's a pleasant day for an outing in the countryside, wouldn't you agree?"

"We are farmers," said Uncle Jacob without looking at him. "We don't take outings in the countryside. We live in it."

"Quite right, sir," said Cyrus genially. He glanced at Dorothea; she gave him an apologetic shrug. "Those of us who live in town are not so fortunate."

Uncle Jacob snorted, but before he could say anything more, Dorothea quickly asked, "What brings you this way, Cyrus? Surely you didn't come so far just to bid us good morning."

"I wish I could flatter you by saying I had, but as you surmised, I am out on a matter of business."

His gaze shifted away from hers before he finished speaking, which told her he did not wish to elaborate. At once she suspected he had been to see Mr. Nelson, as his stepfather was on the school board.

"We're on our way to the Wright farm," she told him, ignoring the urge to press him about the visit. She did wish to know what Mr. Nelson had thought of her pupils, but suspected he was unlikely to have said anything favorable about them or Dorothea's teaching.

His eyebrows rose. "Are you?"

"There's plenty of work if you want to help," said Uncle Jacob.

"I wish I could, but I'm afraid I have obligations elsewhere." Cyrus returned his attention to Dorothea. "I see you are too busy for me at the moment. I had hoped to speak with you about the upcoming benefit for the library."

"I was not aware of any benefit," said Lorena. "You're welcome to call on us at home to discuss it. I'm sure we would all be glad to assist such a worthy cause."

Dorothea's father glanced dubiously at Uncle Jacob, who hunched his shoulders but otherwise ignored them. Since he voiced no objection aloud, Dorothea said, "Please do call on us."

"Is Sunday too soon?"

"Not at all," said Lorena, and it was quickly agreed that Cyrus would come out the next Sunday afternoon. Then he bade them good-bye, turned his horse around, and headed back toward Creek's Crossing.

Shaking his head, Dorothea's father murmured something to

Lorena, who let out a laugh and murmured something back. "What are you whispering about?" said Dorothea, amused.

Lorena shrugged. "We were merely agreeing that it is good to see a young man so committed to improving our city's access to fine literature."

"I quite agree," said Dorothea. "And naturally, as the former schoolteacher, I ought to be involved."

"I wonder if the new schoolmaster will want to be involved as well," said Robert.

Dorothea frowned. "Surely Cyrus would know better than to invite us both after—" She broke off when she realized her father was teasing her. "I for one would welcome Mr. Nelson's advice. No doubt he has seen the country's finest libraries and would be delighted to tell us exactly how and to what degree our plans fall short."

Not long after that, the Wright farm came into view. From a distance Dorothea spied Mr. Wright already at work in the fields; closer to the house, a tall woman in a head scarf worked in the kitchen garden. A dog barked, another answered, and suddenly the pair burst from a nearby field and raced down the road to the wagon. The dogs escorted them to the house, tails wagging in a frenzy of welcome.

Mr. Wright greeted them outside the barn with a courteous nod and handshake for Uncle Jacob and warmer smiles for Dorothea's parents. Constance Wright hung back, unsmiling, even as Mr. Wright proudly introduced her to the visitors. When he spoke Dorothea's name, Constance's gaze fixed on hers in a silent, bold challenge, and Dorothea looked away first. She had not expected Mrs. Wright to be a girl close to her own age, as Mr. Wright was nearly as old as her parents. Nor had she expected such a cold welcome.

"Congratulations on your marriage," said Lorena, clasping one of Constance's hands in hers. "And on your emancipation."

Constance allowed a small nod. "Thank you."

"We hope you'll not think us too forward, but we hoped you would indulge us in a belated wedding celebration. We brought a cake, if that will tempt you to say yes."

Lorena handed over the covered cake plate, which Constance accepted with some surprise. "We jumped the broom two years ago," she said, peeking under the cover. "Seems a little late to celebrate."

"Does that mean you don't want the cake?" teased Lorena, reaching for it.

At this, Constance gave a tentative smile. "I didn't say that," she said, holding it out of reach. "I suppose a little party won't hurt none."

"Our daughter has a gift for the bride," said Robert. "Dorothea?"

With a start, Dorothea remembered and returned to the wagon for the quilt. Constance wiped her hands carefully on her apron before accepting the bundle, then slowly unwrapped the muslin dust cover. She said not a word as she held it up, arms outstretched, face expressionless.

"My," said Mr. Wright. "That sure is a pretty quilt."

"It's a new style fashionable in Baltimore, or so my brother tells me," said Dorothea as Constance studied the quilt, and, in an echo of her mother, added, "You can quilt it if you like, or leave it as it is for a summer quilt."

"Thank you." Constance carefully folded the quilt top and wrapped the muslin around it. "I'll quilt it and keep it nice for company."

It was soon agreed that Dorothea would assist Constance in the garden while Lorena prepared a meal and the men worked in the fields. "We'll take these inside first," said Lorena, indicating the cake and baskets of food, still in the wagon.

"This should go in, too," said Constance, handing the quilt to

Dorothea as the men left for the fields. Caught off guard, Dorothea almost dropped it. Without another word for her guests, Constance headed for the garden.

"I rather hoped she would show us where she would like us to put things," murmured Lorena as they carried the baskets and bundles inside.

Dorothea had rather hoped she would have shown a trifle more appreciation for her quilt top. "Where shall I put this?" she asked as they entered the house. It was small and tidy. Mr. Wright had managed well for a bachelor, but as far as Dorothea could discern, Constance had made few changes since her arrival. A vase of flowers stood on a corner shelf in the house's front room, but Mr. Wright could have arranged the decoration for his bride. A sewing basket sat on the floor beside a chair loaded with a pile of clothes, likely for mending.

"Leave it in the bedroom, I suppose."

As her mother went to the kitchen, Dorothea found the bedroom but lingered in the doorway, studying the quilt already spread upon the bed. It was an unusual string-pieced star pattern, one Dorothea had never seen before, probably stitched from the leftover scraps or even remnants of older quilts.

"Dorothea?" Lorena joined her in the doorway and spotted the quilt that had captured Dorothea's attention. "Perhaps you should place the appliqué sampler over it."

"Why?" The fabric in the quilt did not appear to be new, but the colors had held fast, the stitches were small and even, and the binding was not worn. Perhaps the quilt had been made more recently than it appeared. "I think it's rather striking."

"Yes, but it is not quite the thing for a bridal chamber."

Dorothea thought of the elaborately pieced, appliquéd, and stuffed creations some of her friends had made as their own nuptials approached—beautiful, decorative, and often too fine for daily use. Her best friend and her husband, married only seven months, had last slept beneath their quilt on their wedding night, although Mary was considering releasing it from the hope chest for their first anniversary. In comparison, Abel Wright's quilt was less lovely and impressive, but far more comfortable and enduring. She wondered how he had come to own it. He did not piece quilts himself, as far as she knew.

"Perhaps it is not a proper bridal quilt," said Dorothea. "But it is a perfect marriage quilt."

"I suppose so." Dorothea's mother put her arm around her daughter's shoulders as she regarded Abel Wright's quilt. "A summer quilt is not enough for these cool autumn evenings, anyway. Since Mr. Wright is not a quilter himself, he is not likely to have anything more suitable, and Constance was unlikely to bring a wedding quilt with her, much less the thirteen pieced tops required of a bride of fashion in this county. It is a pity we no longer have yours. All those tops would have made a fine wedding gift, quilted or not."

"They would have, indeed," said Dorothea, managing a tight smile. "The appliqué sampler top will have to do."

She saw no reason to tell her mother she never would have agreed to give away all her quilt tops. Why confess her selfishness when such a sacrifice was impossible, as the seven quilt tops she had pieced, appliquéd, and tucked away in her hope chest had been lost in the flood that had taken their farm? Dorothea had intended to re-create them and complete the thirteen that, according to local custom, would have shown she was properly trained and prepared for marriage. Lorena had her own ideas of proper training, however, and with so many more important items to replace, a new hope chest remained a luxury they could not afford. With home, land, and livestock lost, thirteen unquilted tops for Dorothea's own use in some distant and uncertain future were a secondary, even frivolous concern. What no one in the family had yet admitted aloud was that Dorothea, with no wealth of her own, was unlikely to need even one wedding quilt.

Her throat constricting, she set the muslin-wrapped bundle on a pine bureau. "I should help Constance in the garden," she said, and left the house.

Constance did not look up as Dorothea approached, nor did she respond when Dorothea asked where Constance would prefer for her to begin. "I suppose I'll start over here, then," said Dorothea brightly. Constance made a noise of assent, so she set herself to work. On her hands and knees, she dug onions, brushed the dirt from them, and stacked them in the grass beside the garden.

After a few minutes of silence, Dorothea said, "How was your journey north?"

"You can see for yourself we made it safe."

"Have you had an opportunity to go into Creek's Crossing? It's not a large town, but it has some fine shops and friendly people."

"I saw enough."

"We also have a lending library, although it's not much at the moment—two dozen books on a shelf in the post office. As long as I've lived in Creek's Crossing, there have been plans to enlarge the collection, and possibly even build a room onto the school to hold it. Perhaps now it will finally happen. I understand a benefit is being organized."

"I don't care about no library. I don't read."

"Oh. I see." Dorothea hesitated. "I could teach you. I used to be a schoolteacher—only for six months, but—"

"Maybe you don't understand." Constance stuck her trowel into the ground. "I don't need your charity. Not your teaching, not your help in the garden, not your mama's food, not your fancy quilt. You're here because my husband invited your people. I don't want to be your friend."

"I see." Dorothea sat back on her heels, brushed the dirt from her palms, and shaded her eyes with her hand as she looked up at Constance. "I suppose we needn't fear that happening."

Constance frowned before taking up her trowel again. "There are plenty of colored families around here. I don't see why we need to ask white people for help."

"My uncle and your husband have been exchanging work for years. It's the neighborly thing to do."

Constance barked out a laugh. "You aren't our neighbors. Abel says you live clear on the other side of Creek's Crossing." She chopped at a weed, hard. "I met our neighbor, and he ain't nobody I want to speak to again."

"Whom did you meet? Was it a thin man, loud and unkempt?" Constance's silence confirmed Dorothea's guess. "I know that man, and I can tell you he is a drunkard and a fool. It is uncharitable to say so, but it's the truth. Whatever he said or did, you must not assume all people in Creek's Crossing are like him."

Constance worked on as if Dorothea had not spoken.

"I'm afraid you're wrong about something else, too. There are not plenty of colored families in Creek's Crossing. There are only a handful in the entire Elm Creek Valley, and none of those nearby. I'm afraid you'll have to settle for some white friends unless you're determined to be stubborn and lonely."

Cross, Dorothea pushed herself to her feet, took up the spade, and began overturning earth along the edge of the garden. At first Constance ignored her, but before long, she stopped working to watch.

"What are you doing?"

"I'm adding another row to your garden."

"I can see that. Why? We won't be planting until spring."

"Because every spring for the past three years, my mother has traded some of her seedlings for some of your husband's cheese. Last year it was pumpkins. This year I believe it will be sweet potatoes."

"I didn't know about no sweet potatoes."

Dorothea was tempted to retort that there seemed to be a good deal that Constance did not know, but instead she said, "If I overturn the earth and mix in some manure with the grasses, in the spring, the soil will be richer for my efforts."

Constance watched her work for a while, then picked up the hoe and began to help. When the new row was nearly complete, Dorothea left Constance to finish and went to the barn for a wheelbarrow half-full with manure. Facing each other on opposite sides of the new row, they mixed the manure into the freshly overturned earth.

"A man came to the farm my second night here, so drunk he could barely sit his horse," said Constance eventually. "He had a torch and said he was going to set fire to the barn, and if we didn't clear off after that warning, he'd set fire to the house. He slid off his horse and made like he was going to fling that torch into the hayloft, but all he did was scare his horse so it lit off down the road the way he came. He stumbled around and swore, all red in the face, and went into the barn saying we owed him one of our horses for the one that ran away. When he came out with a horse but left the torch behind, Abel ran to the door, but I wouldn't let him leave the house. So Abel set the dogs on the man. They just nipped him a bit to make him let go the horse. They chased him away and came right back to the house once he was off our land, but from the way he was screaming, you'd have thought they'd taken his legs off. Abel and I both ran out to the barn, but the torch had just fell on a bare spot of ground. But not two feet away was a bale of hay. If he'd dropped the torch there instead—" Constance shrugged, studiously overturning soil. "I guess Abel would have asked you all to come help with a barn raising today instead of harvesting."

"You must have been terrified."

"The man didn't have no gun. It could have been worse." Constance looked away, her eyes sweeping from the barn to the place where the road from Abel's barn met the main road. "He stood right there hollering that he'll be back with friends to finish the job."

"He wouldn't dare. You must inform the authorities at once."

"Why? They wouldn't do nothing. They can't lock up every drunk who swears at colored folks, not even here in the North."

"He did much more than swear at you."

"I'm not afraid of him." Constance stuck her hoe firmly into the ground. "If he comes back, Abel's going to shoot him."

Dorothea felt a sickening shiver of dread. "If he should kill him—"

"Then he's as good as dead himself. I know. You white folks don't take kindly to having a colored man kill a white man, even a white man you don't like."

"Constance—" Dorothea did not know what to say. "If you go to the authorities, they will warn Mr. Liggett to leave you alone."

"Liggett. So that's his name." Constance nodded, satisfied. "Abel wouldn't tell me. I figured he didn't want me to find out how close he lives. He lives close?"

Dorothea nodded reluctantly. "His farm lies no more than a mile away, in the direction of town."

"Too close." Constance gazed off to the northeast, to the thick mass of elms and oaks that hid Elm Creek from view.

"It may be some small consolation to know that one part of his threat rings hollow," said Dorothea. "Mr. Liggett does not have any friends, so if he does return, there will be no one to help him, as he put it, finish the job."

"I guess that's something." Constance took up the hoe again and resumed her work. "I knew we'd have trouble with white folks up here. Abel didn't tell me what it would be like, but I knew."

"But you came anyway."

"Of course. What choice did we have? He couldn't live with me on the plantation, him being free and me not. He wouldn't have wanted to leave this farm anyhow, nor all his goats." She snorted and shook her head, but she could not conceal a smile, or the affection in her voice. "He could have saved himself a lot of work and trouble by marrying some free girl up here instead of me."

"But he chose you."

"Lord knows why. Maybe he knew I'd say yes if he promised to buy my freedom."

Dorothea regarded her with surprise. "Is that how it happened?"

"No, no. He always said he'd get me free, even before he ever said he loved me. I just thought he was the crazy cheese man, trying to fill my head with notions just like folks had warned me he would." Constance stuck the hoe into the earth again and rested her chin upon it. "Every few months he would come by with that wagon selling his cheese. My master's wife loved it and always bought some. Of course I noticed Abel, being as he was the only free colored man I had ever seen, but I didn't know he had taken any notice of me until one day he gave me a big wheel of cheese and said he had brought it all the way from Pennsylvania especially for me."

Dorothea smiled. "He wooed you with cheese."

Constance grinned and nodded. "He brought me other presents, too. I liked his stories about the North best, about how he could go where he wanted, when he wanted. About how he had his own house and farm and didn't answer to no one. Then he started talking about me running away—" Abruptly Constance fell silent.

"Running away, or running away with him?" prompted Dorothea.

Constance shrugged. "Both, I reckon. I wouldn't do it, though. I didn't know him all that well, for all his stories and gifts." She looked abashed. "I was too scared."

"You had every reason to be."

"I don't know about that. Others have done it. Abel thought I didn't want to go because it wasn't proper, us not being married."

Constance shook her head. "That wasn't it at all, and I told him so. Once we jumped the broom and I still wouldn't run off, well, then he believed me."

"You must have been so lonely when he left."

She considered. "I was, but I always knew he would come back for me. The mistress liked me and she liked Abel, so she thought it was real sweet. My master hated us being married, though. He only had ten slaves and didn't want any of us to think about being free."

"How could he expect you not to think about it?"

Constance shrugged. "Lord knows. My master was real sorry he ever said we could get married, so when Abel finally understood that I wasn't going to run away, he asked about buying my freedom. He told Abel to pay two thousand dollars."

"Two thousand?" Dorothea echoed, aghast. It was an enormous sum and yet shamefully little for a human life. "How did he expect Abel to raise so much?"

"Well, he didn't. We figured he expected Abel to tire of visiting me only now and again and either leave me, and stop being a nuisance, or settle down there. My master thought he would get another slave out of the bargain, but he didn't know my Abel. Or his own wife. She made him lower the fee to one thousand, and a few months later, Abel paid it."

Dorothea smiled. "And here you are."

"And here I am." Constance waved a hand toward the house, the barn, the fields, the goat pens, shaking her head in disbelief. "Never thought I'd be working in my own garden on my own piece of land. Abel's a good man, too. I don't suppose I'll ever know why he fell in love with me, but I thank the good Lord he did."

"He must love you a great deal to have fought for you so determinedly."

"Most days I think so." Constance grinned. "Some days I think he just didn't want to lose to my master. Abel's quiet, but he's like an old dog that's got hold of a bone. Try to take it from him, and you might never hear him growl before he bites you." She glanced toward Mr. Liggett's farm. "Some folks around here haven't yet learned that, but they will."

Dorothea, too, looked off to the northeast in silence. She could not imagine what had possessed Mr. Liggett to try to frighten off the Wrights. She hoped it was nothing more than the drunken notions of a lazy man who would abandon his hateful promises once he sobered up.

Just then Dorothea's mother emerged from the house and called them to dinner. Dorothea and Constance gathered their tools and returned them to the barn before going to summon the men.

As they strode out into the fields, Constance said, "I still don't need no reading lessons."

"And no friends, either, I assume."

Constance gave her a sidelong look. "I guess I don't mind that part so much. I don't need no reading lessons because Abel is teaching me."

"That's good. Where reading lessons are concerned, I'm sure a devoted husband would be more agreeable company than an old schoolteacher."

"And I already have a wedding quilt."

Dorothea thought of the string-pieced star quilt in the bedroom. "I know. I saw it."

"It ain't as fancy as yours, but I'm sure I can sew as fine a seam as you." Constance kept her eyes fixed on the men in the fields as they walked. "I saved scraps from what the mistress threw out ever since I was a little girl, ever since I was old enough to understand that every nice thing on that place belonged to the white family and not me, and that none of those pretty things could ever be mine. I saved all those scraps and kept them clean, and when Abel asked me to be his wife I started the quilt. I gave it to him when he came to bring me home. He said it was the prettiest patchwork ever made, and until today I'm sure he truly thought it was."

Dorothea was ashamed. "I'm sorry. I had no intention of insulting you with my gift. If I had known—"

"I know. Now I know. And that's why I suppose I'll keep it." Suddenly Constance grinned at her. "I'm not contrary or foolish enough to give it back. I did say I like pretty things."

AFTER DINNER, THE GRANGERS and the Wrights worked on until nearly dusk, when they hastily ate a cold supper so the Grangers could leave while there was still enough light to travel by. On the return journey, Uncle Jacob did not circumvent the town of Creek's Crossing but passed along its main streets, knowing they would be quiet at that hour. Dorothea looked for, but neither saw nor expected to see, any of her friends. She did glimpse a slender man in spectacles—who might have been Mr. Nelson—entering a tavern, but she could have been mistaken.

They were the only travelers on the ferry, so Dorothea stretched out in the back of the wagon, determined to rest as long as she could until Uncle Jacob ordered her to sit up and act like a lady. She watched the stars appear in the darkening sky, and the next thing she knew, the wagon jerked as the horses pulled the wagon from the ferry to the landing. She sat up properly again, returned a smile from her mother, and absently picked dried mud from the hem of her skirts.

"Niece," said Uncle Jacob suddenly. "If you truly need work to occupy your idle hands, and since you are so inclined to give away your quilts, maybe you would make one for me."

Dorothea and her mother exchanged a look of surprise. "Of

course," said Dorothea. "Did you have a certain pattern in mind?"

She expected him to say no, since few men admitted to being able to distinguish one quilt pattern from another, but instead he nodded. "A scrap quilt like one my mother once made," he said. "I will draw it for you. And I will need it by winter."

Chapter Three

THE NEXT EVENING after the chores were done, Dorothea was making the most of the fading daylight by reading the last chapter of a borrowed book when Uncle Jacob interrupted to show her a sketch of a block he wanted in his quilt. Dorothea had not thought he would expect her to begin the quilt so soon, but she hid her reluctance and set the book aside. He lit the lamp and gestured with his pen as he explained the various features of his small, neat drawing.

"It resembles the Delectable Mountains pattern," remarked Dorothea, studying the arrangement of large right triangles set at right angles to each other, with smaller right triangles lining their shorter sides. Uncle Jacob nodded brusquely, frowned at the interruption, and directed her to make the blocks exactly as he had drawn them, with clear and distinct points.

Dorothea declined to assure him that she was not known for sloppy piecing. "I assume you mean for me to fill in these blank places with light-colored fabric?" she inquired, indicating a diagonal row of squares from the upper left corner to the center of the quilt. In an ordinary Delectable Mountains quilt, those squares would have been part of larger triangles of background fabric.

"Do no more and no less than you are told," said Uncle Jacob.

"I'll need more time to sketch those squares. Make the part of the quilt I have drawn first and do the rest later."

Delicately, because her uncle had clearly given his design a great deal of thought, she said, "It will be difficult to assemble the rest of the quilt with these important blocks missing, especially the center. Perhaps I should wait until you have completed your drawing."

"I've watched you sew," her uncle retorted. "I've seen how long it takes you to stitch two little triangles together. If you wait until my drawing is done, you'll never finish the quilt in time."

Dorothea managed to keep from sighing. "Very well," she said. "What colors would you like?"

"Serviceable colors. Whatever scraps you have in your sewing basket will be fine."

"You have said nothing about how large you would like your quilt to be."

"The usual size will do."

Abruptly as that, he departed for the barn, calling over his shoulder for Dorothea's father. Dorothea watched the men go, mystified. A quiltmaker would never spend so much time on the design for a quilt only to dismiss qualities as important as color and size. Of course, Uncle Jacob was no quiltmaker, despite the care he had lavished on his drawing, or he would have known it was no simple matter to leave empty spaces in a quilt top to fill in later. Perhaps he did know, but did not mind the extra work and difficulty it created, since he was not the one to sew it.

Since her uncle had neglected to douse the lamp, Dorothea got to work, beginning by calculating how large one Delectable Mountains block should be in order to make a finished quilt suitable for Uncle Jacob's bed. Then she made templates out of stiff paper, trimming the edges carefully, since even an error the width of a pencil mark, when multiplied over the many pieces that made up a quilt top, could alter a quilt's size considerably.

"I hardly know what colors to select for such a quilt," said Dorothea to her mother as she set the completed templates aside.

"I believe some bright pinks and blues and cheerful butter yellows will suit your uncle nicely," advised Lorena, looking up from her darning to grin at her daughter.

Dorothea laughed and opened the scrap bag. She searched through the pieces of cloth and retrieved scraps of brown, tan, Turkey red, and somber blue, as well as lighter shirting fabrics for the background; Uncle Jacob typically wore such colors, so she supposed they could be considered his favorites. The fabrics were serviceable, just as he had requested, since they were the leftover scraps from the household sewing.

Every evening thereafter Dorothea took up her needle and triangular scraps and worked on the quilt. If she happened to take up mending instead, she felt the weight of her uncle's disapproving glare until she switched to his quilt. She forced herself to think of it as a gift, since the task was more tolerable if she pretended he had not all but commanded her to make it.

Within three days she had completed two blocks and Uncle Jacob had brought her another sketch, a lopsided, four-pointed star. One point was longer than the others, reaching from the center of the star all the way to the upper left corner. Uncle Jacob asked for the original drawing and indicated that the new block was to be inserted in the very center of the quilt. When she asked if the other blank spaces in the design were to be filled with similar stars, he said, "You have plenty of work to do now without worrying about the work that will come later."

"It would be easier—and faster—to make your quilt if I knew the entire design," she told him.

"You've made more difficult quilts than this one," he said shortly. "But if you can't manage on your own, get your mother to help you."

It was her uncle's cooperation, not her mother's help, that Dorothea needed, but of course she could not say so. After he left, Dorothea studied both drawings and realized that her uncle's design was not as well crafted as she had first thought. While the lines were straight and precise, she detected some accidental variation among the Delectable Mountains blocks. Most of the larger triangles had four smaller triangles along each side, but a very few had only three, and some five. Dorothea was tempted to point out his error to him, since he took so much grim pleasure in finding the faults of others, but such impertinence would alarm her parents, who were sure that one single offense would be enough to compel Uncle Jacob to strike the Grangers from his will. Instead Dorothea decided to spare his pride and correct his mistake without drawing attention to it.

Sunday came, bringing with it the promised diversion of Cyrus Pearson's visit. He arrived promptly at two, and at the sound of his horse's hooves on the road, Uncle Jacob broke his customary rule about keeping the Sabbath as a day of rest and made excuses about harnesses that needed mending. He withdrew to the barn, but it was Dorothea's father who met Cyrus and helped him tend to his horse.

Dorothea and Lorena sewed in the parlor while they waited for Dorothea's father to bring in Cyrus. When she heard their boots on the floor, Dorothea wondered fleetingly what Cyrus would think of Uncle Jacob's austere furnishings compared to the grandeur of his stepfather's home, but when he entered wearing the same cheerful grin with which he greeted her in brighter surroundings, she forgot her worries.

Lorena invited him to sit, and Dorothea went to the kitchen for tea. "Tell us, Mr. Pearson," said Lorena as Dorothea poured. "What do you have in mind for the library?"

"Yes, do tell us we are finally going to expand beyond a single shelf of books," said Dorothea, taking the chair beside her mother. "I believe I could recite all sixteen verbatim."

"You needn't boast of your cleverness," said Cyrus, a naughty twinkle in his eye. "You are famous in Creek's Crossing for your prodigious memory."

"I was not boasting," protested Dorothea. "I merely meant because I have read them so often, lacking other choices."

"Mr. Pearson, please do not tease my daughter or I shall have to ask you to leave," said Lorena, smiling. "I would hate to do that, because you've piqued our curiosity. What is this grand scheme of yours?"

"I cannot take all the credit for it," said Cyrus, accepting the cup Dorothea handed him. "My mother is the catalyst that motivates me. Her new husband is so occupied with matters of business that my mother needs other diversions. She insists that a few volumes of poetry and novels would not sustain her for long, but her new husband has neither the funds nor the space in his home for the number of books that would suffice. Therefore, expanding the town library seems the best solution."

"Agreed," said Dorothea. "Unfortunately, the good people of Creek's Crossing seem far abler at settling upon a solution than implementing one."

"Dorothea," said her mother, gently chiding. To Cyrus, she added, "Perhaps we could look to local benefactors to donate funds."

"My stepfather has already agreed to a substantial gift," he replied. "More to appease my mother than out of any literary interest of his own. Other prominent families have also promised donations, although not enough for a separate building. In fact, we will need quite a bit more if we are to afford an addition to the school and new books to fill it."

"It is perhaps too much to hope that one wealthy patron would contribute enough for an entire building," said Dorothea. "Even for the privilege of having his name over the door."

"Have you asked Mr. Nelson?" Lorena asked Cyrus. "After all, his father did pay to have the school built."

"Ah." Cyrus allowed a polite cough. "I believe—well, I did approach Thomas Nelson and was rebuffed."

"But he's the schoolmaster," said Dorothea. "He has a decided interest in the establishment of a proper library in Creek's Crossing. Think of the benefit to his pupils."

"I did remind him, but he was unmoved." Cyrus shrugged apologetically and looked almost as embarrassed as he had the night of his mother's party. "I do not think we can rely on his support."

"How disappointing," said Lorena. "When I think of how his father supported intellectual pursuits in the Elm Creek Valley, I confess I am surprised by his son's disinterest."

"We do not need the younger Mr. Nelson's support," said Dorothea determinedly. "Perhaps no one person can afford to donate an entire building, or even an addition to the school, but many could surely donate something a trifle smaller but no less essential. Those who contribute three dollars, for example, could have their names engraved on a plate affixed to a bookshelf."

When Lorena and Cyrus nodded their approval, Dorothea continued. "We could ask those less able to donate the gift of their labor. We will need people to build the addition."

"Of course," said Lorena. "Mr. Pearson, you should consult Mr. Wright. His carpentry skills are unparalleled in the valley and I'm quite certain he would design your addition free of charge. He would be an excellent choice for construction foreman."

"Mr. Wright?" said Cyrus, puzzled. "Do you mean Abel Wright?"

"The same. He's a good friend of ours. Use my name when you call on him and I'm sure he'll agree to help."

Cyrus looked dubious. "I cannot imagine he would be interested." He shrugged, his smile returning. "I think that we should impose only upon members of the community, people who would be likely to use the library."

"The Wright farm is not that far away," said Lorena, regarding Cyrus curiously. "I'm sure the Wrights will use the library as much as anyone else."

Dorothea thought of Constance Wright, how she was only just learning to read, and how she had declared she had seen as much of Creek's Crossing as she cared to see. She wondered if Cyrus had already met Constance or if he was simply more insightful than he appeared.

"These are all excellent ideas," said Cyrus. "I knew you would come through for me, Miss Granger. This is precisely why I told my mother you should be named secretary of fund-raising on the new library board."

"Secretary of fund-raising?" asked Dorothea. Lorena beamed at her.

"Of course. You would be ideal. My mother insisted on assuming that role herself, naturally, but she would very much appreciate your assistance."

"While I would like to help—" Dorothea shook her head, uncertain. "I was not expecting to play such a prominent role. I have my obligations to my uncle—"

"Surely he would release you from your chores occasionally so you might assist in such an important community effort."

"Mr. Pearson," said Lorena dryly, "have you met my brother?"

"I suppose it was too much to expect that you could be spared. I continue to underestimate the amount of work required by every member of a farmer's family, including the ladies." Cyrus looked endearingly disappointed. "I had so hoped you would be able to assist us. Your status as the schoolteacher lends credibility to a cause that has often floundered, and I had looked forward to seeing you more often in town."

"I am only the former schoolteacher," Dorothea reminded him. "Considering how briefly I held that position, I suspect I have little credibility to lend."

"You underestimate the esteem this town holds for you." The familiar mischievous light returned to his green eyes. "And my esteem, too. But very well. If the thought of a well-functioning lending library does not tempt you, if the prospect of escaping the drudgery of farm chores for what I hope you would consider pleasant company does not move you, if my personal appeals to your generous nature do not persuade you—" He rose. "I confess the latter wounds me the most, but—"

"Mr. Pearson," said Dorothea, laughing. "You have persuaded me. I want a library as much as your mother does, and I will assist in the effort as much as I am able."

"I cannot tell you how much this pleases me. My mother would like you to call on her at three o'clock Thursday afternoon for the first meeting of the library board. May I tell her you will be there?"

Dorothea nodded. She would obtain her uncle's approval somehow.

"Perhaps I might also escort you to the meeting?"

"Thank you," said Dorothea, "but I do not believe that will be necessary."

"I think that is a fine idea," said Lorena. "It is possible you will not be able to take our wagon. Your uncle may need the horses."

Dorothea reconsidered. Her mother was wise to anticipate an objection that might prevent her from attending. They agreed that Cyrus would come for her a half-hour before the meeting and bring her home afterward.

Cyrus lingered long enough to finish his tea, but left soon thereafter, citing other necessary errands. Dorothea changed out of her

Sunday dress and met her mother in the kitchen garden. That morning at breakfast, Uncle Jacob had announced that he did not want any preening young peacock of a man to interfere with the gathering of the potatoes. Dorothea was determined to show her uncle she could have callers and still complete her chores.

"What are you thinking, Mother?" Dorothea asked when her mother worked a long while in silence.

"I'm thinking that it seems as if the new library may at last become more than a fond wish," she said, brushing clumps of soil from a potato. "I also think it is very fine that you are wanted so badly on the library board. However . . ."

"Yes?" prompted Dorothea.

Her mother hesitated a moment longer before saying, "Nothing. I suppose it is good that Cyrus is so devoted to his mother."

Dorothea laughed. "You would fault him for being attentive to his mother's needs?"

"Only if it means he neglects the needs of others. Of course, there is no reason to assume he will." Lorena smiled ruefully. "I suppose if I did not dislike his mother so, his attentiveness would not bother me in the least."

Dorothea's mirth dimmed. She had not considered that joining the library board would mean more time in the presence of Cyrus's formidable mother.

DOROTHEA AND LORENA HURRIED, but they did not finish in the garden by the time they needed to begin making supper. Since only the potato rows were left, Lorena suggested they finish in the morning, since Uncle Jacob would likely not notice the neglected garden but would certainly notice a late meal. They washed quickly at the pump and ran to the kitchen, but although they raced through supper preparations, Uncle Jacob still sat at the table a full five minutes before his plate was set before him. They learned soon enough a further reason for his displeasure: As he cut into his bread, he announced that Lorena would return to the garden after her regular chores were through and remain there until the last potato was collected.

Lorena nodded without a word; Dorothea took a drink of water and tried to maintain the appearance of calm. Later, when her mother went to the back door, Dorothea followed.

"Where are you going?" said Uncle Jacob, reading his Bible in the fading daylight.

"To the garden with Mother."

"You have other work to do." He gestured to her sewing basket on the floor behind her usual chair.

"It's my fault we didn't finish the potatoes. I should help her."

"You should attend to your own business." He returned his attention to the page, holding the book close.

"It will be dark before she finishes."

"Dorothea." Lorena shook her head and reached for the lantern hanging on the peg beside the door.

"Leave it," said Uncle Jacob.

"It will take her twice as long in the dark as in the light," said Dorothea.

"Dorothea," said her father. "Mind your uncle."

"It's all right," murmured her mother. "I won't be long."

Lorena threw a shawl over her shoulders and slipped out the door. Simmering with anger, Dorothea stormed across the kitchen to her seat by the fireplace, unlit now though the early autumn evening was cool. She sat, fuming, hands clasped in her lap.

Uncle Jacob closed his Bible and put away his reading glasses. "You ought to get to work on that quilt."

"I ought to be helping my mother," said Dorothea. "Better yet, she ought to come inside. The garden can wait until morning."

"And fall behind on every chore entrusted to her tomorrow?" Uncle Jacob countered. "That is no way to run a farm, niece. I should think your father's failure would have taught you that."

Her father never looked up; Uncle Jacob might have been speaking of a stranger for all he seemed to care. "Thrift Farm was lost to a flood," said Dorothea tightly.

"Thrift Farm was in serious decline long before the waters claimed it. Elm Creek merely put it out of its misery."

"I have the milking," said Dorothea's father suddenly. He touched Dorothea's shoulder in passing and left out the back door, taking the lantern. Dorothea yearned to follow, but she understood her father's unspoken request and grudgingly opened her sewing basket. She sewed the pieces of her quilt block in silence, glancing at the door at the slightest noise for her parents' return. Her father entered first, without the lantern; she guessed where he had left it and, unfortunately, so did Uncle Jacob. He ordered her father to go and fetch it, but Dorothea announced that she would do it and left her sewing behind on her empty chair.

She found her mother on her hands and knees in the potato plot, working by lantern light. Dorothea swiftly knelt to help her.

"You should get back inside," said Lorena. "Your uncle will be furious."

"I don't care."

"You will care well enough if he should see fit to switch you."

At her words Dorothea could almost feel the sting of the hickory branch. "He hasn't switched me since I began wearing corsets and long skirts. I don't believe he will do so now."

Lorena sighed, pulling furiously at the weeds. "The older you get, the more you provoke him."

"Someone ought to stand up to him."

"Dorothea—" Lorena sat back on her heels. "You don't understand."

"I do understand. How long must we endure this? We don't need

Uncle Jacob or his farm. We can go out west, to Kansas, to California. We can stake a claim and make our own farm." She was almost in tears. "We can summon Jonathan. He will come. Surely they need doctors in the west."

"That's a very romantic notion, but your brother is only sixteen. We cannot interrupt his training now, and he is unlikely to receive a proper education in unsettled country." Lorena picked up the spade and stabbed at the earth. "Your uncle is right in one respect: Your father and I were very poor farmers. We would have no chance of establishing a farm in unfamiliar climate, on ground that has never felt a plow."

"We have learned a great deal in eight years."

"Not enough to risk our lives when we stand to inherit a well-tended farm right here."

Dorothea knew the argument was useless. She yanked on a fistful of weeds and said, "Uncle Jacob is likely to leave the farm to someone else just to spite us."

"To whom would he leave it? He has no friends and no other relations."

"Then he will probably live forever." Her anger spent, Dorothea listlessly brushed soil from a potato, shadowed and strange in the flickering light. "He sent me to fetch the lantern."

"Then you should take it to him." When Dorothea hesitated, Lorena smiled. "Go ahead. I'm almost finished."

"Very well," said Dorothea, but she stayed with her mother until the last potato was harvested.

Dorothea waited until Thursday morning at breakfast to tell Uncle Jacob she had been specifically requested as the former schoolteacher to assist with the creation of a new library.

"Why don't they ask the new schoolmaster?" asked Uncle Jacob.

"They did. Mr. Nelson refused."

"So once again you are their second choice."

Dorothea refused to be baited. "I suppose I am. Nevertheless, the request is a great honor, and I am obliged to assist them."

Uncle Jacob shook his head. "I cannot spare the horses to take you into town."

"That is your only objection?" asked Lorena, piling more flapjacks on her brother's plate.

"It is." Uncle Jacob waved her away before she buried his plate entirely. "But it is reason enough."

"Then you will be pleased to know Dorothea does not require the horses," said Lorena brightly. "Mr. Pearson has offered to escort her."

Uncle Jacob's jaw tightened. "I see." He knew he had been tricked, but he could not retract his words. "See that you return home promptly afterward. Your chores will be finished before you go to bed if you must stay up all night."

"Thank you, Uncle," said Dorothea, but he spared her only an irritated glare as he pushed back his chair and rose from the table.

"Never mind him," said Lorena as they cleared the table. "I will finish your work as well as my own. You are a young girl and you deserve a pleasant outing."

Riding into Creek's Crossing to attend a board meeting at the home of Mrs. Violet Pearson Engle was hardly Dorothea's idea of a pleasant outing, but she was interested in the library, and Cyrus never failed to be an engaging companion. For all the friendliness between them when they met in town, they did not truly know each other well. They had attended school together only one year, a brief interval immediately following the Granger family's arrival in Creek's Crossing and preceding Cyrus's departure for a boys' academy in Philadelphia. When they were in school together,

Cyrus had sat in the back row with the other older boys who thought themselves too old for school, laughing in whispers and genially ignoring the teacher, the sweetly befuddled Miss Gunther. Dorothea did not care for such disrespect and laziness, and she had ignored Cyrus and his friends except when her best friend Mary's lovesick admiration forced her to notice him. While Mary mourned when Cyrus left Creek's Crossing, Dorothea never missed him. To her pleasant surprise, however, when she encountered him during his rare visits home for holidays and summers, it was evident that his time back east and abroad had greatly improved him. He behaved in a far more gentlemanly fashion than he had as a boy, and if he did tend to tease, a manner Mary now derided, Dorothea found it a welcome and refreshing departure from Uncle Jacob's mercurial tempers.

Cyrus arrived, not in a wagon as she had expected, but driving a gleaming black carriage pulled by two lively Morgans. Uncle Jacob glared balefully from the barn door as Cyrus helped her inside, neither bidding them good-bye nor forbidding her to go. "He's not an easy fellow to live with, I presume," Cyrus said as they rode away.

"He has given us a home," said Dorothea, reluctant to appear ungrateful. "But he can be . . . difficult."

Cyrus grinned. "I'm sure you're being kinder than he deserves."

They chatted easily as they rode, and when they crossed on the ferry, Cyrus placed a hand on her elbow to steady her—unnecessarily, for she was quite comfortable on the river—and alternately alarmed and amused her with stories of his boyhood exploits on the riverfront. "It's a wonder your mother survived such a mischievous son," she remarked as they climbed back aboard the carriage and left the ferry.

"It is indeed, but my mother is a wonder herself." Cyrus's grin turned rueful. "I suppose I should be grateful that Mr. Engle recognized that as well."

Dorothea regarded him curiously. "You objected to the marriage?"

"I did not. Mr. Engle is a decent sort, and my mother cares for him. Still . . ." He shrugged. "She did not need to marry again. I was rather surprised she did not realize that."

"Perhaps she did not marry for need, but for love."

Cyrus looked as if the thought had not occurred to him. "I suppose it's possible. I also suppose that if I had been engaged, the promise of my upcoming wedding would have been inducement enough to encourage her to remain unmarried."

Dorothea laughed. "Now you say she married because she longed for the gaiety of a party! Goodness, Cyrus, can you not admit it is possible she loves your stepfather?"

Cyrus frowned thoughtfully at the horses. "When you put it that way, I suppose she must adore him. I feel quite foolish for not noticing before."

"Now you're teasing me."

"Not merely now, Dorothea. I tease you every chance I get."

They had left the older section of town behind and were just about to turn on to the Engles' street when a man seated unsteadily on horseback rounded the corner at a canter. His clothes were dusty as if he had taken a hard fall or two on the road into town, his filthy hat pulled down low over unkempt hair. In the moment it took Cyrus to avoid a collision, Dorothea recognized the rider as Amos Liggett.

His bloodshot eyes widened at the sight of them. "Pearson," he rasped, wheeling his horse around. Tobacco juice dribbled into the dark stubble of his beard. "I was just coming to talk to you."

Cyrus straightened. "To me?"

"Yes, yes. That matter we talked about. I took care of it. I mean, I *will* take care of it. But I need a little money first. Just a bit more, like last time."

Cyrus's brow furrowed, but his voice was polite when he replied, "I'm afraid I don't understand."

The man sawed at the horse's reins. "You remember. At the tavern. You asked me—" Suddenly his eyes narrowed as his gaze shifted to Dorothea. "Say. Ain't you the Granger girl? When's your uncle gonna pay me what he owes?"

At once, Cyrus chirruped to the horses and the carriage pulled away. "Call on me at my office if you have business to discuss," he called over his shoulder as they continued around the corner. To Dorothea, he said, "Please accept my apologies. I never should have paused long enough for him to address you."

"What business would you have with Amos Liggett?" said Dorothea, shaken.

"No business at all. I have no idea what he is talking about. However, sometimes it is expedient to humor men in his condition." He shook his head, frowning. "I don't know what Creek's Crossing is coming to when drunkards can accost young ladies in the street."

Dorothea managed a smile. "I hardly feel as if I had been accosted." She did not care for Mr. Liggett, especially after what he had done to Charley Stokey, but she had to admit he was right: Her uncle ought to pay him something for the days he had worked. She turned around to see what Mr. Liggett would do next, but he was nowhere to be seen. "He seemed convinced you had hired him for some chore."

"Either the liquor has confused him or he has pride enough to disguise the request for a handout. Or . . ."

"Yes?" prompted Dorothea.

"I should not bring it up. I would hate to be accused of spreading tales. But perhaps he has mistaken me for someone else. After all, he could not have been on his way to call on me. He already passed my house."

"Who, then?"

He leaned closer and grinned. "If I tell you, will you think me a vile gossip?"

"If you do not tell me, I will be quite furious with you."

"I could not bear that. Very well. Thomas Nelson."

"Mr. Nelson? Why?"

"Some people claim we bear some resemblance to each other."

Dorothea had to laugh. "I do not see it."

"Really?" Cyrus pretended to be wounded. "But most women of my acquaintance say Mr. Nelson is a handsome man. Do you mean to say I am not?"

"I mean to say nothing on that subject at all. You will not trick me into flattering your vanity."

"And yet you have done so, by revealing it would be flattery." Cyrus stopped the carriage in front of his stepfather's house and smiled wickedly at her. "Perhaps you are not as clever as your reputation would have us believe."

Dorothea opened her mouth to protest and felt heat rise in her cheeks as she realized he was right. His grin broadened at her speechlessness, and he jumped down from the carriage. "I have heard that Mr. Nelson has recently been hiring farmhands," she said as Cyrus assisted her down from the carriage. "But why would he hire a man of Mr. Liggett's reputation?"

Cyrus shrugged and offered her his arm. "A man hires another man to do what he cannot do, or what he will not do. But he usually hires a man of like mind."

Not in Uncle Jacob's case, Dorothea thought. "If you are right, I fear for the pupils of Creek's Crossing."

Cyrus laughed, but Dorothea's misgivings ran deep. Mr. Liggett was bad enough. It was unsettling to think of what a like-minded man in a position of influence and authority might do.

❁

TO HER DISAPPOINTMENT, CYRUS departed shortly after seeing her inside, promising to deliver her home once the meeting concluded. She had assumed he would be on the library board as well.

Five women had already gathered in the parlor, which with its furniture and rugs restored looked much different than it had on the night of Mr. Nelson's welcoming party. Mrs. Engle sat on the overstuffed sofa by the front window with the others seated in pairs on her right and left hand, giving her the air of a queen presiding at court. The others glanced up as Dorothea entered: Mrs. Deakins, the mayor's wife; Mrs. Collins, married to the banker; Miss Nadelfrau, the timid dressmaker; and Mrs. Claverton, who smiled a welcome and beckoned Dorothea to come and sit beside her. Dorothea murmured an apology and seated herself; she had not realized she was late.

"Before you entered, Miss Granger," said Mrs. Engle, "we had just decided that your suggestion about selling nameplates for bookshelves was inspired."

"Thank you," replied Dorothea. Cyrus must have told his mother, for Dorothea had not.

Mrs. Engle smiled graciously. Her glossy black hair was piled in formal curls on top of her head and tied with a white velvet ribbon. Her skin was very fair, and her slight plumpness gave her an appearance of softness despite her sharp green eyes, which were as haughty as her son's were mischievous.

"Still," piped up Miss Nadelfrau, the dressmaker, who was known to be good with figures of all sorts, "it will not be enough."

"So, assistant to the secretary of fund-raising," said Mrs. Claverton, nudging her. "What ideas have you brought us?"

"I think we would be wise to consider a social event," said Dorothea as they watched her expectantly. "Something so splendid no one would dream of missing it."

"And no one would mind spending their money to attend," added Mrs. Claverton.

"I know the very thing," declared Mrs. Engle. "An evening of musical celebration. My cousin is a former soloist with the Philadelphia Opera. I'm sure I could persuade her to donate her services."

The other women murmured their agreement. "That does sound wonderful," agreed Dorothea, thinking of how much her mother would enjoy it. Unfortunately, they had no suitable auditorium large enough to suit a soloist and still accommodate the crowds Dorothea hoped to draw. "But I thought perhaps a celebration with dancing and a covered-dish supper."

Mrs. Collins tittered. "One does not dance to opera."

"I also would not expect my guests to bring covered dishes," said Mrs. Engle. "My cook is capable of a truly remarkable feast."

As the others discussed a possible menu, Dorothea gradually understood. "You mean to hold the event here?"

"Of course." Mrs. Engle waved a plump hand gracefully. "Unless one of you would prefer to offer your home."

Miss Nadelfrau, Mrs. Collins, and Mrs. Deakins hastened to assure Mrs. Engle that no one would prefer their homes to hers, while Mrs. Claverton watched Dorothea with a tolerant smile, waiting to see what she would say.

"As lovely as your home is, Mrs. Engle," said Dorothea, "and it is, truly, the loveliest in Creek's Crossing, it would not accommodate the entire town."

The other women exchanged glances. "You mean to invite everyone?" asked Mrs. Collins.

"Yes," said Dorothea. "After all, it is a fund-raiser. The greater the attendance, the more money we shall raise."

"My dear," said Mrs. Deakins. "We cannot expect common farmers to be interested in a library. It is unkind to take the hard-earned money of people who will never peruse the collection."

"I expect quite the opposite will happen. I am sure many people will make use of the library who were not able to offer a cent at the fund-raiser."

All but Mrs. Claverton, who hid a smile behind her handkerchief, regarded her incredulously. Then a nervous smile flickered on Mrs. Collins's lips. "You must excuse young Miss Granger," she said. "She is an idealist. As a former schoolteacher she has an exceptionally high regard for books and assumes all others feel the same."

"She has a very good point, however," said Mrs. Claverton. "As the wife of a common farmer, I plan to visit the library frequently. Since most of the citizens of Creek's Crossing are farmers, we would be foolish to ignore the potential of their accumulated contributions."

"I suppose it would do no harm to open the event to the whole town," said Miss Nadelfrau. "If they are interested enough in a library and if they can pay the admission charge, I suppose they should be welcome."

"Just as everyone will be welcome at the library," said Dorothea, fervently hoping that she would not have to argue that point, as well. "The more people who are involved in creating the library, the more community support we will have, and the greater our chances for success. Which brings me to my second idea."

The others looked wary. "And what would that be?" asked Mrs. Engle.

"An opportunity quilt."

The others looked so relieved that Dorothea was tempted to ask them what they had expected her to say. "What a charming idea," said Mrs. Engle. "I believe I might have a quilt I could donate."

"I'm sure everyone in the Elm Creek Valley would be thrilled to own a quilt made by your hands," said Mrs. Deakins. "We will sell a thousand tickets, surely!"

Dorothea hid her exasperation. "That is very generous of you,

Mrs. Engle, but I believe this occasion calls for something unique. I thought instead we might make a quilt of Album blocks."

Mrs. Claverton and Mrs. Nadelfrau nodded, intrigued, but Mrs. Deakins glanced nervously at Mrs. Engle, who said, "A what? I've never heard of such a thing."

"I'm sure you have," said Mrs. Claverton. "Any variety of patterns might be used, as long as there is a piece of plain muslin at the center, upon which the quilter signs her name, her place of residence, the date, and so forth. A lady might collect a variety of such blocks from the ladies of her circle, then embroider over the ink, sew the blocks together, and quilt a delightful remembrance of her friends."

"Since we are raising funds for a library," said Dorothea, "I thought we might write to our favorite authors and ask them to send us scraps of muslin bearing their signatures. We shall embroider the names and piece the blocks ourselves. Think of the excitement that will grow in town as we announce what illustrious autographs have arrived in the post."

"The social event can be a quilting bee," Mrs. Collins guessed, delighted.

Dorothea nodded. "But we'll make it more than a quilting bee. We will have a dance, a covered-dish supper, and of course, the drawing for the quilt."

"Such a quilt would be quite valuable," mused Mrs. Engle. She glanced upon the sofa, as if imagining the Album quilt draped over the back.

Dorothea cast her final hook. "Quite valuable indeed, especially if we include the autographs of local persons of note, including, of course, the president of the library board and the mayor's wife, if they would condescend to participate."

Mrs. Deakins beamed, and Mrs. Engle smiled indulgently. "Indeed we would. Well, Miss Granger, I must congratulate myself for including you on the library board. You have already been of great service to us."

Dorothea thanked her, but confessed that her motives were completely selfish. She wanted a library and was willing to do almost anything to ensure that one was built as soon as possible.

After some discussion—in which Dorothea repeatedly had to gently remind the others that they could not have the quilting bee within a month and call it a Harvest Dance, charming though the idea was, because they had to allow time for writing to the authors, receiving their replies, and piecing the quilt top—they settled on the end of February. It was a dreary month much in need of brightening with festivity, Mrs. Engle thought, while Dorothea and Mrs. Claverton noted that the weather would be favorable for travel, but not mild enough to interfere with spring planting.

Before they parted, Mrs. Claverton assigned everyone a part of the work of planning the event. Dorothea's task was to compose the letter that would be sent to the authors. Mrs. Engle also instructed each of them to make a list of ten authors who should be contacted. Already Dorothea could think of twice that many, and she was sure her parents would be eager to contribute more names.

On the ride home, she told Cyrus how the meeting had gone and queried him about his favorite authors. "What men and women of letters would you like to see immortalized in our quilt?" she asked. "For whose autograph would you be willing to buy a chance?"

"Shakespeare and Homer."

"That helps me not at all," she scolded him.

"The only person of letters whose autograph I would care to possess is your own. If your name is embroidered on that quilt, I would offer twenty dollars."

"Then you would very likely win the drawing," said Dorothea, trying to hide her astonishment. "Since the chances will likely cost only twenty-five cents."

He shrugged. "If that is what I must do to be assured of winning, then that is what I shall do."

At first, Dorothea could not find the words to reply. She was not certain if he was in earnest, if he only meant to flatter her, if he thought her a silly, giddy girl who would be impressed by such a lavish show. She could not deny being pleased that he would be willing to spend so much money for a quilt with her name on it. "The library board will be very grateful for your contribution," she eventually said, but he merely smiled.

That evening after chores were done, Dorothea drafted a letter to the authors, then set it aside to revise later. She took up the pieces of a quilt block for her uncle's quilt, eager to finish it so that it would not interfere with the Authors' Album once the autographs began to arrive. Lorena worked on her mending on the opposite chair, suggesting writers the library board should contact. "Knowing where to send the letters will be the trick," she mused, threading a needle. "Some writers are reclusive, others are itinerant, and many are both."

Uncle Jacob, mending a boot sole in the light of the fire, snorted. "You could sign the names yourself and no one would know the difference."

"We may resort to that if none of our authors favors us with a reply," said Dorothea seriously, with a wink for her mother.

Uncle Jacob looked up. "If I thought you might engage in such dishonesty—" He peered at the quilt block in her hands. "What's that?"

"This?" Dorothea did not understand. "It's a Delectable Mountains block for your quilt."

"That's not right at all." In two strides Uncle Jacob crossed the room and snatched the quilt block from her hands. Pins scraped her palms. "Why are these triangles pointing this way?" Suddenly he dug into her sewing basket and scattered the completed blocks on the hearth, searching. "All of these squares have four triangles along the side. All of them! Didn't I make a drawing for you? Didn't I tell you to follow it precisely?"

"You did."

"Then why did you deliberately disobey me? Some of the squares were to have three, some five."

"I did not mean to disobey," said Dorothea, astounded by his fury. "I thought those were errors. I meant only to correct—"

"Don't be presumptuous, niece. If I give you a drawing and tell you to reproduce it exactly, it is not your place to add or subtract a single stitch."

"Jacob, it is only a quilt," said Robert. "Dorothea meant no harm."

"I assure you I will fix my mistakes." Dorothea's voice shook with surprise and offense. "Your quilt will be precisely as you have drawn it."

"See that it is," her uncle growled. He retreated to his chair and took up his torn boot again. "And do not think I will allow you to work on this library quilt until you have finished mine."

"Of course, Uncle."

She lowered her gaze so he would not see the anger she could not mask. There was no need; already he had returned his attention to his work, ignoring her. On hands and knees, she gathered the scattered quilt blocks, setting aside those she would have to rip apart to suit her uncle's whims.

Chapter Four

DOROTHEA RIPPED OUT the seams and made over five of the Delectable Mountains blocks according to her uncle's drawing. She had no idea why he insisted on his peculiar design, but in her less charitable moments, she believed his only intention was to be contrary. He provided her with three additional sketches: one with curved pieces like a Fool's Puzzle in disarray; one with narrow, pieced lines like a braid; and one that resembled the Spiderweb block with eight pieced triangles seamed together to make an octagon. When she remarked that such unique blocks would stand out, surrounded as they were by the traditional Delectable Mountains blocks, Uncle Jacob thought for a moment, jabbed a thumb at a piece of light shirting fabric, and said, "Make those blocks from that lighter fabric."

"All of the pieces?" queried Dorothea, who had assumed that he wanted his original designs to attract attention.

"Not the star in the middle. It is fine as it is. The other three blocks."

Dorothea tried to convince him that this was a mistake, since the individual pieces would be indistinguishable from one another, but he refused to listen. "What is the point, then?" she asked her mother after he had left the room. "I might as well use solid fabric if the piecing is going to be all but invisible. He said he wanted a quilt like his mother's, but I cannot imagine Grandmother making any quilt like this."

Lorena admitted that she could not recall such an unusual quilt among her mother's creations.

Dorothea contented herself with using slightly darker tones for some of the pieces so the elements of his designs would not entirely disappear. She also suggested adding a border of blue cotton salvaged from a worn coverlet to frame the quilt. Uncle Jacob considered, and replied, "I guess that wouldn't do any harm." It was a less than enthusiastic response, but she decided to add the border anyway, for her own satisfaction if not his.

Dorothea complied with his wishes as well as she could, and once, when he seemed in an agreeable mood, she asked if she might make one slight change to his design to reduce the number of seams. He objected without explanation, so she resigned herself to repeated tests of her sewing dexterity until his quilt was finished—except on one later occasion, when Dorothea forgot prudence and remarked that a certain new sketch resembled a ladder. Uncle Jacob frowned at the paper, then turned it ninety degrees and added four angled lines. "There," he said, leaving Dorothea with a design that required three additional seams and that still resembled a ladder, albeit a crooked ladder on its side. After that, she learned to keep her artistic commentary to herself.

The first of November came, and the first snowfall. Uncle Jacob grew increasingly impatient for Dorothea to complete the quilt, to her mother's consternation. "He already has three wool blankets for his bed," she reminded Dorothea, as they took advantage of one last sunny day to boil the winter bedding in the washhouse. "He is in no danger of freezing without his precious new quilt."

"I imagine he is eager to see his artistic vision realized," replied Dorothea. "No, I am quite certain he is simply growing more disagreeable with age. I am glad you and Father have managed to keep your senses of humor, although I suppose Uncle could not be expected to keep something he never had."

"I never thought I would say this, but I am determined that you should marry."

"What?"

"You should marry and leave this farm."

Dorothea forced a smile. "Are you that eager to be rid of me?"

"It is my fault you are not married yet." A deep groove of worry appeared between Lorena's brows as she stirred the boiling kettle of laundry with a stick. "Other mothers—and how I disdained them for it—train their daughters from an early age how to attract a suitor and win his undying devotion. In my hubris I thought I should train your mind instead."

"And I am heartily glad you did."

"But if you had married, you would have a home of your own now and be out from beneath your uncle's thumb."

"Firstly, Mother, I am only nineteen and may marry yet. Secondly, it is entirely possible I would have married into a situation less pleasant than this." Dorothea fed one of her father's newly cleaned shirts into the mangle. "Do not despair. I suspect you shall be rid of me eventually."

She did not tell her mother how often she had imagined having a home of her own, with an affectionate husband rather than a sour old uncle as her companion, but she did not blame her lack of suitors on her upbringing. No man she would consider marrying would disdain an educated wife, so the love for learning they had instilled in her would not have kept a prospective husband away. Her lack of any wealth aside from her saved wages, however, did act as a deterrent. Young men in love did not mind if their beloved lacked thirteen quilts, but their mothers did, and mothers and fathers alike cared if a young woman brought nothing to the marriage except herself.

It was little wonder that Lorena and Robert had cast their principles aside when opportunities arose to secure their son's future. Charlotte Claverton was demure, lovely, and the only child of one of the wealthiest farmers in Creek's Crossing. After Jonathan inherited Uncle Jacob's farm and married Charlotte, he would be master of the largest farm in the Elm Creek Valley. If he preferred, he could continue to practice medicine and leave the management of the farm to his family. Either way he would provide for them—as long as everything came to pass as Robert and Lorena hoped. The engagement, if one could call it that, was an agreement between the parents alone, even though Jonathan or Charlotte would likely find it difficult to refuse when both sets of parents were so eager for them to marry. The Clavertons did seem to favor the match as much as the Grangers, although they had hinted that they would withhold their consent if Jonathan and Charlotte did not learn to be fond of each other, or if Jonathan did not inherit his uncle's farm. Still, it was a future, one that left Dorothea alternately appalled and envious.

"I have only myself to blame for your unhappiness," said Lorena.

"Mother, I assure you I am content."

In truth, she was somewhat less than content. She had been more content by far when she was Creek's Crossing's schoolteacher. But she knew marriage was not the only road leading from Uncle Jacob's farm. And, too, there was Cyrus.

He called for her every other Thursday to carry her to his mother's house for meetings of the library board. He came even after Uncle Jacob approached as Cyrus was helping her from the carriage and told him gruffly that he need not call for Dorothea anymore. He would drive her himself, and if he was too busy, she was more than capable of driving herself. To her satisfaction, Cyrus declared that he would not think of inconveniencing Uncle Jacob when escorting Dorothea brought him so much pleasure. "Nevertheless, it is not necessary for you to return," said Uncle Jacob. When Cyrus appeared the following second Thursday as usual, Dorothea enjoyed seeing her uncle thwarted almost as much as she delighted in realizing that Cyrus came for her because he wanted to, not because she had no other way to get to his mother's house. He was becoming a good friend, even if he did tend to tease and joke any time she tried to engage him in more thoughtful discourse.

Still, his merry conversation was a welcome diversion from Uncle Jacob's sour grumblings, and planning the library benefit made her feel useful again, as she had when she was the schoolteacher. She knew little of how the school fared without her. If she encountered a former pupil in Creek's Crossing, she could query him only so much without seeming to be eager for bad news. All she knew was that the students appeared to be progressing in their lessons, their parents seemed satisfied, and, to her chagrin, her darling pupils did not seem to miss her as much as she had secretly hoped.

Dorothea speculated that, since the young people of the town seemed to think well of him, time in Creek's Crossing must have softened the new schoolmaster's heart toward its inhabitants. Her theory was soundly disproven one Sunday when Mr. Nelson walked his bay stallion onto the ferry she and Cyrus had already boarded. They had left the carriage to stand by the rail, and when Cyrus called out a polite greeting, Mr. Nelson gave him a curt nod and offered Dorothea a wordless glance before continuing forward. After securing his horse, he took a position at the far opposite side of the ferry near the pilot, although Dorothea and Cyrus were the only other passengers on board.

"How is that dreadful irritation, Mr. Nelson?" Dorothea called to him brightly. His back was ramrod straight, and she knew that he had heard her, though he did not turn around. "You see how he shuns me," she added in only a slightly lower tone to Cyrus, not caring if Mr.

Nelson overheard. "He is so offended by the presence of an ignorant country girl that he must stand at the far side of the ferry."

"Perhaps he wants to avoid the embarrassment of another intellectual thrashing. If the most agreeable woman in Creek's Crossing would trounce him at his own welcome party, what might she do elsewhere?"

Dorothea flushed with pleasure and shame. She was pleased that Cyrus found her so agreeable, but until that moment she had not considered that it might have been inappropriate to point out Mr. Nelson's ignorance of local customs and flora at his first introduction into Creek's Crossing society. Then she remembered how he had provoked her and she hardened her heart. "I wonder if any mortal creature could hope to win his approval."

"A more puzzling question is what occasions his travels today," mused Cyrus. "Do you suppose he is on his way to visit your uncle, or perhaps your parents?"

"I doubt that very much," said Dorothea with a little laugh. "He has never called upon us before, and my uncle's reputation is usually enough to keep away even the most determined uninvited guest."

"If it is any consolation, I strongly suspect he wishes to avoid me, not you."

"I thought you were friends." They had seemed companionable enough at Mrs. Engle's party.

"Merely acquaintances, and recently less than that." Cyrus shifted so that his back was to Mr. Nelson, an unnecessary gesture since Mr. Nelson's attention was studiously fixed on the distant shoreline. "His ungentlemanly behavior at my mother's party concerned me, especially since I know the school board hired him solely on the basis of his father's recommendation. I hope you will not think ill of me that I decided to inquire into his background."

"Not at all." Dorothea could not help feeling wounded that she was so readily replaced by a man about whom the school board had known so little. She hoped for her former pupils' sakes that he at least had earned the university degree credited to him. "What did you discover?"

"While his father's reputation is beyond reproach, I regret that Thomas Nelson's is not. He has some decidedly questionable views on the subject of slavery, opinions that led to certain actions, which, in turn, led to imprisonment."

"You're joking." Astonished, Dorothea stole a look at Mr. Nelson. He chose that moment to look their way, and his gaze locked with Dorothea's. She raised her chin and met his gaze boldly, determined to show him she was unafraid, despite hearing the worst of the rumors about him confirmed. She had thought from their first encounter that his eyes burned too brightly for the solemn scholar he purported to be, and now she knew why.

"I wish it were not true, but it is." Cyrus frowned and shook his head. "He spent two years in prison but was released before completing his sentence, it is said, because his father exerted his influence upon the local judiciary."

Dorothea knew all too well what influence the elder Mr. Nelson wielded. "I assume you told your stepfather," she said, looking away from Mr. Nelson to Cyrus at a sudden thought. "Surely the school board was not happy to discover he had been falsely represented."

"On the contrary, they had known all along. After the school board agreed to make Thomas Nelson schoolmaster but before he came to Creek's Crossing, his father disclosed his son's incarceration, although he declined to reveal the particulars of the crime. Mr. Nelson the elder assured them that his son had repented entirely and asked only that a compassionate, Christian town allow him the opportunity to redeem himself through useful service."

"So he will stay on as schoolmaster?"

Cyrus shrugged. "My mother says the school board was moved by his father's pleas, and since he has all the other necessary qualifications and no other likely candidate has appeared, he will suffice as long as his criminal activities remain a part of his past."

"I see." No other likely candidate, indeed. Dorothea crossed her arms, drawing her shawl around herself at a sudden chill gust of wind from the creek. How could the school board entrust the impressionable minds and characters of the young people of Creek's Crossing to a man whose objectionable opinions about slavery had driven him to commit criminal acts? For that matter, what had he done? Beaten a fugitive slave in the streets of Philadelphia? Set fire to a school for freedmen? Dorothea could easily imagine a dozen possible offenses, each reason enough to keep Mr. Nelson far from the Creek's Crossing school, despite his respected father's entreaties.

Cyrus eyed her and chuckled. "Now, Dorothea, don't be cross. The school board was pleased with your efforts, but they never expected you to stay on. A young woman with your prospects— well, they had already recently lost one maiden schoolteacher. They did not want to so soon lose another."

Dorothea shrugged and forced a smile as if she understood the school board's judgment, when in truth she found it unfathomable. Then, when she thought of how Miss Gunther had been "lost," the smile came easier, and with it, a blush. She turned so Cyrus would not see the color rising in her cheeks, knowing he enjoyed any opportunity to tease, and her eyes met Mr. Nelson's again. She gave him her brightest, most cheerful smile, as if they were the very best of friends, and was delighted to see him turn away again, frowning in irritated bewilderment.

By the end of November, the harvest was complete, Uncle Jacob had drawn the last odd patch for his quilt, and the other members of the library board had debated and revised Dorothea's letter for what felt to her like the hundredth time. Delicately, not wishing to appear overly protective of her prose, she suggested that they allow her to send out the most recent version without further revising, or they would have no time left to complete the quilt.

To Dorothea's enormous relief, they agreed at last. "Now that we have a suitable letter," said Mrs. Engle, "to whom shall we send it? I do hope each of you remembered to make up a list of proper candidates."

"How many authors and personages of note do we require?" asked Mrs. Collins anxiously, clutching a sheet of paper in her lap. Dorothea glimpsed a list of perhaps five names, half the number Mrs. Engle requested from each woman present.

"I think we should send out a great many invitations," said Miss Nadelfrau, glancing to Mrs. Engle for approval. "It will mean more letter-writing and more postage, but not everyone will respond, and the more requests we send out, the more signatures shall be returned."

Mrs. Engle nodded, and Dorothea also agreed, but Mrs. Collins hesitated. "What if we receive too many autographs? We would not want our quilt to be too large and cumbersome or it will seem ridiculous."

"We should be fortunate to have such a problem," said Mrs. Claverton. "If we receive too many signatures, we can stitch the extra blocks to the back of the quilt."

"We shall do no such thing," declared Mrs. Engle. "That is a fine way to insult a renowned author, to tell him his signature is good enough only for the back of the quilt. No, if we receive more than we need, we shall choose those written in the most pleasing hand. The others we shall discard. If a discarded author should ever view the quilt and wonder what became of his signature, we shall feign ignorance and pretend his autograph was lost in the post."

Dorothea was about to object to this plan when Mrs. Deakins

said, "A splendid solution. This will give us the opportunity to pick and choose."

"Which brings us again to our proposed authors." Mrs. Engle turned to Mrs. Collins. "Hester, would you be so good as to record the names?" Mrs. Collins nodded and lifted her pen to indicate her readiness. "My list is as follows: President Zachary Taylor, of course; Mrs. Zachary Taylor; Governor William Freame Johnston; Mrs. Johnston; Mr. Charles Dickens; Sir Walter Scott; Miss Catharine Maria Sedgwick; Mrs. Ann Sophia Winterbotham Stephens; Miss Maria Jane McIntosh; and Mrs. Ann Radcliffe."

"I believe Sir Walter Scott is deceased," murmured Miss Nadel-frau. "Mrs. Radcliffe, as well."

"Is that so? Very well, then. Scratch out their names and substitute mine and my husband's. That should make ten."

Mrs. Collins nodded, scribbling.

Next, Mrs. Claverton read her list—which boasted Washington Irving and James Fenimore Cooper as well as the painter Thomas Cole—followed by Mrs. Deakins. "Nearly all of my authors have been named," wailed Mrs. Collins when Mrs. Deakins had finished, and insisted upon reading her own list next, before every person on her list had already been proposed.

Then it was Dorothea's turn. "It was too difficult to choose only ten, so I have twelve," she said, unfolding her paper. "Ralph Waldo Emerson, Henry David Thoreau, Walt Whitman—"

"Goodness gracious, no," said Mrs. Engle.

"Who is Walt Whitman?" asked Mrs. Collins.

"I believe he is the lieutenant governor," replied Mrs. Deakins, looking to Mrs. Engle for confirmation.

"He is without question the most disgraceful poet of our age," declared Mrs. Engle. "My dear Dorothea, I cannot imagine you have read his notorious works or you would have known better than to suggest him."

"I did not know the lieutenant governor wrote poetry," murmured Mrs. Collins to Mrs. Deakins.

Astounded by the objection, Dorothea asked, "Mrs. Engle, have you read his work?"

"I most certainly have not. I would not have any such trash in my house, nor the name of its purveyor in my quilt."

"But if you have not read his work, how do you know it is trash?"

Mrs. Engle tittered, but her mirth carried an edge. "I do not need to be kicked by a horse to know it is not a pleasant experience."

"We can't expect to like all of one another's choices," said Mrs. Claverton, with a look that, while sympathetic, suggested Dorothea forgo further argument. "Besides, controversy may sell tickets. Dorothea, please continue reading your list."

"Margaret Fuller," said Dorothea, pretending not to notice the hard stare Mrs. Engle now leveled at her. "Robert Browning and Elizabeth Barrett Browning. William Cullen Bryant."

"Absolutely not," Mrs. Engle broke in.

Dorothea lowered her paper and suppressed a sigh. "He is a writer, and a personage of note. Why should he not be included?"

"Apparently we must make our criteria more specific," said Mrs. Engle. "Dorothea, dear girl, I do not blame you. I am sure you have no idea what sort of radical diatribes in the guise of literature these so-called authors on your list have shamelessly paraded in front of the public. Your parents likely fed you these names, taking advantage of your innocence to turn our quilt into a political tool."

Dorothea smiled, but regarded Mrs. Engle levelly. "I have read every one of these authors, and I do not understand how including a certain writer is any more political than including a governor or a president."

"Presidents and governors are meant to be political," explained Mrs. Collins. "A writer is supposed to enlighten and amuse."

Dorothea looked around the circle of women, eyebrows raised. "I have found the writers on my list to be quite enlightening."

"Let us agree that we shall include men who practice their politics overtly by running for office, and exclude those who conceal their politics in writing," said Mrs. Engle. "Now go on, Dorothea, and finish up."

Dorothea knew the rest of her list would not make the other women any happier. "Elizabeth Cady Stanton, Lucretia Mott, William Lloyd Garrison, James Russell Lowell, and Frederick Douglass."

The women drew in a collective gasp, all save Mrs. Claverton, who seemed to be struggling to contain her laughter. "You do seem determined to shock us," she said.

"I did not mean to." Dorothea handed her list to Mrs. Collins, who, she had observed, had not added any of her proposed names to the official list. "I confess I do not understand why these men and women would not be worthy additions to our project."

"We will simply have to come up with more names on our own," said Mrs. Engle to the others. "Dorothea has done us more harm than good today."

"She cannot help how she was brought up," said Miss Nadelfrau. "She did write a fine letter, and the quilt was her idea."

As all but Mrs. Claverton nodded and agreed, Dorothea decided she had had quite enough of being discussed as if she were not present. "I beg your pardon," she began, but Mrs. Claverton reached over and clasped her hand. In an undertone she urged Dorothea to allow Mrs. Engle to have the last word in the argument. She would never back down today, not after expressing her opinion so forcefully, but later she might be persuaded to tolerate the signatures of authors she did not necessarily admire, especially if the quilters fell short of their goal of eighty Album blocks. With some regret, Dorothea complied. Life with Uncle Jacob had taught her the unpleasant necessity of occasional outward compliance to conceal inner dissent.

The rest of the afternoon was devoted to cutting pieces of muslin to send with the invitations, because, as Miss Nadelfrau pointed out, the male authors were more likely to respond if they did not have to first obtain the proper fabric from their wives. As they cut, they proposed additional names for the list. Mrs. Collins and Mrs. Deakins noticeably flinched whenever Dorothea spoke. Dorothea was amused but indignant; she would have spoken up more staunchly for her authors if not for Mrs. Claverton's request and for her own reluctance to further offend Cyrus's mother. She held her tongue when, at the conclusion of the meeting, Mrs. Engle assigned each of them a portion of the list, distributed the scraps of muslin, and instructed them to send invitations to the authors. Of Dorothea's candidates, only Emerson, Thoreau, and the Brownings remained.

Cyrus must have sensed a certain tension in the air when he arrived to take her home, for he regarded her quizzically as they left the house. "Mother seems disturbed," he remarked. "Did something upset her?"

"I regret that I was the source of her displeasure," said Dorothea as he helped her into the carriage. As they rode toward the ferry, she gave him a brief, lighthearted account of the afternoon, taking care not to insult his mother's taste or judgment.

"This is most unfortunate." Cyrus's characteristic grin had fled. "Mother's good opinion, once lost, is rarely regained."

"I assure you, I will do such a fine job on this quilt that she will forgive me entirely," said Dorothea, studying him, not certain if he was once again teasing her, and would at any moment laugh with her about his mother's behavior.

"I do hope so." He shook the reins and chirruped to the horses, frowning.

He remained all but silent as they crossed Elm Creek, lost in a brood, but as the carriage brought her closer to home, he assumed a close approximation of his usual joviality. When he assisted her from the carriage and promised to call for her two weeks hence, she nodded, troubled by his obvious displeasure.

That evening after supper, Dorothea recounted the events of the afternoon for her mother as they layered Uncle Jacob's eccentric quilt top with a pieced muslin lining and an inner layer of cotton batting. Lorena listened thoughtfully, but looked surprised when Dorothea told her how much the other women's objections had astounded her. "Are you surprised that they object, or that they object so strenuously, without any appearance of shame for their opinions?"

Dorothea considered. "Both, I suppose." She was not so naïve as not to readily understand the reason for their dismay, but she had not expected these particular women to react in such a manner. If Creek's Crossing were a southern village, she might have expected objections to including abolitionists, advocates of woman's suffrage, and freedmen in the quilt, but not so in the free commonwealth of Pennsylvania. If anyone did harbor secret prejudices, she would have expected them to be too ashamed to allow them to be detected.

"You assumed you were among like-minded women," said Lorena, threading a tapestry needle. She tied a knot on the end of the thread and began basting the three layers of the quilt with large, zigzag stitches.

"I did," admitted Dorothea. She'd had no reason to, but she had also had no reason to do otherwise. She had never talked politics with any of the women but Mrs. Claverton, whom she knew despised slavery. "They seemed sensible enough, so naturally I assumed they would agree with me."

In his usual chair by the fire, Uncle Jacob snorted, but did not look up from his Bible. She thought of the often silly prattle of Mrs. Deakins and Mrs. Collins and silently agreed that perhaps sensible was too generous a term.

"Sometimes it is best to keep your opinions to yourself until you have discovered what those around you believe," said Robert.

Dorothea felt a spark of indignation. Her list had contained several of his favorite authors. "The philosophy of Thrift Farm was to speak one's own truth, whatever the consequences to oneself."

Chagrined, her father shrugged and nodded. Dorothea would have been happier if he had scolded her for showing such disrespect.

"The philosophy of Thrift Farm," muttered Uncle Jacob, shifting in his chair. "Write poetry about the Oversoul, allow your children to run wild, and hope the wheat learns to sow and harvest itself."

Lorena ignored him. "What of Mrs. Engle? Why did you assume she shared our enlightened ideals? You have read what her husband has published in the *Creek's Crossing Informer.*"

"Those articles expressed her husband's views, not hers."

"She chose to marry the man who holds those views."

Dorothea hesitated. "I suppose knowing how Cyrus feels, I assumed his mother would be sympathetic to the inclusion of abolitionists, or at worst, indifferent."

"And how does Cyrus feel?"

She was aware of her uncle's sudden keen interest, though he had not moved a muscle. "He jokes and teases so much I do not know how he feels on any serious subject," she admitted. "I do know it distresses him to see his mother offended."

Uncle Jacob radiated animosity. "In my day we had a word for a young man like that. He squires young ladies about in a fancy carriage, but he hasn't worked a day in his life."

"You do not believe any man works if he does not own a farm," said Dorothea.

"Dorothea," warned Lorena.

"It is unfair to condemn Cyrus for the political views of his step-father, a man who did not raise him, a man who has been married to his mother for less than a year." Dorothea struggled to keep her composure as she worked her needle with broad, furious stitches. "Even if Cyrus's opinions are not widely known, our family's are. Surely he would not seek out my company if he found our views in any way objectionable."

Uncle Jacob slammed his Bible shut. "Maybe he doesn't seek out your company for your conversation, or haven't you thought of that? I should forbid him to set foot on my property for your own sake, since you're apparently determined to be as foolish and as easily deceived as all of your sex."

They stared after him as he stormed from the room.

"Mother, Father." Dorothea took a deep, shaky breath. "I have done nothing to provoke such censure. I assure you Cyrus Pearson has never been anything less than a gentleman in his conduct."

Her mother reached for her hand. "Of course, dear. We know."

Her parents exchanged a worried look, but her father said, "He's in a sour temper today because a calf was stillborn last night. Say nothing more, and he will forget about it by morning."

But if anything, her uncle's temper worsened overnight. At breakfast he chastised Lorena for serving flapjacks instead of eggs, although Dorothea had heard him request flapjacks before heading to the barn to milk the cows. In the days that followed, his demands became more exacting, his sudden bursts of anger more swift and vengeful. He hovered over Dorothea whenever she sat at the quilt frame, glaring as if he suspected her of quilting slowly just to vex him. He left the house mornings and evenings alone, saying only that he would be at his sugar camp. Once Dorothea was sent there to fetch him, but although the scuffled dirt around the fire pit and a newly mended roof on the shack indicated recent activity, he was nowhere to be found. Another time, while gathering hickory nuts, she could have sworn she heard him arguing with someone, but when she ran to see what was the matter, she found him alone, with no reasonable explanation for wandering about the forest on the westernmost edge of the property after he had said he would be working in the barn. When she asked to whom he had been speaking, he first denied that he had spoken at all, then said he had been praying. Dorothea knew of no psalm that encouraged believers to make an angry noise unto the Lord, but she pretended to believe him.

Uncle Jacob's increasingly erratic behavior made her long to unburden herself to Jonathan, the confidant of her childhood. She wrote to him often, but found it difficult to strike the appropriate balance of care and confession, to share her concerns with him without provoking any undue guilt or worry. She knew she had failed when he wrote back to thank her for her cheerful letters and praised her for accepting their uncle's eccentricities with grace and humor. As Christmas approached, she grew ever more anxious for his impending visit. When he came home, he would see for himself how their uncle had worsened with age. Perhaps—she seized upon a wild hope—he might sympathize with her plight and invite her to spend part of the New Year in Baltimore with him.

But when his letter arrived a week before Christmas, she did not have to read it to know that her hopes were in vain. Her mother's expression as she scanned the lines told her that he would not be coming home. One of his mentor's patients, a young boy with unexplained recurring fits, took more comfort from Jonathan than the doctor himself. The boy's parents begged Jonathan to remain in Baltimore so that their son's final days would be eased by the presence of a trusted friend. Jonathan apologized for canceling a second visit and assured them he would find some excuse for the boy's parents should his parents find themselves unable to do without him.

Lorena, though obviously disappointed, said that she did not have the heart to deny the grieving parents their one small measure of comfort, and she wrote back to tell him he should remain.

Lorena asked Uncle Jacob's permission first, of course. He told her that Jonathan might as well stay in Baltimore where he might do some good, since he had already missed spring planting and the harvest, when he was needed on the farm the most. Lorena tried unsuccessfully to hide her dismay at his apparent indifference to his nephew and presumptive heir, and both she and Robert were especially attentive to Uncle Jacob for the next few days, a display Dorothea regarded with disgust.

Her disappointment over Jonathan's prolonged absence made her ever more determined to finish Uncle Jacob's quilt so that it would not annoy her any more, and so she fixed herself a deadline of Christmas Eve. That way, she thought somewhat meanly, she would not be obliged to get him any other present, and she could enjoy the holidays without him hovering over her at the quilt frame. Besides, already a few authors had returned autographed pieces of muslin to the library board, and she was eager to join in the work of piecing Album blocks. She had not forgotten her uncle's decree that she sew no other quilt until his own was complete. The more blocks she sewed, the greater her role would be in determining which authors were included—and since she had disregarded Mrs. Engle's instructions and sent invitations to her own authors as well as those assigned to her, she could not afford to be left out of the selection process.

She sewed the last stitch into the binding of Uncle Jacob's quilt on the morning of Christmas Eve. She concealed the finished quilt in her attic bedroom until the next morning, wistfully recalling long-ago Christmases on Thrift Farm, the curious amalgam of tradition and whimsy, solemnity and joy, the fragrance of candles and gingerbread and Yule log, the sound of Bach's Christmas cantatas on dulcimer, fiddle, and organ. One of the founding members of the community would read the story of the Nativity, bringing it to life for Dorothea and Jonathan and the other children so vividly that Dorothea was filled with a rush of awe and reverence and gratitude. They would exchange gifts, but only things they had made or had found in nature. Looking back, Dorothea had to smile recalling how her father had once given her mother the second of the Four Brothers, the mountains framing the north end of the Elm Creek Valley, and how it had seemed a perfectly normal thing to do.

The gift of a handmade quilt would have met with approval on Thrift Farm, but Christmases at Uncle Jacob's were a more subdued affair. He permitted the giving of gifts since the magi had brought gifts to the Christ Child, but there was no music save the hymns at church services, and certainly no parties. Dorothea had been invited to several Christmas Eve gatherings, one at her best friend Mary's new home with her husband Abner, but Uncle Jacob would not allow her to attend. He emphatically forbade her to attend a sleigh riding party with Cyrus; anticipating this, she would not have bothered to ask him except Cyrus repeatedly entreated her, and she had promised she would.

Christmas morning church services were too festive for Uncle Jacob's taste, but he could not very well forbid the family to attend church on Christmas. Dorothea could almost forget her longing for Jonathan in the merriment of the day. The people of Creek's Crossing were cheerful and smiling as they wished one another a Merry Christmas, forgiving disagreements and past quarrels, if only for the day. The Ladies' Auxiliary had arranged for a magnificent Christmas tree to adorn the sanctuary, and when services concluded, all were invited to take ribbon-tied oranges and wrapped parcels of roasted nuts down from the boughs. Most of the congregation lingered in the pews to share fellowship and laughter, but just as he did every year, Uncle Jacob urged his family toward the door as soon as the final hymn was sung. They had nearly reached it when Lorena spotted Abel and Constance Wright amidst the throng and broke away to greet them; as Uncle Jacob scowled after her, Dorothea felt a tap on her shoulder.

She turned to find Cyrus dangling a small parcel by its ribbon, so close it almost brushed her cheek. "There were toys on the tree for the children, too. Dolls for the girls and drums for the boys. Didn't you get yours?"

"I must have forgotten," she said, returning his smile.

"I thought you might, so I took the liberty of fetching yours for you. And now, before the crotchety old geezer turns around, I'll have my Christmas present from you."

Before she knew it, he kissed her swiftly on the cheek and disappeared into the crowd.

Too astonished to worry that Uncle Jacob had seen, she stood rooted in place. A moment later her mother was at her side. "Constance brought chestnuts for the dressing and said she'll make the pudding at our place." Lorena peered at her daughter. "What's that in your hand?"

Dorothea glanced down and saw the ribbon-tied parcel. "A gift. From Cyrus."

She quickly slipped it into her coat pocket, but not before Uncle Jacob turned around and spotted it. He scowled and urged Dorothea and her parents outside.

The parcel seemed heavy for its size as it weighed down Dorothea's pocket on the ride home. The Wrights, having been invited for Christmas dinner, followed in their own wagon. Her parents conversed cheerfully, even laughing aloud as they rode, but Dorothea was as silent as Uncle Jacob. She had not expected that Cyrus would give her a gift. It had not even occurred to her to get him one.

At home, as the men tended to the horses and the women went

to the kitchen, Dorothea slipped away to her attic bedroom to unwrap Cyrus's gift. She untied the ribbon, unwrapped the paper, and discovered inside a hand mirror and comb, intricately worked with carvings of vines and roses, gilded in silver.

She had never owned anything so fine.

She sat on the bed with the gifts in her lap, then, hesitantly, lifted the mirror and ran the comb through her hair. Her reflection showed flushed cheeks and startled eyes; with a sudden jolt of embarrassment for her vanity, she quickly wrapped the comb and mirror in the paper and tucked them into the drawer of the pine table that served as her nightstand.

She hurried back to the kitchen and tied on her apron. Her mother and Constance were so engrossed in a discussion of the best way to dress a goose that they did not seem to notice her absence. The men returned from the barn and settled in the parlor, where Uncle Jacob took up his Bible and Dorothea's father and Mr. Wright played draughts. After a game, Mr. Wright came into the kitchen, stole a kiss from his wife, and offered to help the women prepare the meal. At first they refused, but when Robert drawled, "Better let him help, if it will get the meal on the table faster," they laughingly tied an apron on Mr. Wright and threatened to put Robert in one, too. Lorena and Constance teased Mr. Wright as he picked up a paring knife and offered to take care of the vegetables, but he worked diligently if not swiftly. Dorothea surmised he had gained a great deal of practice living as a bachelor. She doubted Cyrus would be so proficient in the kitchen, having first his mother and then a housekeeper to cook for him, but she quickly severed that train of thought.

At Lorena's request, Dorothea set the table with the fine china her grandparents had brought over from England, the plates and bowls and tea service that spent most of the year wrapped in linen and tucked away in a lined chest decorated in golden fleur-de-lis.

Translucent white with a border of roses, they were so delicate she was almost afraid to handle them, knowing that a single place setting was worth more than she was likely to earn in her lifetime. She had once asked her mother why people prosperous enough to own such treasures would have left their homeland to immigrate to the New World. Lorena had told her that the china had been the entirety of her grandparents' fortune. Her grandfather, a soldier, had been given the trunk and its contents for saving the life of his commanding officer in battle in France. Upon his discharge, he sold enough pieces to purchase second-class passage to America for himself and his wife, determined to start a new life far from the seemingly endless warfare of Europe.

Plainer fare adorned the table service than its original owners could have imagined, but the food was plentiful and delicious. Even Uncle Jacob's dour blessing seemed heartfelt that night, and although Dorothea ached for her absent brother, she could not dwell on her own misgivings after Constance remarked that she had never sat at a finer table. It suddenly occurred to Dorothea that this was Constance's first Christmas in freedom. Truly it was a blessing, Dorothea reflected, to have Constance among them at Christmas, as a reminder that so many people still waited to be redeemed from their suffering.

After the meal, they exchanged gifts. Her parents had bought Dorothea a fine edition of Henry Wadsworth Longfellow's anthology, *The Poets and Poetry of Europe*, and an autobiography, *Narrative of William W. Brown, an American Slave*. Dorothea wondered how welcome the latter would be on the shelves of the Creek's Crossing library, but Constance took a special interest in it and reflected that one day she might write her own story. Dorothea was pleased to hear this, for her gift to Constance, as yet unwrapped, was a pen with several nibs, a primer, and a copybook.

Uncle Jacob gave his sister and brother-in-law nothing, but he offered the Wrights two large cakes of his best maple sugar; since the Wright farm did not have enough maple trees to support their own sugaring, the gifts were much appreciated. To Dorothea he gave a collection of the Proverbs, with a narrow strip of brocade fabric marking the thirty-first. Since the verses praised the pious, thrifty, industrious wife, Dorothea knew the placement was no accident.

Then Dorothea returned to her attic bedroom for the Delectable Mountains quilt. "For you, Uncle," she said, placing the folded bundle in his arms. "I trust it is exactly as you wished it. I hope it pleases you."

He unfolded the quilt and studied it. "I think it will do. You did justice to my drawings. Thank you, niece."

"It is lovely handiwork," said her mother, since her uncle did not.

Dorothea thanked them both. She had hoped for more pleasure in her uncle's expression, but she should have expected no more than his taciturn approval of her accurate reproduction of his sketches. He took no true delight in anything and was not capable of offering greater appreciation.

The Wrights were examining her quilt—out of politeness, she thought. Mr. Wright looked over each of the blocks in turn, and Dorothea could see him pausing to count the triangle points on the blocks that had three or five when most had four. He looked over the other, odd squares her uncle had drawn, arranged in a diagonal line amidst the Delectable Mountains blocks, looked at Uncle Jacob, then glanced at Dorothea. "Sure looks warm," he said, returning the quilt to its new owner.

"You did not need to make it so fine," murmured Constance to Dorothea, so low no one else knew she had spoken. Dorothea glanced at her in surprise and hid a smile. She used her finest quilting skills out of pride, not because her uncle deserved them.

"It'll do," said Uncle Jacob, folding the quilt and placing it on the back of his chair. There it sat for the rest of the afternoon and into the evening, while they told stories of Christmases past, while the women brought out pie and tea for dessert, when the Wrights bade them good-bye and headed home, and after Uncle Jacob and Robert left to do the chores. It remained there still when Dorothea came down to help her mother prepare breakfast the next morning.

After all of his demands, after all of Dorothea's exacting labor, he had not even put it on his bed. "Perhaps he is saving it for company," suggested Lorena, trying to spare Dorothea's feelings.

"When do we ever have company?" said Dorothea. "Constance was right. Uncle Jacob did not deserve my best handiwork."

She deliberately chose not to resent his indifference. The quilt was finished, she had done her best, and now she could move on to a project much more pleasing to her. Seven autographed pieces of muslin had already arrived at Mrs. Engle's home, and two more belonging to authors that Mrs. Engle had rejected had been sent to Dorothea directly.

At the previous meeting of the library board, Dorothea had been assigned the task of sketching a plan for the quilt, something that would suit the varying skills of the participating quiltmakers and something that could be adapted easily according to the number of Album blocks they made. She and Miss Nadelfrau had joined forces to convince the others to use the traditional Album block, even though Mrs. Engle had balked when Mrs. Deakins remarked that she knew the pattern by another name, Chimney Sweep. Dorothea had needed five minutes of her most tactful persuasion to reassure Mrs. Engle that the block's association to another, less distinguished profession would not offend the authors, should they learn of it. Miss Nadelfrau's point that the block would be easy to assemble since it had no curves or set-in pieces ultimately won the argument. Mrs. Engle was less willing to consider that she might receive fewer than the eighty blocks she wanted, as she was accustomed to receiving everything she desired. She insisted that the eighty blocks would be arranged in ten rows of eight, the most pleasing rectangular ratio, and cut short any "pessimistic" suggestions to the contrary. Dorothea decided not to waste breath on further argument and to plan alternative settings secretly, just in case.

At the same meeting where Dorothea would present her sketch, Miss Nadelfrau would bring swatches for them to consider, and—assuming they could reach a consensus—the meeting would adjourn to the dry-goods store, where they would purchase and divide up the fabric. Board members would piece blocks at home, completing all blocks by the end of January and the entire quilt top by the last week of February in time for the dance. Dorothea was confident she would find some way to sneak her banned authors into the quilt at an intermediate step.

Dorothea and her mother were so busy making up for the usual chores they had neglected the previous day that it was almost suppertime before Dorothea noticed that Uncle Jacob's quilt had been removed from the back of his chair. When she was sure he was out of the house, she passed by his bedroom and peered inside, but she did not see it. She was tempted to ask if he had put it in his chest for safekeeping or passed it on to one of the horses, but knew any reply he gave was unlikely to please her.

That evening, as she worked on the drawing and idly pondered more polite ways to inquire about the whereabouts of the quilt, her mother suddenly said, "Goodness, Dorothea. I had completely forgotten Cyrus's Christmas gift. Have you opened it?"

"Yes," said Dorothea, wishing her mother could have chosen a different time to ask, preferably when Uncle Jacob could not overhear.

"What was it?" asked Robert.

"A silverplated comb and mirror."

Uncle Jacob snorted. "That would be a fine gift for himself. I have never met a young man more likely to enjoy gazing at his own reflection."

"I cannot imagine you know him well enough to determine that."

"Dorothea," said her father mildly.

Dorothea set down her pencils. "I am sorry, Uncle, but I do not care to hear my friend so unfairly maligned, especially when he is given no opportunity to defend himself."

"Then by all means, let us give him opportunity," said Uncle Jacob, a hard glint in his eye. "Tomorrow when he calls for you, let us have him stay for supper. We will have him make both his character and his intentions plain."

"He is not coming to call," said Dorothea. "He is coming to take me to the library board meeting."

"After he brings you home, then," thundered her uncle.

Dorothea could not see any way out of it. "I shall ask him."

"See that you do."

The room was silent for the rest of the evening. The others went to bed—first her uncle, then her parents—but Dorothea remained to finish her sketch by candlelight. She was nearly done when she heard a creak on the floorboards behind her. She turned to find her uncle, still in his nightshirt and cap.

"Niece," he greeted her gruffly.

Dorothea hurriedly drew a last stroke and began clearing the desk. "I am sorry if the light kept you awake."

"I am only looking out for what is best for you." Uncle Jacob crossed the room in long, slow strides. "He is no good for you and I know you do not love him."

So he wanted to speak of Cyrus. She almost smiled. She had never known him to be kept awake, troubled by an argument. Usually his confidence in his own perfect judgment provided him suffi-cient righteousness to sleep soundly every night.

"I have seen nothing to persuade me he is *not* good," said Dorothea, "and I never claimed to love him. We are friends. Noth-ing more."

"Don't be coy. A young man does not call on a young lady so many times unless he has intentions."

Dorothea gathered up her papers. "If he has any, time will reveal them."

"By then it might be too late." He clasped her shoulder and spoke earnestly. "Niece, if you must marry, choose a good, God-fearing man. If you can't find one in Creek's Crossing, then go out west, where a woman is valued as much for her strength as for her beauty."

The steadiness in his voice turned to trembling as he spoke; his eyes were strained and pleading as they pooled with tears. A tear slipped from his eye, ran down his cheek, and disappeared into his scruff of beard. Dorothea stared at him in stunned disbelief. Sud-denly he seemed to come to his senses; he glanced at his hand rest-ing on her shoulder and snatched it away. Dorothea clutched her papers to her chest, too astonished to speak as her uncle hurried from the room, scrubbing his eyes with the back of his fist. In another moment he had disappeared down the hallway. She heard the door to his bedroom close and the latch fall into place.

Chapter Five

DOROTHEA SLEPT LITTLE, but she woke when the first gray light of dawn touched the attic windowpane, worry fluttering in her chest like a trapped bird. She did not know what to do about her uncle's unexpected tears. In all the years she had known him, she had never seen him weep. And he had seemed as shocked by his sudden emotion as she.

Dorothea did not like to keep such a troubling secret from her parents, but she knew she must keep silent. Uncle Jacob had too much pride to endure such shame. Any mention might compel Uncle Jacob to banish them from the farm rather than acknowledge his weakness. She could not cost the family Jonathan's inheritance.

She lingered as long as she dared before going downstairs to help her mother with breakfast, where she learned that her uncle had taken a cold breakfast with him to the sugar camp. "He has gone several times a week since late summer," remarked Lorena. "Perhaps someone should remind him that this is not the time of year to tap the trees."

Dorothea knew he had left early that morning to avoid her. "Let's not tell him, or he might not spend so much time away from the house."

Lorena allowed a small smile, but she looked worried. "I wonder . . ." She hesitated. "I wonder if he is, perhaps, not altogether well."

Dorothea held herself perfectly still. "What do you mean?"

"Have you not noticed he has been even more irascible than usual? He is more forgetful, more snappish. Do not forget he is fourteen years my senior, and he drives himself hard."

"He drives us all hard." Still, her mother's words brought Dorothea a small measure of relief. An illness would pass.

Her uncle did not reappear even for lunch, and while Lorena wondered aloud if someone ought to run to the sugar camp to look for him, Dorothea was glad he remained absent. She spotted him trudging through the old wheat field, now shorn and muddy and dusted with snow, as she went outside to meet Cyrus's carriage. In her eagerness to leave, she climbed inside without waiting for Cyrus to assist her.

She delivered Uncle Jacob's invitation to supper as they crossed Elm Creek on the ferry, the water too turbulent there to freeze over completely during all but the coldest winters. Cyrus seemed pleased to be asked, but he declined, citing the presence of two important out-of-state business associates. When she inquired what business, he grinned and said, "The pursuit of lucre. I regret that I do not engage in the altruistic profession of teaching, such as yourself, or the essential craft of farming, like your uncle."

Dorothea noticed he did not mention her father. Robert might spend the rest of his life working Uncle Jacob's land, but no one who knew him considered him a farmer. Dorothea often thought he would be happier living in a rented room in a city back east, writing philosophical essays at the behest of an indulgent patron.

She brightened considerably as the distance increased between herself and her uncle, now that the unhappy prospect of subjecting Cyrus to his baleful scrutiny had been averted. The library board meeting passed pleasantly, the members settling on a popular green, Turkey red, and Prussian blue color scheme, then leaving for Mrs. Engle's favorite dry-goods store to purchase fabric. Dorothea had brought some of her saved wages, believing that each of them would be responsible for purchasing her share of the fabric, but to her surprise, Mrs. Engle insisted on paying for it all.

"She thinks she's going to win the quilt," said Mrs. Claverton to Dorothea when the others were in another part of the store selecting bolts of calico. "She doesn't mind buying so much fabric for a quilt for herself."

Before Dorothea could reply, a thunder of horses' hooves passed just outside, followed by loud shouting somewhere down the block. Dorothea and Mrs. Claverton were the first to the door. From the front steps they saw three men on horseback leveling their rifles at the door to Schultz's Printers. One man slid down from his horse, pounded on the door, and shouted for Schultz to come out. Dorothea saw the flicker of a curtain in an upstairs window, but no other sign of life within. Then from somewhere unseen came another cry, a furious shout that Schultz had escaped through the back door and was fleeing down Water Street. The man at the door leapt back onto his horse and raced off with the others, vanishing around the corner.

The rest of the women had crowded onto the steps after Dorothea and Mrs. Claverton, but none of them knew what to make of the commotion.

"Isn't the eldest Schultz girl a friend of yours?" Mrs. Claverton asked Dorothea.

Dorothea nodded. "A very dear friend."

"Well, go on, then." Mrs. Deakins nudged her. "Go find out what's the matter."

Dorothea, who had been on the verge of dashing over to the printers to see if she could help, now resolved to stay away. "Mary would not be there. She's married with a home of her own."

Mrs. Deakins sniffed and went back into the store, disappointed that her appetite for gossip would not be satisfied. The rest of the library board followed, Dorothea last of all. For the rest of the shopping trip, the other women speculated on the curious incident, but Dorothea was too worried about Mary's father to participate in the conversation. No one knew who the men were, or what their purpose with Mr. Schultz could have been. Mrs. Collins declared that one of the strangers resembled a cousin's husband, but when she admitted he was a farmer in Maryland, no one was inclined to believe her.

As Cyrus drove Dorothea home a few hours later, she recounted the scene to him and asked him what he made of it. As it happened, he had been on Water Street at the time and had witnessed the three men apprehending Mr. Schultz. He stood accused of assisting a fugitive slave across the Maryland border by concealing him in his wagon. The men claimed to be law officers and announced as a warning to other would-be lawbreakers that they were taking Mr. Schultz to Maryland to stand trial.

"They cannot," gasped Dorothea.

Cyrus shrugged. "They can take him since they have him, but I doubt much will come of any trial. No one has any evidence Schultz aided runaways in the past, and he can always claim that the runaway climbed aboard his wagon and hid amongst his freight when Schultz was not looking. His son-in-law and brother have already headed south to fetch him. On one point, however, the constables are quite correct: Schultz did break the law."

"A law that has existed for more than fifty years without this manner of enforcement. The people of Pennsylvania would never stand for it."

Cyrus grinned. "That is precisely the problem. The southern states have had enough of northerners mocking federal laws that support slavery. Until a stronger law is enacted—and it is coming, mark my words—it's little wonder they believe they must enforce the laws themselves."

Dorothea felt sick at heart thinking of Mr. Schultz's wife, of Mary and her younger sisters. "If they are as adamant as you say, I cannot see how this will end without violence."

"Schultz should have thought of that before choosing a time of heightened animosity to help runaways."

Dorothea could not reply. She never would have imagined the unassuming Mr. Schultz capable of such courage. Likely he had acted on noble instinct, helping the fugitive in an instant of need without thinking of the potential consequences to himself. Circumstances requiring heroism often did not permit contemplation or forethought.

Suddenly she had another thought. "What became of the fugitive slave Mr. Schultz assisted?"

"I gather he escaped, which is unfortunate for Schultz. Perhaps they would have been satisfied with the return of the runaway."

Dorothea shuddered, thinking of the various dreadful punishments captured runaways received at the hands of slavecatchers: beatings, starvation, amputations. "Unfortunate for Mr. Schultz, but fortunate indeed for the runaway. Perhaps Mr. Schultz considered it a worthy sacrifice."

Cyrus chuckled. "That would not surprise me."

Dorothea supposed it was amusing that Mr. Schultz had outsmarted the slavecatchers, but she could not manage even a smile. She marveled at Cyrus, who seemed to have a depthless well of good cheer to draw upon even in the face of horrors.

LORENA WAS DISAPPOINTED THAT Cyrus could not stay for supper, but she seemed to forget the invitation when Dorothea told her about Mr. Schultz. "We must send word to Mrs. Schultz that we will help her however she needs." Lorena wiped her hands on her apron and sent Dorothea for a pen and paper. "She will need a lawyer familiar with Maryland law. Dr. Bronson will surely know someone."

While her mother wrote to Mrs. Schultz and Jonathan's mentor in Baltimore, Dorothea packed a basket of food for the family. Lorena sealed the letters and tucked them into the basket as Dorothea threw on her wraps, instructing her to ask her father or uncle to drive her to the Schultz's if the men were in the barn, and to take a horse and ride alone if they were not.

Dorothea hurried outside, and when she entered the barn, she found her uncle alone, sitting on a bench cleaning mud from his boots. "I'm looking for my father," she asked, peering around for him. She was reluctant to ask her uncle to drive her or to try to ride off on horseback against his wishes, because he would surely forbid the errand.

"Last I saw he was bringing in the cows."

"I will meet him." As she turned to go, Dorothea glimpsed a familiar cluster of color amid the folds of the rag her uncle rubbed over his boot. "What's that?" Before the words were past her lips, she knew. "My quilt. That's my quilt."

He glanced up at her, unconcerned. "No, it's my quilt."

She could not comprehend it. "You are using the quilt I gave you for Christmas—the quilt we both put much thought and labor into—to clean mud from your boots?"

He studied her for a moment before saying, "I told you I wanted serviceable fabrics. It can be washed."

"Even the most thorough scrubbing could not remove those stains. Surely you know that." Dorothea could not bear to look upon the ruins of her quilt any longer, and she suddenly no longer cared if Uncle Jacob attempted to stop her. Without a word of explanation, she saddled her mother's horse and rode off down the road to the Elm Creek ferry. Absorbed in his work, Uncle Jacob did not interfere.

Either her uncle was crueler than she had ever supposed, or he was going quite mad.

The Schultzes lived on the upper story above the printers, and Dorothea arrived to find several horses and wagons already tied up outside. She could hear fervent and angry voices on the other side of the door as she knocked. Mary answered, her face ashen and eyes rimmed in red. Dorothea embraced her and offered words of comfort and asked about Abner, but Mary was so upset she could only cling to Dorothea and choke out that she had not heard from any of the men yet.

Mary took Dorothea into the other room, where other neighbors and friends surrounded Mrs. Schultz. Dorothea gave her Lorena's letter and said, "My mother sends you her most sympathetic regards and offers her services in helping you obtain a lawyer."

Mrs. Schultz managed a wan nod. "Thank you, my dear. Your mother is very kind, but we have already made arrangements."

"The Marylanders have sent word already," said another man, whom Dorothea recognized as the editor of the *Creek's Crossing Informer.* "They have levied a fine and will release Mr. Schultz when it is paid."

"How could they have so swiftly determined his guilt?" asked Dorothea. "They apprehended him mere hours ago."

"There was no trial," said Mrs. Schultz. "They are holding him for ransom, pure and simple."

"They will take cash payment or the return of their slave," another man said.

Dorothea shook her head. "This cannot be legal."

"Slavecatchers live by their own laws," said the newspaper editor. "Make no mistake, Schultz is not in the hands of legitimate authorities. It was sensible of Abner to accept Nelson's offer to go along. He will help sort this out."

"Mr. Nelson?" echoed Dorothea. "The younger Mr. Nelson?"

The others nodded and resumed their discussion, oblivious to her astonishment. Then she understood. Of course it made perfect sense to include Mr. Nelson; as a southern sympathizer he would not engender the Marylanders' offense. He could speak to them in a language they understood. And naturally he would have no compunction against the return of the fugitive slave. Dorothea prayed the unfortunate man was far away in some safe haven.

He was, but not in the manner Dorothea had hoped.

The following week, as Dorothea and Cyrus crossed on the ferry, they spotted a knot of men on the opposite shore. As the ferry drew closer, Dorothea recognized the undertaker's black carriage and saw the men reach for something tangled in the weeds on the riverbank.

"Dorothea, avert your eyes," ordered Cyrus, but she did not. Transfixed by horror, she watched as they hauled the corpse from the creek, paused to rest, then loaded it into the undertaker's carriage. The undertaker had driven off by the time Dorothea and Cyrus came ashore, but a few onlookers still lingered, and from their remarks, Dorothea was able to piece together what had happened. The body had been identified as that of the runaway slave. He had tried to cross the creek upstream at Widow's Pining, but the ice had not held, and he had plunged into the frigid waters. Bone-chilling cold and treacherous currents had hastened his drowning.

"He can't be returned to his owner now," remarked Cyrus as they left the scene behind them. "That will be unhappy news for the Schultzes."

Dorothea doubted they had ever had any intention of trading the runaway for Mr. Schultz. "It shall be unhappy news for this unfortunate man's family, as well."

"If they ever learn of it," said Cyrus.

Dorothea did not reply. She could not disagree with him, but something in the lightness of his manner annoyed her. Almost always she enjoyed his perpetual good humor, but sometimes circumstances warranted more gravity. He did not seem to know this, or he was concealing his concern to spare her more worry. Either way, she did not care for it.

Before taking her to his mother's house, Cyrus drove her to the post office so she could mail a letter to Jonathan. She had needed two pages to tell him of recent happenings in their once-quiet town. A letter awaited Dorothea, and when she saw the New York return address, she realized it must have come from one of her banned authors. She slipped it into her pocket to read later. Cyrus was certain to inquire if she opened it in the carriage, and he might feel obliged to inform his mother.

With Mary's father gone, it was difficult to think of anything but his safe return. The library board meeting went on as usual, except that talk of Mr. Schultz's captivity dominated the conversation. Everyone had some bit of news to report, though Dorothea wondered how much truth was in the rumors. Abner and Mr. Schultz's brother had returned from Maryland to report that Mr. Schultz was in good spirits but concerned for his family, and he refused to declare whether he had knowingly helped the runaway or if the runaway had stolen aboard without his knowledge.

"Mr. Schultz's silence is confession enough," said Mrs. Engle with a trace of disapproval in her tone. "He surely helped the runaway." Nevertheless, it was she who suggested they have the tickets for the opportunity quilt printed at Schultz's, to give the family the commission in their hour of need. Dorothea would have been more impressed with her generosity if Mr. Schultz's were not the only printer in town, the nearest rival ten miles away in Grangerville.

The Schultzes would need every penny. According to Mrs. Collins, the fine, or ransom, was five hundred dollars. Dorothea was aghast, knowing Mary's family could never raise such an enormous sum without selling the printing press and sacrificing their livelihood. She suggested to the rest of the library board that they use the proceeds from the opportunity quilt to free Mr. Schultz. Her idea was met with laughter and scorn by all but Mrs. Claverton, who privately told Dorothea that her heart was in the right place, but the quilt was not even finished, would probably not raise five hundred dollars, and would not raise any amount as swiftly as Mr. Schultz needed. "Late is better than never," retorted Dorothea, frustrated by the consensus opposing her. The others seemed to believe that Mary's family should solve their problems unassisted. Mr. Schultz got himself into his present circumstance and ought to get himself out.

Dorothea complained about their lack of compassion to her mother that evening as they cleaned up after supper. "What happened to Mr. Schultz could have happened to any one of us."

"Not to just anyone," said Uncle Jacob, returning from an errand outdoors in time to hear. "Only folks who decide to help runaways."

Dorothea snapped off her apron. "Are you saying Mr. Schultz should have ridden right past that poor man without stopping?"

"Not at all." Uncle Jacob shrugged out of his coat. "I'm saying he should have hid him better."

Dorothea, who had been expecting a different reply, opened her mouth and closed it again without a word.

"Mr. Schultz's act of courage should not be mocked," said Lorena.

"Helping runaways is a dangerous business and those who don't know what they're doing shouldn't meddle in it." Uncle Jacob settled into his usual chair and opened his Bible. "Schultz is a prisoner and the runaway is dead. If Schultz had left well enough alone—"

"The runaway might still be dead, or recaptured, but not likely any closer to freedom." Dorothea gestured to the Bible in his hands. "Look up John 15:13 while you contemplate Mr. Schultz's choices. Aunt Rebecca was a Quaker. What do you think she would have done?"

"Dorothea," her father warned. "That's enough."

Deliberately, Uncle Jacob closed his Bible and set it on the table. "You did not know my wife," said Uncle Jacob, his voice a quiet warning. "You have never risked your life for anyone. Without giving the matter any thought, you praise Schultz for his actions, but would you have done the same?"

Dorothea hesitated. "It is what I would have wanted to do."

"But would you have?"

"I—I don't know. I like to think I would have shown sufficient courage. I suppose I cannot know for certain, having never been confronted with such circumstances."

"Well." Uncle Jacob almost smiled, but no mirth touched his eyes. "An honest answer at last."

"Leave her alone," snapped Lorena. "At least she considers such actions, which is more than you have ever done for the abolitionist cause. Mr. Schultz is a better man than you by far."

Uncle Jacob opened his Bible again. "Then you will be gratified to learn he is coming home."

They all stared at him. "Coming home?" echoed Robert.

"Yes, I heard it from Abel Wright this afternoon. The ransom has been paid and Mr. Schultz was set free. He is on his way home if he is not there already."

Dorothea and her mother exchanged a look of astonishment. "How did Mrs. Schultz obtain the money?" asked Lorena.

Uncle Jacob turned a page and drew the lamp closer. "It did not occur to me to ask such an intrusive question."

Dorothea was too overcome to speak at first, but then she snapped, "You knew he had been released and yet you did not tell us. Instead you prolonged our worry and tormented us with this silly argument."

"Such cruelty is beneath you, brother," said Lorena in a softer tone. "What you did to your niece's quilt was bad enough, and now this—"

"I needed a quilt to keep up at the sugar camp. I did not ask for finery."

"You were very particular about every detail," countered Lorena. "If you had told us your purpose I could have given you any number of suitable quilts. You did not need to mock my daughter's efforts by treating the work of her hands so indifferently."

"Take a lesson from Mr. Schultz," growled Uncle Jacob. "Keep to your own affairs."

Dorothea wanted to declare that the matter of the quilt *was* her affair, but when Lorena pressed her lips together and turned away, she knew the argument was over. She helped her mother finish cleaning the kitchen, then took her sewing basket to a chair by the fire. Only then did she remember the envelope she had received at the post office earlier that day. She retrieved it from her coat pocket and discovered inside a piece of muslin bearing the signature of William Lloyd Garrison. He had also enclosed a brief letter. "What an immense pleasure it is to assist in a benefit for the town that has recently become the home of a longtime acquaintance," he had written. "Please give my regards to Mr. Thomas Nelson if you should meet him."

Dorothea read the letter over, thunderstruck. How could it be that Mr. Nelson was acquainted with Mr. William Lloyd Garrison, newspaper editor and renowned abolitionist? She read the letter a second time, scrutinizing each line. Mr. Garrison had called him a "longtime acquaintance," not a friend. Perhaps Mr. Garrison was a friend of Mr. Nelson's more amiable father, and knew little of the son's quite different inclinations. Or perhaps Mr. Garrison had indulged in a bit of sarcasm; after all, he did not say to give Mr. Nelson his "best regards" or "warmest regards." The greeting could have been a taunt, mocking Mr. Nelson in his exile.

It did not matter, as Dorothea had no intention of delivering the message, should she be so unfortunate as to have the opportunity.

An event Dorothea had anticipated with almost as much eagerness as the quilt raffle fell upon the following Saturday: the Creek's Crossing school annual exhibition. Last year she had directed the students in their recitations and various displays of their academic accomplishments, and was pleased to hear it declared a resounding success. She was determined to attend this year's program and satisfy her curiosity regarding how her students fared under Mr. Nelson's tutelage.

Like nearly everyone else in Creek's Crossing, her parents also wanted to attend, but on the evening of the exhibition, Uncle Jacob found additional work for them that he insisted must be completed before morning. Robert accepted this without a word of complaint, but Lorena protested on her daughter's behalf. Dorothea's absence would be conspicuous since she was the former schoolteacher, and that would reflect badly upon the entire family. At first Uncle Jacob resisted, saying that even if he did not object to Dorothea driving into town at night alone, he needed the wagon himself, but Lorena convinced him to leave Dorothea at the schoolhouse before his errands and pick her up afterward.

Dorothea was reluctant to ride alone with her uncle, but since the alternative was to remain at home, she accepted the arrangement. They rode in silence until they had nearly reached the ferry, when her uncle said, "My sugar camp quilt washed up well."

"Yes, Mother managed to rid it of nearly all the stains." She could not help emphasizing *nearly all*.

"I told you to use scraps and serviceable colors."

"You have reminded me of that already. You might be surprised to discover what beautiful works may be created from those same materials."

They reached the ferry. Uncle Jacob drove the wagon on board, but Dorothea ignored his hand as he reached to help her down. He scowled at the rebuff, but followed her to the railing. "If I had known you and your mother would be so upset, I would have made my intentions more clear."

Dorothea sighed. "If that is an apology, Uncle, then I accept."

"You're right, too, what you said about your aunt. Rebecca."

He spoke her name carefully, as if it were a word in an unfamiliar language, a taste he had craved and never thought to savor again. Dorothea was so astonished to hear it she could not form a reply, only stare at him as he gazed out upon the creek. She hoped he would say more about the aunt whose passing had left him so crippled with grief that the Grangers understood implicitly they were never to mention his lost family, but if he intended to speak, their arrival at the schoolhouse rendered further confessions unspoken.

He left her at the door with a warning to be ready to leave at half-past eight even if the exhibition was not over. Dorothea went inside and tried to find a seat in the crowded schoolroom. Even the choir loft, included in the design at the senior Mr. Nelson's request so that the building could double as a church on Sundays, was full of eager spectators—and numerous parents giving last-minute instructions to their nervous children. Dorothea spotted Mary waving to her on the main level. Mary had saved her a seat with her and her husband, and as Dorothea sat down, she observed that Mary clutched Abner's arm tightly as if to reassure herself that he had indeed returned from his dangerous journey to Maryland.

"How is your father?" asked Dorothea.

"He is faring well," said Mary, "but my mother will not let him out of her sight."

"You did not have to mortgage the print shop to raise the ransom?"

"Oh, no. Didn't you hear? They released him without receiving a penny from us. I don't know what Mr. Nelson said to them, but it was evidently very persuasive." Mary gave a little shudder and drew her shawl around her shoulders, tightening her grasp on Abner's arm. "One scarcely knows what to think about that man."

"On the contrary, one knows precisely what to think," said Dorothea. "No doubt he threatened violence, and with his prison background, I'm sure he knew how to make the threats convincing."

Abner leaned forward. "I don't care what he said or did. He obtained Mary's father's release, and that is good enough for me."

Mary and Dorothea exchanged a look of knowing exasperation. Men too often confused success with moral worth. They could say no more about it, though, for at that moment, Mr. Nelson stepped up to the front of the schoolroom and introduced himself, an unnecessary formality given the size of their town and the speed with which news traveled when there were few other novelties to distract its citizens. His spectacles caught the lamplight, emphasizing his scholarly air, though he was neither as pale nor as slender as he had been upon his arrival in Creek's Crossing. Apparently the climate of their little hamlet agreed with him. If he did not manage to escape, in a few months he might become almost robust.

Mr. Nelson introduced his twenty-two pupils in ascending order according to age, then led them through an exercise in grammar. Next followed an examination in arithmetic, with the youngest pupils solving simple addition and subtraction problems, and the very eldest presenting geometric proofs. Dorothea was surprised by this; she had not taught them any advanced geometry, but she would have, she told herself, if she had been given the opportunity. The students made so few errors that she whispered to Mary that they had surely been given the problems in advance. Mary giggled and whispered back that they simply remembered all Dorothea had taught them. Someone shushed them, so Dorothea contented herself with silently correcting the pupils' errors before Mr. Nelson did, and guiltily wishing there were more of them.

She forgot to criticize when the students began their recitations in history and poetry. The youngest children were so earnest, their voices so sweet as they carefully repeated the pieces they had memorized. The eldest class, nearly all girls, recounted the history of Pennsylvania so well that she found herself regretting the end of the presentation. She applauded as loudly as anyone present, putting aside, for the moment, Mr. Nelson's part in the students' success.

"They did very well," remarked Abner.

Dorothea had no choice but to agree. Despite his other faults, Mr. Nelson was apparently an adequate teacher. Perhaps better than adequate. Mary must have sensed her ambivalence, for she hastily added that the students would have performed just as well, if not better, had Dorothea been their teacher.

After a few closing remarks, Mr. Nelson dismissed his pupils to another round of applause. Dorothea accompanied Mary to the cloakroom, but when she did not see Uncle Jacob in the vestibule, she gathered her wraps and returned to the warmth of the schoolroom. Others filed past her. Mothers and fathers praised their children; young men met young ladies at the door to see them home. The schoolhouse steadily emptied, but although the clock on Mr. Nelson's desk read a quarter to nine, still Uncle Jacob did not appear.

Dorothea checked the vestibule again, and even peered outside to see if he had decided to wait in the wagon rather than push against the departing throng, but he was nowhere to be seen. She returned to the classroom, but stopped short at the sight of Mr. Nelson, alone, wiping down the blackboard.

She decided she preferred the chilly vestibule, but before she could turn to go, Mr. Nelson looked up. "Is there something you require, Miss Granger?"

"I did not mean to disturb you. My uncle is coming for me, but he has not yet arrived."

His eyebrows rose slightly. "Your uncle, not Cyrus Pearson? I rarely see you in town except upon his arm."

Something in his tone made her bristle. "Yes, my uncle. Mr. Pearson had a pressing business engagement that prevented him from attending your exhibition. You should not consider it a slight."

"On the contrary, I consider it a stroke of good fortune." Mr. Nelson nodded at the coal stove in the corner. "I will keep the fire going until I have finished straightening the classroom. You are welcome to wait in here."

"Thank you," she said, and took a seat at the desk nearest the stove. She sat in silence, staring at the door rather than watch Mr. Nelson dust off the chalk railing and replace books on the shelves. The clock chimed the hour just as she realized Mr. Nelson was straightening the bookcases slowly and methodically, postponing the completion of his tasks rather than put her out of the schoolhouse.

She rose and began putting on her wraps. "It appears my uncle has been delayed. I'm sorry to have kept you. Good evening."

"You can't mean to walk home."

"I have a friend in town. I will leave a note on your door for my uncle and stay with her until he comes for me."

"Nonsense." Mr. Nelson closed the dampers on the stove, dousing the light. "You do not need to impose on your friend. I will take you home."

"So that I might impose on you instead?" Dorothea laughed shortly and wrapped her muffler around her neck. "I think I would prefer Mary."

He followed her into the vestibule, pausing only to snatch his coat from the cloakroom. "I will have to escort you wherever you decide to go. I would prefer to escort you to my horse and carriage, which is just next door, rather than to the edge of town and back on foot."

"My uncle's farm lies to the north. Your farm is to the west."

"If you mean that I will be traveling out of my way, I cannot dispute that." Mr. Nelson reached up to turn down the oil lamp hanging beside the door. "If we are fortunate, we will encounter your uncle along the way, and he can carry you the rest of the way home."

His manner was so abrupt, so completely without courtesy, that she almost told him she would rather spend the night in Mary's rocking chair than in debt herself to him, but she knew her parents' worries would increase the longer she stayed away. "Very well, Mr. Nelson," she said. "You may take me home."

He frowned at the condescension in her tone, but he offered her his arm.

His horses were a perfectly matched team of Arabians; his carriage not new, but well fashioned and comfortable. The wind had picked up, and though it blew from the southwest, it was biting. The ride home would have been much colder in Uncle Jacob's wagon, the company only a trifle more pleasant. She wondered if her uncle had forgotten their arrangements. Perhaps she had not accepted his apology regarding the sugar camp quilt graciously enough, but of course, it had not been graciously given.

When they turned on to Water Street, Dorothea suddenly remembered. "I forgot to leave a note for my uncle."

"I will do so upon my return."

"Thank you." Dorothea felt that she ought to say more. "Your students conducted themselves quite well this evening. You must be proud."

"They performed adequately, but they are no match for their counterparts in the east," said Mr. Nelson. "It is not through any fault of their own. Their intellectual capacity is comparable, but they have lacked the necessary resources and guidance."

"I see."

He glanced at her. "And I see that you have chosen to take

offense. Do so, if you insist, but be aware that I do not blame you for their deficiencies. You could hardly be expected to pass on a better education than you received."

She smiled thinly. "That is generous of you."

"Furthermore, you were their teacher for only six months, which is hardly long enough to have much influence upon them."

"It was eight months, actually. Please, Mr. Nelson, do desist. If I hear any more of such praise I shall be compelled to fling myself into the creek."

"It was not my intention to praise you."

"Then you have succeeded," said Dorothea. "Oh, and before I forget, I was asked to pass along a message to you. Mr. William Lloyd Garrison sends his regards."

Mr. Nelson did not so much as flinch. "How did you come to possess a message from Mr. Garrison to me?"

"He was kind enough to respond to my request for an autograph for the library board's opportunity quilt. However did you come to meet Mr. Garrison?"

Mr. Nelson gave the barest of shrugs. "Our acquaintance is long-standing. I do not recall how or when we met."

"Perhaps you met him in prison," exclaimed Dorothea, as if inspired. "I understand Mr. Garrison has quite a reputation for engaging in charitable works. Perhaps he visited you there to offer you words of comfort."

Mr. Nelson kept his gaze fixed on the horses. "You are quite right," he eventually said. "Mr. Garrison was kind enough to visit me in prison. Several times, in fact."

He said nothing more, but it was confession enough. Dorothea was torn between triumph and astonishment. She had not expected him to so readily acknowledge the criminal past he surely had assumed was unknown in Creek's Crossing. Part of her had even disbelieved the rumors as too shocking to be true. Now she had his own admission, but he made no attempt to excuse his crimes or beg her to tell no one. Perhaps at last he regretted his offensive behavior since his arrival in their town. If he had been less insulting, less arrogant, she might have agreed not to reveal what she had discovered, had he asked.

They reached the ferry dock. The pilot had left the craft for the warmth of the boathouse, but he soon emerged and allowed them to drive the carriage aboard. "You got here just in time," he remarked. "I was about to go home for the night."

"Has my uncle crossed recently?" asked Dorothea.

The ferryman shook his head. "Not since earlier this evening when you both came over together."

Troubled, Dorothea asked him to tell her uncle, if he should appear before the ferry ceased operating for the night, that she was already on her way home.

"I gather this is not typical behavior for your uncle," said Mr. Nelson after the ferryman left them to push away from the shore.

"Not at all. Ordinarily he is as conscientious as he expects everyone else to be."

But he had not been his usual self for months. His forgetfulness, his outbursts of anger—perhaps her mother was right and he was not well.

Mr. Nelson seemed unconcerned. "It is likely he has preceded you home."

"Yes." She forced confidence into the words and settled back into her seat. "Very likely."

When they reached the road up the hill to Uncle Jacob's farm, the distant light from the house's windows offered a soft welcome. Mr. Nelson asked if he could water his horses in the barn before departing. Dorothea consented, and as soon as he swung open the doors, she saw that neither Uncle Jacob's wagon nor his horse was inside.

"Thank you for seeing me home," said Dorothea, climbing down from the carriage. "Please take whatever you need for your horses."

She ran toward the house, in her haste forgetting to invite Mr. Nelson to warm himself by the fire before he left. She opened the door with a bang, startling her parents, who looked up from their chairs in alarm, which faded when they saw her. Lorena set down her knitting and smiled. "How was the exhibition? We did not expect it to run so late."

"Is Uncle Jacob here?"

"No," said her father. "Didn't he bring you?"

"He never arrived. Mr. Nelson brought me home instead."

Her parents exchanged a look of puzzlement and joined her in the kitchen. At her father's request, Dorothea repeated what Uncle Jacob had said regarding the time and place he planned to meet her. "It is unlike my brother to be so late," said Lorena, turning quickly at the sound of a knock on the door. She hastened to open it, but it was only Mr. Nelson.

"Is Mr. Kuehner missing?" he asked.

"Missing or delayed," said Robert.

Mr. Nelson addressed Lorena. "You know his habits best. Is it too soon to begin a search?"

"If it were a temperate night, I would say yes, but because it is so cold . . ." Lorena shrugged helplessly.

The men quickly agreed to ride back to Creek's Crossing. Mr. Nelson would search south of town on the route toward his home while Dorothea's father inquired at the houses of Uncle Jacob's few acquaintances. Lorena and Dorothea would search the farm. As the men rode off, Lorena investigated the outbuildings while Dorothea headed for the sugar camp.

The lantern in her fist swung as she ran, casting stark shadows on the ground. Frozen tufts of grass crackled underfoot; her nostrils prickled and lungs burned from the cold. She began calling for her uncle as soon as the lantern light lit up the shelter and the large log tripods that had once suspended an enormous black kettle over the fire at sugaring time. There was no reply. She reached the shelter, but inside she found only the quilt she had made him, draped clumsily over a wooden bench.

She searched the forest next, stumbling over tree roots and windfall hickory nuts the squirrels had abandoned. She called for him, but listened in vain for a reply. She then began to search the fields, following the post-and-rail fence that marked the boundary of Uncle Jacob's property, and met her mother coming from the opposite direction. Her search of the outbuildings had yielded not a single clue as to Uncle Jacob's whereabouts.

Their faces and limbs were numb from the cold, their throats aching and hoarse from shouting. Lorena decided that they should return to the house, await word from Robert, and keep the kettle on the fire in anticipation of the men's return.

Hours passed with no word. Dorothea and Lorena fell asleep in their chairs beside the fire, bundled in quilts. The first pale pink shafts of dawn were appearing on the horizon when Dorothea's father returned, haggard and shaking from fatigue. He had found no sign of Uncle Jacob.

"Perhaps Mr. Nelson—" Dorothea began, but her father interrupted her with a shake of his head. Mr. Nelson, too, had searched all night. They had encountered each other southwest of town; Mr. Nelson suggested they concentrate their search in that region, since the last sighting of Uncle Jacob's wagon located him heading south, following the road along Elm Creek.

None of them could imagine what he might have been doing there at that hour. Robert suggested a second, more thorough search of the farm now that daylight had arrived, but Lorena insisted he rest while she and Dorothea combed the grounds once more. He wearily agreed, but when they returned two hours later, they found him in the barn doing the chores.

"Someone's got to tend to these animals," he said before Lorena could scold him. He was right, of course; together they completed the usual morning chores. They forgot about breakfast until it was nearly lunchtime, but when Lorena prepared a meal, none of them could eat more than a mouthful. Dorothea felt sick and apprehensive. Something dreadful had happened, and now all they could do was wait until they discovered what it was. Suddenly an image flashed before her mind's eye: the fugitive slave, bloated and decaying, being dragged from the reeds along the creek bank.

She jumped up from her chair. "Someone should go in to town to see if there is any word."

Her father nodded, but at that moment, they heard horses coming up the road toward the barn.

Dorothea reached the door first and dashed outside, the cold wind biting her cheeks and whipping her dress against her legs. She hugged herself for warmth and halted in the middle of the road, shivering, as her parents caught up to her. Her mother drew in a sharp breath, her father murmured something, but Dorothea was insensible to everything but the wagon and riders coming slowly toward them.

It was Uncle Jacob's wagon, but an unfamiliar horse pulled it, and the man driving it sat stiffly, shoulders hunched against the wind. Two men on horseback flanked the wagon: Charley Stokey, a scar running the length of his face where Mr. Liggett had cut him with the scythe, and Linus Donne, the county constable. The wagon rolled awkwardly, its front corner smashed, the wheel wobbling uncertainly.

The men would not meet their gaze as they approached. That and the condition of the wagon told Dorothea that Uncle Jacob was dead.

Chapter Six

THE WAGON HAD been found overturned in Elm Creek, but since the wounds upon Uncle Jacob's body were merely scratches and bruises, they knew the crash had not killed him. Mr. Donne speculated that Uncle Jacob had been felled by an apoplexy, and, unable to control the horse, he had driven the wagon down the riverbank.

The accident had occurred in the woods belonging to Mr. Liggett, who had chanced upon the scene earlier that morning. According to Mr. Donne, Mr. Liggett insisted that he had not been expecting a visit from anyone, least of all Uncle Jacob. He had not known that Uncle Jacob was missing or that others had been searching for him. Charley Stokey added that he had seemed less concerned with Uncle Jacob's death than with figuring out why Uncle Jacob had been on his land. Dorothea and her parents were equally bewildered. The scythe had been returned long ago, and they could think of nothing that would have compelled Uncle Jacob to seek out Mr. Liggett's company.

When Mr. Donne and Charley offered their condolences, Lorena took a deep breath and said, "Thank you for your kindness. It was a terrible accident, but we will take comfort in knowing my brother is now in a better place."

"An accident." Mr. Donne's brow furrowed. He scratched his

head and rolled the brim of his slouch hat. "Only one thing bothers me."

"What's that?" asked Robert.

"Where's his horse?"

Charley looked grim. "We should check Liggett's barn."

Donne shook his head. "Now, Charley, I told you. Just because it happened on Liggett's land don't make him responsible."

Charley absently fingered his scar. "I'm not saying he done it, but maybe he saw a chance to steal a horse whose owner wouldn't miss it."

"This isn't the time or place to talk about this."

"That horse didn't unhitch itself."

Charley's voice rose, but Mr. Donne cut him off with a low word. Dorothea was numb to the exchange. All she could think of was Uncle Jacob, lying dead on his bed, wrapped in a coarse sheet.

Mr. Donne asked Dorothea's father if he could do anything more for the family, but when Robert shook his head, the visitors departed. Alone, the Grangers sat silent and motionless in their chairs.

Lorena broke the silence with a murmur. "The Lord be praised, we are delivered."

"Mother," exclaimed Dorothea.

Lorena shot her a frown. "Don't look at me that way, Dorothea. I do not celebrate your uncle's death, but I cannot help feeling that a great yoke has been lifted from my shoulders."

"We must see to his burial," said Robert, rising woodenly from his chair. "He would want to be buried on his own land, and he would want prayers said."

"Mr. Donne should have taken him to the undertaker's rather than bringing him here," remarked Lorena.

"Perhaps they thought his family would want him," said Robert, a new sharpness in his voice.

"All I mean is that the ground is too frozen for you to dig a grave. He will need to be buried in the town cemetery."

Privately, Dorothea agreed. Each fall, the undertaker had the grim task of estimating how many citizens of Creek's Crossing were likely to perish before the spring thaw. Before the first snow, he would arrange for the corresponding number of graves to be dug, plus a few more in the event of unforeseen dire circumstances. A few years earlier, an outbreak of typhoid fever filled all the prepared graves before January, and the remains of the additional deceased had to be stored in the undertaker's barn until late March.

"He would want to be put to rest on his own land with Rebecca and the children," said Robert more firmly. He took pen and paper from the desk and dashed off a letter, which he handed to Dorothea. "Please take this to the reverend. I'll get to work on a grave."

Dorothea nodded. She was halfway to the barn when the numbness of her hands woke her to the realization that she had left the house without her wraps. She returned inside and threw on her coat and muffler, but as soon as she stepped outside again, she discovered she no longer carried the letter. Her frantic search of the kitchen called her mother to the doorway, but Lorena did not ask what she was doing and it did not occur to Dorothea to explain. She stopped short in the middle of the room, pressed her palms to her head, and squeezed her eyes shut, willing the noise and confusion from her mind. Slipping her hand into her pocket, she grasped the familiar roughness of paper. She withdrew the letter, threw her mother a look of helpless apology, and tucked the page back into her pocket.

"It will be all right," said Lorena. "Everything will be all right."

Dorothea could not find the words to reply.

As she rode to the ferry, she tried not to think of how long her parents had waited for Uncle Jacob to die, how often they had all wished him dead. Now that their wishes had been satisfied, she almost thought she could sense her uncle just beyond the range of sight, scowling at her accusingly, as if their anticipation had brought about his death.

He had probably died from an apoplexy, Mr. Donne had said. He had investigated many scenes of death and understood them more thoroughly than any man should be obliged to. But what, indeed, had happened to the horse?

There was no visitation. Uncle Jacob would not have appreciated such a gathering in life and would not gain anything from one in death. He was buried beside his wife and sons the next day, with only his closest kin and the minister in attendance. With a pickax Dorothea's father had hewn a grave in the icy ground within the maple grove not far from the sugar camp, which they surmised must have been his favorite place on the farm. No one wept. Mired in shock and disbelief, Dorothea could not mourn her uncle because she could not believe him truly gone.

The ceremony was brief, flat and empty despite the minister's words of comfort. Lorena had suggested that Robert play a hymn on the fiddle after the last prayer, but he had refused, flexing his fingers and rubbing his callused palms together as if unaware that he did so. Although Dorothea longed for the solace of music, she was relieved by her father's reply. To play hymns at the grave of a man who considered music a frivolity would be to mock him, powerless as he was now to enforce his wishes.

Dorothea left her parents at the gravesite while Robert covered her uncle's coffin with earth. Listless, she wandered through the maple grove to the sugar camp, to the sturdy, windowless sugarhouse and the outdoor workspace that had preceded it. A heavy chain still hung from the timber Uncle Jacob had secured between two sturdy oaks and the ring of large stones beneath it remained, but the enormous cast-iron kettle that had once been suspended from the chain over the fire had been stored in the barn for years, ever since Uncle Jacob decided that a series of smaller kettles produced a far superior syrup than one large kettle alone. Why he had left the kettle stand and fire circle in place after building the sugarhouse, Dorothea did not know, unless it was to mislead curious rivals.

She crossed the camp to the sugarhouse, passing beneath the suspended timber, her fingers brushing the chain, shoes kicking up black soot from the accumulated cinders of seasons past. Since the sugaring season lasted only a few weeks, other farmers made do with crude log shacks, but Uncle Jacob had built a sugaring house large enough for three or four adults to work in relative comfort, protected from the elements, with a loft for storage.

Each year her father helped Uncle Jacob collect hundreds of gallons of sap, and she and her mother did their part to boil the clear liquid into syrup, but Uncle Jacob alone decided when the work would begin. In mid-February, Uncle Jacob would begin taking careful note of the weather, marking the time of the sunrise, observing if the temperature had risen above freezing during the day before dropping at night, consulting his meticulous notes from previous years. A few days before he thought the sap would begin running, he and Robert would traverse the maple grove, drilling a hole in each trunk, inserting wooden spiles, and hanging buckets beneath the spouts to collect the sap. Uncle Jacob never failed to tap the trees at precisely the right time, though sometimes he chose the last days of February and other years the first weeks of March. He always managed to collect the pure, precious sap in abundance, even in seasons when their neighbors complained of stubborn flows from their trees or woody flavors in the sap.

Each day the men would empty the buckets into barrels loaded on the wagon and haul the sap to the sugarhouse, where Dorothea

144 ~ Jennifer Chiaverini

and her mother boiled it down in three kettles hung in a row over an open fire, which they were careful to keep burning steadily. As the sap boiled and thickened in one kettle, they would ladle it into the next and replenish the first, holding back their skirts from the flames, wincing when an errant splash of bubbling syrup struck their hands or faces. When the syrup in the last kettle had thickened enough, Dorothea or Lorena would stir and stir as the liquid turned into grains of sugar. Together they would pour the maple sugar into the wooden molds Uncle Jacob had fashioned and then set them aside to harden.

Occupied though he was with collecting sap, Uncle Jacob still kept a watchful eye on the women's work, never too busy to remind them to stoke the fire or chide them if their attention seemed to wander from the boiling kettles. And to Dorothea's chagrin, the time-consuming labor required to boil forty gallons of sap down into a single gallon of syrup did not relieve the women of their ordinary chores. They rose early to fix breakfast and tend the livestock; at midday and late afternoon either Dorothea or her mother would race back to the house to prepare another meal. Often, long after the men had returned from the barn and had gone off wearily to bed, Dorothea and Lorena labored over the housekeeping neglected during the day—the baking, the churning, the never-ending laundry and mending.

Dorothea's thoughts went back to the previous year, to a sugaring season when the days dawned sunny and nightfall brought new snow that dusted grassy slopes and underbrush. The lingering pattern of daytime thawing and nighttime freezing had extended the sap run. Uncle Jacob, hardly able to contain his satisfaction, expressed his enthusiasm by working his family harder than ever. Dorothea was alone in the sugarhouse stirring a kettle when her uncle entered, peered at her through the clouds of steam, and inquired as to her mother's whereabouts.

Dorothea brushed damp hair back from her forehead, the sweet scent of maple clinging to her skin, her hair, her clothing, and told him Lorena was back at the house preparing dinner. He nodded, but did not depart as she expected. Instead he took the long-handled spoon from her hand and checked the sap in the center kettle, which had thickened and acquired a rich, amber hue. "Some people think I begin my sugaring earlier than most folks because I'm too impatient to wait when there's work to be done," he said. "That's nonsense. I start as soon as the sap runs because the early run of sap is the sweetest. Better sap means better sugar. This syrup is ready to be moved to the next kettle. Quickly, now."

Dorothea obeyed without a word, and after the task was done, Uncle Jacob began to ladle boiling sap from the first kettle into the second. "You must care for the trees just as you do the fields and livestock," he instructed. "Keep the sugarbush thinned. Don't tap them too young or use more than one spile per tree or tap anything but sugar maple."

"The Craigmiles say they have used red and Norway maple with no discernible difference in taste."

"This is not the Craigmile farm. You are my niece and you will do it my way." He handed her the ladle. "Finish this while I fetch more fresh sap."

Dorothea nodded, taking the spoon, wondering why he had chosen that day to share his sugar-making secrets and her as his confidante.

Uncle Jacob hefted a barrel of fresh sap and poured some into the first kettle. "Some folks can work the land all their lives and never learn a thing from it. You have to tend the sugarbush as you would any crop. Not like Amos Liggett." He nearly spat the name. "The fool man chops into the tree with an ax to get to the sap instead of drilling a hole. All that does is injure the tree and allow pestilence and infection to ruin the sap in years to come. I've seen trees on his land that had six buckets around them collecting the sap that dripped from those hatchet cuts. Six holes on one tree! It's no wonder his sugar tastes like burnt sand."

He had gone on to instruct her in the proper carving of a spile from a branch of sumac, but Dorothea had not paid as much attention as she would have had she known he would not see another sugaring season. At the time she had wondered, idly, how her uncle had come to discover how Mr. Liggett's sugar tasted, since they never traded work and were definitely not friends. Now, a new realization struck her: Uncle Jacob must have observed Mr. Liggett's trees firsthand in order to know such specific details of his sugaring methods. Evidently the night of his death was not Uncle Jacob's only occasion to visit Elm Creek Farm.

Troubled, Dorothea swung open the door to the sugarhouse and stepped inside. Uncle Jacob's tools lay in their proper places, exactly where he had left them. Dorothea tried to imagine sugaring without him, but her mind's eye refused to form the pictures.

One object out of place caught her eye: The quilt she had painstakingly created from her uncle's drawings lay on the ground beside an old wooden bench. She remembered last seeing it draped across the bench, but she must have jostled it in her haste to search for her uncle. She bent down to pick up the quilt, brushing dirt and stray bits of crumbled maple leaves from the fabric. Her gaze traced the path the triangles made, lingering upon familiar scraps she recognized from sewing her uncle's work shirts and Sunday trousers. Without realizing it, she had made him a memorial quilt.

She folded the quilt and tucked it under her arm.

"We must send for Jonathan," said Lorena as the family walked back to the house from the gravesite. Dorothea felt a stirring of feeling then, a distant gratitude. Jonathan would surely come to hear the will read. If, as they all hoped, he inherited Uncle Jacob's estate, he might even decide to stay and continue his studies with the local physician.

Once Uncle Jacob was safely beneath the ground, Lorena began sorting through his papers. She found his ledger and the will, which she wanted to open but declined to do so without his lawyer present, lest anyone accuse her of tampering with it. Dorothea knew a simple comparison with the copy on file with the county clerk would clear her of any such charges. She suspected her mother hesitated to read the will out of fear that it would not fulfill her hopes.

A steady flow of condolences came once the death notice appeared in the *Creek's Crossing Informer.* Friends visited with gifts of food and words of comfort. All who came agreed that he had been a hard man, but decent and God-fearing, and that surely he would receive his just reward. "The Lord is merciful and I am confident he will reward my brother as he deserves," Lorena always replied.

Dorothea wanted to remind her that it was not always a mercy to receive what one deserved.

A WEEK AFTER UNCLE Jacob's death, Abel Wright came to pay his respects. Dorothea took him to the grave and stood some distance away while he bowed his head in silent prayer. Then he looked up and said, "I have something to tell you and your folks."

Dorothea took him back to the house, where her mother had been emptying Uncle Jacob's bedroom of his clothes and books and his few other possessions. She could not dispose of anything until after the will was read in case the worst happened and Jonathan did not inherit, but she wanted to have the room ready for her son should he decide to take it, or for herself and Robert if Jonathan declined.

Lorena put the kettle on and sent Dorothea to the barn for her father while Mr. Wright took a seat in the front room. He shifted uncomfortably in his chair while Dorothea poured, but gave her a kindly smile and thanked her as he took his cup. His expression grew more serious as he returned his attention to her parents.

"There's something about your brother you need to know," he said. "I can tell you why he was on Liggett's land that night."

Startled, Dorothea set the teapot on the table too hard, rattling the china. She murmured an apology, sank into her usual seat by the fire, and picked up the pieces of an Album block with trembling hands. She held her breath and waited for Mr. Wright to confirm Charley's suspicions: Mr. Liggett had been involved in her uncle's death.

Robert began, "How—"

"I remember now," Lorena interrupted. "You saw him that day. He said you had told him of Mr. Schultz's return."

"I saw him later, too." Mr. Wright hesitated. "He was coming from my place. He was going to cross Elm Creek at the place where it narrows in Liggett's woods."

"Why?" asked Robert. "Why not use the ferry?"

"He couldn't be seen crossing so many times in one night. Folks might ask questions."

"Questions? What questions?" asked Dorothea. "Why could he not be seen?"

"He didn't want any of you folks to know." He directed his gaze at Dorothea. "Except you. He was proud of you. He thought maybe you could be told. The older he got, the more he wished he could ask for your help. But he knew it was too dangerous."

Robert's voice was slow and direct. "What was too dangerous?"

"Helping runaways."

The room was silent.

"My brother—" Lorena paused and began again. "My brother was no abolitionist."

"He didn't talk about it, but he was," said Mr. Wright. "Do you really think I saved up enough money to free Constance selling cheese?"

"But he objected to your trip," said Lorena. "If it had been up to him, Constance would have perished enslaved."

"No," said Dorothea, suddenly remembering. "He objected to the timing."

"He objected to putting a single penny into the pockets of slavers, too," said Mr. Wright. "He wanted me to help Constance escape, like we helped the others. That's what I wanted at first, but when Constance wouldn't run, I agreed to do it her way. When we couldn't wait any longer, Jacob gave me the rest of the money I needed."

"You brought escaping slaves north in your wagon after delivering your cheeses in the South," said Robert.

"Sometimes. Other times I just brought them things they needed. Directions, false papers, money, things like that."

"Why did Jacob not tell us?" asked Lorena, bewildered. "He knew we loathe slavery. We would have assisted him."

Mr. Wright almost allowed a smile. "Sure, he knew how you felt. So does everyone else in town. Jacob thought you two were too free with your opinions. You might not have been able to keep quiet."

Insulted, Lorena said, "That is just like my brother. Selfish even in his altruism, not to allow us to share in his mission."

"Well, you can surely share in it now. We need this station. We already lost one on this route when the Carters left—"

"The Carters?" echoed Robert.

"Goodness," gasped Lorena. "Are there any more abolitionists in this town who have not dared to reveal themselves to us?"

"Some serve the cause of abolition by speaking out, and others by operating in secrecy," Dorothea broke in. "Clearly Uncle Jacob was able to assist runaways because no one, not even his family, would have suspected him."

"Be that as it may." Lorena lifted her palms and let them fall to her lap. "I only wish we could have helped him."

Mr. Wright said, "Dorothea already has."

He exacted their solemn vow that they would never reveal the rest of the tale before he agreed to explain.

The escape route through the Elm Creek Valley was relatively new, as the southern pass through the Appalachians was difficult to navigate except by those who knew it well. Most stationmasters knew little about the other stations along the route, a necessary precaution should any one of them be compelled to confess what he knew. The safe havens for runaways ranged from the house proper, in the case of the Wrights, to a secret cellar beneath a stable, to Uncle Jacob's sugar camp. "He wasn't so protective of his sugar-making secrets," said Mr. Wright. "He just pretended to keep folks away. He thought it was right funny anyone believed it."

Mr. Wright knew of at least one station between his farm and the southern pass; there could be more, but he wasn't speculating. It was safer not to know too much about any station but one's own and the next one down the line. Runaways who reached the Wright farm used to travel on foot to Two Bears Farm two miles to the north, making a risky journey across Mr. Liggett's property in order to ford Elm Creek at its narrowest point.

Two Bears Farm was lost to them after the Carters moved away, since no one knew Mr. Nelson well enough to ask him to continue the dangerous work. Until then, Uncle Jacob had occasionally allowed runaways to spend the night in his barn out of respect for his late wife's beliefs, but with the Carters gone, he had agreed to assume a more significant role and became a stationmaster. Unwilling to risk his family's safety and reluctant for them to discover his clandestine activities, he made his sugar camp the station. Unfortunately, the distance between the Wright farm and Uncle Jacob's was too great to navigate on foot in a single night. For the past eight months, fugitives had been forced to find shelter in corn fields or woods between the Wright farm and Uncle Jacob's sugar camp, unless Mr. Wright could carry them north in his wagon or Uncle Jacob could travel south to fetch them. This was not always possible, as frequent travel between the two farms would draw unwanted attention. To conceal the truth from the Grangers, Uncle Jacob would pretend to have an appointment with his attorney.

"But he made frequent visits to his attorney long before the Carters moved away," interrupted Lorena. "And on occasion I saw him bring back legal papers. Did he forge those, as well, merely to deceive us?"

"No, many of those visits were genuine," said Mr. Wright. He gave a rueful shrug, either to apologize for Uncle Jacob's behavior or for what he intended to say next. "He said you folks were always on your best behavior after he met with his lawyer. That's why he considered it such an advantageous excuse."

"Well," huffed Lorena. "I hardly know what to think."

But Dorothea knew. So much of her uncle's strange behavior now made perfect sense—his self-enforced isolation in the sugar camp, the occasions when he could not be found when needed, the meals he carried with him as he went off to work early, his frequent visits to the attorney. He had not been changing his will at the slightest offense after all, as he had encouraged them to believe. In hindsight Dorothea was certain he had enjoyed deceiving them.

"You said I helped him," said Dorothea, "but I cannot imagine how."

"Do you still have that quilt you made him?"

Dorothea nodded and retrieved the Sugar Camp Quilt from her attic bedroom. Mr. Wright unfolded it and ran his hand across its surface. "Your uncle never knew when runaways would come, and since he couldn't wait around the sugar camp to greet them, he had Dorothea make this quilt. It marked the sugar camp as a safe haven, of course, but it also told runaways where to go next, in case they had to leave before Jacob had a chance to explain."

Robert shook his head. "The *quilt* told them?"

Even as he spoke, Dorothea understood. "Those odd blocks my uncle drew—the varied number of triangle points on the Delectable Mountains blocks. This is a map."

"In a way it is." Mr. Wright held out the quilt to Dorothea. "It's more like a list of directions."

"Where do they lead?" asked Lorena, gazing eagerly at the quilt as Dorothea draped it over her lap.

Even as Mr. Wright confessed that he did not know, Dorothea began to puzzle it out. "These represent the Four Brothers mountains to the north of the Elm Creek Valley," she said, indicating the upper left portion of the quilt where the three- and five-triangle edged blocks stood apart from those that had the traditional four. She wondered how she had not noticed before how the number of triangles in the blocks mirrored the most prominent peaks of the mountain range. "And these . . ." She examined the five blocks Uncle Jacob had so deliberately sketched. "These must be intermediate steps along the safest route north."

"My brother's insistence on accuracy at last becomes clear," said Lorena, a trifle dryly. "He could not leave a map or written directions at the sugar camp where a slavecatcher might discover them."

Nor would written instructions have been useful to fugitive slaves who could not read. Dorothea thought of her uncle's request for scraps of serviceable fabrics, of the mud he had wiped from his boots. He had wanted the quilt to seem old and worn, nothing so precious that it could not have been left behind in a sugarhouse.

Dorothea stroked the quilt and was suddenly struck by a profound sense of loss. Her uncle had concealed his brave secrets, unwilling to incriminate his family but also wary that they might expose him. What an unnecessary effort his secrecy had been. The Grangers were outspoken in their views, but they were not fools. They would have been a great help to him, had they but known. He had underestimated his family, and it may have cost him his life. Dorothea could have assisted him on the night of the school exhibition. She could have helped him think of a plausible excuse for crossing on the ferry. If only Uncle Jacob had trusted her, he would not have been alone on Mr. Liggett's land when the apoplexy befell him.

But he had not been alone. "What became of the runaway who was with Uncle Jacob on the night he died?"

From Mr. Wright's expression, she knew he had been expecting the question—and dreading it. "I figure he continued on north, on horseback."

"Of course. What other choice had he?" said Lorena briskly. "He could not have done anything for my brother in any event."

"I hope he at least tried," said Robert.

He spoke quietly, but there was an odd note of contempt in his voice that drew Dorothea's attention away from the quilt.

"Robert," said Lorena steadily. "There is no reason to believe that this unfortunate fugitive killed my brother for his horse. He had no need. Jacob was transporting him in greater safety than if he attempted to go alone."

"I'm not saying he killed him," said Robert, "but perhaps he left him to die."

"The runaway didn't know the way to the next station," Mr. Wright reminded him. "He needed Jacob."

"All he needed to know was how to get to the sugar camp. If he gave the horse her lead, she would have taken him right past it on the way to the barn. Once the runaway saw the quilt, he would have known where to go."

Lorena reached out and stroked his arm. "You heard what Mr.

Donne said. My brother almost certainly died instantly. There was no sign of any struggle, any suffering. Can you imagine how terrified the runaway must have been? Would you have expected him to stay rather than flee for safety? Why? Out of respect for the deceased, out of concern for our sensibilities?"

"Sam," said Mr. Wright. His face was stone. "His name is Sam. This runaway is a man. He has a name. He is not some killer on the run. He is fleeing *for* justice, not from it."

Robert looked away. "We'll never know that, will we?"

Dorothea studied the quilt. "It may be possible." She addressed Mr. Wright. "You said you do not know where the signs in this quilt are meant to lead?"

He shook his head. "It's better that I don't know."

"One of us must find out." She plunged ahead before her parents could object. "One of us must know where the next station lies if we mean to continue Uncle Jacob's work. We do mean to continue?"

Mr. Wright tensed almost imperceptibly, but only Dorothea saw it. Her parents were looking at each other, debating their decision without saying a word. A moment later they turned back to Dorothea and Mr. Wright and nodded. "Of course," said Lorena. "We would have helped before if your uncle had allowed."

"You should think carefully before you decide," cautioned Mr. Wright, though his relief was evident. "There are laws against helping runaways, and folks like Liggett who would give you up in a heartbeat."

Dorothea thought of how Uncle Jacob had disparaged Mr. Schultz for following his better nature. "I am not afraid," she said, emboldened by her disappointment that Uncle Jacob had not shown more faith in them. "Were we not already exposed to prosecution by virtue of my uncle's actions? Had he been detected, who would have believed that we had not known?"

"No one would have considered a girl your age complicit in any crime, Dorothea," said her father. He nodded to Mr. Wright. "I will figure out the riddle of this quilt tonight. Tomorrow morning, I will follow wherever it leads."

"No, Father," said Dorothea. "I should do it."

They regarded her with surprise. "It is good that you want to help," said her mother, "but you are too young. It is too dangerous."

"I am a grown woman and I know the Elm Creek Valley better than anyone." Only Jonathan knew the forest and fields so well, and if he were there, Dorothea knew he would insist upon going instead of her parents, who never left the well-traveled roads. "It is as Father said: No one would suspect me. That is why, like Uncle Jacob, I should be the one to do this. I know I can."

They looked doubtful, even fearful. She thought they would forbid it outright. Instead they sent her from the room to begin supper while they discussed it. By the time she called them to the table, they had decided.

Dorothea would follow the route depicted in the Sugar Camp Quilt to discover where it lay and to meet the stationmaster there. He and Mr. Wright would advise them how to proceed. The Grangers knew little of the operations of the Underground Railroad, but they would learn. The sugar camp would remain a haven for runaways. There was never really any question of doing otherwise.

Together the Grangers would continue the work Uncle Jacob had begun, the work he had not trusted them to share.

SNOW FELL OVERNIGHT, BUT the next morning dawned clear and brisk. Dorothea set out after completing her chores, bundled warmly against the cold. Her breath ghosted through her muffler in faint white puffs as she broke a trail to the sugar camp, the quilt under one arm. She and her father had begun studying it as soon as

Mr. Wright had departed the day before, and they had stayed up late into the evening, uncertain how to decipher the patchwork symbols. Lorena had searched through Uncle Jacob's belongings for a journal, letters, anything that might explain the meaning of the quilt's design. Mr. Wright had warned them this would be a wasted effort, for like any good stationmaster, Uncle Jacob knew better than to put his secrets in writing. Some might consider even the wordless symbols of the Sugar Camp Quilt too great a risk. Sure enough, Lorena's search turned up nothing. Even the sketches Uncle Jacob had made for Dorothea were gone.

Eventually the Grangers concluded that the designs had so many potential meanings the quilt was, perhaps intentionally, incomprehensible to anyone who could not see their actual counterparts. Since Dorothea was fairly confident she understood the first clue, she decided to proceed and hope she recognized the other landmarks when she encountered them.

She committed the patterns to memory and draped the quilt over the bench as she had seen it the night Uncle Jacob went missing. On the day of his burial, she had found it on the ground and had assumed she had knocked it down in her haste, but gazing at it now, she wondered if the runaway named Sam had done so. Perhaps her father was right and he had let the horse lead him there before continuing north. Perhaps her father was right about Sam in other matters.

Dorothea shook off the thought and focused on the five unusual blocks Uncle Jacob had sketched. The star in the center of the quilt, with its longest point directed to the upper left corner, had seemed off-kilter and strange to her before, but now that she understood the quilt's true purpose, the design resembled a compass rose pointing to the northwest. Since the Four Brothers were depicted in the upper left corner of the outermost border of Delectable Mountains blocks, and since the real mountains lay northwest of the farm, Dorothea surmised that the fugitives were supposed to bear in that direction.

She studied the quilt one last time and left it behind in the sugar camp, regretting the necessity. She would have liked to bring it along in case she had neglected an important detail in the patterns, but she could not afford to be seen using the quilt as a map. Uncle Jacob's compass was a reassuring weight in her pocket as she made her way through the maple grove, her footsteps muffled by the thin layer of snow covering the fallen leaves. Her father had insisted she take the compass, though she had argued she probably would not need one, since the fugitives did not and had to be able to follow the quilt regardless. Now she was glad he had insisted.

At the last moment her father had also urged her to travel on horseback rather than walk. Mr. Wright had told them stations were ideally no more than ten miles apart, a long day's walk even in fair weather. Dorothea had been tempted, but Uncle Jacob would have assumed the runaways would travel on foot. The landmarks might be so subtle that she would miss them if she rode. So she packed food and dry stockings in her coat pockets, hoped the stationmaster would allow her to spend the night by his fire, and prayed the journey would not be long.

An old worm fence marked the boundary between Uncle Jacob's land and his neighbor's, zigzagging off in both directions and disappearing into the trees. Dorothea lifted her skirts and climbed over it, glancing up through the bare-limbed trees for the position of the sky to be sure she still headed northwest. She considered checking the compass when, with a sudden flash of insight, she halted and peered over her shoulder at the fence. It resembled a crooked ladder on its side, or the quilt block she had inadvertently encouraged her uncle to redraft.

She hesitated, uncertain. The fence did seem to run almost due north, the logical direction for a runaway slave to go, but if she were mistaken, she could find herself wandering far from the correct route until nightfall with no shelter from the cold. "Any wrong choice will have the same consequences," she said aloud. The air seemed colder when she stood still, so she approached the fence and rested her hand upon it. She had to keep moving; she had to choose.

The crooked ladder block lay in the ring of blocks encircling the central compass rose. If the center indicated the beginning of the route, the crooked ladder clue, which could indeed depict a worm fence, would be the second clue, the first landmark.

Lacking any reason to choose otherwise and unable to conceive of anything that would resemble Uncle Jacob's sketch more than the fence, Dorothea decided to follow it north. She quickly dismissed the troubling thought that the fence snaked off to the south as well as to the north, and that even if she had found the right landmark, she might be traveling in the wrong direction.

Twenty minutes later, she emerged from the maple grove at the bottom of a low slope that rose to the west. She followed the fence to the top, from where she looked out over acres of old cornstalks sticking up through the snow. A house, barn, and three smaller outbuildings sat at the far edge of the fields. Dorothea searched her memory for the name of the family. "Wheeler," she murmured. They had eleven children and had sent only the youngest boys to her school. She was not sure how they would feel about her trespassing on their land, or what excuse she might invent for her presence there.

Walking would be easier on the open ground on the Wheelers' side of the fence, but she quickly climbed back to the eastern side and concealed herself in the woods. She could still glimpse the fence through the tree trunks as she made her way north, but she feared she might miss the next landmark entirely. The next concentric square of Delectable Mountains blocks contained a patch that resembled a narrow braid stretching from left to right on a slight angle. She assumed that was the next block pattern to interpret since it followed the sequence moving outward from the center.

Her dress caught on a tree branch; she tried to pull free but stopped at the sound of fabric tearing. She stopped to untangle herself, wishing Uncle Jacob had been more explicit despite the need for secrecy. It was a wonder Uncle Jacob's runaways had not given up and returned to the sugar camp for better directions.

She continued, stumbling through the underbrush with the worm fence six paces to her left. She passed the Wheelers' house and barn. In the distance, she heard a dog bark, but she did not see it nor any sign of the home's inhabitants, save a thin trace of smoke curling from the chimney.

The corner post of the fence appeared. Dorothea paused to catch her breath, regarding it with misgivings. The fence continued west along the road directly in front of the Wheeler farm. Anyone walking alongside it could easily be spotted from the house or barn.

Uncle Jacob surely would not have sent the runaways so close to an unknown household. She considered, for a moment, that the Wheeler farm might be the next station, but she could not be more than two miles from the sugar camp and had three clues yet to follow. She held perfectly still and listened for the sound of horses on the road, but heard only the wind in the trees. Reassured of her solitude, she made her way stealthily through the woods, drawing closer to the corner fence post. Suddenly she tripped over a low depression in the ground; naked branches scratched at her face as she stumbled and struck her shoulder on the rough trunk of an oak. Instinctively she pressed her lips together to hold back a cry of pain. She quickly regained her footing but had to pause to collect herself. Her shoulder ached. She rubbed it with a mittened hand and searched the ground for the obstruction. It was not a hole, as she had assumed, but a narrow patch where the undergrowth had been worn away to bare earth.

With the tip of her boot she cleared away fallen leaves from one end of the patch. When she found more worn ground, she eagerly looked up and detected an indistinct path winding to the northeast for a few yards before it disappeared into the forest. It was an old Indian trail, abandoned for decades—or perhaps not entirely abandoned. The path did lie along the same angle as the next block in the Sugar Camp Quilt, and the braid appearance could be meant to evoke an association with Indians.

Dorothea concealed the part of the path she had uncovered and set off to the northeast. The trail that had seemed all but invisible until she knew what to look for widened slightly a quarter mile east of the Wheeler farm, wide enough for a horse and rider. Years ago, Dorothea and Jonathan had explored old Indian trails that crossed Thrift Farm, and they had followed one all the way from Widow's Pining to the foothills of the Appalachians at the southern end of the Elm Creek Valley. Such trails laced the valley; European settlers had widened some into roads, but most remained overgrown and forgotten. Pennsylvania remained difficult to traverse despite the rise of towns such as Creek's Crossing. Most easterners traveling to points west still preferred the water routes to the south along the Maryland and Virginia border rather than the national roads through Pennsylvania's mountains. Mr. Wright had said that the rugged terrain of the Elm Creek Valley had compelled weary fugitives to find easier routes to the north, but as slavecatchers increased their patrols along the more well-traveled crossings, more runaways would be forced into their valley.

The sun rose higher in the sky as Dorothea followed the Indian trail through the woods. It was past its peak when she finally had to stop to rest and eat. Her shoulder still hurt where she had slammed it against the tree; her hands were cold, but not numb. Her feet were cold inside the work boots she had borrowed from her mother, but they were dry, and the three pairs of socks she wore would hold off frostbite.

Dorothea saved half of the bread, cheese, and meat for later and sated her thirst with a handful of snow. She shivered from the cold but took another mouthful before pulling her muffler over her mouth and nose and continuing on.

Another hour passed, or so Dorothea guessed. She had meant to note how long the journey took, but the passage of time had become a blur of weariness and cold and the glare of sunlight on snow. Her feet ached in the overlarge boots; despite the three pairs of socks, a blister had formed on her left heel, and cold had crept into her bones. Her hand, nose, and feet steadily grew colder until they became numb. She longed to stop somewhere to warm herself, but the woods surrounded her. There was no place to go, and she could not be certain that home was closer than her destination.

Runaways could not turn back. She pressed on.

She should have taken the horse, she thought as she floundered through a thick patch of underbrush. Once she lost the trail, but found it again. The next block in the sequence was the one that resembled the curves of the Fool's Puzzle block. The Indian trail must eventually cross another path, perhaps a circuitous or hilly road. She shook off the anxieties that had been growing ever since she left the familiarity of the worm fence. She told herself she would recognize the next landmark when she saw it.

Another hour passed, or perhaps more. She stopped to rest on a fallen tree, to remove her boots and rub feeling back into her toes. The temperature had steadily dropped as the sun descended in the sky. It could be no more than midafternoon, but she was as fatigued as if she had walked from dawn until sunset. Wave after wave of weariness overcame her as she sat rubbing and pinching her feet. They tingled a bit and she could still move her toes, but she yawned as she tried to work sensation back into them, great, enormous yawns. Her hands moved ever slower.

She woke with a jolt as her hip struck the ground. Dazed, for a moment she did not understand what had happened. When she did she yanked on her stockings and boots and laced them, shivering from fear as much as from cold. She had dozed off and fallen from her seat on the log. If she had not, she might have slept until she froze to death.

Fright sped her footsteps. The trail grew more difficult to discern as the forest thinned and shadows stretched out longer and longer. The trees grew more sparse, the path all but invisible. Disbelieving, she came to a halt as the trail ended. She must have missed the road. The Indian trail surely would have crossed it. She turned slowly in a circle, heart sinking. She would have to retrace her steps and look more carefully. But how far off the route had she wandered? How many needless miles and hours had she added to her journey?

Fighting despair, she closed her eyes and whispered a prayer for courage. Uncle Jacob expected fugitive slaves to make this journey, men and women and even children who had not that morning left the comfort of their home and family, who could not expect a cordial welcome at any farm in the valley. Unless her uncle was a fool, he had known that the people following the symbols in his quilt would be tired, hungry, frightened—and possibly pursued. He would not have made the quilt so difficult to follow. Unless she believed her uncle to be a fool, she would have to trust the message he had left behind.

With her eyes closed, she heard the wind blow through the trees. The few dried leaves still clinging to the trees rustled. Bare boughs squeaked as they scraped against each other. Behind it all, she heard another sound: a gentle, almost musical burbling.

Her eyes flew open and she hurried toward the sound. She recognized it now: the trickling of water. The curving road she sought was a stream, shallow and rocky, nearly frozen over.

She looked down upon it from the snowy bank, laughing aloud

from relief even as tears sprang to her eyes. She had found it, she was sure of it, but this was only the third of four landmarks. She could not endure another walk as long as the Indian trail to reach the fourth.

She took a deep breath and gave only one quick, worried glance to the sun nearly touching the horizon. The creek flowed to the east, but instead of following the current, she chose west and hurried on.

She should have started out from home earlier. She should have taken the horse. She should have let her father go instead. Her feet slipped on snow-covered pebbles as she hurried to beat the sunset. The last symbol in the quilt, a square in the upper left corner between the last ring of Delectable Mountains blocks and the sawtooth border, was the most cryptic of all. While piecing it, she had noted the similarities to the Spiderweb block, with its eight slender triangles meeting at a point in the center, but the bases of the triangles were made of narrow rectangles. Surely she could not be looking for something as transient as a spiderweb.

Racing the fading light, she reached the origin of the stream, a broad, fast-flowing creek—not Elm Creek, she was sure, but one that ran from the northwest between cultivated fields. On the other side of the creek was a road, and beyond that, a banked barn and farmhouse. Her hopes rose, and she forgot for a moment the cold and the dull ache of her hands and feet. Though she might not reach the end of her journey before nightfall, she would not freeze to death. Unlike the fugitives for whom the Sugar Camp Quilt had been created, she could seek shelter at one of the farmhouses.

Newly energized, she quickened her pace. Scattered houses appeared more frequently until she was sure she had reached the outskirts of a town. A wagon passed on the road on the opposite shore, but if the driver regarded her curiously, he could not surely consider her behavior suspicious.

Then, suddenly, the sound of the creek altered. She rounded a bend and gasped. Another wagon and a man on foot passed on the road, but she barely noticed them.

Up ahead, turning steadily in the fading light, was the water wheel of a mill. Just beyond it were a bridge and the gray-board buildings of a town.

Relief flooded her. In moments she had reached the road and hastened across the bridge. The sun was nearly gone by the time she pounded on the door of the millhouse, heedless of any passersby who might wonder at her urgency.

The door opened, and a woman with piercing eyes and streaks of white in her dark hair regarded her with concern. "What is it, my dear?"

The moment had come and Dorothea knew not what to say. "I— I'm Jacob Kuehner's niece."

The woman did not hesitate. "Come in. Come in at once and warm yourself."

Muffling a sob, Dorothea stumbled inside.

Chapter Seven

THE WOMAN SHUT the door and guided Dorothea to a seat by the fire. Dorothea fumbled with her wraps, her eyes tearing from the sudden warmth and light. Her hands were stiff and useless. The woman swiftly removed Dorothea's muffler and coat, then knelt to remove her boots and stockings. Dorothea began to shiver, shaking so uncontrollably that she could not have spoken even if she could have summoned enough strength for words. Within moments the woman placed a cup of hot tea in her hands, and, once assured Dorothea was thoroughly cold but not frostbitten, began to scold her.

"I cannot imagine what your uncle was thinking, sending you out so late and in such cold," she said, using a long-handled hook to pull the iron arm of the kettle crane out of the fireplace.

"He didn't send me." Dorothea drank deeply of the tea, her shaking hands rattling the cup against her teeth. "He is dead."

"I see." The woman stirred the kettle, tasted its contents, and swung the arm back into the fireplace. The aroma of beef stew made Dorothea's head swim and mouth water. "The last passenger told us so, but I had hoped he was mistaken."

Passenger. "You mean Sam. He did come here."

"Yes, riding your uncle's horse. She's in our barn." The woman set out plates and spoons on a wooden table in the center of the room. "You will ride her home, of course, but not tonight. You'll spend the night here."

"Thank you." Dorothea glanced around the large room for a sign of the runaway, but her hostess was not that careless. "Is Sam still here?"

"He continued on north the day after he arrived." The woman gave her a searching look. "We had snow that day. He should have remained with us until the storm passed, but he was terrified to have northerners as well as slavecatchers pursue him. He feared he would be blamed for your uncle's death."

Dorothea thought of her father's suspicions. "Very few know Sam was present when my uncle died. Only one voiced any concern."

"You will have to set that one straight, then. Sam had nothing to do with it."

"Did he tell you what happened?"

"Sounds like an apoplexy, the way Sam described it. He was hidden in the wagon beneath a tarpaulin when the wagon lurched and left the road. Sam peeked out and saw your uncle slumped over in the wagon seat, still holding the reins. He drove the wagon right off the path and into a river—some tributary of the Juniata, I suppose."

"It was Elm Creek," said Dorothea softly, picturing the scene. Uncle Jacob must not have died instantly after all. She wondered if he had lived long enough to realize what was happening to him.

"That horse of his is a capable creature. She didn't buck or panic when the wagon overturned, but waited patiently for someone to unhitch her." The woman set a loaf of bread and a ball of butter on the table. "Your uncle wasn't breathing, nor did his heart beat. Sam spied a cabin and considered asking for help there, but instead he took the horse and gave it its lead home."

"He was wise not to knock on the door of that cabin. The man within would have turned him over to the next band of slavecatchers to pass through the valley."

"They pass through far too frequently these days." The woman sighed and settled into a chair opposite Dorothea's. "We never used to see more than one group every two or three months around here."

"Where, precisely, is here?"

The woman's eyebrows rose. "You don't know? You're in Woodfall, dear. You've walked eleven miles, nearly halfway to Clearfield."

Dorothea gave a shaky laugh. "That explains why I'm so weary."

"Indeed," the woman said dryly. "You look hearty enough, but one wonders why your father did not come instead."

"He wanted to, but I thought I would be less likely to raise suspicions."

"Oh, certainly. A young woman wandering about alone on a cold winter's eve. No one would think twice about that." She regarded Dorothea with amusement. "So the children make the rules around your house now that your uncle's gone, do they?"

Before Dorothea could reply, a door on the far wall opened. Dorothea glimpsed the machinery of the mill in the room beyond as a barrel-chested man with sandy hair and whiskers entered. He shut the door and halted at the sight of Dorothea shivering beside the fire. "Well, who's this now?" he asked, his voice deep but friendly.

"This is—" The woman gave a small laugh. "My goodness, I don't know her name."

"I'm Dorothea Granger."

"She's Jacob Kuehner's niece."

The miller's eyes filled with sympathy. He shook her hand and offered his condolences. "Your uncle was a good man," said the miller, whose name was Aaron Braun. "His death is a great loss to the abolitionist cause."

"My parents and I intend to continue to run his station."

The husband and wife exchanged a look. "I see," said the miller slowly.

"This is not a task entered into lightly," said his wife. "To the young it may seem a romantic adventure, but it is a dangerous business."

"The fugitives depend upon us not only for their freedom, but often for their very lives," said Aaron Braun. "And we depend upon each other's secrecy for our own survival."

At once, Dorothea understood the reason for their concern, the dread that lingered not far below their calm exteriors. "My parents and I realize we must scrupulously conceal our activities. We will, of course, rely on your advice."

"What if our advice is to abandon your plans?"

Dorothea straightened in the chair and met his gaze levelly. "Then I would tell you that would be unwise. You have already lost the Carters, and as I have myself discovered, the journey from Creek's Crossing to Woodfall is too far to venture without a safe haven along the way."

A smile flickered in the corners of Mrs. Braun's mouth. "Most slaves are wise enough not to attempt an escape in the dead of winter."

"Some have no choice. Sam, for example."

The Brauns exchanged a look. Dorothea had no idea why Sam had fled to the north in January rather than waiting for spring, but she could imagine various reasons. She felt a flush of shame at allowing the Brauns to believe she knew more than she did, but securing their confidence was too important.

"They already know enough to betray us," Mrs. Braun told her husband after the doubtful silence dragged on unbearably long. "We might as well let them help."

"Our uncle's activities have already exposed us to the dangers we would face as stationmasters," said Dorothea. "We are prepared to face them knowingly, now."

"So it is to be 'in for a penny, in for a pound'?" said the miller, but his voice was kindly.

His wife's expression was graver. "If we allow you to do this, we will be putting our lives into your hands."

"We would die before we would betray you."

"Would you, indeed." Mrs. Braun smiled, but deep grooves of worry appeared around her mouth. "My dear, you cannot make that promise on anyone's behalf but your own. Especially when you will be expected to keep it."

MRS. BRAUN BECKONED HER husband and Dorothea to the table and served them steaming plates of fragrant beef stew with thick slices of fresh bread. Ravenous, Dorothea thought she had never eaten anything more delicious. While they ate, she expected to query the Brauns about the operation of the Underground Railroad, but they put two questions to her for every one she asked them. They asked how she had found the route to the mill and why her uncle had not confided in her family. She told them about the quilt and answered their other questions as honestly as she knew how. By the time the meal was over, Dorothea felt as if her memory had been put through a mangle and squeezed dry. She had learned almost nothing about the Brauns' station. They did not reveal by so much as a word or a glance whether they hid their passengers in the mill itself or their adjacent residence.

It was late in the evening when Mrs. Braun ordered Dorothea to bed, in a motherly way, affectionate but unyielding. When Dorothea protested, Mr. Braun promised her they would continue their discussion in the morning. Dorothea nodded and resolved that it would not, however, proceed in the same fashion. She had only a few hours to learn all she could from her hosts, and she could not do that if they subjected her to more questioning.

Mrs. Braun led her to a small bedroom on the second story. Dorothea undressed to her shift and climbed beneath the layers of quilts, shivering until she grew warm. She fell asleep almost immediately and woke, hours later, to the sound of the low, steady grinding of the mill. The whole house seemed to tremble.

She dressed swiftly, judging from the sunlight outside it was past eight o'clock. Mrs. Braun was already working in the large room downstairs, which seemed to be kitchen, front room, and parlor all at once. The Brauns had eaten their breakfast earlier since Mr. Braun had to run the mill, but Mrs. Braun invited Dorothea to the table and soon placed a hot plate of potato pancakes and sausages before her.

Mrs. Braun poured them each a steaming cup of tea, and as she seated herself, Dorothea said, "There is much my parents and I need to know about running a station."

"Yes." Mrs. Braun sipped her tea. "So a good night's sleep did not clear your thoughts of such foolish notions."

"They are not foolish notions, and like it or not, you need our help. The situation is so desperate I must wonder why you would turn us away."

"Forgive me, but your uncle did not think your parents capable."

Dorothea felt a surge of loyal anger. "He did not know them as well as I. We found you, did we not?"

Mrs. Braun nodded in acquiescence. "*You* did. Very well, then." She set down her teacup and folded her arms on the wooden table. "I will tell you what you need to know."

Dorothea drank in every word as Mrs. Braun explained the coded language preferred by the stationmasters and conductors, how to conceal one's tracks in the forest, various means to convey a fugitive north, and so much else that Dorothea felt she could not absorb it all. There was too much to remember, and as Mrs. Braun gravely recounted stories of friends and acquaintances whose stations had been discovered and what they had suffered, Dorothea felt her confidence wavering. A fine her family could bear, but imprisonment? The seizure of the farm? The responsibility was so great, as were the consequences. If they failed, they could be worse off than when Elm Creek claimed Thrift Farm. They could be rendered destitute. They could fail those who depended upon them.

Then she thought of what Constance Wright had endured until her husband bought her freedom, and what so many others like her endured every day while Dorothea lived in safety and comfort with her loving family.

She inhaled deeply and sighed. Mrs. Braun studied her. "Are you having second thoughts?"

"Of course," said Dorothea. "But how can I refuse to help? Whatever I might face is nothing compared to what the runaways have suffered. I cannot turn my back."

At last, Mrs. Braun smiled with a warmth that lit up her eyes, and Dorothea knew instinctively that she was speaking with a kindred spirit, the sort of woman she would like to become.

"That is precisely how I felt when Aaron and I embarked on this journey together," said Mrs. Braun. "I have never regretted my decision. May you never have reason to regret yours."

They talked at length, until Dorothea felt she was as prepared as she could be for the task her family had undertaken. Mrs. Braun sent her husband's apprentice to saddle Uncle Jacob's horse while Dorothea put on her wraps, bracing for the cold ride home.

"Do not tarry," advised Mrs. Braun. "The air smells like snow coming."

Mr. Braun instructed her to follow a different route home rather than backtracking along the Sugar Camp Quilt trail. The journey home was much swifter on horseback along the main roads, but Dorothea still did not reach home until after noon. Her parents must have been watching the road, for they ran to meet her before she reached the barn. Their relief was so obvious that Dorothea almost wished she had left the Brauns' at daybreak and spared her parents a few hours of waiting, but she had needed that time with Mrs. Braun.

She recounted for them every detail of her journey from the moment she left the sugar camp until she departed the stable behind the mill. Lorena seemed most interested in Mrs. Braun's guidance for running their station; Robert, on the fate of Sam. He seemed to accept that the runaway had had no part in Uncle Jacob's death. Dorothea accepted Mrs. Braun's word. Robert took as evidence the safe return of the horse.

Dorothea's parents had news of their own to report. Cyrus Pearson had called for her earlier that day, and he had seemed most disgruntled to discover her absent. He asked to wait for her, but Lorena invented an ill friend and said Dorothea would be tending her for at least the rest of the day. He left, reluctantly, with a message: His mother was eager to complete the quilt and wanted to know when Dorothea would be willing to bring her blocks so they could finish piecing the top.

For a moment, Dorothea thought he meant the Sugar Camp Quilt, and then she remembered the Authors' Album. She had not thought of the opportunity quilt or the library board since the night Uncle Jacob went missing. For that matter, she had not given a single thought to Cyrus, who had once occupied so many of her idle musings. She might have missed two board meetings, or perhaps three. Cyrus had not come by the farm to fetch her for them or she would have been reminded. He had probably assumed that the family was in mourning and that she would not have gone. Still, it would have been thoughtful of him to pay his respects to Uncle Jacob out of consideration for Dorothea. Perhaps he knew the older man had not liked him and did not want to appear a hypocrite.

"I have only one block left," said Dorothea. "I will finish it tonight and take the blocks to Mrs. Engle's house tomorrow rather than wait until next Thursday." Her mother had not mentioned that Cyrus planned to come for her then, and she was reluctant to ask.

"There is more news," said Lorena, withdrawing a folded paper from her pocket. "Jonathan has sent a letter. He is coming home."

Dorothea scanned the letter eagerly. Jonathan apologized for his absence and declared that he planned to come as soon as he was able. The needs of his patients and the difficulty of winter travel rendered him unable to provide his family with the specific date of his arrival. If he would be delayed more than two weeks, he would send them another letter to tell them so, but otherwise they should expect him before the end of January. Dorothea's happiness at this news dimmed as she read the letter over more thoroughly. He did not say so, but he implied that after the visit, he intended to return to his studies in Baltimore.

"The post must have been delayed," remarked Lorena, indicating the date written at the top of the page. The letter was almost two weeks old. "Jonathan is probably even now on his way."

"Or a second letter apologizing for his delay is," said Dorothea, but she was so pleased by the prospect of his imminent arrival that she could forgive him all the earlier, canceled visits.

The snowstorm the miller's wife had predicted reached the farm while Dorothea and her mother prepared supper. The flakes flew thick and fast, but after the evening chores were done, Dorothea lit a lantern and made her way to the sugar camp. Inside the sugar-house, snow had blown in through the weathered boards and had collected in drifts in the corners. Uncle Jacob would have immediately set to work finding and sealing the spaces, but Dorothea could not tarry. The cold nipped at her cheeks as she covered a basket of her mother's dried apples with the Sugar Camp Quilt, apparently undisturbed since her last visit. She glanced up at the loft and envisioned a runaway hiding above in fearful silence while she and her mother stirred boiling kettles of maple sap below. She hesitated before climbing the ladder to check, but no one now hid among the stored tools.

As she completed the Album block bearing William Lloyd Garrison's signature that evening, Dorothea pondered the sugar camp and its fitness as a station. Uncle Jacob had chosen it because it provided concealment from other farms and from his own family, not because it was comfortable and safe. Weary fugitives would be far better off in the house, or even in the barn, especially in winter.

She shared her thoughts with her parents, who agreed they must make more suitable arrangements. They needed a place where one or more runaways could rest comfortably, and yet remain entirely hidden from both friendly visitors and slavecatchers.

Lorena shuddered as they all imagined slavecatchers forcing their way into the house. "Perhaps the sugar camp is safest after all," she said, "for both the runaways and ourselves. If they are discovered, we could pretend we did not know they were hiding there."

Robert said nothing, and even Dorothea was at a loss for words. She could not imagine Mrs. Braun disavowing the fugitives in her care.

The next morning, Dorothea hitched up Uncle Jacob's mare and drove the wagon into Creek's Crossing. Elm Creek had frozen over, the ferry stowed ashore in the boathouse until the spring thaw. Only the tracks of horse's hooves and wagon wheels marked the crossing over the ice.

At the Engles' home, the housekeeper took Dorothea's wraps and led her to the parlor. Mrs. Engle bustled in a few moments later. "I do not usually expect callers so early," she said, taking her customary place in the armchair near the front window. "It is not time for tea. Will you take coffee instead?"

"No, thank you. I won't keep you long. I only stopped by to give you my finished blocks for the Authors' Album."

Dorothea opened her satchel and steeled herself for the inevitable shriek of horror when Mrs. Engle discovered the signatures of several authors she had expressly banned from the quilt.

"Give your blocks to me?" Mrs. Engle asked, bemused, giving the satchel the barest of glances. "It would seem you've misunderstood my son's message." She rose and retrieved a muslin-wrapped bundle from behind the divan. "I was not expecting you to come for these until Thursday, but I suppose this is better. Perhaps you will finish the top before our next board meeting."

Mrs. Engle handed Dorothea the bundle before she was ready for it, and it fell into her lap. "Finish the top?" she echoed.

"Most of the blocks are already stitched, but you will need to assemble the top. Including your own blocks, of course, which I assume will bring the total to eighty." Mrs. Engle folded her hands and smiled. "We did not think you would mind, since you missed our last three meetings and the rest of us have done so much more work than you have. This quilt was, after all, your idea. We assumed you would want to have at least some hand in the making of it."

Indignant, Dorothea nonetheless managed a pleasant smile. "You assumed correctly, although I cannot promise I will complete the top by our next meeting."

"Just so long as you attend." Mrs. Engle took her chair again, sitting with a grace that belied her stout form. "We have much to do and the quilting bee is only weeks away. You'll probably want to get started right now."

Dorothea recognized the dismissal and rose. "Of course. Good day, Mrs. Engle."

"Good day," said Mrs. Engle cheerily. "Oh, Dorothea?"

Dorothea paused in the doorway. "Yes?"

"Please accept my condolences on the loss of your uncle."

"You are very kind."

"I understand his will has not yet been read?"

"No." Dorothea tucked the bundle of quilt blocks into her satchel. "My uncle's lawyer prefers to wait until my brother returns from Baltimore."

"I suppose that would be necessary. Well—" Mrs. Engle smiled and nodded. "Good luck, dear."

Dorothea gave her a wordless nod in return and left the room.

TWO DAYS LATER, JONATHAN came home, tall and solemn in his black suit, which Dorothea later learned he had borrowed from his mentor's nephew since he had no suitable mourning clothes of his own. Lorena was so happy to see her son that she flung her arms around him, laughing and crying and clinging to him, impeding his progress through the doorway. He felt so good in Dorothea's eyes that she almost ached from it.

Her baby brother had grown taller, his face more thin, but the thick shock of brown curls was the same, forever tousled no matter how much he tried to slick down the locks, giving him the perpetually windblown look of someone always rushing off on horseback.

He wanted to visit Uncle Jacob's grave, but Lorena insisted he eat and warm himself first. "It will be a pleasure to eat good home cooking again," he said, taking off his coat and sitting down at the table in the chair the family still referred to as his although he had not used it in more than a year.

"Doesn't Mrs. Bronson feed you?" teased Lorena, setting a plate before him.

"Yes, and she's a fair enough cook, but I'm usually so busy I take my dinner at the tavern."

Dorothea saw her parents exchange a look. Jonathan quickly added, "I haven't taken to drink if that's what worries you. Taverns are different in the city. The one I frequent is more like an inn."

"You forget I used to live in a city and I know very well what a tavern is like," said Lorena dryly.

Jonathan grinned. "Of course, Mother."

Dorothea and her parents had so many questions and Jonathan so much to tell that they lingered at the table long after he had finished eating. It was late afternoon before he pushed back his chair and reached for his coat. Dorothea offered to accompany him to the gravesite, but he said he preferred to go alone. Dorothea was sewing in the front room when he returned nearly a half-hour later. He paused in the kitchen and as he bent to kiss his mother on the cheek, she said, "We still have a while before dinner. Why don't you ride over to the Claverton farm and call on Charlotte?"

Jonathan straightened, a barely perceptible frown appearing as he shrugged out of his coat. "I don't know that Charlotte would appreciate an unexpected visit."

"Unexpected? You mean you didn't write and tell her you were coming?"

"I came to see you and pay my respects to Uncle Jacob, not to court a thirteen-year-old girl."

"She is fourteen." Lorena dusted flour from her hands and reached for his coat. She helped him back into it, and after a half-hearted attempt to stop her, Jonathan acquiesced. "If you expect Charlotte Claverton to marry you someday, you must at the very least call on her while you're in town."

Dorothea watched surreptitiously as Jonathan, about to protest, heaved a sigh and nodded. He promised to return soon and left, reluctant obedience evident in his every step.

Lorena resumed kneading bread dough in silence. A few moments later, she said, "I suppose he needn't have gone today. He could have waited until tomorrow or the next day, when he would be more inclined to see Charlotte."

She had spoken as if thinking aloud, but Dorothea ventured a reply. "I am not certain he would be any more inclined tomorrow or any other day."

"I suppose you're right. It was just as well I sent him today. Tomorrow we are going to the lawyer, and there may not be enough time for visiting the Clavertons. Jonathan has not said how long he intends to stay, and he could hardly come home without calling on his fiancée, could he? I'm sure he would agree with me."

Dorothea did not know what to say. Deliberately or not, her mother had misunderstood her. Dorothea gave her a thoughtful nod and a shrug, making a noncommittal noise that could be interpreted in any number of ways. If she said what she really thought, there would be an argument, and she did not want an argument to spoil Jonathan's visit.

She spent the afternoon working on the Authors' Album quilt while Lorena carried fresh linens to Jonathan's old bed in the attic and prepared a welcome-home feast. The other members of the library board had evidently used their very best needlework, for each block lay perfectly flat with small, even stitches and precisely matched seams. The green, Turkey red, and Prussian blue calicos gave the quilt a lively, stylish air, and the signatures were as varied and splendid as the people who had inscribed them. The only complaint Dorothea could have made was that one of the quilters had used indigo embroidery thread to backstitch over the inked signatures, while everyone else had used black. She decided the variation added a note of humor to the quilt, and rather than pick out the indigo stitches and do them over in black, she decided to scatter those blocks throughout the quilt so that the differences would appear part of the pattern.

The nine blocks Dorothea contributed brought the total to sixty-one, far short of Mrs. Engle's expected eighty. After considering several arrangements, Dorothea decided to set the blocks on point and separate them with muslin sashing. Before threading her needle, she took pencil and paper from Uncle Jacob's desk and sketched the quilt layout so that she would have a guide to follow while assembling the rows. A sudden memory came to her of working in that same place as she turned Uncle Jacob's drawings into usable templates, and she felt a stab of regret that she had not known him well enough while he lived. She had never suspected his courage. She would have respected him more had he not kept the best part of himself hidden.

Her drawings completed, she began sewing the rows of blocks together. It was repetitive, painstaking work, but it allowed her time to her own thoughts, since her mother was too preoccupied in the kitchen to chat.

Jonathan returned just as Dorothea was setting the table. He apologized for his lateness, adding, "Mr. Claverton had so many questions for me I scarcely had a moment to speak to Charlotte."

"Did you manage to get her to speak to you in return?" said Dorothea innocently.

Jonathan grinned. "She did, and you don't need to tease me about her shyness. Or her youth. She is a charming girl and she will make a fine wife."

"And the combined lands of the Claverton-Granger alliance will make a fine farm."

"Dorothea," said Lorena reprovingly as Robert came in for supper. "You needn't be so vicious."

"What?" protested Dorothea as she placed the platter bearing her mother's roasted chicken in the center of the table. "I'm merely repeating an observation that you and Father have made many times."

"Charlotte also allowed me to sample an apple tart she had baked and showed me her needlework," said Jonathan hastily, in a poorly disguised attempt to forestall an argument. "She is quite an accomplished seamstress. Do you know she already has seven quilt tops pieced for her hope chest?"

Dorothea smiled tightly as she filled the water glasses. "I do indeed know that, since her mother finds nearly every opportunity to update me on her progress. I wonder. Charlotte started so early but she has yet to reach thirteen finished quilt tops. Perhaps she is wiser than all of us and is sewing slowly to delay the wedding."

"Seven quilt tops is far more than you have been able to complete for your hope chest," retorted Lorena.

"Since my hope chest and the eight quilt tops within it lie at the bottom of Elm Creek, I am forced to agree with you."

Robert looked from his wife to his daughter and back, bewildered. "Dorothea has made far more than seven quilts. She made at least three this year alone."

Lorena took her husband's plate and began to serve him. "We're talking about bridal quilts. Dorothea has none of those, but it doesn't matter anyway because she doesn't need them."

Dorothea set down the pitcher. "I may not be as young as Charlotte Claverton, but I am not a spinster at nineteen."

Jonathan's brow furrowed. "If I had known how much my visit would upset everyone—"

"Heavens, no." Lorena placed a bowl of cucumber pickles on the table with a bang. "You have been away too long as it is. If I had known how rarely you would come home, I might never have allowed you to study under Dr. Bronson. Don't let a silly quarrel make you regret your visit."

"I meant my visit to the Claverton farm," said Jonathan. "But you are right to chastise me for not coming home more often. I should have come for the harvest. Uncle Jacob wrote and asked me even after you gave me permission to remain in Baltimore, but I refused, without bothering to write and tell him why."

The room was still. Eventually Jonathan said, "Mr. Claverton inquired about my studies, but mostly he was curious about Uncle Jacob's will. It is clear he wants to know if I will inherit."

"He is thinking of his daughter's welfare," said Robert. "That is all."

Jonathan picked up his fork, but he merely poked at his food, brooding. "I hope my negligence of my uncle's pride will not give you reason to be disappointed."

"If it has, there is nothing to do about it now," said Lorena. "If we lose this farm, too, we will manage."

Robert nodded and clapped Jonathan on the back in a gesture of reassurance. Dorothea murmured her agreement, ashamed of her spiteful remarks about Charlotte, who, Dorothea had to admit, was a sweet and gentle girl. Charlotte could not be blamed for obeying her parents. Perhaps she even wanted to marry Jonathan. He was handsome and kind, and Charlotte probably saw him as a dashing older man. That is, if she were not too terrified to think of him at all.

Jonathan steered the conversation to other matters, and the rest of the family was gratefully diverted. He told them of his studies, the patients he cared for, and the Bronson family, with whom he boarded—the doctor, his wife, and their seven children. Since the eldest were girls, Jonathan shared a bedroom with the two youngest boys, aged four and two years. He confessed he had always considered sharing a small attic bedroom with his elder sister a great hardship until boarding with the Bronsons gave him a new perspective.

Jonathan talked and his family plied him with questions until long after the last bite of Lorena's sour cream cake had been eaten.

It was such a comfort to be together as a family once again, despite the conspicuous absence of Uncle Jacob, that they forgot their quarrel. This time when Lorena asked Robert to play for them, he agreed. They waited in expectant silence as he tuned the long-abandoned fiddle, but when the first pure, sweet notes of a melody flowed from his bow, Dorothea felt suddenly refreshed, as if relieved of a burden she had not known she was carrying. After the second song, Lorena said, "If only we had an organ for Dorothea, so you could play together again, as you did on Thrift Farm." Dorothea knew from her mother's expression that she was thinking of Uncle Jacob's will. Dorothea would not allow herself to hope that Uncle Jacob might have made some small provision for her, so she hurriedly said that she had not played in so many years that she had likely forgotten.

Eventually, their father reluctantly put away his fiddle and went to the barn to get a late start on the evening chores. Jonathan offered to help, so Dorothea and Lorena were left alone to clear away the dishes and tidy the kitchen. They had nearly finished when Lorena reminded Dorothea to check the sugar camp for visitors.

No one had passed through their station since Sam, and recalling Mrs. Braun's remark that most runaways escaped in fairer weather, Dorothea thought nightly visits to the camp might be unnecessary until spring. Leaving food regularly was surely a waste. Still, she put on her wraps, took a lantern from the hook by the door, and ventured outside.

A light flurry brushed her face as she trudged past the barn, but the night was not as bitter cold as it had been. Uncle Jacob would have been consulting his notes, noting the temperature day and night, checking the sugar molds, carving new spiles. The Grangers had done none of those things, distracted by his passing and learning anew how to run a farm without his supervision. Sugar season would be upon them before they were prepared. If they did not need the sugar and the income from the sale of the surplus, Dorothea would not have been surprised if her parents decided not to tap the trees that year.

"Dorothea," called Jonathan, behind her. "Where are you going?"

She hesitated only a moment. "The sugar camp."

She waited for him to ask why, but instead he said, "Want some company?"

"Certainly."

He broke into a trot and caught up to her. They walked side by side through the snow, Dorothea following the path she had broken the evening before, Jonathan wading through the deeper drifts. She realized too late that her brother was sure to notice. After a few paces, he indicated the old trail and said, "You've been to the sugar camp recently."

"Yes. Last night."

"To tap the trees? Already?"

She shrugged. "Just to be sure the camp is in order."

He shook his head, hands buried in his pockets. "It won't seem like sugaring time without Uncle Jacob. So you're going to try to do it without him?"

"I suppose so, assuming we'll be able to keep the farm." Quickly she added, "I'm sure you'll inherit."

He barked out a laugh. "I am not as confident as you. All that our uncle wanted was my attention, and instead I showed nothing but indifference to him and his farm. I don't want to be a farmer. I want to be a doctor."

"Other men have done both."

"But I am happier in Baltimore. If not for you and our parents, I would not care if Uncle Jacob left the farm to a perfect stranger."

She gave him a sidelong look. "If not for me, our parents, and Charlotte, you mean."

"Yes. Charlotte." He was silent a moment. "I wonder if she would like to live in Baltimore."

Dorothea could not believe he was actually considering it, but she said evenly, "If you have been disinherited, or if you relinquish the farm, the impetus for you to marry Charlotte no longer exists."

"She would probably refuse me in any event." Jonathan looked suddenly to the southwest. "What was that?"

"What?"

"Over there, through the maple grove. It sounded like a dog barking." He paused. "There it was again."

That time Dorothea heard it plainly. "A neighbor's dog got loose, I suppose." Her heart began to pound with dread, but she reassured herself that they had heard only one dog, and slavecatchers surely traveled with several. Nevertheless, she quickened her pace. "I'm getting cold, aren't you? Let's have a quick look around the sugar camp and get back inside to the fire."

He agreed, and they hurried on through the snow. Dorothea was almost running by the time the lantern light touched the old kettle stand, the abandoned chain suddenly resembling a hangman's noose. "I'll be just a moment," she called over her shoulder as she ducked into the sugarhouse. There she stopped short and choked back a gasp.

Jonathan called out in reply, but Dorothea did not hear him.

A man sat on the wooden bench, huddled in the Sugar Camp Quilt. He squinted and raised a hand to shield his eyes from the lantern's light. "A dog got me," he said through clenched teeth. He moved the quilt aside to reveal torn trousers soaked in blood. "I couldn't run no more."

"That dog sounds like it's coming this way, fast," remarked Jonathan as he entered the sugarhouse. He halted at the sight of the bedraggled man. "Good Lord."

Swiftly Dorothea set down the lantern and went to help the fugitive to his feet. "We have to get him to the house."

Jonathan's expression plainly showed he understood the urgency. "Can you walk, with assistance?"

The man nodded and gasped in pain as they lifted him. On either side of him, his arms over their shoulders, Dorothea and Jonathan guided him out of the sugarhouse. Outside they could hear the dog barking louder now, nearly in a frenzy. It had surely caught the scent.

They hobbled toward the lights of the house. Dorothea thought in vain of the instructions Mrs. Braun had provided for concealing one's tracks in the snow. There was no time now.

They reached the house and burst into the kitchen. Lorena froze at the sight of them.

"A dog is on our heels," Jonathan told her as they brought the man inside. "It may be merely a stray, but we cannot take chances."

Instantly Lorena snapped into action. "Jonathan, take him upstairs and hide him. Dorothea, run to the barn and warn your father."

Dorothea nodded and fled. The dog's furious barking had drawn her father to the door of the barn, where she breathlessly told him about the runaway. He glanced worriedly toward the southwest, but told her he would finish the chores rather than raise suspicions by leaving them half-finished. "We must go about our usual business," he said. "Tell your mother I will make haste."

Dorothea nodded and ran back to the house. The barking had grown louder, but the dog had not yet appeared. A dog running alone would have reached the house by that time. It must be leashed.

Dorothea hurried indoors and took off her wraps. In the front room, Jonathan had removed his coat and boots and was seated beside the fire, apparently engrossed in the *Creek's Crossing*

Informer. Lorena was rocking in her chair, her knitting needles clicking busily. Dorothea sat down across from her and snatched up her sewing basket. Her fingers trembled as she pieced together narrow strips of muslin for the sashing of the Authors' Album quilt. She desperately wanted to know where Jonathan had concealed the runaway, but she dared not ask.

The dog sounded as if it were almost upon them, and all at once came a furious pounding on the kitchen door. "Granger," a man yelled. "I know you're in there. Open up!"

Dorothea and her mother stared at each other, shocked. The voice, though distorted by rage, was familiar.

The pounding on the door came again, more furious. "Granger!" shouted Mr. Liggett. "Open this door or I'll break it down!"

Jonathan began to rise, but Lorena shook her head and stood. "No. Let me."

Dorothea shot Jonathan a desperate look as they heard their mother greet Mr. Liggett, and then say, "If you wish to speak to my husband, he is in the barn." They heard the strain in her voice and a scrabbling of the dog's toenails on wood as if Mr. Liggett were trying to push past Lorena into the house. Jonathan bounded out of his chair and strode into the kitchen, Dorothea right behind. Their mother struggled to shut the door on Mr. Liggett's dog as Mr. Liggett tried to shove it open. Dorothea snatched up the broom and swiped at the snarling cur until Jonathan shoved it outside with his foot.

"What's the meaning of this, Liggett?" said Jonathan. His frame nearly filled the doorway, and Dorothea was suddenly aware of how much he had matured since she had last seen him, how much authority his manner now commanded.

Mr. Liggett's face was red with fury, but he yanked on the dog's chain and ordered him to heel. "You 'uns got a runaway in there. My dog tracked him here clear as anything all the way from my place. Got a piece of his leg, too."

Dorothea swallowed and suppressed a shudder. "There's no one here but us."

He glared at her. "I'll just see that for myself."

"You are not bringing that dog into my house," said Lorena. "Nor will you set one foot in it yourself. My brother told you to stay off his property, and though he's gone, I'll abide by his wishes."

Before Mr. Liggett could retort, Robert emerged from the darkness behind him. "What's going on here?"

The dog lunged at him, but Liggett held fast to the chain. Robert did not even flinch. "You 'uns are hiding runaways," Liggett spat. "There's a reward out for runaways and I mean to get this one."

Robert shook his head, feigning puzzlement. "There aren't any runaways here."

"I saw him. I tracked him here."

"You heard my father," said Jonathan. "You're obviously mistaken."

"Or drunk," said Lorena disdainfully. "Again."

Mr. Liggett shifted his weight and cinched the dog's chain. "I know what I saw. I saw tracks in the snow, and blood besides. There's blood on the floor of that shack at the sugar camp. Then the tracks go here, and my dog led me right to your door."

"Or perhaps you led the dog," said Dorothea. "You were so certain of your destination."

Robert held up his hands in a conciliatory gesture. "We aren't denying that there might be a runaway out there somewhere, but he isn't hiding here. You're welcome to search the farm if you like, but it's a cold night. Why don't you have a drink first?"

Mr. Liggett hesitated. "I saw tracks in the snow. Someone broke a trail."

"I did," said Jonathan. "My uncle was put to rest in the maple grove. I was out that way paying my respects right before you arrived. Perhaps my presence threw your dog off his original quarry."

"He's a better dog than that." Mr. Liggett eyed him, then turned to Robert. "A drink, you say? What're you pouring?"

"Whiskey."

Dorothea almost started. Uncle Jacob forbade liquor. There had never been a drop of it on the farm except for that which was already in Mr. Liggett.

"Maybe I can stay for a minute," Mr. Liggett said, jerking his head in a nod. He wrapped the dog's chain around a tree branch and ordered the animal to sit. "I could use a drop for warmth."

Jonathan lingered in the doorway, frowning, but after a warning look from his father, he stepped aside and allowed Mr. Liggett to enter. Lorena led their unwelcome guest to the front room, and to Dorothea's astonishment, her father reached into Uncle Jacob's desk and pulled out a bottle of amber liquid. She wondered if her parents had purchased it with Mr. Liggett in mind.

Dorothea knew she must endeavor to maintain appearances, so she resumed her seat and took up her sewing. In a moment her mother's knitting needles were clicking away again, and though Jonathan sat scowling at the fire, Robert engaged Mr. Liggett in conversation. Mr. Liggett had little to say about crops or cattle, but he was eager to boast about a new horse he had procured and his plans to breed champions. He stayed much longer than a minute and took far more than a drop. The bottle was little more than a quarter full by the time Mr. Liggett hauled himself to his feet and declared that he needed to resume the hunt before the runaway fled too far. "I would be much obliged if your pretty daughter would see me to the door," he slurred, his eyes red and bleary.

Lorena's mouth tightened, but Robert gave a slow nod, so Dorothea folded the rows of quilt blocks and placed them on her chair. She escorted Mr. Liggett to the back door, opened it, and said, "Good evening."

He smirked. "Good evening," he echoed in a mincing tone. "Miss Granger, may I ask you a question?"

She nodded.

"Do you folks often leave a burning lantern in the sugarhouse?"

"Only on those evenings when we feel most melancholy for the loss of my uncle. You will recall, of course, that the sugar camp was his favorite place on the farm."

He nodded, disappointed, his eyes searching her face, hungry for more. She kept her features smooth and impassive until he frowned, tugged on the brim of his hat, and left the house.

She shut the door behind him too quickly and stood with her hands pressed against it as if to block his return. She looked for him through the kitchen window, but it was too light inside for her to see more than her own panicked reflection in the glass. Surely Mr. Liggett knew they were hiding something.

Back in the front room, her parents and Jonathan were speaking in hushed voices. "He is a greedy fool," Lorena was saying. "He will likely wake in the morning with a dreadful headache and no recollection of what passed this evening."

Robert looked hopeful, but Dorothea shook her head. "He is a drunkard, but he is no fool." She repeated his remark about the lantern.

Her mother blanched. Jonathan said, "He may have believed Dorothea's excuse, but either way, we will have to be extremely cautious as long as that runaway remains beneath our roof."

"Son," said Robert, "we will have to be cautious longer than that."

Jonathan searched his family's faces until his expression began to shift into comprehension.

Lorena said, "We have much to tell you."

"It will have to wait." Jonathan glanced up. "Dorothea, I will need your assistance."

She nodded and followed him upstairs. Inside the attic bedroom, he knelt beside Dorothea's bed and said, "It's all right. You can come out now."

The runaway emerged from beneath the bed, his face wrenched in pain. Dorothea and Jonathan helped him onto the bed. Dorothea went to remove his shoes and saw that he had only wads of burlap wrapped around his feet and tied with twine. She left them as they were and waited while Jonathan dug into his black leather bag.

"That dog—" The runaway's teeth were clenched in a grimace of pain. "He caught me in the woods, but ran off when I got to the creek—"

"He returned with his owner in tow," said Jonathan, grim. "But now they've left."

"They won't be back." Dorothea patted the man's shoulder and tried to smile reassuringly. "You're safe here."

With a groan, the man fell back upon the pillow and let Jonathan tend to his wounds. The worst injuries were the deep gashes in his left calf where Mr. Liggett's dog had sunk his teeth. As Jonathan washed the wounds, applied a salve, and bound them, Dorothea gently removed the burlap wrappings from the man's feet. She washed and rubbed them to get the blood flowing, but the two smallest toes on his right foot looked shriveled and burned. Silently, Dorothea directed Jonathan's attention to them. Her brother took one look and nodded in assent.

Shortly thereafter, Lorena brought a tray of food upstairs. They helped the man sit up and left him alone to eat and rest, retreating to the front room to discuss his condition. Jonathan asserted what Dorothea had feared: The frostbitten toes would have to come off.

"Perhaps when he reaches safety in Canada—" Lorena began.

"He cannot wait that long," said Jonathan. "The putrefaction will spread. He will sicken and die if his injuries are allowed to fester."

"Can you do it?" Robert asked his son.

"I assisted Dr. Bronson in an amputation once." Jonathan hesitated. "I did none of the cutting myself, but—" He nodded.

At Jonathan's request, Dorothea accompanied him upstairs to deliver the news. As the words sank in, the man began to tremble, but his eyes were angry rather than fearful as he said, "Ain't nobody cutting off my toes. I need my feet if I'm going to run."

"You cannot run in this condition," said Dorothea gently.

"I made it this far."

"It is a long way to Canada," said Jonathan. "Perhaps you will not need to run. Perhaps we can contrive some other means to transport you. We have a wagon."

The man shook his head. "No, sir. You're not taking my toes." Gingerly, wincing with pain, he began to rise from the bed. "Thank you for the food and the tending, but I think I best be going."

"There's a man out there hunting you," said Dorothea, incredulous. "You'll never make it to the next station."

"I made it all this way from Alabama on my own two feet, and it's the same way I'm crossing into freedom."

"This is madness," said Jonathan.

"No, you thinking I'm gonna let you take my toes is madness."

Frustrated, Jonathan ran a hand through his unruly locks. "Very well. Stay. Rest here in safety until tomorrow night. I will not treat you if the alternative is to send you out to a certain death."

The fugitive eyed him. "You swear?"

"You have my word."

Satisfied, the fugitive climbed back into bed and drew the quilt over himself. Dorothea and Jonathan returned downstairs.

"You said 'station,'" said Jonathan as they entered the front room. Their parents looked up expectantly. "Can I assume that you are not unaccustomed to events of this sort?"

They told him everything. Lorena even seemed apologetic about their clandestine activities, deferring to her son as the presumptive future master of the farm. He listened, shock and disbelief on his face, as they explained how they had discovered Uncle Jacob's secret, how Dorothea had followed the clues in the quilt to the next station. How they had resolved to continue Uncle Jacob's work.

When the tale had been told, Jonathan looked drained. "We have not satisfied Liggett's suspicions. He will plague you continuously."

"We will be vigilant," said Dorothea. Her brother abhorred slavery. Why did he look so wary? Had so much time in Baltimore rendered him accustomed to slavery? Resigned to it?

"A man like Liggett would do anything for money," said Jonathan. "Vigilance might not be enough."

It was still dark when a hand on Dorothea's shoulder woke her with a jolt. "Dorothea," said her mother, shaking her gently. "It's time to get up."

Dorothea sat bolt upright. *Mr. Liggett has returned,* she thought. *The slavecatchers are here.* "What's happened?"

"Nothing. All is well," Lorena quickly assured her. "We need to make ready. The will. Remember?"

In the excitement of the previous night, Dorothea had forgotten. The will would be read that morning. They were due at the lawyer's office at eight o'clock sharp.

Dorothea told her mother she would come downstairs presently, and as Lorena left, Dorothea rose and washed herself in the basin of water on the nightstand. Her teeth chattered as she bared her skin to the cold air and the even colder water, then swiftly pulled on her red flannels and second-best wool dress. She unbraided her hair, brushed it out, and braided it up again, coiling the long brown braids at the nape of her neck. She had done her hair by herself in the attic before dawn so often she needed neither mirror nor light to complete the task.

The previous evening, they had moved the runaway—whose name was Zachariah—to the larger and more comfortable bed in Uncle Jacob's old room. Jonathan had slept in the front room at his own insistence, to keep watch. Dorothea paused to check on Zachariah on her way to the kitchen and found him still sleeping. Jonathan and Robert were just returning from the barn. Lorena had already finished cooking breakfast, so all that was left for Dorothea to do was set the table.

They ate in near silence. Dorothea could hardly force herself to swallow a bite. The fate of Uncle Jacob's farm would be decided that day, and yet she could hardly think of the will for the images of Zachariah and Mr. Liggett crowding her mind.

Zachariah emerged just as the family was about to depart. He hobbled into the kitchen, bracing himself with one arm against the wall. "You should be in bed," said Jonathan, going to his side.

Zachariah waved him off. "I'll be fine." He winced as he lowered himself into the chair Lorena held out for him at the kitchen table. Dorothea brought him a cup of fresh milk, cooled now, and a plate of food, which he began to eat hungrily, eyeing the Grangers as they put on their wraps.

"We have some business in town," said Robert. "We will be home before noon."

"When we return, I'll have another look at those toes," said Jonathan. "When you're finished eating, you should get back into bed."

"Into bed or under it?" Zachariah grimaced and looked away to Lorena. "Thank you for the food, ma'am."

"You're welcome." Lorena hesitated. "The man who pursued you here yesterday might not have been put off for good. He may return."

"It would be wise for you to remain hidden," said Robert. "He is not above entering our home in our absence."

Zachariah made a humorless chuckle. "I might be safer at the next station."

"You won't be safer traveling in daylight," said Dorothea. "Lock the doors and stay away from the windows. Take my bed in the attic just to be sure. You will be fine."

She forced certainty into the words as she imagined Mrs. Braun would have done, but Zachariah looked dubious even as he agreed to do as they suggested. After they closed the door behind them, she heard the solid thunk of the bolt sliding into place.

Robert had hitched up the sleigh, and as the horses pulled them smoothly over the snow-covered road, Dorothea glanced back at the house. There was no sign anyone remained inside. "Do you think Zachariah will be there when we return?"

Her father shrugged, and the gesture seemed to mirror Jonathan's thoughts. Lorena said, "Of course he will. Surely he knows to wait until nightfall to depart. Besides, I threw out those old burlap rags of his and he hasn't any shoes."

Dorothea recalled the look in the man's eye when he had rejected Jonathan's medical treatment and thought that Zachariah might very well decide to limp off in the snow barefoot, if it came to that. She feared that it might. All the way into town, from the farm that might no longer be theirs, across the frozen creek, her thoughts dwelt on what might be happening behind her. Even at that moment Mr. Liggett might be lurking about their farm, following the trail through the snow, examining the bloodstains on the floor of the sugarhouse, letting his dog lead him again and again to the Granger's back door. She thought of what might befall Zachariah should he not wait for Dorothea to return and explain to him the secret route stitched into the Sugar Camp Quilt, and how he would fare if he did not consent to Jonathan's treatment.

The meeting with the lawyer, which had loomed large and foreboding in their imaginations for years—the day they would either

secure their futures or be forced to leave Uncle Jacob's farm forever—had been diminished by the previous night's events. Even
Jonathan's admission that he had not done all he could to secure his
uncle's affection did not fill them with dread as it might once have
done. Dorothea knew from her parents' distracted expressions that
they, too, were preoccupied with thoughts of their hunted guest.
Lorena confirmed Dorothea's suspicions when, upon entering the
lawyer's office, instead of encouraging her family regarding the
possible outcomes of the meeting, she said, "Likely Mr. Liggett will
be sleeping off his inebriation well into the afternoon. We will be
home before he even rolls out of bed."

Later, Dorothea wondered if they had surprised the lawyer with
their lack of elation when he declared that Jonathan Augustus
Granger was the sole heir to his uncle's estate, with the exception
of a few smaller gifts to his family and his church. The Grangers
were so eager to return home that they barely stayed long enough
to sign the papers. Only Dorothea managed a laugh when she
learned of Uncle Jacob's bequest to herself: his best steamer trunk,
three hundred dollars, and a book about the western territories.
His plan for her was clear. She mused that if he had wanted to guarantee she follow it, he should not have left the farm to her brother.

The Grangers hurried home. As many times as Dorothea had
thought of this day, she had never envisioned her parents quiet and
pensive as they returned to what could at last be called *their* house,
their land. Only once did a sense of triumph overcome Lorena's
uneasiness. As the farm came into view, she declared, "From now
on we shall call this place Thrift Farm the Second."

Jonathan shifted uncomfortably.

"No," said Robert. "We will call it the Granger farm."

Lorena shot him a look of surprise, but something in his expression silenced her intended protest.

While Jonathan and Robert remained behind in the barn to

unhitch the horses, Dorothea and her mother hastened to the house. Dorothea's heart leaped into her throat when her mother tested the kitchen door. It swung open easily. The bolt had been drawn back.

Lorena hurried to check Uncle Jacob's old room while Dorothea raced upstairs. She found Zachariah resting in her bed, the Sugar Camp Quilt spread over him.

"Where else did you reckon I'd be?" asked Zachariah, bemused. "Did you think I was fool enough to go my own way in daylight?"

"The bolt was drawn back. We thought you had left us, or—that you had been taken."

"That bolt locks from the inside," he told her. "If that man did come back and found the door bolted, he'd know someone was in here. I thought it best to leave it as you folks would have."

"What if Mr. Liggett had returned and come inside?"

"What if he'd been watching the house when you came home and saw you folks knocking on the door and calling out for someone to let you in? He'd know for sure you had someone in here."

Dorothea was stumped for a moment, but she said, "At least the bolt would have kept him out until our return."

Zachariah shrugged. "Maybe, unless he thought to kick in a window. This is a nice place, but it ain't a stockade. You can't keep out someone who's bent on coming in, not unless you got a rifle."

"We do not believe in violence."

He snorted. "Just because you don't believe in it don't make it any less real."

Dorothea had no reply to that. She changed the dressing on his leg as Jonathan had taught her and brought him a cup of water, then returned downstairs to help her mother prepare dinner. When her father came in from the barn to inquire after Zachariah, Dorothea told him of their scare. Robert shook his head and said, "We must contrive a better hiding place."

Jonathan went upstairs to check on his reluctant patient, and when he returned he wore a disgruntled expression. He drew on his coat and announced he was going back into town for something for Zachariah's foot.

Not long afterward, when Dorothea carried a tray upstairs to Zachariah, she drew a chair closer and explained the route to the next station, using the quilt draped over him as a guide. "Remember these patterns and you'll remember the way," she told him.

"What about that doctor brother of yours?" he asked. "Think he'll let me go?"

"He would never keep you here against your will."

"Where is he?"

"He went into town for something for your foot."

"What would that be? A hacksaw?"

Dorothea rose and gathered up his dishes. "He means the best for you. You would do well to take his advice."

"It's not his foot. It's not his choice."

"That is certainly true." Dorothea paused and sat down again, the tray on her lap. "You would risk your life rather than sacrifice two toes. Do you mistrust his skill so much?"

"His doctoring don't have nothing to do with it. Don't you know what they do to runaways they catch? They cut off their feet—and not just so they can't run no more. It tells everyone he's a runaway. He's a slave."

"It's just two toes, not your whole foot. Two toes to purchase your life."

"I'm not going to die because of two shriveled toes."

His expression was resolute, and Dorothea knew further argument was futile. "Summon me if you need anything," she said quietly, and left him to rest and memorize the quilt.

She helped her mother complete the day's housework, then settled in the front room to sew while Lorena knitted. Robert passed through on his way to Uncle Jacob's old room carrying his toolbox and an armload of boards of all sizes. All afternoon while Dorothea and Lorena worked and discussed measures they should take to improve their station—in hushed voices as if they expected to discover Mr. Liggett crouched outside beneath a window—the sounds of sawing and hammering came from Uncle Jacob's room. Just when their curiosity could not bear another moment, Jonathan returned with a paper-wrapped bundle beneath his arm.

"What's that?" asked Dorothea.

"Did Dr. Bremigan ask why you needed the medicine?" Lorena added.

"I didn't go to see Dr. Bremigan." Jonathan shrugged out of his coat. "I went to see Mr. Hathaway."

The cobbler? Dorothea and her mother exchanged a look of bewilderment as Jonathan began to tear off the paper wrapping.

"If Zachariah's going to travel on foot, he'll need boots," said Jonathan, holding them up so the women could see. "Before you ask, no, I didn't tell Hathaway why I really needed them."

"But they're too small for you or your father," said Lorena, drawing closer. They were good work boots, solid and warm. If only Zachariah had had them weeks ago. "Even if they did fit you, everyone knows you are not here often enough to need them. Mr. Hathaway is sure to wonder."

Jonathan grinned. "He did wonder. I told them they were for Dorothea."

Dorothea laughed. "You must not think much of my sense of fashion if you considered that a credible story. Don't you think Mr. Hathaway will wonder when he does not see me clomping about the streets of Creek's Crossing in these boots?"

"Now that you mention it, Mr. Hathaway did say he didn't remember you having such large feet."

Lorena said to Dorothea, "Between now and the time you buy a new pair of shoes, you will have to think of some reason to explain how your feet shrank."

"That, or purchase my shoes in Grangerville."

"I don't believe that will be necessary. Mr. Hathaway was so glad to have the sale that he didn't question my story." Jonathan grinned at his sister, amused. "One other customer was more curious, though. He overheard our conversation and said that he didn't recall ever seeing you wearing anything so coarse. I believe he said you had much too delicate a foot and too graceful a manner to wear such things."

Immediately Dorothea thought of Cyrus. "What did you say in reply?"

"I said that obviously he had never seen you stomping outside to milk the cows in the winter before dawn, and that you have the most enormous, clumsy feet of any woman alive."

"You didn't," protested Dorothea. "You could have simply agreed with him."

"On the contrary. I'm your brother. Someone has to dispel your suitors' illusions."

"Jonathan," scolded Lorena, feigning displeasure. "Cyrus Pearson has danced with Dorothea many times. He surely saw through your exaggeration."

"He might have, except he wasn't there," said Jonathan. "The man was not Cyrus Pearson."

"Not Cyrus?" asked Lorena.

"Who, then?" asked Dorothea.

"No one I had ever met. The cobbler called him Mr. Nelson."

"You must be joking," said Lorena. "You must mean Mr. Nelson the elder. He must be in town visiting his son."

"This man did not seem more than a few years older than Dorothea."

"Then you must have misunderstood his manner," said Dorothea.

"What you interpreted as flattery was certainly intended as sarcasm. Mr. Nelson has never had a kind word for me."

Jonathan's eyebrows shot up. "So I was speaking to Mr. Nelson, the schoolmaster?"

"I know of no other Nelsons in Creek's Crossing." Heat rose in Dorothea's cheeks. Why had her brother felt it necessary to ridicule her in front of a man who would relish her humiliation all too well?

Jonathan frowned, dubious. "This man did not seem as unkind as you have described him. In fact, he rebuked me for speaking about you unfairly."

Dumbfounded, Dorothea said, "He rebuked you?"

"Yes. He said he had seen you dance and that it was grossly inaccurate to describe you as clumsy."

Lorena shook her head at Dorothea in wonder. "Who would have imagined a compliment from that man?"

"I am not so sure it was a compliment," said Dorothea flatly. "Did Mr. Nelson mention he is a former convict? I am sure he is quite capable of lying convincingly."

Taken aback, Jonathan said, "He made a far different impression upon me. He seemed a trifle stern, but he did not seem dishonest. Besides, is he not the son of—"

"His father has a wonderful reputation, of course," interrupted Dorothea. "From what I have seen, his son deserves nothing of it. None of us even knows the crime for which he was imprisoned."

"Considering that he is the head of the school, I hope it was nothing violent," said Jonathan.

Dorothea agreed, but she did not have time to ponder the secrets of Mr. Nelson's past, or why he had spoken so civilly about her to her brother. He was too deliberate a man to have made those remarks casually. Then she remembered: He had helped search for Uncle Jacob that fateful night. Perhaps, out of pity for her loss, he regretted his earlier rudeness.

Just then, her father peered out from Uncle Jacob's old room. "It's finished," he said, and beckoned them inside. "If you cannot find it, I'll consider it a job well done."

Dorothea scanned the room, but it appeared unchanged from when her uncle had inhabited it. Jonathan knelt to look beneath the bed. "I suppose that's the first place anyone would look," he remarked as he rose, brushing dirt from his knees.

Dirt? Dorothea peered more carefully at the floor by her brother's feet. She had swept the room just that morning. While her mother and brother searched elsewhere, she paced slowly through the room, studying the floor carefully.

"What's that you're doing?" asked her father.

Dorothea merely smiled and did not allow herself to be distracted. What at first glance appeared to be dirt was really sawdust. She found traces of it in several places, most likely where her father had worked with his tools. Occasionally she also spotted a larger sliver of wood. She paused where the debris seemed to be most concentrated: directly in front of her uncle's wardrobe.

She pulled open the doors, peered inside, even shifted aside some faded work shirts. She was about to shut the door when her mother said, "Who returned those old shirts? I know I put them in the rag bag."

Dorothea smiled over her shoulder at her father, who was doing his best to look innocent. She reached deeper into the wardrobe and her fingers brushed the wooden back sooner than she expected. Rapping upon the boards, she heard a faintly hollow report. She spun around to her father and announced, "Here. It's here. You made a false back."

She watched as her father's face assumed its old uncertainty, and it occurred to her that she had not seen it since the night Uncle Jacob died.

"You found it so quickly," he said. "You're a clever girl, much cleverer than Liggett, but maybe I should build something else."

"No," said Dorothea quickly. "It is a fine hiding place. If you had swept the sawdust away, I would never have found it."

"The wardrobe is so narrow, no one would think to look for a false back," added Lorena.

"It's more than a false back," said Robert, and he showed them the hidden latch that allowed the false back to fold away, revealing a compartment inside just large enough for two men to stand shoulder to shoulder. On the floor was a handle, which Robert lifted to reveal a hole sawed through the floorboards. None of them could see anything below but empty darkness. Robert explained that the hole went straight through to the cellar, and that he intended to partition off a small, hidden room below by building shelves, one with hinges to act as a door. A space large enough for two or three people to sit comfortably would be undetectable to all but the most determined searcher. Now fugitives could hide inside the wardrobe if Mr. Liggett or anyone else searched the house, and could pass from Uncle Jacob's bedroom to the cellar and outdoors, if necessary.

"Let us pray it never will be necessary," said Lorena fervently. Silently, Dorothea agreed.

ZACHARIAH REMAINED WITH THE Grangers for two more days, until the wounds from Mr. Liggett's dog had begun to heal. He left at twilight with a sack of bread and dried meat on his back and the new boots on his feet. The night was cold but clear, with a bright half moon providing enough light to find the landmarks by. He assured Dorothea he would remember the symbols in the quilt, but if they failed him, he would "follow the drinking gourd" and make his own way north.

At breakfast, Jonathan announced that he intended to leave the next day. Lorena was dismayed. "But the farm is yours now," she said. "Don't you wish to stay and take charge of it?"

"Mother, we all know that the farm is really yours and Father's."

"But you could stay on here." She reached across the table and clasped his hand. "You've always liked Dr. Bremigan. You can continue your studies with him."

His mouth curved in a rueful half smile. "If you considered him an adequate tutor, you wouldn't have asked Dr. Bronson to take me on."

"Now that we're running a station, we could use your help more than ever," said Robert. "Zachariah is not the only fugitive who will need a doctor's care."

Jonathan rubbed a hand over his jaw. "There is something I need to tell you." He hesitated. "I have been admitted to Harvard Medical College. Dr. Bronson helped me secure a scholarship. I enrolled last week and will begin my studies there after I conclude our business here."

"Harvard Medical College?" All the color drained from Lorena's face. "But . . . that is so far away, and it will take so long. Years."

Jonathan nodded. "And when those years are over, I will be a proper doctor, not merely some well-trained assistant."

"But we need you now," protested Lorena. "No one else can provide the help you can here."

"There is so much I still need to learn," said Jonathan. "Allow me to study at the college. Then I will return and do all you ask of me. I promise."

Dorothea could see that he was resolved, that he would do as he wished regardless of his parents' reply. She saw in her mother's eyes that she knew it, too.

"I will hold you to that promise," said Lorena softly. Then she nodded.

Robert drove Jonathan to the train station early the next morning. The house felt strange and empty with only herself and her mother in it, so Dorothea was glad for the brief walk out to the sugar camp to leave the quilt. She should have taken it earlier, but Zachariah had seemed to find comfort in it, and he had needed to memorize the symbols. Circling the shelter, she found unfamiliar boot tracks in the snow. Only Mr. Liggett could have left them, but there was no way to determine if he had done so on the night of Zachariah's arrival or if he had returned more recently. Suddenly Dorothea felt a crawling sensation on the back of her neck as if she were being watched. She draped the quilt on the wooden bench inside the shelter and hurried back to the house.

Soon afterward, the jingling of sleigh bells called her from her housework to the window. She had not expected her father to return from the train station so soon. "Who is it?" called Lorena from the kitchen as Dorothea looked out upon the front road.

A single horse pulled a cutter and driver up the road. She had never seen the cutter, but she recognized the horse. "It's Cyrus Pearson."

"On a Saturday?" Lorena came to the window, but the horse and sleigh had already passed. She gave her daughter a quick, appraising glance. "Take off that apron. Your dress and hair are fine, but you have a smudge of dust on your nose."

"If he comes unexpectedly, he should be prepared to see me as I truly am," said Dorothea, but she rubbed her nose with the back of her hand and smoothed the skirt of her dress. Thus she was somewhat presentable when she answered Cyrus's knock. He declined her invitation to enter and instead invited her to go riding. Lorena gave her permission, so Dorothea put on her wraps and took Cyrus's hand as he helped her into the cutter. They bundled up beneath the heavy blankets, Cyrus chirruped to the horse, and they rode smoothly off.

"Please accept my condolences on the loss of your uncle," Cyrus began.

"Thank you."

"I would have been by sooner, but I did not want to intrude on a family matter."

"That's quite all right," said Dorothea, thinking of all the neighbors who had not considered their kindness an intrusion. She was suddenly troubled by his long absence. Something in his manner seemed distant, chilly.

"Oh, by the way, how is your friend?"

"My friend?"

"The ill friend you were caring for when I last called for you."

"Oh. She is fine. She made a full recovery." Dorothea silently scolded herself for forgetting the ruse. "I was gone only for the day."

"Then I should have returned sooner." He grinned at her, his good humor apparently restored. "You will forgive me, but I thought you were out driving with some other fellow and had left your poor mother to invent a story to protect you."

"Do you really think I would have done such a thing?" said Dorothea stiffly.

"Of course not. You are goodness itself." Then, with a sudden edge to his voice, he added, "If you tell me you were nursing a sick friend, I will believe you."

"I assure you, I was not out riding with anyone."

He nodded, satisfied. Dorothea buried her chin into the blankets, emotions roiling. Her friend Mary thought a man's jealousy spoke well of his feelings for a woman, but Dorothea felt unsettled and displeased by Cyrus's concern. She was relieved that he seemed to accept her half-truths, but resentful that he had required them.

"My mother sent me with a message about your library business," said Cyrus.

"You could have delivered it in the warmth of our kitchen."

"And deny myself the pleasure of your sole company? I wouldn't dream of it, especially since it seems that our regular Thursday drives will no longer be necessary."

"What do you mean?"

"My mother has decided to cancel the library board meetings now that the event you have been planning for is so quickly approaching. She says everyone's efforts will be better spent preparing for the quilting bee." He glanced away from the horse to grin at her. "You, especially, are expected to spend all your waking hours completing the quilt top. Neglect every other duty if you must, just as long as you bring the finished quilt top to the quilting bee."

"Your mother said this?"

"Not in so many words, but her intention was clear."

Uncertain, Dorothea said, "Doesn't your mother want to see the quilt top ahead of time? I have already sewn the rows together as I thought best, but I expected her to want to examine my work."

"She would like to, but there isn't enough time. She says she has faith in your ability to complete the task as instructed."

Dorothea suppressed a sigh. She had designed the quilt and would not concede that Mrs. Engle or anyone else on the library board had instructed her. Still, while this arrangement would ensure that the banned authors were included in the quilt, she had intended for Mrs. Engle to learn of it well before the quilting bee.

She ought to tell Cyrus what she had done and ask him to inform his mother. She almost did, but then she thought of Mrs. Engle's patronizing manner and Cyrus's annoying jealousy, and said instead, "You're certain your mother wishes for me to finish the quilt top according to my best judgment?"

"I'm sure that would satisfy her."

"Very well." Dorothea could not hide a smile. "I will do so."

Cyrus peered at her quizzically, then shrugged. "I have never understood this fascination with making bedcoverings." He tugged on the reins to turn the horse in a wide circle until the cutter was heading for Dorothea's home. "For purely selfish reasons, however, I regret that this particular quilt is nearly done. I will miss our Thursday drives."

"I have enjoyed them, too. It is pleasant to have an outing to look forward to during the week."

"I hope that means you enjoy the company."

Dorothea decided to exclude that day's drive from her assessment. "I have, indeed."

"Then perhaps we might continue our drives even if they have no practical purpose."

She had to laugh. "My uncle would have said that is too much of an indulgence, but I think my parents would allow it."

"Then I will call for you next Sunday as long as the weather is fair." He paused. "I understand your brother is in town."

"He was. He left only this morning."

"I'm sorry I missed him. Did he return to hear the will read?"

"Yes." A corner of one of the blankets came loose and flapped in the wind. Dorothea tucked it beneath her feet. "We visited the lawyer yesterday."

"Since I did not see your parents loading the wagon, I assume the news was favorable to your family."

Did everyone in the Elm Creek Valley know the Grangers' circumstances? "Yes. My uncle was generous enough to leave his estate to my brother."

"Splendid," enthused Cyrus. Then he glanced at her. "You don't mean the entire estate?"

"Well, no. He bequeathed a substantial gift to the church and provided smaller sums to friends and acquaintances."

Cyrus's smile seemed frozen in place. "And to you? Did he leave nothing to you?"

"As a matter of fact, he did leave me a most impressive steamer trunk, a book on the western territories, and more than enough money to purchase comfortable accommodations on the next train headed in that direction." Dorothea laughed and shook her head. "The message might not be apparent to someone who did not know my uncle well. He thought I should seek my fortune out West."

"Did he."

"He told me so, not long before his death."

"He could not know how hard life out West is for a woman or he never would have suggested it. Surely you need not resort to such drastic measures. Have you no inheritance forthcoming from your father's side, from your relations in Grangerville?"

"I regret that I do not. My father's beliefs put him at odds with the rest of his family long ago. When he and my mother asked for their share of the land to build their earthly utopia, his brothers bought him out of his share of the family farm rather than have such an embarrassing spectacle so close to home. It was a substantial portion, enough to buy Thrift Farm, but of course all was lost in the flood. I am sure you have heard that part of the story."

"Yes," said Cyrus. "That little I knew."

Dorothea tried to make light of the family misfortune, knowing how quickly Cyrus wearied of any tale of woe. "We are, as far as I know, the only Grangers forced to leave in disgrace the town my grandparents founded, the town named after our family. Perhaps my uncle has a point, encouraging me to venture farther afield. But of course, I will not follow his advice. If I were to go anywhere, it would be back East, to a city such as Boston."

"Boston is quite pleasant," said Cyrus. "As for me, I prefer New York."

They had turned onto the road up to the Granger farm—how easily the family had begun to think of it by that name, as if it had never been called by any other name, as if Lorena had never suggested they burden it with the title of their first, ill-fated farm. The meeting with the lawyer had indeed changed everything, even though the inheritor was even at that moment traveling eagerly eastward to a city and a life he much preferred.

Cyrus brought the horse to a halt a few paces from the back door. He demurred when she invited him in for tea, saying that he had other messages to carry for his mother. So she bid him a cheerful good-bye and returned inside to finish the housework, work she no longer minded now that the house was the Grangers' own.

Chapter Eight

A HEAVY SNOWFALL prevented Cyrus from coming on Sunday, and when he did not come the next Sunday, either, Dorothea surmised he had decided it was too cold for a long ride. Still, even without the pleasure of an outing, the two weeks passed swiftly. Dorothea managed to finish the quilt top and, with her mother's help, she made over her best winter dress for the dance. Though Dorothea declared it perfect, Lorena fretted over the dress, insisting that Dorothea should have used some of her inheritance money to purchase a few yards of silk brocade for a proper dancing gown. When Dorothea decided Creek's Crossing did not host enough dances to warrant the expense, Lorena said, "You could wear it for other things besides dancing." Dorothea knew she meant it would be a fine wedding dress, but teased her mother by saying she would wear it to milk the cows, and that she knew Mr. Hathaway could help her find the perfect men's work boots to wear with it.

She did spend three dollars of her inheritance to purchase a bronze plate for a shelf for the new library. She had heard from Miss Nadelfrau that nearly twenty plates had sold. If the opportunity quilt earned only half as much, Dorothea would be well pleased.

In all that time, only two other fugitives passed through the

Grangers' station. They had come from Virginia, but thankfully had secured warm clothing before entering Pennsylvania. One of the men told Dorothea they had been planning their escape for a year and had intended to wait until spring, but when word came that their master intended to sell them to another plantation owner farther south before spring planting began, they fled. With regret, Dorothea realized she had never asked Zachariah why he had been compelled to flee to the north in the midst of winter. She wondered what had become of him. It was tempting to ride to the Brauns' mill and ask what they knew, but Dorothea knew she must limit contact between their families to divert suspicion.

She also knew that when spring arrived, traffic through their station would increase. Robert completed the secret room in the cellar and rode out to the Wright farm to tell them to direct fugitives to the house rather than the sugar camp. Runaways could rest comfortably in Uncle Jacob's old room, only a few steps away from a secure hiding place should they need it. The Sugar Camp Quilt would adorn the bed, giving the runaways ample opportunity to learn its patterns by heart. Dorothea was relieved to know that her nightly treks to the sugar camp would cease, for she always felt as if Mr. Liggett was watching her from the darkness of the maple grove. Even Lorena acknowledged that the new arrangements were for the best, as the increased safety of the runaways was worth the greater risk to themselves.

On the last Saturday evening in February, Dorothea and her parents rode into town dressed in their finest. Lorena had made a chicken pie for the covered-dish supper, and Dorothea carried a sour cream cake in a basket on her lap. The completed Authors' Album quilt top lay in the wagon, folded and wrapped in a clean muslin sheet. Although Dorothea was tempted to get it in the quilt frame before Mrs. Engle inspected it too closely, she knew it would be wiser to inform Mrs. Engle about the banned authors before she discovered on her own that they had been included in the quilt. Mrs. Engle might not be above ordering Dorothea to rip out stitches even in front of all the assembled guests if she thought Dorothea had intended to deceive her.

Dorothea had not seen any of the other library board members for several weeks, so she was as curious as any other guest to see what the ladies had done to transform the school into a suitable ballroom. Mrs. Collins greeted the Grangers at the door, beaming. The whole town seemed to be turning out for the Quilting Bee Dance, and so many people had purchased tickets for the quilt based on its description alone that they might sell out. Mrs. Collins was so pleased with the board's success that at first she urged the Grangers to enter without paying the admission fee, but they insisted.

"Where is Mrs. Engle?" asked Dorothea, the quilt bundle in her arms. From inside the school came the sounds of people talking and laughing. A fiddle, banjo, and bass were tuning up, and after the barest pause, they launched into a merry tune.

"She's meeting with Mr. Schultz to see how long it would take to print another batch of tickets," replied Mrs. Collins, raising her voice to be heard. "You'll find Miss Nadelfrau's quilt frame in the front corner. Mrs. Engle said for you to put the quilt into the frame as quickly as you can."

"Doesn't she want to see it first?"

"There's no time! Ladies are milling about with their thimbles and nothing to do." Mrs. Collins broke off for a moment to collect money from a small crowd of revelers eager to enter. "She left strict instructions that you are not to waste a moment on anything else until the quilting is under way."

"You had better do as Mrs. Engle wishes," added Lorena, unable to conceal her amusement.

"I guess I'll take this for you, then," said Robert, indicating the sour cream cake he carried for his daughter.

Dorothea thanked him and followed her parents inside. It was too late to do anything else.

They left their wraps in the cloakroom, and while her parents took their contributions to the covered-dish table, Dorothea hurried to the quilt frame. Miss Nadelfrau stood beside it, fidgeting anxiously with her chatelaine, but she heaved a sigh of relief when Dorothea appeared. Swiftly they layered the backing, batting, and quilt top in the frame as a crowd of admirers gathered about them. Dorothea waited for Miss Nadelfrau to mention the banned authors, but in her haste she seemed not to notice.

Four women sat down to quilt as soon as Dorothea and Miss Nadelfrau pulled up chairs. "It seems everyone wants to be the first to put a stitch in," said Miss Nadelfrau, with the first smile Dorothea had seen from her that evening. She smiled back, weakly, and excused herself to find Mrs. Engle.

The room was steadily filling with people, but Dorothea did not spy Mrs. Engle among them. All of the desks had been pushed back against the walls and a few were arranged end-to-end along the back wall to hold the covered dishes, from which delicious aromas wafted. Couples took the floor and the musicians began a schottische. Dorothea saw her parents among the dancers and her best friend, Mary, with her husband, Abner. Mary called out something, but Dorothea could only smile and shake her head to indicate that she had not heard.

Just then she heard Mrs. Engle bark out a command near the back of the room. Dorothea wove through the crowd of onlookers lining the dance floor and steeled herself as she approached Mrs. Engle, who was giving directions to a group of frightened-looking girls apparently drafted into service as servers, judging by their aprons and the speed with which they scurried to the back tables once Mrs. Engle dismissed them.

Dorothea touched her lightly on the arm. "I beg your pardon—"

Mrs. Engle spun about, the skirt of her royal blue velvet dress swirling. "Ah! There you are, my dear. Is the quilt in order?"

"Yes, but there's something I—"

"Let's have a look at it, then, shall we?"

With an indulgent smile, Mrs. Engle turned and made her way toward the quilt frame. The crowd parted before the formidable woman and closed just as quickly behind her so Dorothea was forced to dodge passersby and groups gathered in conversation. She tried to call out to Mrs. Engle, but her voice was lost in the din.

When she finally caught up to Mrs. Engle, she was standing rigid and wide-eyed at the side of the quilt frame. Two other women had joined the original six, and already they had completed a significant portion of the quilt with meticulous, feathery quilting.

Mrs. Engle did not even turn to look at her. "What is the meaning of this?"

"I meant to tell you—"

"As you should have done!" Two spots of red appeared in the plump ivory of Mrs. Engle's cheeks. "I distinctly recall stating that this man—" She jabbed a finger at one block. "—And this man—" The finger again pointed accusingly. "Were not suitable for this quilt!"

The quilters looked up cautiously but did not pause in their work. Dorothea took a deep breath. "You did indeed tell me that, but I thought—"

"You thought?" Mrs. Engle trembled with anger and disbelief, her powdered jowls shaking from the effort of controlling her temper. "You were not placed on the library board to think. You were included because we thought your uncle might make a donation on your behalf!"

Dorothea could not imagine why they had thought such a thing. "I regret that you were disappointed in that regard," she said. "However, you did include me, and therefore I was obligated to do my very best to make this fund-raiser a success. While you do not care for these authors, their works are widely read and respected in the community, and thus their inclusion increases the value of the quilt."

"You do not know the reading habits of our community very well if you believe that," retorted Mrs. Engle. "What am I to do when people demand their money back once they become aware of this— this debacle?"

Dorothea thought of her inheritance. "In the unlikely event that anyone should do so, I will reimburse them for their tickets—up to a certain point."

Mrs. Engle sniffed. "That is the very least you can do. You will forgive me, of course, if I request your resignation from the library board before you can do any more damage."

Stung, Dorothea was suddenly aware of a lull in the noise around them and the watchful eyes of the women waiting for their turn at the quilt frame. Others, men and women drawn by the sounds of argument, peered at the quilt and whispered to one another as if trying to deduce which authors were not supposed to have been included.

"Why, I declare," said a woman loudly. "This Henry Brown here isn't Henry 'Box' Brown, is he?"

Dorothea turned and saw Constance Wright standing on the other side of the quilt frame, indicating the Album block nearest her right hand. Her feet were planted and she regarded Mrs. Engle with defiance.

"The one and the same," said Dorothea, grateful for the distraction.

"That's worth another dollar from me," said Constance. "I'm going to buy myself some more tickets."

"Who is Henry 'Box' Brown?" asked a young man, apparently curious despite being disappointed that Constance had interrupted Mrs. Engle's tirade.

"Why, don't you know?" said Constance. "He was a slave in Virginia who escaped by having himself shut up in a crate and mailed to abolitionists in Philadelphia."

A wave of incredulous laughter went up from the onlookers.

"Utter nonsense," said Mrs. Engle, looking more outraged than ever. "No one could endure it. Furthermore, I would never abide the inclusion of a—"

"As incredible as the story may seem, it is nevertheless true," said Mr. Nelson, emerging from the crowd. "I lived in Philadelphia at the time and it was in all the papers. Mrs. Engle, you are too modest to claim that you were not aware of his name on your quilt. It was a stroke of genius to include people who were bound to provoke interest and discussion. How appropriate for a library full of books destined to do the very same. While we dance, you must tell me how you arranged this."

He held out his hand to Mrs. Engle with such brisk authority that she could only stare at him, dumbfounded, before taking his hand. He led her off to the dance floor without so much as a glance for Dorothea or the quilt that had sparked such controversy. The spectacle over, the onlookers returned to enjoying the dance.

Dorothea joined Constance on the other side of the quilting frame as she took a chair vacated by another quilter. "You arrived at precisely the right moment. If she had gone on much longer I might have said something I truly regretted."

"Don't regret what you say so long as it's the truth. That's what I do." Constance nodded in the direction Mr. Nelson had taken Mrs. Engle. "If you ask me, he's the one who showed up just in time."

"Mr. Nelson? Oh, yes. One can always rely on him to appear at the moment of my greatest humiliation."

Constance had unrolled a huswif on her lap and was frowning thoughtfully at several needles arranged in a neat row. "I'm just glad she's gone." She kept her voice too low for the other quilters to hear, which Dorothea considered wise. Mrs. Engle had friends and admirers everywhere.

Constance selected a needle and asked the woman seated at her left to pass the thread. "I think we both know she was about to say she wouldn't abide no colored folks' names in her quilt. I don't think she would abide one stitching on it, either."

"We're glad for your help," said Dorothea, just as she remembered she was no longer on the library board and ought not to say "we."

"Tell that to the lady at the front door who almost wouldn't let me in."

"Mrs. Collins?" Dorothea's heart sank, but she said firmly, "The library will be for everyone, white and colored alike, and don't believe anyone who tells you otherwise."

Constance regarded her with weary skepticism. "We'll see what happens when the library opens. You know the men told Abel they wouldn't need his help in the building."

"I didn't know that. One would think they would be grateful for an experienced carpenter."

"One might think that if one was a nice young white girl like you who don't know any better." The woman on Constance's left sniffed and abruptly abandoned her seat, her thimble still on her finger. Constance seemed not to notice. "Anyway, I'm here to help so that later, no one can say I can't borrow books because I had no part in the building of the library. We bought a bookshelf plate, too."

Another quilter gathered her things and rose. This time Constance glanced up and followed her with her eyes. "I take it your lessons are going well?" asked Dorothea, hoping to distract her.

Constance shrugged. "Good enough."

"So here is the infamous quilt," said Mrs. Claverton, approaching with her arm linked through her daughter's. Charlotte wore a dress of ivory crushed velvet with a rose velvet sash and a matching ribbon around her neck. Her dark hair hung in thick ringlets upon her shoulders.

"Yes. Quilt upon it if you dare," said Dorothea with a smile. As Mrs. Claverton and Charlotte seated themselves in the vacant chairs, Dorothea clasped Constance's shoulder and promised to speak with her later.

Dorothea left the quilt frame behind and went in search of her parents to tell them what had occurred with Mrs. Engle before a worse version reached their ears. She spotted them in the supper line, but before she could reach them, Mary called out to her and came hurrying over. "I hoped to warn you," said Mary, taking Dorothea's hand, "but I can see from your expression that I'm too late. Please do compose yourself. Don't give them the satisfaction of knowing they have upset you."

Dorothea immediately smoothed the strain from her features. "Thank you, Mary. It is my fault, really. I should have been more forthright."

"Your fault? Why on earth do you believe that?" Mary cast an indignant look over her shoulder. "He's truly despicable, as I seem to recall warning you. I never liked him—well, not in recent years, anyway."

"Are you talking about Mr. Nelson?"

Mary regarded her with utter bewilderment. "What? Of course not. Why would I—" She drew in a breath sharply. "Then you don't know."

"I don't know what? If we aren't discussing Mr. Nelson and Mrs. Engle—"

"Dorothea." Mary bit her lip, put her hands on Dorothea's shoulders, and gently turned her toward the dance floor. "Look over by the window."

Dorothea complied. "Mr. Hathaway is sipping from his hip flask. You're right. It's scandalous."

"Not there. The other window."

Dorothea laughed but obliged. She saw men and ladies circling on the dance floor. Farmers she hardly knew and townsfolk she had known for years sat side by side enjoying the covered-dish supper. Against the far wall couples stood chatting near the center window. Among them she spotted Cyrus with his head bowed near the ear of a pretty red-haired young woman Dorothea recognized from church; all Dorothea knew of her was that she had been several years ahead of Dorothea in school and that her father's farm lay between Creek's Crossing and Grangerville. Cyrus looked up and met her gaze. She smiled and nodded; he returned a quick, close-mouthed grimace and quickly resumed his conversation.

Suddenly she understood. "Am I supposed to be jealous merely because Cyrus Pearson is speaking to another young lady?"

"He is not merely speaking to her. Rumor has it they are nearly engaged."

"How can they be nearly engaged when Cyrus took me driving only two weeks ago?"

"He is fickle and she is nearly twenty-seven."

Dorothea laughed. "Oh. Now everything is made clear." She kept her voice light, but a hollow of confusion and disappointment had formed inside her. "I never had any claim on him, and although I am fond of Cyrus, I do not love him. If he has found happiness with someone else, then I will be the first to congratulate him."

"No, you will be the second," said Mary darkly, glaring across the room. "One can tell by the look on his face that he has been congratulating himself for days. Her parents are aged, you see, and she has no brothers and sisters with whom to divide their farm."

"I see." Indeed, Dorothea did, now. "Thank you for the warning, but I assure you my heart has not been broken."

Mary squeezed her hand. "You are too good for him, Dorothea. Don't lose hope. You will meet a man as fine as my Abner someday, I am sure of it."

Dorothea smiled. "If I meet a man even half as fine as your Abner, I will snatch him up so quickly he will not know what hit him."

As Mary peered at her, not certain whether she spoke in jest, Dorothea bade her good-bye and went off to meet her parents, who had carried their plates to a desk near the front of the room. The delicious aromas from the back table no longer appealed to her, but she kept her parents company while they enjoyed their supper. She told them what had passed between herself and Mrs. Engle, but a reluctant embarrassment kept her from mentioning Cyrus.

She resolved not to dwell on Mary's rumors until Cyrus himself had confirmed or denied them. Before long one of Abner's friends invited her to dance, and after him another young man, and after that she was rarely without a partner long enough to more than quickly check the progress on the Authors' Album. Already the rails had been adjusted twice to allow an unquilted portion to replace a section already completed. Miss Nadelfrau had remained beside the quilt nearly all evening, and while she seemed anxious to avoid being seen talking to the disgraced former library board member for too long, she expressed sincere approval for the quality of the quilters' work.

After one of these brief examinations of the quilt-in-progress, Dorothea found herself face-to-face with an abashed Cyrus. "Hello, Dorothea," he greeted her. "Would you care for a dance?"

She agreed, so he took her hand and led her to the dance floor as the fiddler began a cheerful polka. Cyrus was uncharacteristically somber as they danced, which told Dorothea that Mary's tales were most likely true. When the dance was over, Dorothea thanked him and began to move away, but he held fast to her hand.

"I suppose you've heard."

"Indeed." Dorothea smiled brightly. "I understand congratulations are in order."

"Well—" He glanced over his shoulder. Dorothea forbade herself to see if the red-haired farmer's daughter waited there. "Not quite yet, but perhaps soon."

"I see. Well, I will be sure to congratulate you when the time is right and give the lucky girl my best wishes."

"Dorothea, I always said you were kindness itself." His grip on her hand tightened. "I think I should explain—"

"It truly is not necessary."

"But you see, my father left my mother with little more than her personal belongings, and my stepfather has children of his own from his first marriage. They will benefit from his success, whereas I will receive nothing." He regarded her with earnest remorse. "A man with property of his own may make choices a man without it cannot."

"I understand perfectly. You need say no more." She placed her other hand upon his, smiled encouragingly, and freed herself. "I wish you the best. I sincerely do."

She turned her back and walked away, willing her features to reveal nothing but glad serenity. Then, the absurdity of how badly the evening had gone struck her, and she could only laugh. She touched a hand to her brow and murmured, "I should have remained at home. Things cannot possibly get any worse."

"That is where we differ, Miss Granger," a man's voice spoke at her side. "I believe that matters can always get worse."

She closed her eyes, sighed, and turned to find Mr. Nelson. "I must confess, Mr. Nelson, that at the moment I find myself quite unable to dispute that."

His eyebrows shot up. "And I find myself quite astonished to discover you without an argument at hand."

Mrs. Claverton chose that moment to walk by. "Oh, she is not always as sharp-tongued as she seems. And she is a fine dancer." She gave Mr. Nelson a pointed look. "You ought to see for yourself."

"Thank you, Mrs. Claverton," said Dorothea, "but I would not want to inconvenience Mr. Nelson."

"Nonsense! I saw him twirling Mrs. Engle about not long ago. If he will partner an old married woman he would surely consent to dance with a lovely young girl such as yourself."

Dorothea intended to explain—and to caution Mrs. Claverton not to refer to Mrs. Engle as "old" too loudly given the temper she was in—but Mr. Nelson spoke first. "It would be my privilege to partner Miss Granger."

Dorothea muffled a sigh and agreed. Mr. Nelson escorted her to the dance floor where couples were forming lines. Mary had taken the floor with Abner, and as the musicians began to play, she stood in place staring at Dorothea with astonished sympathy until another dancer bumped into her. Dorothea smiled ruefully in return to show she was resigned to her fate, but she smothered a laugh when she realized that Mr. Nelson had witnessed the entire silent exchange.

She resolved to be civil company until the dance concluded, but Mr. Nelson made even fewer attempts at conversation than Cyrus had. Finally Dorothea spoke up. "I suppose you expect me to thank you for whisking Mrs. Engle off like that."

"I expect nothing from you."

Dorothea did not know quite what to say to that. "Then I will be happy to oblige."

He nodded curtly.

They danced in silence for a time, an isle of cool civility lapped by waves of laughter and happy chatter.

"Mrs. Claverton is wrong about you," Mr. Nelson said suddenly.

"What do you mean?"

"You are outspoken to a fault." He scrutinized her. "I suspect you deliberately provoked Mrs. Engle. Surely you could have found some moment to tell her about the unexpected signatures she would find in the quilt, but you chose to wait until she discovered them on her own, knowing it would be too late for her to change anything."

"That is not true," retorted Dorothea, but when her conscience pricked her, she added, "Well, perhaps it is partially true. I took the blocks to her home once, but she could not be troubled to look at them. I suppose I could have insisted."

"Or you could have omitted the authors she objected to, but I suspect that never occurred to you."

"I did not see any reason to leave them out." She raised her chin and met his gaze defiantly. "And I do not care who objects to their inclusion."

"I see. Raising money for the library was a secondary consideration for you. Nevertheless, I commend you on managing to have your own way on this. I do believe it will result in more money for the library after all."

The dance ended. Mr. Nelson made a perfunctory bow and released her hand. She nodded and left without thanking him for the dance. She was not certain if he had praised or insulted her. It was quite possible he had managed both.

It was no simple matter to avoid Mrs. Engle, Cyrus, and Mr. Nelson in a schoolroom that suddenly seemed much too small, but Dorothea endeavored. Several hours into the dance, a murmur of excitement went up from the people surrounding the quilt frame: The thread of the last quilting stitch had been knotted and cut. Dorothea joined in the work of attaching the binding, and before long Mr. Collins and Mr. Claverton stood upon a small riser at the front of the room and held up the finished quilt for all to see. Dorothea's heart swelled with pride and pleasure that even Mrs. Engle's criticism could not diminish. It was a beautiful quilt and honored the people of Creek's Crossing as well as those whose names had been enshrined upon it—regardless of what Mrs. Engle thought.

Everyone began to clamor for the winner of the masterpiece to be chosen. Mr. Engle brought forth a large locked box with a slit carved into the lid, used as a ballot box in election time. As Mrs. Deakins filled the box with ticket stubs, the other library board members gathered in a half-circle behind her. Dorothea, standing with her mother and father, did not move to join them. Her mother put an arm around her shoulder, but Dorothea felt no need to be consoled. She had already received everything she had sought from making the Authors' Album. She did not need applause and acclaim as well.

Mrs. Deakins deferred to the mayor, who lifted the lid and withdrew a single slip of paper. Dorothea clasped her hands together and hoped.

"And our winner is—" The mayor paused dramatically. "Cyrus Pearson!"

Exclamations of delight and moans of disappointment filled the room. Dorothea watched as Cyrus strode to the front of the room to claim his prize, accepting congratulations as he went. It pained her to remember how he had told her he would pay any amount to have a quilt made by her hands. She wondered if he would have said such a thing if he had not imagined her inheritance to be much greater than it was. She wondered if he had meant anything he had ever said to her, and if he meant what he told the pretty red-haired girl now.

"He is never happier than when he has an audience," said Lorena for Dorothea's ear alone as Cyrus made a show of beckoning his mother to the front of the room. She came willingly at first, but her pace slowed when she realized Cyrus meant to give the quilt to her. She demurred, but as the clapping and whistling of the crowd swelled, she took the quilt, pretended to admire it, and kissed her son on the cheek. No one who had not heard her outburst earlier that evening would have known how much she disliked it, but Dorothea observed the distasteful curl of her lip and the speed with which she folded the quilt and set it aside. Suddenly she realized that with Cyrus nearly betrothed to someone else, she no longer had to worry about Mrs. Engle's good opinion. It was an enormously relieving thought, and it cheered her immensely.

She saw Mrs. Collins take Mrs. Engle and Mrs. Deakins aside, and when they withdrew into the vestibule, Dorothea knew they were going to the cloakroom to count the evening's earnings. Miss Deakins hastily scooped up the Authors' Album quilt Mrs. Engle had left behind.

The fiddler struck up a sweetly melancholy waltz, a tune Dorothea knew well and loved. She listened wistfully, but when she saw Cyrus glide past with the red-haired girl in his arms, she did not feel a single twinge of regret. She liked him, and any woman with eyes to see him must admit he was handsome, but she knew they did not suit each other well for anything more than a weekly ride in the cutter. She was too serious, he too merry. They would be at each other's throats if forced to remain in each other's company for the rest of their lives.

Just then Dorothea felt someone watching her. She looked over her shoulder and was not entirely surprised to find Mr. Nelson there. Too weary to provoke him, she merely nodded and returned her attention to the dance floor.

To her surprise, he said, "If you are not too tired, I would appreciate the favor of a dance."

She was tempted to refuse on the grounds that a woman does not like to hear that she looks tired, especially when she is dressed in her best at a dance, but she merely nodded again and took his hand. She would enjoy the music if not the company.

Mr. Nelson, however, chose to converse, spoiling any chance she might have had of enjoying her favorite waltz. "You were quite complimentary to my students on the night of the school exhibition."

So many things of greater significance had happened that night that Dorothea had to think before she could recollect what she had told him. "Yes. I thought they performed beautifully."

"I think you give them undue praise."

"I think you tend to offer undeserved censure, for your students and everyone else."

He ignored the bite in her tone, but she knew it had not gone unnoticed. "They are not progressing as well as I had hoped."

"Perhaps the job is too much for you," she said innocently. "Perhaps you should resign and allow someone who actually does like children to take over."

"One does not need to like children to instruct them."

"One most decidedly does!"

"At any rate, that is beside the point, because I do like children. Miss Granger, if you would allow me to speak more than one sentence in succession, I would be able to come to the point much sooner."

Dorothea, who had assumed the point was to annoy her, inclined her head to indicate he was free to speak without interruption.

"The number of students and the differences in their ages is significant enough now to warrant dividing the school into two groups. Obviously I cannot teach both simultaneously, so I wondered if you would consider teaching the younger group."

She stared at him, speechless. Finally she managed, "You would ask me this after criticizing my teaching?"

He had the decency to look embarrassed. "It is possible that my criticism was a trifle premature. While it is true that the students had received only a passing introduction to the more advanced subjects and concepts, their understanding of the fundamentals was quite thorough in all their subjects. I did not discover this until after I made . . . several remarks that I now regret."

"Mr. Nelson, if I did not consider you to be entirely without a sense of humor, I might suspect you are playing a prank on me."

"Do you accept the offer or not?"

"We have not discussed wages, and—" She hesitated. "I am not certain the school board would hire me."

"I have already spoken to them. They agreed or I would not have asked you. Your salary will be the same as when you last taught." He regarded her with barely concealed impatience. "Do you accept or must I find someone else?"

"I would like five dollars more each term," said Dorothea. "If that condition can be met, I would be delighted to accept your proposal."

"I will have to consult the school board, but I think they will be agreeable."

"When you know for certain, please inform me."

The last note of the waltz faded away. Dorothea suddenly became very conscious of Mr. Nelson's hand lingering on the small of her back. "Thank you for the dance," she said, and quickly walked away.

Before she could find Lorena and tell her the astonishing news, Mrs. Engle and the remaining members of the school board approached the stage at the front of the room. "We have our final count," Mrs. Engle called out as everyone gathered around to hear. "The library board is pleased to announce that thanks to the generosity of the people of Creek's Crossing and surrounding environs, we have raised five hundred dollars for the founding of a new library!"

A cheer went up from the crowd. Thrilled, Dorothea joined in the applause. Whatever else befell her, at least she would be able to enjoy a library one day soon.

"We will break ground in spring," Mrs. Engle continued. "Every man who wishes to assist in the building will be gratefully welcomed."

Dorothea thought of Constance and Abel and hoped Mrs. Engle spoke the truth.

Mrs. Engle thanked everyone for attending and stepped down from the stage. Before anyone could depart, Mrs. Claverton quickly asked for their attention again. "We have one more announcement. The Authors' Album quilt that the ladies of Creek's Crossing have so beautifully fashioned has been donated to the library board so that it might be displayed in the library for all to enjoy!"

A rousing cheer went up from the people, but Dorothea was too surprised to join in—and, if she was not mistaken, Mrs. Engle was equally astonished. Mrs. Engle quickly regained her composure, however, and graciously acknowledged the applause. Apparently word of Mrs. Engle's revulsion for the quilt had not spread far or the onlookers would not have found her so generous.

After that, the Quilting Bee Dance ended. Dorothea offered to help Miss Nadelfrau disassemble her quilting frame, but Miss Nadelfrau hastened to assure her she had enough help. Thus rebuffed, Dorothea collected her basket and cake plate from the covered-dish table, bade good-bye to Constance and Mary, and left with her parents.

On the cold ride home, Dorothea told her mother and father about Mr. Nelson's offer. Robert was dubious, but Lorena was pleased. "It is about time they realize what a fine teacher they had in you."

"So you plan to accept?" asked Robert.

"If you think I can be spared from the farm. It is nearly sugaring time, and after that, spring planting. With Uncle Jacob and Jonathan gone, we will be shorthanded."

"We will hire hands, as we have done in the past," said Lorena. Her mouth was concealed beneath her muffler, but her eyes smiled. "You can help me with the garden in the mornings and on Saturdays. We will manage."

"Then I shall accept the position, assuming the school board can scrape together the extra five dollars."

Robert chuckled. "I think you asked for that additional five dollars just to spite them, not because you felt underpaid before."

"I will not deny it," said Dorothea. "If anyone else but Mr. Nelson had offered me the position, I probably would have accepted my original wages."

"This has been quite a successful night for you," remarked Lorena. "You have your position back at a higher salary, your quilt was an overwhelming success—"

"Not entirely," Dorothea reminded her.

"It earned a great deal of money for the library and that's what counts."

"It was a successful night for me, too," said Robert.

His wife peered at him quizzically. "How so?"

"From what I hear, I will no longer have to dread Cyrus Pearson becoming my son-in-law."

He shuddered so comically that Dorothea had to join in her parents' laughter, though she was mortified that they had heard through gossip what she was too embarrassed to tell them herself. Worse yet was the genuine relief she detected beneath their sympathetic humor. If they were so disinclined for her to marry Cyrus, why had they not spoken up when he seemed to be courting her?

FOR ALL OF THE unexpected happenings on the night of the Quilting Bee Dance, two more equally astounding revelations awaited her.

The first came two days later. The school board had sent word that they agreed to the requested raise. After dropping by Mr. Engle's office to sign her contract, she paid a call on her friend

Mary, who was eager to share an intriguing bit of news. Mrs. Engle had not donated the quilt to the library, nor had Mrs. Claverton erred in saying the gift had been made. According to one of Mr. Schultz's printing customers, who had witnessed the exchange, Mr. Nelson had purchased the quilt from Mrs. Engle for five dollars and had immediately given it to Mrs. Claverton for the library. "Perhaps Mr. Nelson thought Mrs. Engle would donate the five dollars to the library," said Mary, "but she kept it. So in the end, Mrs. Engle came out well ahead."

"Unless you deduct her expenses. She did purchase all the materials for the quilt."

Mary tossed her head scornfully. Dorothea was trying to be charitable, but they both knew Mrs. Engle had spent far less than five dollars on fabric, batting, and thread. Why she had accepted the thanks of the crowd when she had not been the one to donate the quilt—and why Mr. Nelson had not claimed rightful credit for the deed—was a mystery neither Dorothea nor Mary could explain to their complete satisfaction.

The second revelation came in a letter from Jonathan. He had thought about Mr. Nelson often since leaving Creek's Crossing, and his curiosity and concern plagued him so much that he was compelled to send an inquiry to an acquaintance in Philadelphia. "Thomas Nelson was in prison for a crime he did without a doubt commit," wrote Jonathan. "That much was never in dispute. However, I think it will interest you to know that he was convicted of helping runaway slaves."

Mr. Nelson had lived in Philadelphia, but he had often traveled to Virginia on business for his father. He used his frequent travels as a cover for business of his own. He routinely carried with him money, false identification papers, forged bills of leave, and other useful items for slaves determined to run away, which he distributed to plantations and households throughout several southern states. He earned the enmity of influential slave owners who conspired to catch him in the act. He was tried and convicted of forgery and assisting runaway slaves, and he was sentenced to six years in prison. He served two before his father managed to secure his early release on good behavior, with the understanding that any additional infractions would result in a lengthy imprisonment with no chance of leniency from any judge. Most people believed the senior Mr. Nelson had paid substantial bribes in order to have his seriously ill son freed just in time to save his life.

After a lengthy recuperation, Thomas Nelson's father made him swear an oath that he would tell no one the reasons for his imprisonment, and that he would obey the law no matter how much it tested his moral convictions, for following his conscience had almost killed him. After the Carters informed him of their intention to stake a claim out West, the senior Mr. Nelson sent his son to live on the family estate in Creek's Crossing rather than find a new tenant family. It was believed that the father thought his son safer in a place far from his old temptations; it was also said that the senior Mr. Nelson could not bear to watch his son struggle with his decision to obey his father.

"As you can see," concluded Jonathan, "the scholars of Creek's Crossing could do far worse than Mr. Nelson as a moral influence, although I wonder how long a man of his convictions will be able to keep the oath his father wrested from him. Though you might be tempted to speak to him on these matters, I urge you to refrain. Apparently the truth is known to only a few close family friends, one of whom disclosed these facts to me due to my concern about the safety of Thomas Nelson's pupils. By all accounts, both the elder and the younger Nelson are determined to keep the entire unfortunate episode a secret, and it is their fervent hope that no one in Creek's Crossing will ever know what has passed."

Of course her brother was right; the secret must be kept unless

Mr. Nelson himself chose to divulge it. Mr. Nelson was fortunate that Cyrus Pearson's inquiries had not uncovered it.

Dorothea wished she could ask Mr. Nelson what part of his secret he considered shameful: that he had helped runaways, or that he had vowed never to do so again.

Chapter Nine

THE NEXT MORNING, Dorothea hurried through her chores, eager to finish so that she could begin planning her lessons. She shivered in the barn as she milked the cow but she hardly noticed, her thoughts on the schoolroom a mile to the south. A few months earlier, Mr. Nelson's offer to teach only the youngest pupils in the choir loft might have insulted her, since she had so recently instructed the entire school on her own. Now the very thought of teaching again, any teaching at all, so gratified her that she refused to see her diminished role as anything but a wonderful opportunity to foster in Creek's Crossing's youngest pupils the important foundation upon which the rest of their education would be built. That she owed her good fortune to Mr. Nelson unsettled her, but not so much that she would reconsider accepting the position. Perhaps, she told herself, her uncomfortable gratitude would remind her to be civil.

As she carried the milk pail back to the house, she slipped on a patch of ice. A wave of white froth spilled over the brim before she could catch her balance. As she brushed the spilled milk from her skirt, she noticed that the ice underfoot had formed in the tracks of wagon wheels. Up and down the road, similar smooth pools of ice filled all the old ruts left in the mud of the previous autumn so that she could trace several distinct trails from the Creek's Crossing road to the barn. Yesterday the entire road had been covered by a half inch of snow.

She ran back to the house and burst into the kitchen, where her mother was frying potatoes for their breakfast. "We had a thaw yesterday and an overnight freeze."

"Yesterday was not the first thaw, either. It is just the first we noticed." Lorena wrapped a towel around the handle of the skillet and pulled it off the fire. "Your father has already gone to the maple grove. He asks you to bring him his breakfast."

"Uncle Jacob—" Dorothea hesitated. "We should have begun tapping the trees days ago."

"I know that is what Uncle Jacob would have done." Lorena gave her a small, regretful smile. "We were so distracted by the Quilting Bee Dance that we neglected his records and ignored the weather. We will have to make up for lost time."

Dorothea ate swiftly as her mother packed the lunch pail for Robert, silently berating herself for ignoring the changing seasons. How many days of the sap run had they squandered? On her way to the sugar camp, she observed that already the rising sun was warming the earth. The sap would run that day, and they were not prepared.

She found her father in the maple grove, moving swiftly from tree to tree, inspecting old spiles, hanging buckets to catch the drips of sap, drilling new holes where necessary. He thanked her for the food but did not interrupt his work to take it from her. When she realized he had forgotten it, and possibly her, Dorothea set the pail on the ground between the roots of a tree and went to help him.

She had never done this part of the work of sugaring before, had only occasionally seen it done, but did not need her father's silent swiftness to understand the urgency. They hurried to complete the neglected tasks, and before long, Lorena joined them. When they had seen to all but the last third of the sugarbush, Robert sent them to prepare the sugaring house. He came by later with the team to replenish the depleted stores of firewood and load the empty barrels into the wagon.

Despite their haste, it was past noon before Robert returned with enough fresh sap to warrant building a fire beneath the three empty kettles. Evening had fallen before Dorothea and her mother poured off the contents of the last kettle into two sugar molds. They had not stopped to eat or care for the livestock, so Robert decided they would resume sugaring in the morning. After finishing the evening chores, they ate a cold supper of bread and cheese and went off to bed. Just before she fell asleep, Dorothea's thoughts drifted to the school and the lessons she had intended to prepare. She promised herself she would rest her eyes for only a moment before retrieving her schoolbooks, but she fell asleep before she could summon up enough willpower to force herself to rise.

At the sugar camp early the next day, Dorothea and her mother built the fire and awaited Robert's delivery of the first barrels of fresh sap. He turned the team back toward the grove as soon as he unloaded the wagon, reporting, with chagrin and annoyance, that some of the buckets had overflowed, spilling their precious contents onto the ground. "I should have known that the trees I tapped first would have had time to refill their buckets. I won't make that mistake again," he said, giving the reins a shake and chirruping to the horses. As she and her mother poured sap into the first of the three kettles, Dorothea reflected that Uncle Jacob had always insisted upon emptying all of the buckets at the end of the day, even those only partially full. The sap retained its quality if it went swiftly from tree to kettle, he had often said, and he deplored wastefulness. She imagined him shaking his head in disgust at the sight of sap backing up into the spiles, oozing down the sides of the buckets.

They grew more assured in their work as the week passed, but they missed Uncle Jacob's advice and gladly would have endured his curt criticism to have his guidance. The sugar seemed to be as fine in quality as ever, though not as plentiful, and Dorothea felt they worked twice as hard as in previous years to get it. Evenings found her too exhausted to tend to the housework or plan her lessons. When she mentioned in passing that the school board expected her to begin teaching in two days, Lorena exclaimed in dismay for her own forgetfulness and sent Dorothea in early. "I can finish this myself," she said, stirring the second kettle and peering into the third.

Dorothea gratefully accepted her mother's offer and returned to the house and her books. She took the time to build a fire in the oven and prepare a hot meal for the family—the first they had enjoyed all week—then turned her attention to her lessons. She set her work aside only long enough to eat with her parents after they came in from the sugar camp, steam-soaked and weary, and begged off helping her mother with the dishes so she could return to her books.

"The temperature hasn't fallen off much since sundown," her father remarked when he came in from the barn, the evening chores completed late. Dorothea and her mother acknowledged his words with a nod. No other reply was necessary. Nighttime freezes prolonged the sap run. Without them, sugaring season would end.

Though Dorothea's work absorbed her, after her father's statement, she brooded over their first attempt to make sugar without Uncle Jacob. They should have been as conscientious as he. Before she doused the lamp that night, unable to put her thoughts to rest, she stole into his room, the sensation of trespass lingering despite the many times she had made up the bed for runaways. Lorena had stored his papers in his steamer trunk—but it was Dorothea's steamer trunk now; he had bequeathed it to her, and she had every right to lift the lid whenever she pleased.

She found his farm journal and paged through the notes on sugaring. From his records she concluded that the sugaring season had indeed come upon them earlier than usual, but still well within the average. But even in years when a caprice of the weather had resulted in an even shorter sugaring season, Uncle Jacob had still managed to produce more maple sugar than the Grangers had done alone.

Dorothea sighed, closed the journal, and returned it to the trunk. They were not finished yet. The sap run might endure another week or more. They would learn from their neglect and be better prepared the next winter.

As she closed the lid, her gaze fell upon a familiar book with a worn cover of black leather. Her heart leaped as she reached for her uncle's Bible. Until that moment, she had not realized how much she missed his blessings at mealtimes, his silent nightly devotions, those infrequent occasions when he would read aloud a verse and query her about its interpretation. At the time she had resented his intrusion into her reading or quilting, and suspected he hoped to catch her in a mistake. Now she wondered if perhaps she had misjudged him.

She opened the cover and turned the thin, well-worn pages, thinking of her uncle and his mercurial tempers, his hidden depths. Her eyes blurred with weariness; she drew a hand across her brow and closed the book, but something written on the flyleaf caught her eye. Holding the page closer to the lamp, she discovered a phrase written in an elegant female hand: "For dearest Jacob on the occasion of our marriage. Deut. 23:15–16." Below the words was a simple sketch of a forget-me-not in bloom.

Dorothea could not recall the verse; likely it was another of her uncle's favorite precepts regarding the proper conduct of a wife. She found the page and read the line, her breath catching in her throat: "Thou shalt not deliver unto his master the servant which is escaped from his master unto thee: he shall dwell with thee, *even among you*, in that place which he shall choose in one of thy gates, where it liketh him best: thou shalt not oppress him."

She studied the verses, wondering whether the message was a request, a promise, a warning, or a directive to her husband-to-be. She wondered if they were instead an acceptance of a request he had made of her. She wished she knew. She knew that she could never know.

The flickering of the lamp roused her from her reverie. Closing the lid of the steamer trunk, she took up the Bible and the lamp and carried them upstairs to her attic bedroom.

THE NEXT MORNING DOROTHEA had to break ice in the well bucket, but the day after, she did not. The Grangers would try to coax the last drops of sap from the maple trees, but the sap run was essentially over. In the final tally, they produced little more than half of the sugar they had the previous year. Robert and Lorena worried whether they would have any left to trade after they set aside the usual amount for their own use, but Dorothea refused to dwell on their unsuccessful first outing. She had long prided herself on knowing the natural world of the Elm Creek Valley better than anyone. Next year she would be mindful of the shifting temperatures, as diligent as her uncle and as intuitive as the Shawnee woman who had taught her herb lore. Next year, she would not fail.

Dorothea resumed teaching on the following Monday, and soon grew accustomed to the pleasant rhythm of the days. Each morning she led the twelve youngest children upstairs to the choir loft, where she gave them their lessons and heard their recitations while Mr. Nelson instructed the twenty-eight elder students in the schoolroom below. Her pupils were sweet and attentive, and they seemed pleased to have their very own teacher and a separate place all to themselves. Sometimes while her students were quietly bent over their books, Dorothea listened to the lectures and recitations below. Mr. Nelson apparently preferred the Socratic method in many subjects, which Dorothea had never tried. It did give his students a great deal of practice in logic and reasoning, skills that Dorothea admitted would be more useful to them once they left school than the endless memorization of facts and dates.

In this fashion they proceeded almost as if they led two separate and distinct schools, but when Mr. Nelson lectured in history, Dorothea took her students downstairs so they could listen. At first she had given her own lectures, but when she observed the younger children straining to hear Mr. Nelson's voice over her own, she gave up and decided one history lecture would serve the entire school. She could not deny that Mr. Nelson's university studies had given him a greater depth and breadth of knowledge than her own in many subjects, but in history, especially, he excelled. He brought the stories of the past to life with such detail and intriguing narrative that the students sat spellbound throughout the lessons. Dorothea had never seen the school so quiet, except for when Miss Gunther's gentle monotone had put half the class to sleep.

"You could have been a university lecturer," remarked Dorothea one day after she and Mr. Nelson excused the students for lunch.

"I was," he said, to her surprise. He had been a tutor in the history department at the University of Pennsylvania for two years and had intended to become a professor.

"Why didn't you?" she asked.

"Other events intervened."

He said no more, and Dorothea did not persist in questioning him. She could only imagine all that he had left behind to keep his promise to his father. It was no wonder he had found little to admire in Creek's Crossing or its inhabitants when he first arrived.

The weeks passed. The sun rose earlier each morning, and before long the temperatures grew mild enough for Dorothea to walk the mile to the ferry rather than ride her mother's horse and board him in Mr. Engle's livery stable during the day. Since she was no longer privy to the plans of the library board, she was surprised one morning to discover that a team of men had broken ground on the vacant lot not far from the school. By the size of the foundation they had marked with pickets and rope, they intended the library to be an impressive size, nearly as large as the Lutheran church. Her spirits soared at the thought of how many books could fill such a space. She only hoped that Mrs. Engle would not somehow contrive to have the building named after herself.

On a particularly warm day, upon noticing that her students were gazing wistfully out the windows more often than at their books, Dorothea suggested to Mr. Nelson that they take the children outside for a lesson in the natural sciences. He agreed, and both classes of students gladly followed as she led them on a walk beside the creek, where she pointed out the various geological features the view provided. Upon their return to the classroom, she assigned the students compositions about what they had learned. She was pleased to find that even the youngest had grasped the concepts of erosion and sedimentation. A few of the boys wrote enthusiastically about turbulence and velocity, which made her glad she had not taken them past Widow's Pining, where they might have been tempted to experiment in the dangerous current.

At the end of the day, after the students departed and she and Mr. Nelson were tidying the classroom, he remarked, "That was a very instructive lesson. I believe I learned something today."

She smiled and continued wiping the blackboard. "You are merely being kind."

"Not at all." He paused. "I am never merely kind."

She almost laughed, but she could not deny it. "Perhaps later in the spring we might venture out again to study plants, when there are more to see."

He readily agreed. That very night, Dorothea began preparing her next natural science lesson so that she would be ready when the time came. Spring planting would soon begin, and the eldest boys and even some of the eldest girls and younger children would leave school to work on family farms. Her lesson on the flora and fauna of the Elm Creek Valley could not wait much longer if she wanted all the students to benefit from it. Besides, with so many pupils gone, Mr. Nelson would likely consolidate the two classes and dismiss her until after the harvest.

Fair weather also brought more passengers through the Grangers' Underground Railroad station: a husband and wife from Virginia, whose necks and shoulders bore thick scars from many beatings, fleeing so that their unborn child could never be sold away from them. Two young girls who dressed as boys and walked off the plantation unrecognized by their overseer. A man, promised emancipation upon his master's death, who rode off on a stolen horse when the master's son and heir refused to honor his father's wishes. Their harrowing tales chilled Dorothea to her core, and she often could not sleep at night for thinking of the others, so many others, who could not run away or who had died trying. The Grangers' efforts to help a handful of runaways reach the North seemed pitifully inadequate, no more than a gesture—except to those few who found their freedom. So much more was needed, so much more than they could ever do.

The hiding place Dorothea's father had made in Uncle Jacob's old room was tested twice in the weeks the winter snows melted and warmer winds began to blow from the southwest. Mary and Abner paid an unexpected call on a sunny afternoon, forcing the Grangers to hide a mother and her young son behind the false back of the wardrobe. Dorothea was dizzy with alarm the whole duration of their visit, waiting for the child to wail and betray them. As soon as the unexpected guests had departed, Dorothea and Lorena rushed to the wardrobe to free its occupants. They found the young boy asleep in his mother's arms, the mother herself anxious but calm, and safe.

The second test came a week later as two men scarcely older than Dorothea lay sleeping in Uncle Jacob's room. Someone pounded upon the back door of the kitchen, but before anyone could run to warn the fugitives, the door opened and Mr. Liggett stuck his head in. "Mornin', folks," he said awkwardly, startled to find Dorothea and her mother there. "I didn't think you 'uns were home."

"Are you in the habit of entering our house when you believe us to be elsewhere?" Lorena inquired.

"No, no, but since I came all this way I thought I'd leave you a note."

Lorena stood fast, blocking his view of the rooms beyond. "How fortunate that we are home and you will not have to bother."

"Yeah." Disappointed, Mr. Liggett still tried to peer around Lorena. "I just thought I'd check and see if you 'uns are hiring for the planting. Since your brother never paid me from last year, I thought you could just tack on what I earn this time to what you owe me."

Dorothea saw the line of her mother's jaw tighten. "I do not believe my husband will require your services this year. Thank you just the same."

Baleful, he said, "Then I'll just take what you owe me and go."

He shoved open the door. Lorena protested and grabbed hold of his coat, but he shook loose, knocking her to the floor. Dorothea, too, tried to block his path, but he shoved her aside and stormed into the front room. He scanned it, and, finding nothing, squared his bony shoulders and turned down the hallway toward Uncle Jacob's room.

Dorothea heard her mother choke back a gasp as Mr. Liggett

swung open the door and stepped inside. He lifted the Sugar Camp Quilt to peer under the bed; he flung open the doors to the wardrobe and rifled through the old clothes hanging within. Dorothea held her breath as he looked left, right, then backed out of the room and headed for the attic stairs.

When Dorothea heard his footsteps overhead, she dashed into Uncle Jacob's room. The two runaways were nowhere to be found, and the door to the wardrobe was ajar. She closed it without a sound and returned to the hall where her mother stood, her eyes fixed on the ceiling, darting back and forth in response to the creaks of the floorboards. Dorothea linked her arm through her mother's as they listened to Mr. Liggett tearing about upstairs, her mind racing with plans of what to do if Mr. Liggett found any sign of the fugitives. Her father was off in the northwestern fields; he could not come to their aid.

Mr. Liggett stomped downstairs, glowering. "The cellar," he snarled at Lorena.

Her back was ramrod straight, but her grasp on Dorothea's arm tightened. "I cannot comprehend why you believe you have any right to subject us to this search. If it's money you seek—"

"Never mind. I'll find it myself." He disappeared around the corner into the kitchen. They heard the cellar door swing open and the scuff of his boots on the steps.

Dorothea tore free of her mother and ran upstairs. Her small attic bedroom was in a shambles, quilts and clothes and books strewn over the bed and floor. Swiftly she retrieved the book her uncle had bequeathed to her and removed the stack of bills from within the front cover. She counted out some of her inheritance and raced back downstairs. She reached the kitchen just as Mr. Liggett returned from the cellar.

"Here," she said, holding out the money. "The wages my uncle neglected to pay you. Please take it and leave us in peace."

Mr. Liggett snatched the folded bills and thumbed through them. "This ain't enough."

"It's the wage you agreed upon."

"That was a year ago. I want something for my trouble and for the wait."

"That's all I can give you."

He jerked his head toward the front room. "Then I'll just have that whiskey and call it even."

Lorena quickly retrieved the nearly empty bottle from Uncle Jacob's desk and thrust it at him. "Take it and go."

He shook the bottle, scowling to see how little remained, and tucked it into his coat. "Thank you kindly. Good day, ladies."

Lorena slammed the door behind him and slid the bolt in place. "That will remain locked, day and night, from this moment on." She placed a hand on her chest, breathless. "I declare that man is a demon. He was not looking for money, or even for whiskey. That much is evident despite his words."

Dorothea felt a slow churning of anger growing within her. "We should not have allowed him to invade our home like that."

"Allowed him? I do not see how we could have prevented it."

"If Jonathan had been here—"

"They very likely would have come to blows. Your brother would have thrashed Mr. Liggett soundly, making him hate us all the more. Now Mr. Liggett has seen for himself that we have nothing to hide, and he will not return."

Dorothea was not so certain.

They went to the window, expecting to see Mr. Liggett trudging off on foot, but they caught a glimpse of him on horseback before he disappeared into the trees. They hurried down to the cellar and eased open the door Robert had concealed in a row of shelves. In the dim light, Dorothea saw the two men crouched warily, prepared to run.

"He is gone," she said. "It is safe to come out."

"If you don't mind, we'll stay put for a while," said one of the men. The other nodded his assent.

"As you wish." Dorothea handed them some bread, dried apples, and a jug of water, and closed the hidden door.

MR. NELSON SCHEDULED DOROTHEA'S second lesson in natural sciences for a Friday, on the same morning her father, at breakfast, had announced that the ground was thawed enough for plowing. He had already hired hands to help with the work, and the men would begin the next day. She walked to school that morning slowly, reluctant for the day to begin and speed toward its end. While she welcomed the work of springtime more than in previous years—now that the farm was the Grangers' own—she would miss her students, the daily walks to school, the cordial lunches in the classroom when she and Mr. Nelson would discuss books or the news from back East. She resolved to fill her hours with work so she would not miss the schoolhouse until they needed her again.

After lunchtime recess, Dorothea and Mr. Nelson gathered the children and set off on foot to the meadow and woods southwest of town. Dorothea showed them the early signs of spring pushing up through the earth, natural herbs useful in medicines, berries and roots that were safe to eat, and poisonous plants they must never touch. The children were so inquisitive and interested in all she had to show them that she lost track of time, and they wandered farther than she had intended. When she finally remembered, she apologized to Mr. Nelson and turned the children back toward school, wondering why he had not reminded her that the hour was growing late. The end of the school day was nearly at hand, and he would not have time for his history lecture.

Usually one of them walked at the head of the group and the other at the end, with the children in between, but this time Mr. Nelson followed behind the children with Dorothea, remarking that the students knew the way to the schoolhouse without a guide, and this way, he and Dorothea could both watch them.

"Another fine lesson, Miss Granger," he said. "Raised in the cities as I have been, I never knew what wonders lay on my family's own land."

"Your land?" asked Dorothea. "We walked far, but not all the way to Two Bears Farm."

"Indeed we did. The strand of oaks beyond the far edge of the meadow marks the boundary of our property."

"I had no idea." She and Jonathan had played there often as children, thinking the land belonged to no one.

"You seem to know every species of plant and animal in the Elm Creek Valley."

"Not every one, I'm sure." She brushed a hand along the long blades of grasses growing on the side of the road, plucking one and raising it to her nose. It smelled like fresh, green wheat. "I have lived in the valley all my life, however, and my brother and I explored every bit of it we could."

They reached the town with its hard-packed dirt roads and flat board sidewalks. The children's pace slowed the closer they came to the schoolhouse. "They think we won't notice their attempts to prolong our outing," said Mr. Nelson dryly. He returned to the front of the line and began walking more briskly so that the students were forced to hurry after him. Dorothea muffled a laugh and quickened her pace to keep up with them.

They were only a block from the schoolhouse when a man stepped out from the doorway of a tavern and seized her by the upper arm. Her exclamation of surprise was cut short by the sharply foul odor of liquor and tobacco juice and unwashed skin.

"I know you 'uns are hiding something," Mr. Liggett muttered, tightening his grip as she struggled to free herself. The children continued on to the schoolhouse unaware. "Something you wouldn't want your sweetheart to know about, eh? You pay me again what you paid me last time, and I won't tell him."

Suddenly Mr. Nelson strode toward them. "What is the meaning of this, Liggett? Release her at once."

Mr. Liggett did. Dorothea backed away from him, rubbing her arm. The children had halted and were watching them curiously.

Mr. Liggett ducked back into the tavern. "Don't forget," he called to Dorothea as she ushered the children on their way, fighting to conceal the sickening dread in her heart.

"Perhaps you would care to explain that," said Mr. Nelson in an undertone.

She would not care to at all. "Mr. Liggett had a long-standing disagreement with my uncle. He persists in troubling my family about it."

"He said something about a sweetheart. I assume he means Mr. Pearson."

Dorothea forced a laugh. "I have no idea what he is talking about. Mr. Pearson is certainly not my sweetheart." She gave Mr. Nelson a searching look. "Perhaps you would have some influence with him."

"I? With Mr. Liggett?"

"Why, yes. I understand he used to work for you."

"Mr. Liggett has never worked for me, nor shall he ever. I assumed he was employed by your sweetheart."

"Cyrus Pearson is not my sweetheart," said Dorothea impatiently. Then she stopped short. "Why would you think Mr. Liggett works for Cyrus Pearson?"

Mr. Nelson shrugged. "I have frequently seen them together in town. One occasion was at the bank, where Mr. Pearson made a withdrawal, which he then gave to Mr. Liggett. I assume it was a payment for services rendered."

Dorothea could not imagine what services. Mr. Liggett rarely did any work but farming, and Cyrus had no farm. "Do you recall when this was?"

"Shortly after my arrival in Creek's Crossing."

Dorothea's thoughts flew back to a day when Mr. Liggett had confronted her and Cyrus as they rode to his mother's house. Mr. Liggett had asked Cyrus for money—more money—and Cyrus had seemed not to know what he meant. Suddenly she remembered that it was Cyrus who had told her Mr. Nelson had hired Mr. Liggett. At once came a cascade of other memories: Cyrus saying that Mr. Nelson had questionable opinions on the subject of slavery; Cyrus surprised that Lorena should recommend Abel Wright as foreman of the library construction; Cyrus doubting that any of the Elm Creek Valley's colored families would care to use the library; Lorena questioning what Dorothea knew of Cyrus's opinions and her own assurances that he must share her own well-known views or he would not have sought her company. But of course, it was never her company, or even Dorothea herself, that had interested him most.

"Miss Granger." Mr. Nelson was regarding her with concern. "Are you all right?"

She had never been less so. A man she had considered a friend may have been more deceitful and conniving than she ever could have imagined, and she had been blind to his manipulations. "Yes, I am fine, thank you."

"If you wish, I will speak to him."

"No! No. Please do not trouble yourself. Anything you say will merely antagonize him."

"If he is as troublesome as you say—" Something in her expression made him break off. "Of course. If that is what you wish."

"It is."

They had reached the schoolhouse. Mr. Nelson held open the door and allowed the students to pass inside. When the last straggler had entered, he said, "I am sure you would prefer for Cyrus Pearson or your father to handle this matter."

"Why are you forever bringing up Mr. Pearson? Are you so engrossed in your books that you hear none of the gossip in this town? You were at the Quilting Bee Dance. Were you standing about with your eyes closed? Are you the only person in town unaware that Cyrus Pearson is engaged to someone else?"

He hesitated. "I was . . . not aware of that."

"Well, now you know." She marched past him into the classroom, where her own young pupils beamed down at her curiously from the choir loft stairs and Mr. Nelson's hid smiles as they wrote upon their slates or pretended to be engrossed in their books. Dorothea flushed with embarrassment and wondered how much they had overheard.

Fortunately, only enough time remained in the school day for Dorothea and Mr. Nelson to assign new lessons and bid farewell to those students who would not return the next week. Dorothea went upstairs and cleaned the choir loft thoroughly before helping Mr. Nelson tidy the main classroom. They did not talk as they worked. Mr. Nelson was in a brood, frowning over some matter—possibly how Dorothea might have brought down scandal upon the school with her public altercation with Mr. Liggett.

When she could linger no longer, Dorothea approached him. "Since the classroom seems to be in order, I will say good-bye."

He did not look up from packing books into his satchel. "Until Monday, then."

"But—" Dorothea did not know what to say. "I did not think you would need a second teacher anymore, with so many of the students gone until after the harvest."

"Did you sign a contract for the entire term?"

"Well, yes, but—"

"Are you asking to be relieved of your obligations?"

"Of course not." She took a deep breath and clasped her hands at her waist. "I merely assumed that you intended to consolidate the classes."

"I intended no such thing. However, if you wish to resign, I will not stop you."

"No, Mr. Nelson, I do not wish to resign." In consternation, Dorothea snatched up her satchel. "I will see you on Monday."

She glimpsed his answering nod as she hurried for the door.

She would be grateful for the respite of the weekend, she thought as she crossed the street on her way to the ferry. She and Lorena had mapped out the garden and were eager to begin planting. Lorena had been nurturing seedlings indoors for weeks, waiting until the danger of frost passed. They had been a fortnight now without a freeze, and Lorena decided the time had come to put her plants into the ground.

Dorothea heard the steady clop of horse's hooves on the street behind her as she descended the hill to the ferry crossing. A horse and rider followed her aboard, and to her dismay, she saw that the man was Cyrus.

She forced a nervous flicker of a smile and turned her back to lean on the rail and gaze out at Elm Creek. Cyrus ignored the hint and came to stand beside her. "Good afternoon, Miss Granger," he said quietly, with none of his usual mirth.

"Good afternoon, Mr. Pearson."

"It is a pleasant day for a crossing, isn't it?" Then he made an impatient gesture of disgust. "This is nonsense. For months you have called me Cyrus and I have called you Dorothea. We laughed at each other's jokes and had a jolly time. Can't we be friends again?"

"I would like that," said Dorothea carefully. "But you must understand, I cannot go riding with another woman's fiancé as if we were courting. You can imagine, I'm sure, what people would say about that."

"I never thought you one to tailor your behavior according to what other people think."

"I do so when I agree with them." She hesitated. "If we are to be friends again, however, we must have complete honesty between us."

"Of course, Dorothea." His mouth twisted in a rueful grimace. "I understand perfectly why you would need my assurances on that point."

"Indeed, I have many questions for you, many uncertainties," said Dorothea. "For one, I wondered why you and your mother allowed everyone to believe that she rather than Mr. Nelson donated the Authors' Album quilt to the library."

Cyrus was taken aback, but he quickly composed himself. "I cannot agree that we did any such thing. If I recall correctly, Nelson was given credit for his gift."

"You do not recall correctly. Mrs. Claverton announced the donation. You and your mother accepted congratulations from one and all without a word of thanks to Mr. Nelson."

"I regret the oversight, but Nelson is not one to draw attention to himself. I am quite confident he was relieved not to be hauled onto the stage. Furthermore, my mother and I did not accept congratulations for the donation. If you recall, I accepted congratulations for winning the drawing. My mother accepted congratulations for running a successful event."

"I see."

"What do you see?"

"I see that we are not going to be completely honest with each other after all. Or rather, you will not be so."

He frowned, annoyed. "Any explanation that does not satisfy a conclusion you have already reached must be a lie?"

"I suppose it might seem that way to you. Let us move on, then. Why were you so eager for me to believe that Mr. Liggett worked for Mr. Nelson when in truth you were his employer?"

He studied her for a moment. "That day in the carriage. Of course. I hope you can forgive me a momentary lapse in judgment. I confess I was not entirely truthful. I could not think of any other excuse for Mr. Liggett's behavior, and, knowing how you despise him, I did not want to admit that he worked for me. I valued your good opinion and did not want to lose it."

"That accounts for why you lied, but not this particular lie. Why not simply deny that Mr. Liggett worked for you? Why attribute your own actions to Mr. Nelson?"

"I thought you did not like him, so your own prejudice against him would make my tale more convincing." He spread his palms and shrugged. "You wanted complete honesty. Very well. You shall have it. I also realized that you two had much in common, with your love of books and pursuit of ideals. I did not want you to prefer him to me. I knew that as soon as you discovered he had paid for your friend's father's release—"

"What?"

His eyes widened, and his grin had a hardness to it she had never seen before. "Is it possible you did not discover it?"

"Mr. Nelson paid Mr. Schultz's ransom? How would you know such a thing?"

"I heard it from the recipients themselves. They are . . . men with whom I occasionally do business."

She let that sink in. Cold fingers of certainty and regret clutched her heart. "Cyrus, tell me plainly. Did you hire Mr. Liggett to threaten Constance and Abel Wright?"

Cyrus leaned against the railing and gazed at the approaching shoreline. She thought she heard him sigh. When he said nothing, she knew.

"Why would you do such a thing?" she asked him. "Do you know he could have burned down their barn?"

"I only meant to frighten them away. I offered Abel Wright a good price for his land, but he refused. I confess I can be an impatient man. Rather than wait months or even years for him to realize on his own that he would be happier among his own kind, I decided to encourage him to depart."

"So they would sell to you at whatever price you offered."

"Come now, Dorothea. Let us have complete honesty on both sides. Do you really want their kind in the Elm Creek Valley? You must know Abel has a colored woman living with him now. Soon colored children will be running around in our streets, taking up seats in our schools, and more colored families will think themselves welcome here."

"They *will* be welcome here."

He shook his head, regarding her with lingering fondness. "You can be so innocent, Dorothea. That is an endearing quality in a woman, but it may lead to your disappointment. You do not know the people of Creek's Crossing as well as you think you do if you believe more share your principles than mine."

"I do not believe it."

"Like it or not, it is true. Not only in Creek's Crossing, but in the entire nation." He reached for her hand, but she pulled away. "Dorothea. Reconsider. You will not want to find yourself on the wrong side."

"I will allow my conscience and not public opinion to determine which, for me, is the right side."

"Suit yourself. But be careful. It is not wise to make enemies of your betters. Think on Miss Nadelfrau."

"What do you mean?"

He smiled coolly. "Is the schoolhouse so cozy that you no longer care about the happenings in town? Or is Mr. Nelson such pleasant company that you no longer visit Mary to catch up on your gossip?"

"What has happened to Miss Nadelfrau?"

"I leave that to you to discover. If you are wise you will take a lesson from her example."

The ferry reached the northern shore of Elm Creek. Untying his horse's reins, Cyrus added, "Despite our disagreements, I still care about you, Dorothea. If I had the carriage, I would offer you a ride."

"If you offered, I would decline."

His eyes snapped in anger. "Apparently it will be impossible for us to be friends after all."

Dorothea made no reply. Cyrus led his horse from the ferry and rode off at a gallop without a backward glance.

DOROTHEA REPEATED CYRUS'S CRYPTIC remarks about Miss Nadelfrau to her parents, but they were just as mystified as she. They were less shocked to learn of his deception than she had been, though, and more incensed by his veiled threats. When Dorothea proposed that they warn the Wrights immediately, however, Lorena assured her that Cyrus was unlikely to persist in his plan to frighten the couple off their land, now that he had been exposed. Dorothea worried that the erratic Mr. Liggett might act on his own, but she agreed that informing the Wrights could wait until the following week, when they planned to meet in town to swap Lorena's sweet potato seedlings for some of Abel Wright's cheese.

Spring planting began. Jonathan had written that he would try to come, but Dorothea and her parents did not expect him, nor were they surprised when in a second letter he apologized and told them of the many fascinating cases and assignments from his professors that compelled him to remain at college. As if to make up for his absence, he sent Dorothea sketches of quilt patterns he had observed before leaving Baltimore. They were made in the same intricate appliquéd style she had used for the quilt top that she had given to Constance. She could not conceive of making such an elaborate quilt twice in one lifetime, but she admired his drawings and tucked them away for future reference and inspiration.

From time to time over the next two days, Dorothea felt a surge of strange, exuberant melancholy as she worked alongside her mother in the new garden. Spring planting always brought with it a sense of hope and expectation, but she missed her brother and, to her surprise, she even missed Uncle Jacob. Her gladness that she would be able to finish out the term at the Creek's Crossing school was tempered by Cyrus's revelations and her fear that he and Mr. Liggett would not cease their maltreatment of the Wrights. Most of all, she was proud of her family's station but anxious that Mr. Liggett would persist in troubling them. If his mistaken belief that Cyrus was her sweetheart was all that restrained him, she dreaded what he would do if he discovered the truth.

Every daylight hour of Saturday and Sunday was filled with tasks of the spring planting, so none of the Grangers could spare the time for a trip into town to inquire after Miss Nadelfrau. Robert, who stated that Cyrus's ability to lie was inversely proportionate to his capacity to love, thought that likely nothing was amiss, and that Cyrus had spoken as he had only to upset Dorothea, knowing that she would not be able to investigate for several days. Dorothea hoped her father was correct, but on Monday morning she left for school early so that she would have time to stop by Miss Nadelfrau's dressmaking shop.

The blinds were drawn but the door was unlocked, so she proceeded inside, where she found Miss Nadelfrau draping sheets over her dressmaker's forms and sewing machine. No lovely finished gowns hung in their usual places in the front windows, and the bolts of satins, silks, wools, and brocades ordinarily artfully arranged in the front of the store to tempt ladies inside were rolled up and stacked in a corner.

Dorothea took in the sight and said, "This looks for all the world as if you are closing your shop."

Miss Nadelfrau looked up, startled out of a mournful reverie. "The shop is not closing. I am just taking the little that is mine and sorting the rest for the new owner."

"New owner?" As soon as the words left her lips, Dorothea guessed. "Not Mrs. Engle."

Miss Nadelfrau nodded. "She is a rather fine seamstress and apparently she is restless with so little to do now that the library benefit is over. She decided her own business was just the thing to satisfy her need to occupy her time and her desire to express her artful impulses."

Miss Nadelfrau's voice was uncharacteristically bitter. "Forgive me," said Dorothea carefully, "but you do not seem entirely pleased by these arrangements. I am curious why you sold to her."

"I had no choice." Miss Nadelfrau made a brittle laugh and dabbed at her eyes with a handkerchief. "I did not want to sell. I have no other livelihood. Unfortunately, when I opened my shop five years ago, I made the mistake of borrowing money from Violet. She charged a lower interest rate than the bank and I thought my future more secure if entrusted to a friend. When Violet decided our friendship had ended, she called in the loan. Of course I did not have enough to pay her in full." She tucked her handkerchief away. "Of course I do not blame you, Dorothea. No true friend would have turned so quickly against me."

Bewildered, Dorothea asked, "Am I the cause of Mrs. Engle's enmity toward you?"

"Oh, unwittingly, I'm sure. That quilt, you know—the Authors' Album. I helped you put it into the quilt frame. I was in such a state of nerves that evening that I did not even notice the names Violet found so objectionable, but since I saw the quilt top and said nothing, she is convinced I knew all along. She accused me of conspiring with you to go against her wishes."

"For this she would take away your livelihood?" exclaimed Dorothea.

Miss Nadelfrau nodded. "But she has allowed me to retain my apartment upstairs."

"How very decent of her," said Dorothea, fuming. "I will speak to her and set the matter straight."

"Don't bother. I am resigned to my fate, and she would not listen to you anyway." Miss Nadelfrau tried to smile. "She has every reason to suspect me, since she has seen works by those very same notorious authors on my own bookshelves."

Dorothea did not know what to say. "Is there anything I can do to help?"

"No, no. I'll be fine. I am glad for your sake that you have no outstanding debts to the Engles."

Dorothea thought of Mr. Engle's position as head of the school board. For all his apparent faith in her abilities as a teacher, Mr. Nelson could not force them to hire her for the autumn term. "What will you do?" she asked.

Miss Nadelfrau shrugged and lined up spools of thread in a neat row on a table. "I have a little money tucked away, and I might be able to take in a bit of sewing from my most loyal customers. If my savings run out before I find another position, my brother in Pleasant Gap will take me in. He has a farm and seven children, but his wife is sickly. They tell me they would be grateful for my help and that I would not be a burden."

"I am sure you would be an enormous help to them."

"And perhaps someday I will try again." She looked around the walls of her shop, teary-eyed. "Who knows? Perhaps Pleasant Gap needs another dressmaker."

Dorothea hugged her and offered the most encouraging words she could manage. It was an outrage that Mrs. Engle saw fit to punish poor, hapless Miss Nadelfrau for some imagined complicity rather than confront Dorothea directly.

Dorothea could not reflect on the unfolding of recent events without considering that it might have been better had she never sewed a single stitch of the Authors' Album. She certainly regretted what had befallen Miss Nadelfrau. Yet she did not regret including the banned authors in the quilt or the results of her choice. The quilt was not to blame for creating the animosity and mistrust on the rise in Creek's Crossing. It had merely illuminated cracks and crevices that had always existed in the shadows. She was disappointed by what she had discovered about Cyrus, Mrs. Engle, and others, but it was better by far that she knew it. The truth was always preferable to a lie.

She hurried on to the schoolhouse, where she discovered Mr. Nelson in a foul mood. He greeted her curtly and called his students to attention as soon as the hour struck, without his usual dry pleasantries. From the choir loft she overheard his increasing impatience with his students' errors, which, she observed, bewildered them into making even more errors. She had come to know that Mr. Nelson was a clever and quick-witted man, but caustic when vexed. When he nearly brought one slow but dutiful older girl to tears as she struggled through her geography lesson, Dorothea wished she could intervene, but dared not compromise the students' respect for their teacher.

An opportunity to speak frankly did not arrive until they dismissed the students for lunch. "You seem especially displeased with your students today," she said after the last little boy ran outdoors.

Her remark seemed to surprise him. "Do I? They are no worse than usual, though regrettably, no better, either."

"Helene is a sensitive girl. She tries her best, but she never even held a book before she started school only two years ago. I found that a gentle approach, with a great deal of encouragement, worked best with her."

He did not bother to look up from unpacking his lunch from his satchel. "Do you know her so well?"

"I was her teacher myself not so long ago, and I would appreciate the courtesy of a respectful reply. I am not one of your students."

Immediately he looked up. "My apologies, Miss Granger. Of course you are right. Helene cannot be bullied into learning."

"May I suggest that most children cannot?" She regarded him. "I do not believe the students are to blame for your ill temper."

"No." He yanked out his chair and sat down, then glanced up as if surprised to see her still standing. "Are you going to eat or aren't you?"

"I think I might prefer to eat outdoors with the children than remain in your delightful company."

He almost smiled. "I'm sure they would enjoy that."

"I would, too." But she did not leave. "If I knew the reason for this foul mood, I might be able to help—for the students' sake."

He scowled. "You cannot help." The venom in his tone astonished her. "You cannot, and I cannot. There is nothing we can do here in this patch of wilderness that will effect any change whatsoever."

"Our students might not be the dedicated scholars you taught in the East—"

"I am not speaking about our students." Abruptly he rose and strode to the window. "A letter came yesterday, from my sister. Her husband is a representative to Congress. Do you know there is a bill before them that would require all law officers to hunt down and capture all runaway slaves and return them to their owners? Not only in the South, but also in states where slavery has been banned. Harboring or assisting fugitives in any fashion would also be against the law."

Shocked, Dorothea said, "But there are already similar laws on the books. People pay them little attention."

"A new law would signify an increased commitment to the perpetuation of slavery for the entire nation. It cannot and must not be allowed to pass." He paced back and forth, scowling morosely. "The bill must be fought and defeated. My sister's husband is doing his part, while I—" He halted, his shoulders slumped in defeat. "While I reprimand children for not knowing the major water routes of Asia. What can I do here that will make any difference? Nothing. I am utterly useless."

"You have already done a great deal to ease the suffering of slaves."

He shot her a sharp, curious glance before uttering a brittle laugh. "You sound like my father. I made my contribution and now must let others carry on the fight. I tell you, Miss Granger, that resolution suits me very ill indeed."

There are other ways to fight, she almost told him. Two Bears Farm had been a haven for fugitives once and could be again. Then she remembered the promise his father had exacted from him and what would befall him should he break the law again. She thought of Cyrus and how she had once imagined, wrongly, so much goodness in him because that was what she wanted to see. What if she had confided in Cyrus as she now wanted to with Mr. Nelson?

The risk was too great. Instead she said, "That law, if it should come to pass, does not bind your hands entirely."

"And what am I to do from Creek's Crossing, Pennsylvania?"

"You can vote," she said sharply. That was more than she could do. "You can put that university education of yours to good use by writing letters, newspaper articles, books— You could write about your prison experiences, how your sacrifice was worthwhile because you brought others to freedom. If that *is* what you believe, because frankly, your true feelings on the subject are difficult to discern through all this self-pity."

His gaze bored into her. "Is that how you regard me?"

"Mr. Nelson, I confess that self-pity is one of the lesser faults I have accused you of possessing since first we met."

He paused. "I am quite sure I deserved your censure."

"You did, indeed."

His laugh echoed hollowly in the empty classroom. "At last, Miss Granger, a point on which we agree."

She managed a smile in return. She did not share with him her disconcerting observation that they had, in fact, disagreed very little recently, and that they had more in common than she would have imagined possible a few months before.

Chapter Ten

As the week passed, Mr. Nelson made an effort to moderate his ill humor, but he was not entirely successful. While he was no longer unduly stern toward his students, several times Dorothea caught him in a brood, gazing out the window or paging through a book without seeing what lay before him. She was struck by the similarity of his expression to what she herself had felt on many occasions—when her brother wrote of his studies or when Lorena reminisced about her childhood in Boston.

Mr. Nelson had never been what she would call cheerful, but she could not bear to stand by and watch him sink deeper into gloom. On Friday morning—after asking Lorena to be sure she no longer needed them—she collected older issues of abolitionist newspaper the *Daily Advocate* and presented them to Mr. Nelson at lunchtime. He was immediately absorbed, and at the end of the day, he was so greatly encouraged that he walked her to the ferry so he could share his ideas about forming a local abolitionist group modeled after the Anti Slavery Society of Pittsburgh. She offered to assist him, but as soon as she spoke, she realized that this was precisely the sort of activity Uncle Jacob would have condemned for drawing unwanted attention to their other activities. She could hardly rescind her offer so soon after making it, however, nor did she wish to. The Grangers' views on slavery were already common knowledge. Helping Mr. Nelson form an antislavery society would not create any new risks for their station's passengers.

On Saturday, Lorena and Dorothea rode into Creek's Crossing to meet Constance in front of the dry-goods store to exchange Lorena's sweet potato seedlings for several wheels of Abel Wright's cheese. Constance also had unexpected news: Two nights before, a conductor had guided a party of six runaways to the Wright farm. Among their number were an elderly man, two men of middle years, a younger woman, and two children. Their astounding means of escape had been nearly two years in the planning. The two younger men, grooms on the plantation, had stolen horses and a carriage from their master, while the woman had taken from her mistress clothing, a trunk, and other accoutrements of southern womanhood. They had fled under the cover of darkness, but once far enough away so their master's horses and carriage would not be recognized, they kept the children out of sight and passed themselves off as a shy southern belle traveling with her servants. The ruse served them well until they reached Maryland, where by a stroke of good fortune the eldest man spotted a posted handbill describing their disguise and offering a substantial reward for the return of the slaves and stolen property. They immediately abandoned their disguises, and ever since they had traveled on foot led by a conductor, a former runaway who had reached Canada but who had chosen to return time and time again to guide others to freedom. He usually traveled along a westerly route through Uniontown and Pittsburgh, but this time he had been diverted into the Elm Creek Valley by slavecatchers hired by the fugitives' determined and vengeful master. The slavecatchers and their pack of hounds evidently had traveled through the Elm Creek Valley before, given their swift progress through what was to the conductor unknown terrain.

Abel Wright and the conductor had made the difficult decision to divide the group in two, send them north along different routes, and reunite them in Canada. The woman would not be parted from the children, nor could the elderly man keep pace with the two younger men, so the groups were determined by practicality. The two younger men would travel to the Granger farm that night.They were in good health and would not need to rest more than a day before continuing northward.

The other four presented a problem. Of necessity their master's horses and carriage had been abandoned in Maryland, and the children and elderly man could not travel swiftly on foot. More troubling, their conductor did not know the routes through the Elm Creek Valley as well as the Wrights and the Grangers, who knew only the stations directly before and after their own.

After much deliberation, the Wrights and the conductor had concluded that their greatest chance lay in another disguise. The handbills warned to search for a colored slave posing as a white woman with her servants, but they said nothing of a freed black woman traveling with her aged father and two children.

If the Grangers could provide one horse, Abel Wright would offer a second as well as his wagon. With false baptismal certificates and a bill of sale for a fictitious plot of land in New York, the fugitives could pass themselves off as free coloreds from New York returning home from a visit with family. If they traveled lesser-known routes, they might avoid confrontation altogether. Enough colored families lived in the Elm Creek Valley that if they acted with assurance, it was possible no one would suspect them of being runaways.

Constance, Dorothea, and Lorena had strolled down the block from the dry-goods store while Constance spoke, but Lorena still glanced over her shoulder before shaking her head and saying, "They ought to conceal themselves and follow the tried and true routes through the valley. I have grave doubts this ruse will be any more successful than their first."

"Their first disguise *was* successful," replied Dorothea. "They made it all the way to Maryland in perfect safety. If their pursuers had not sent word ahead of them, they would be using it still."

"I thought like you did, at first," said Constance to Lorena. "But if Liza can fool folks into thinking she's a pampered white girl too shy to leave her carriage, she can surely make them believe she's a free colored."

Eventually Lorena agreed that they had little alternative. If the four runaways relied on speed and stealth, the slavecatchers would surely overtake them.

A soft rap on the door shortly after midnight signaled the arrival of the two men. Robert led them to Uncle Jacob's old room and showed them the hiding place in the wardrobe in case of unexpected visitors. Lorena quickly brought them food and drink, and while they rested, Dorothea used the Sugar Camp Quilt to teach them the route to the Brauns' mill. It seemed ages ago that she had pieced the unusual blocks under her uncle's stern and watchful gaze, unaware of their significance. Since then dozens of fugitives had journeyed closer to freedom following its secret symbols.

Robert checked the locks on the doors twice before turning in for the night. In her attic bedroom, Dorothea slept lightly as she did whenever passengers rested at their station, her ears tuned to the familiar noises of the house, listening for the creak of a window or the baying of a dog. Whenever an unexpected sound jolted her awake, her first thoughts were of Mr. Liggett. Strangely, though she knew him to be a coward, she was more wary of him than of the anonymous slavecatchers she had never seen. She wished that he would grow bored of watching her family and leave them in peace, but Mr. Liggett's anger at Uncle Jacob ran too deeply for that, and some debts could not be paid in coin.

The next morning, the Grangers treaded softly as they moved about the house so that their weary guests could sleep. The two men emerged from Uncle Jacob's bedroom at midmorning and gratefully ate second and third helpings of breakfast. After racing through her morning chores, Dorothea worked at Uncle Jacob's desk on the counterfeit documents the other four fugitives would need to make their disguises complete. As she added an official-looking scroll to a piece of parchment, Dorothea overheard the two men conversing in hushed voices, anguishing over the decision to go on without the others. One of the men, Liza's husband and the father of her two children left behind at the Wrights, was especially troubled. "Won't mean nothing to me to be free if they get sent back," he told his companion, who tried to reassure him.

"They won't be sent back," said Dorothea. The two men regarded her dubiously. "You will all be together again in Canada. You will see."

"That's right kind of you, miss," said the man, "but those slave-catchers are close behind. They got a good look at Liza and Old Dan outside of Harrisburg. Pretending to be some freeborn family won't fool them."

"They didn't get such a good look," the other man contradicted. "It was dark, they were thirty yards away, and they didn't know it was Liza and Old Dan they was looking at. And they never saw the children."

Dorothea forced confidence into her voice. "You've made it this far. You will make it the rest of the way. You'll see."

"We have a long way yet to go," the father said, but he did look less anxious. It struck Dorothea then that the hope and reassurance the Grangers provided did as much as food, clothing, and directions to enable their passengers to journey on. Of course, the fugitives had no choice. They could not stay, and they could not return, having come so far. Slavecatchers and masters liked to make examples of recaptured runaways.

The two men left after dusk—reluctantly, or so it seemed to

Dorothea. She prayed that they would reach the Brauns' mill safely and that they would endure the separation from their loved ones. The rest of the party would be traveling only a few days behind the men, but they would not see one another again for many weeks. Dorothea could not ignore the fact that their reunion was by no means certain.

The next three days passed in a blur of activity—spring planting, teaching, and laboring painstakingly over the documents. Dorothea had apparently inherited her uncle's talent for drawing, for the false papers she created were virtually identical to the real documents she had copied. In addition to the papers affirming Liza and Old Dan's false identities and the bill of sale, she also wrote a letter purportedly from Liza's sister-in-law in Gettysburg imploring her to come visit her ailing brother. Dorothea also contrived a receipt from an undertaker dated several weeks later for the funeral of Liza's fictitious brother. It was a long journey from New York to central Pennsylvania for a social visit, Dorothea thought, but a dutiful sister would willingly travel that distance to bring her father to visit his dying son.

She admired her handiwork, but hoped that Liza and her companions would not be called upon to present the papers to anyone once Dorothea and Constance bid them farewell and they rode off on their own. Then she folded and creased the letter, spilled a bit of tea upon it, and dog-eared the corners. The bill of sale and other papers she crumpled and soiled with ashes from the fireplace, thinking of Uncle Jacob wiping the mud from his boots on the Sugar Camp Quilt. When the papers were suitably aged, she put them in an old leather pocketbook of Lorena's to await the trip to fetch the runaways.

On Tuesday morning, Dorothea rode her uncle's horse to school and boarded him in Mr. Engle's livery stable just as she had in the winter. All day long her thoughts were on the task ahead, bringing the four fugitives across the ferry to the safety of the

Granger farm. She was so distracted that once Mr. Nelson asked her sharply if she were ill and needed to go home. She assured him she was fine and endeavored to give him no more reason to be suspicious, but it was a relief when the school day ended and she could quickly tidy the choir loft and hurry on her way, ignoring Mr. Nelson's questioning glance. Usually she stayed to help him straighten up the main classroom, but since his farm lay along the same road as the Wrights, she must hasten to get enough of a head start so that he would not see her and wonder why she was traveling in the opposite direction of her home.

As she drove up to the Wrights' barn, Constance met her and helped her tend to her horse. While they worked, she assured Dorothea that Liza, Old Dan, and the children were prepared for their journey. The adults had rehearsed the children over and over until they knew their roles perfectly.

"Do you think the children will be able to stick to their story even if challenged?" asked Dorothea.

Constance shrugged. "They're fast learners. They've had to be all their lives. They know how to lie to save their skins. Besides, slavecatchers will most likely talk to the grown-ups and ignore the children. If the children break down and cry because they're scared, that won't surprise nobody none."

They went inside the house. Constance told her that the runaways were upstairs, sleeping in a hidden room in the attic, gathering their strength for the long journey ahead. "Paul was their leader," said Constance, referring to one of the younger men, as Dorothea helped her prepare supper. "He was the courage of this group. Liza tries her best to keep everyone's spirits up now that he's gone on ahead, but it's only worked with the children. Something's gone out of the old man like an old tree hollowed out."

Dorothea felt a quiver of nervousness. "You don't suppose he'll put the others in danger?"

Constance glanced darkly to the ceiling as a floorboard creaked overhead. "You're worried about the children spilling the truth? I'm more worried about the old man."

Night was falling as the four runaways crept quietly downstairs and seated themselves around the table. The two children, girls who looked to be about six and eight, stared at Dorothea with wide eyes as Constance made introductions. Dorothea noted that the four wore the sturdy work clothes of a moderately prosperous farm family, not the garb of slaves. Liza gave Dorothea a polite nod, but Old Dan kept his eyes cast down and did not seem to notice her.

Abel Wright urged them all to eat heartily, but only the children willingly obeyed; Liza choked down her food as if it were the bitterest medicine and Old Dan barely took a bite. After they cleared away the dishes, Constance privately told Dorothea to wrap up as much food as she could. The fugitives, though too nervous to eat now, would be hungry later.

Then it was time to depart.

Liza embraced Constance and thanked her for her goodness. Even Old Dan came to himself enough to shake Abel's hand and murmur that he wished he could repay the Wrights someday. Abel went outside to load his wagon with hay and hitch up the team while the runaways soberly put on their wraps and gathered their few belongings, small bundles that, Dorothea guessed, contained more clothes Constance had sewn for them and food for the journey. They could not rely upon reaching a station every night.

Outside, the stars shone in a clear sky just cool enough to make Dorothea grateful for her shawl. The runaways climbed aboard the wagon and concealed themselves in the hay, with only the smallest mew of complaint from the youngest girl, whom Liza quickly soothed. Dorothea took up the reins as Constance swung up to the seat beside her, chirruped to the horses, and set out for the Creek's Crossing road.

Dorothea and Constance rode without speaking. Dorothea's mouth was dry, her stomach a knot of worry. For all the fugitives who had passed through the Grangers' station, she had never felt so solely responsible for any runaway's fate as she did at that moment, driving to the ferry. As they passed the entrance to the road that led through the woods to Mr. Liggett's farm, the knot in her stomach tightened, but the only sounds were the clip-clopping of the horses' hooves on the hard-packed dirt road. Constance breathed a sigh as they left Mr. Liggett's land behind and approached Two Bears Farm. Dorothea studied the tall, white-boarded house as they rode by; two lights were burning, one upstairs and one below. She wondered what Mr. Nelson was doing at that moment.

They reached the outskirts of Creek's Crossing without encountering another wagon or rider. Dorothea turned east on a back road to avoid the noise and lights of the taverns and inns on the main streets. It was too much to hope that they could pass through the town entirely unobserved, but she would avoid as many eyes as possible.

The few townspeople they passed did not seem to give the wagon a second glance. The tightness in Dorothea's stomach began to ease as they crossed the last few blocks to the ferry. If they could reach the northern shore of Elm Creek unchallenged—

"What's that?" said Constance, nodding toward the ferry dock. A cluster of men stood by the boathouse, horses tied up nearby. Two carried torches. One loosely held the reins of a pack of hounds, sitting lazily at his feet.

"I don't know," replied Dorothea. She slowed the team as they drew closer. Just then, a carriage turned on to the street two blocks ahead of them and slowed as it approached the ferry. The men carrying torches leaped forward and blocked its way. A third man opened the carriage door and leaned inside, then withdrew and shouted something to his companions.

Dorothea did not wait to see if the four men allowed the carriage to board the ferry. She pulled hard on the reins and swung the wagon west on to Second Street.

"They're searching that carriage," murmured Constance, turning in her seat to look back upon the scene. "They ain't the constable's men."

"Indeed they are not." Dorothea urged the team into a trot. "They are slavecatchers."

"How do you know?"

"I know. But even if they were not, they would search the wagon before permitting us aboard the ferry. That is reason enough for us to turn around."

Constance studied her as the horses pulled them briskly away from the ferry dock. "Are you taking us back to the farm?"

"No." Dorothea fought the instinct to make the horses run. "I know another crossing."

"Not on Liggett's land, like your uncle tried?"

"The creek does narrow there. My uncle would have made it if not for his stroke."

"But Liggett—if he sees us—"

"He won't see us," said Dorothea grimly. "He is engaged at the moment."

For Dorothea had recognized the slight, hunched form of the man who had peered within the carriage, and the golden curls and arrogant stance of one of the torchbearers.

Cyrus and Mr. Liggett, working openly with slavecatchers.

THE FOUR RUNAWAYS MUST have felt the wagon turn completely around. They must have sensed their increased speed. Dorothea braced herself for a nervous question from Old Dan or the piping voices of the children, but the fugitives remained hidden.

"What if they saw us?" Constance said in a low voice.

"Let us hope they did not." But Dorothea knew it was possible. They had been only two blocks from the ferry dock when they turned west. Surely Cyrus would wonder about a wagon suddenly veering off as soon as their blockade came into view. Dorothea prayed he had not recognized her or Uncle Jacob's mare.

They passed through Creek's Crossing without incident. As the lights of the town faded behind them, Dorothea strained her ears for any sound of pursuit. All she heard was the steady clopping of the horses' hooves on the road headed south and the gurgling of Elm Creek, unseen in the darkness that fell sharply outside the pool of light their lanterns provided. In the distance Dorothea spied lights from farms, small and fragile in the dark.

They passed Two Bears Farm, the house silent on the top of the hill with only the two lighted windows hinting at warmth within. Dorothea and Constance did not speak. Soon even the sound of the creek died away as it curved around the oxbow to the west. The forest grew deeper; if Dorothea had not known the valley so well, she would have missed the turn onto the road to Elm Creek Farm.

The wagon creaked and jolted over the narrow trail, jarring on rocks and tree roots. Tree branches clawed at Dorothea's face; a lantern pole caught on a limb and snapped. Dorothea pulled the horses to a stop so Constance could get out and retrieve the lantern. The tin was dented, but miraculously, the light had not gone out.

"Seems to me this might be a very bad idea," said Constance as Dorothea started the horse again. Constance held out the lantern at arm's length, but it was a futile gesture.

"If you have a better alternative, I'm listening."

Dorothea's voice was strained from the effort of driving the team. The horses pulled at the bit and tossed their heads, annoyed at Dorothea for steering them into the tangled wood. Dorothea urged them forward, and the wagon jerked and bounded deeper into the woods. Constance nervously clutched at the wagon seat with her free hand, but she did not voice her doubts again. Just when Dorothea thought her aching arms could wrestle the team no further, she glimpsed moonlight on water.

"The creek," she gasped, trying to catch her breath. "We can cross up ahead."

Constance held out the lantern and shook her head. "It's too far off the road. The wagon will never make it."

"We have to try."

Dorothea pulled the team to a halt, jumped down from the wagon seat, and led the resistant horses off the trail into the woods. The horses strained and pulled the wagon into the underbrush, over a rotten log that crumbled onto a carpet of fallen leaves. "Good girl," Dorothea praised her uncle's mare quietly, urging her onward and hoping Abel Wright's horse would follow. They reached the top of a small incline that sloped down a steep hill to the creek bed. The crossing was narrower here, as Dorothea had remembered, but she and Jonathan had been on foot in daylight.

"We can't turn the wagon around here anyway," said Constance. "We might as well go forward." She secured the lantern and climbed down from the wagon seat.

Dorothea nodded and took a deep breath, blood pounding in her ears. She grasped the reins and bridles of Uncle Jacob's mare while Constance took hold of her own horse, and together they pulled the team forward. The horses whinnied in complaint but stepped forward once, then twice, and then quicker steps as the wagon began to roll down the slope of its own accord. Muscles straining, Dorothea held the mare in check as the wagon picked up speed. Suddenly Constance cried out as a wheel jolted against a tree root and sent her sprawling to the ground. The leather reins burned

Dorothea's palms as they tore free from her grasp. She fell to her knees and scrambled out of the way as the horses and wagon sped past her down the steep slope to the creek. There was a rumble and a crash of breaking branches, and then the wagon fell from sight.

A scream strangled in her throat. She crawled forward and spotted the wagon below, upright and stuck in the creek. One lantern lay on the pebbled creek side, the other extinguished, lost in the darkness. Abel Wright's horse whinnied and bucked, then tossed her head and snorted, pacing, still bound to the wagon and Uncle Jacob's mare. After a moment of horrifying stillness, a child's wail broke the night air.

Dorothea forced herself to her feet, choking back a sob. She made her way to Constance, who groaned as she sat up and clasped a hand to her head. Dorothea helped her stand, and together they picked their way down to the wagon, where the runaways were cautiously emerging from the bed of hay. The youngest girl stretched out her arms for Liza, sobbing. As Liza snatched her up, the eldest girl stood and looked around, dazed and silent, picking hay from her hair.

"Where's Old Dan?" said Constance in her ear. They quickly climbed into the wagon bed, and while Liza comforted the girls, Dorothea and Constance dug through the hay, searching frantically for the old man. Then, a flickering of lantern light drew Dorothea's attention to a limp form half in the creek, half on the shore. Her gasp alerted Constance, and together they jumped from the wagon and raced to his side. Dorothea was afraid to move him, but Constance ran her hands over him as if feeling for broken bones. He groaned as she rolled him over. Blood trickled from his brow.

Sitting on the damp shore, Constance drew him onto her lap and shook her head. Her wordless gaze confirmed what Dorothea already knew: Old Dan could not walk.

She left Constance with the injured man and returned to the

wagon, thoughts churning. Liza had calmed the youngest girl, who had quieted her sobs and merely sniffed back tears, thumb in her mouth. "She's more scared than hurt," Liza said quietly. "Please, see to Hannah." She nodded to the eldest child, who stood wide-eyed and wordless in the same spot as when she had first emerged from the hay.

Dorothea approached her gently. "Are you hurt?" No response. Dorothea placed a hand on her shoulder. "Are you all right?"

The girl looked up at her, wordless, but did not even shake her head. Dorothea knelt beside her. "Since you seem to be just fine, I wonder if you could help me. I need someone to hold the lantern while I unhitch the horses. Do you think you could do that?"

Hannah hesitated, then nodded. Relieved, Dorothea helped her down from the wagon and fetched the lantern. Quickly she surveyed the wagon: It had thrown an axle and the right side was smashed in. It was not beyond repair, but they had neither the tools nor the time to attend to it. Dorothea unhitched the mare, who tossed her head and snorted as if to declare that she had warned Dorothea not to try to cross there. Dorothea wished she had taken heed.

She thanked Hannah for helping her. The little girl nodded, lowered the lantern, and ran to her mother. While Liza comforted her daughters, Dorothea and Constance gathered the runaways' bundles, then struggled to lift Old Dan onto the mare. He groaned, semiconscious, but did not struggle.

"We will have to proceed on foot," said Dorothea to Constance as they loaded the bundles on the Wrights' horse.

"At least we're across the creek."

"No thanks to me."

"Hey, now. We both thought this would work."

"We should have gone back to your farm and tried again another night. Those men would have eventually tired of their blockade—"

"Only if they'd moved on to searching houses. And where do you think they'd start? Liggett's already got his eye on you folks, and Abel and I are suspicious just because we're colored."

Dorothea nodded, but silently she berated herself and her poor judgment. She tugged on the mare's reins and ordered her forward, steadying Old Dan with her other hand. Constance walked behind her leading her own horse. Liza followed with the children.

With only the moon and a single lantern to light their way, they made slow progress through the forest. Dorothea led them in a wide arc to avoid the cleared acres and Mr. Liggett's cabin. Old Dan drifted in and out of awareness. Hannah struggled bravely to keep up with the adults, but Liza, Dorothea, and Constance took turns carrying her younger sister.

Suddenly, Hannah piped, "Are we lost?"

"No," said Dorothea emphatically. "Not in the least. This is not the way we intended to travel, but we will reach our destination nevertheless."

She gave the child a reassuring grin and was rewarded with a flicker of a worried smile.

But the journey was long. Dorothea estimated that they would need the better part of two hours to cross Mr. Liggett's land, and her heart sank with dismay, though she kept her true feelings hidden from those who followed her.

At long last, they left Liggett's woods and emerged into a clearing, the border of Two Bears Farm. They climbed a fence and stepped out onto cultivated fields, wide and gently rolling terrain, but clear of underbrush. Their passage would be swifter, but their footprints would be easy to follow in the freshly plowed earth. The open field offered them no protection, no place to hide.

In the moonlight Dorothea studied the white house, alone on the hill. The two lights in the windows had been extinguished, and yet the house seemed a haven.

In a low voice meant for Constance's ears alone, she said, "At this pace, we will not reach the station before daybreak."

Constance indicated the forest with a jerk of her head. "Maybe we can build a fire, make a shelter with branches. Hide out 'til tomorrow night."

"On Mr. Liggett's land? What will we do if he comes home and finds the wagon tonight?"

Constance shuddered, and Dorothea knew she had thought of that. For all they knew Mr. Liggett had already discovered the scene of the accident. He might at that moment be in pursuit.

Dorothea nodded to the house. "We can seek shelter here."

Constance shook her head. "This ain't a station no more. The Carters are long gone."

"Mr. Nelson will aid us."

"I thought you hated that man!"

"I don't. He—he's not a friend, but he is an abolitionist. I do not believe he will turn us away."

Constance halted, bringing the mare to a stop. She glanced back over her shoulder at Liza and the children, struggling several paces behind, exhausted. On the back of the mare, Old Dan slumped lifelessly. They would never make it to the Granger farm without rest.

"I reckon we don't have much choice," said Constance. "I guess . . . I guess we might as well pay a call on the schoolmaster."

They waited for Liza and the girls to catch up, then informed them of the latest change in plans. Liza's expression was haggard, but she nodded and passed her youngest daughter off to Constance. New hope quickened their pace, but Dorothea felt exposed and vulnerable in the open field. When they reached the road, she handed the reins to Liza, ran the last few yards to the porch stairs, and rapped upon the front door. She waited, listening, and knocked a second time, louder. She heard movement within, and after what seemed to be an interminable wait, the door swung open.

"Miss Granger?" Mr. Nelson, clad in trousers and an open shirt, fumbled to put on his glasses. "What on earth brings you here at this hour?"

"A desperate need for your help." She stepped aside and allowed him to observe the party now gathered at the foot of the porch stairs. Constance had helped Old Dan down from the mare, and he mustered his strength to stand, grasping the porch railing for support.

Dorothea heard Mr. Nelson's slow intake of breath. "Runaways, I presume."

She nodded. "We lost our wagon, and as you can see, we have an injured man and children. We cannot go on." Her voice faltered. "I would not ask it of you—of anyone—except I know what you have done elsewhere. I know what you suffered for your compassion."

His expression was unreadable. "Then you know what I will suffer if I am caught helping you."

She hesitated before nodding.

He opened the door and stepped out. Uncomprehending, she moved aside and watched as he descended the stairs. "Take them inside," he told her. "I will return shortly."

He took the horses' reins and led them toward the barn.

Dorothea tore her gaze away from him and beckoned the others. "Inside. Quickly."

DOROTHEA SWIFTLY MADE A fire in the front room fireplace while Constance helped Old Dan, groaning, to the sofa. Liza helped her daughters from their wraps and drew them closer to warm themselves by the fire. Constance dug into one of the bundles and passed around jerky and johnnycake while Dorothea went to the kitchen in search of water. She found a pan of milk and snatched it up as well. The kitchen window looked out upon the southwestern fields they had crossed; Dorothea spared one anxious glance outside before returning to the front room.

The children drank deeply of the milk and ate even the last crumbs Constance rationed out to them. Dorothea tended to Old Dan's injuries as best she knew how. He did not appear to have any broken bones, his cuts and bruises appeared minor, but he had taken a hard fall, and she knew he might suffer from internal wounds. He refused to eat, but gulped the water only to cough most of it back up. She was encouraged by his responses to her questions about the whereabouts of his pain, not only so that she could tend to him but also because they proved the blow to his skull had not addled his mind.

Even so, Old Dan would need time to recover and more medical attention than she could provide. Jonathan would have known what to do for him, but Jonathan was hundreds of miles away.

Dorothea covered the injured man with a quilt folded over the back of the sofa and held his hand until he drifted off to sleep. By the time Mr. Nelson returned from the barn, the children, too, had fallen asleep, curled up under quilts on the floor near their mother. Without a word Mr. Nelson beckoned her from the doorway. She rose and followed him into the kitchen.

"I hardly know where to begin," he said. He kept his voice low enough so that the others would not hear.

"If you mean to scold me, it is a little late for that."

"It would not do any good, anyway." He removed his glasses and rubbed at his eyes, sighing. "You had best tell me everything."

She could not tell him everything, but she told him as much as she dared, including the events of that night. His eyebrows shot up when she described the blockade at the ferry, and she waited for a caustic remark about Cyrus Pearson, but none came. When she told him of the accident with the wagon, his expression darkened.

"How far off the main road is the wagon?" he asked.

"Ten yards, if that. But the gully provides some concealment, especially in the dark."

"If a trail of broken branches does not lead Mr. Liggett right to it."

She had thought of that, too, but it could not be helped. "We must put our trust in Providence—and our faith in Mr. Liggett's foolishness."

"Quite right. I would not peg him as a crack scout." Mr. Nelson almost smiled. "Let us arrange it so that your friends are well out of harm's way before he stumbles upon the latest wagon to overturn on his property."

"Mr. Nelson—" She hardly knew what to say. "I cannot thank you enough for your kindness."

"That is true, so you need not bother trying." He nodded toward the front room. "We should not disturb the old man now that he is asleep, but I will show the rest of you to more comfortable rooms upstairs."

"I will remain below to stand watch."

"Indeed you shall not. You need your rest if you are to lead your party onward tomorrow night."

"But what if—"

"I will stand watch, Miss Granger." He replaced his glasses, folded his arms, and regarded her with what she took to be weary tolerance. "I could not sleep a wink in any event. Not all of us are as accustomed to such excitement as you are."

"No, I suppose not," she murmured uncertainly. He sounded almost as if he were teasing her. "But there is another problem. My parents will worry if we do not arrive by daybreak."

"Will they worry enough to come searching for you?"

"I told them not to."

"But they may not obey their daughter. Very well. I will take word to them myself in the morning, but now I must insist that you rest."

Perhaps it was her fatigue, but his didactic manner did not bother her as much as it once had. She made sure Old Dan was comfortable before gently picking up Hannah. Constance gathered the younger sister in her arms, and together they and Liza followed Mr. Nelson upstairs to simply furnished but comfortable rooms.

Dorothea had one small room to herself. After bidding Mr. Nelson good night, she went inside, undressed to her shift, and was about to climb into bed when she realized that the window faced the southwest.

She went to the window and looked out. The open fields that had so unnerved her as she and Constance led the runaways to the house now provided them protection; neither Mr. Liggett nor Cyrus nor any of their ilk could approach the house unseen. Beyond them, the woods stood dark and silent and still.

She closed the curtains and returned to bed, drawing the quilt over herself. She thought worry and the unfamiliar room would keep her awake, but fatigue soon overcame her and she sank into sleep.

THE ROOM WAS STILL dark when a hand seized her shoulder and shook her awake. "Miss Granger." Mr. Nelson's voice was low and urgent. "Riders from the southwest."

Immediately she threw back the covers and snatched up her dress from the bedside chair. Mr. Nelson disappeared into the hallway to rouse the others. Dorothea swiftly dressed and met him and Constance in the largest bedroom, where Liza was waking the children.

"Stay away from the windows and make no sound," said Mr. Nelson. Just then a heavy fist pounded on the front door below. Hannah gasped. Her sister buried her face in her mother's skirt.

"Nelson," bellowed Mr. Liggett. "We know they're inside."

"Send 'em out and we won't hold you accountable," shouted another man, an unfamiliar voice. Dorothea wished she dared peer out a window to see if Cyrus was among the riders.

As calmly as if the men were guests for tea, Mr. Nelson wiped his glasses and straightened his shirt. "I will have to answer."

"No." Dorothea seized his arm. "They will force their way inside."

"No, they will not." He placed his hand over hers, then released himself from her grasp and left the room.

"Under the bed," Constance ordered. Liza and the children scrambled beneath it while Dorothea and Constance adjusted the quilts to best conceal them. With a flash of terror, Dorothea remembered Old Dan. She fled the room and raced downstairs—only to discover the elderly man nowhere in sight. Mr. Nelson stood before the front door with a rifle cradled in the crook of one arm. He looked over his shoulder at the sound of her footfalls and raised a finger to his lips in warning. She halted at the foot of the stairs, clutching the post, heart racing.

"Nelson." The pounding shook the door, rattling the heavy wooden bolt Mr. Nelson had lowered across it. "We ain't fools. I found the wagon on my land."

His voice steel, Mr. Nelson called back, "My wagon is in my barn."

"So is Dorothea Granger's horse."

This voice was cold and deadly calm, and one Dorothea knew well. A chill prickled down her spine. Cyrus.

Mr. Nelson shifted his weight and adjusted his grip on the rifle, and Dorothea knew he recognized the speaker. He turned to her and said dryly, "My apologies for the damage I am about to do to your reputation." He faced the door again and called out, "Miss Granger is my guest. Since you are engaged to another, it is not any business of yours."

"Don't listen to him. Everyone knows them Grangers help runaways," complained Mr. Liggett.

"Shut up, Liggett," ordered Cyrus. Then, in a kinder tone, he called, "Dorothea, I know you're listening. You're a smart girl. I saw you turn away from the ferry. You know you can't escape. Just give up the runaways and we can all share in the reward."

Mr. Nelson quickly held up a hand to warn her not to answer, but her throat was too constricted for speech.

"That's comin' out of your portion," said a fourth man sharply. "I ain't sharing my reward with them nigger lovers."

"Shut up," barked Cyrus.

Heartsick with dread, Dorothea sank to a seat on the bottom step as the door trembled beneath a man's fist. There had to be another way out. Perhaps if they crept out of a back window, carried the children, sprinted for the cover of the oak grove—but even at a dead run, they had acres to cross. Pursuers on horseback would overtake them easily. And what of Old Dan?

The pounding on the door ceased; the men's voices fell silent. Mr. Nelson turned his head sharply, and Dorothea glimpsed a flicker of a torch as its bearer passed a window. She bolted to her feet.

Mr. Nelson crossed the room in two strides and grasped her arm. "Listen carefully," he said. "Get the others and go into the cellar. Old Dan is already hiding below. In the northeast corner you will find a stack of crates. They conceal a tunnel that will lead you from the house to the barn. Leave the barn by way of the smaller door, on the north side, and go to the ditch nearby. Keep low and follow the contour of the slope all the way to the strand of oaks. Keep running if you can, hide if you must."

"Old Dan cannot run."

"He will have to try." Mr. Nelson handed her the rifle so suddenly that she stumbled from its weight. "Do you know how to use this?"

"Of course."

"Then get moving. I will hold them off as long as I can."

"No." Dorothea shoved the rifle back at him. Surprised, he took it. "I could not fire upon a man, not even those men."

"Don't be a fool." He tried to return the weapon, but she drew back. "It may save your life."

"I cannot run carrying both it and one of the children. You will have greater need of it here."

Without another word Dorothea fled upstairs for Constance and the others. She repeated Mr. Nelson's instructions as they raced downstairs and into the kitchen.

"Nelson," came another shout from outside. "Open up or we'll smoke you out!"

Dorothea tore open the cellar door and sent the others racing ahead of her. She spared one last look for Mr. Nelson. He stalked through the front room, grasp tight upon the rifle, as the furious shouts from outside revealed the men's positions. They seemed to have encircled the house.

Glass shattered as a torch smashed through a window near the front door. Immediately Mr. Nelson was upon it, stomping out the flames. He glanced up and spotted her frozen in the doorway.

"Go," he shouted.

She gasped and descended into the cellar, closing the door behind her.

The air smelled of damp earth. Dorothea stumbled down the stairs blindly. When her eyes adjusted to the darkness illuminated by a single lantern below, she found that Constance had uncovered the entrance to the tunnel. Liza entered in a crouch, still carrying her youngest; Hannah followed on her heels. When Dorothea reached them, Constance had taken Old Dan by the arm and was cajoling him to hasten after them, but he shook his head and pawed at her hand.

"I won't make it," he said. "Just let me be."

"You can't give up now," cried Dorothea.

"I ain't givin' up." With an effort he tore free from Constance and stood proudly, defiantly, before the two women. "I can't run. You can see that plain as day. Somebody's got to put those crates back or those men'll know just where you went."

"I will stay," said Dorothea. She could not leave him to that fate. "They will not hurt me as they would you."

Quietly, Constance said, "No, Dorothea."

"But I cannot—"

"You have to lead us. You're the only one who knows the way." Constance came forward and kissed the man on the cheek. "You're a brave soul, Old Dan." She darted into the tunnel with the lantern.

Overcome, Dorothea hugged him and whispered a word of thanks before following.

The tunnel was low and cramped, braced every few feet by old wooden beams, too narrow to move through except in single file. Dorothea's short stature allowed her to move more easily than the others, save Hannah, and she soon caught up to the group. Constance's lantern bobbed and threw shadows on the earthen walls as they proceeded as swiftly as they dared. Roots brushed Dorothea's cheeks; the soles of her boots slid over dirt and loose stones. The noises from the house cut off abruptly as the crates slid back into place behind them. Dorothea said a silent prayer for Old Dan and urged the others onward.

"I see light ahead," called Liza, in the lead. A few feet later, the tunnel abruptly ended at a makeshift wall of wooden planks. They listened in fearful silence for noises from without, but heard only the whicker of a horse and a cow's low moo. Dorothea scrambled to the front of the group and shoved the planks aside. She peered out cautiously before leading the others from the tunnel. They emerged into an empty horse stall. Uncle Jacob's mare looked down upon her from the next stall and whinnied in recognition.

Dorothea spotted the smaller of two doors and led the others to it. She stole a glance outside before opening the door wide enough for the others to emerge. Constance snatched up Hannah and led the way across the dirt road to the ditch. Liza followed carrying her youngest daughter, and Dorothea brought up the rear. Outside the barn, they could again hear the threats the men shouted at Mr. Nelson's closed door. From the edge of the ditch Dorothea permitted herself one look back. In the light of their flickering torches she recognized the thin, hunched figure of Mr. Liggett, the straight, proud back of Cyrus Pearson. Cyrus stood at the front door, posed as if for a portrait with a hand at his lapel and the other gesturing as he called to Mr. Nelson within. A third man crouched low beneath one of the windows, creeping closer. Cyrus nodded and waved him forward. The other man came even nearer to the window, then lifted his rifle as he rose up on his heels—

"Thomas," Dorothea screamed, but her voice was drowned out by the gunshot.

She had time to witness the men's raucous cheers before hands seized her and dragged her down. "Run," Constance said in her ear.

She struggled to stand. "But Thomas—Old Dan—"

"We can't help them no more." Constance held her fast. "Liza and the girls we can help."

Muffling a sob, Dorothea ran along the ditch after Liza and her daughters. She dared not look back, not even after they reached the safety of the oak grove. They paused only long enough to catch their breath before Dorothea picked up Hannah and urged the others onward. Their entrance unencumbered now, Cyrus and Liggett would search the house and find Old Dan and do to him what they had done to Thomas.

Not ten minutes later, just as they crossed into the Craigmiles' land, the women stopped short at the sound of another gunshot. Liza pressed a hand to her mouth to muffle a cry. Dorothea shook with rage and fear as she whispered a prayer for Old Dan's soul.

"Come," she said, shifting Hannah to her back. "We must make haste."

She could not lead them to the Granger farm. When the riders finished searching Mr. Nelson's house, if they did not find the tunnel, they would think of Uncle Jacob's mare and come after Dorothea, thinking she would flee for the safety of home.

She led them instead across the Craigmile farm to the Shropshires' land, moving always under cover of the trees, shying away from roads and open land. She guided her companions north and east through the maple grove to the old worm fence, which they followed north along the border of the Granger farm to the Wheelers' land. She led them northeastward along the Indian trail to the creek, no longer locked in ice and running swiftly, swollen from recent rains. All the while, to keep her spirits up so that she could in turn encourage the others, to block out images of Two Bears Farm from her thoughts, she pictured the Sugar Camp Quilt and the landmarks she had concealed within its stitches. The Crooked Ladder block. The Sideways Braid. The Drunkard's Creek. The Water Wheel. The patchwork clues would guide her to safety as they had guided others before her.

They walked west along the creek, taking turns carrying the exhausted children. Behind them the sky turned velvet blue, then violet, then rose. The stars faded. Dorothea urged her companions to hurry, but she knew they had drawn on their last reserves of strength to make it that far. They had nothing left to speed their steps.

It was almost dawn when at last the houses and storefronts of

Woodfall came into view. Then she spied the water wheel and the bridge beyond.

"Stay hidden until I summon you," she instructed as she found them a hiding place within a copse of bushes not far from the foot of the bridge. Alone, she crossed the bridge and surveyed the scene. Only when she was sure they could pass undetected did she beckon the others. Liza and Constance, the children in their arms, found new strength with their destination so near, and they fairly ran across the bridge. When they reached her, Dorothea turned and ran for the millhouse. She did not pause to knock on the door; she did not think to be sure all was safe within. Only as she swung open the door and ushered the others inside did she think that perhaps their pursuers had taken the road and arrived before them. Perhaps they waited within. But she had remembered caution too late to call back the others, too late to do anything but enter the station.

The miller and his wife looked up from the breakfast table as Dorothea and her companions burst through the door. A fire crackled merrily on the hearth. They were alone.

"Mercy," exclaimed Mrs. Braun, setting down a serving plate with a clatter. "Shut the door before you are seen!"

Dorothea slammed the door and leaned upon it, breathless, closing her eyes to hold back tears of exhaustion and grief.

Mrs. Braun rushed to attend to them.

"You're safe now," said the miller, his deep voice low and reassuring.

Safe, Dorothea thought dully. Liza and her daughters were safe, but not Old Dan, who had given his life to conceal their escape route.

Nor was Thomas Nelson.

Chapter Eleven

WHEN DOROTHEA GASPED that their pursuers might be close behind, Mrs. Braun quickly ushered them from the residence into the mill. There, in an empty storeroom hidden behind a door fashioned from stacks of barrels, she told them to hide until she could be certain it was safe to emerge. A small, high window provided sufficient light and fresh air, but since it looked out upon the river almost directly behind the water wheel, Mrs. Braun assured them they were in no danger of being observed.

Dorothea helped Liza put the children to bed on the low pallets draped with layers of quilts, then sank down to rest, closing her eyes against tears. She could not drive from her thoughts her last glimpse of Two Bears Farm—the man crouched outside Thomas's window, Cyrus's slow, almost indifferent gesture, the rifle shot.

Not long after showing them to the hiding place, Mrs. Braun returned with food and drink. Dorothea drank a dipperful of water, but her stomach turned at the thought of food. The women spoke little, overcome with exhaustion and the instinct for silence, though the rumbling of the mill would have drowned out any sound quieter than a shout.

An hour later, Mrs. Braun returned a second time and closed the door behind her. "If anyone is chasing you, they are taking their time about it," she said, taking a seat on the wooden floor. "But just in case, you should stay hidden. While we wait, you can tell me what happened today."

But Liza spoke first. "Paul and Jack—did they make it here safe?"

"They did, and they moved on a few nights ago. They told me the rest of their group included a woman, an old man, and two children, and that they would arrive by wagon." Her tone softened. "What has become of the old man?"

Liza's face crumpled in anguish. She turned away.

"I believe he was shot," said Dorothea softly, her voice catching in her throat. "He and . . . a man who tried to help us."

She told Mrs. Braun what had befallen them since leaving the Wright farm.

DOROTHEA AND CONSTANCE STAYED with the Brauns two days and nights. After the first day, Dorothea no longer remained within the hiding place during the day but instead helped Mrs. Braun with her chores in the adjacent house.

While they worked, they made plans for their remaining three passengers. Both Mr. and Mrs. Braun thought it too great a risk to proceed with Abel Wright's original plan for Liza to pose as a free colored woman traveling with her children. She would still carry Dorothea's forged papers in case they were apprehended, but she and her daughters would travel to the next station concealed in Mr. Braun's wagon. The stationmaster there was an innkeeper with ample space for Liza and her girls, and if Liza were spied by a guest, she would easily blend in among his many colored employees. In fact, Mrs. Braun said, runaways were safer there than anywhere in central Pennsylvania. Southerners had learned to spend the night elsewhere after too many of their slaves had been persuaded by the inn's employees to make an escape while their masters slept comfortably upstairs.

Liza and her daughters would remain at the inn until the stationmaster could be certain that their pursuers had lost the trail. Then they would be integrated back into the underground network and guided north through New York State and into Canada.

On the morning of the third day, Dorothea and Constance said farewell to Liza and her daughters and walked back to the Granger farm. They followed the main road as Dorothea had done after her first journey to the Brauns' mill. If they should encounter Cyrus and Mr. Liggett, they would claim to have been visiting a friend and deny any knowledge of the events at Two Bears Farm.

They were nearly a quarter of a mile from Dorothea's house when her parents came running to meet them on the road.

Lorena's cheeks were wet with tears as she embraced her daughter. The Grangers and Abel Wright had been frantic with worry wondering what had become of them and the fugitives in their care. "We hoped for the best," said Lorena, linking her arms through those of her daughter and Constance as they walked back to the house. "Abel found scuffed footprints in the dirt outside the barn, but when he discovered the team still within, he could not determine whether you had left those tracks upon departing the barn, or if Mr. Nelson had left them there earlier when he took the horses inside."

"Liggett and Pearson came by here looking for you that morning," said Robert. "We knew you had sense enough to stay away, so we told them you were off caring for a sick friend."

Dorothea almost managed a smile. "Another sick friend."

"Of course they did not believe us, but what could they do?" said Lorena. "Now tell us, how are your passengers faring?"

Dorothea took a deep breath. "You know, of course, that Old Dan stayed behind."

"Yes, we know." Lorena put an arm around her shoulder and hugged her comfortingly. "It was a courageous and noble act to sacrifice his freedom for that of Liza and her daughters."

"Sacrifice his life, you mean," said Constance.

"Why, no, although I suppose in a sense they are one and the same." When Dorothea and Constance regarded her in confusion, Lorena said, "Cyrus Pearson's loathsome associates captured Old Dan. Mr. Nelson could not say for certain which direction they took after they left Two Bears Farm, but we assume they will return Old Dan to his master. It is a grievous reward for his sacrifice."

Dorothea stopped short. "Mr. Nelson lives?"

"He is badly injured, but he will recover." Lorena's gaze was piercing. "You did not know."

"No." Dorothea felt faint with gratitude. "We heard two shots. We thought—I thought the first ended Mr. Nelson's life, and the second, Old Dan's."

"No, my dear, no." Lorena held her firmly or Dorothea's knees might have given way. "The first shot struck Mr. Nelson in the shoulder, and after that, he was incapable of preventing the men from entering the house. They left Mr. Nelson barely conscious and bleeding on the floor, searched the house, and found Old Dan in the basement. They dragged the poor soul from the house and lashed him to a horse, but before they could continue the search, Abel Wright came upon the scene and fired a warning shot. Though they outnumbered him four to one, the men fled with their single prisoner. Mr. Wright bound Mr. Nelson's wounds and tended him until he was assured he would not bleed to death. Only then did he ride off to fetch Dr. Bremigan."

"The doctor says he lost a lot of blood, but he should make a full recovery," added Robert. "I don't see how he will be able to finish out the school year, though. You might expect the school board to ask you to take over the whole school, Dorothea."

Dorothea nodded, but she thought of Cyrus and Mrs. Engle and could not imagine that Mr. Engle, the school board president, would appoint her. Unless the entire town united against Cyrus, Mr. Liggett, and their slavecatcher associates, she was unlikely to teach for the Creek's Crossing school again.

Lorena must have guessed what she was thinking, for she said, "The story of Mr. Nelson's injury has spread throughout town already. News such as this cannot be kept quiet."

"What do folks say about what happened?" asked Constance. "I don't suppose they like the idea of my husband riding with a gun after a bunch of white men."

Dorothea's parents exchanged a look. Reluctantly, Lorena said, "The townspeople seem evenly divided between those who admire your husband for coming to Mr. Nelson's defense and those who fear his actions will inspire other free coloreds to take up arms against their white neighbors."

"So they're afraid my Abel might become another Nat Turner." Constance shook her head in disgust. "Folks in this town would side with slavecatchers and the local drunk before they side with a colored man, even though he's a farmer and a good man who saved one of their own. All that for a warning shot! What would they have done if he had killed one of 'em?"

"Let us just be thankful that he did not," said Lorena, but Constance scowled, her mouth set and brow furrowed in anger.

"There is much to be thankful for. If Mr. Wright had not come after you . . ." Robert shook his head. "He told us he had been restless and uneasy from the moment you two left in the wagon, so he decided to follow you. He was on the way to Creek's Crossing when he heard the gunshot from Two Bears Farm. If he had not come . . ."

Robert did not complete the thought, but Dorothea knew. Without Mr. Wright's curious inkling that all was not well, Mr. Nelson would have perished.

LORENA URGED CONSTANCE TO stay for dinner, but Constance was eager to return home to Abel. Robert hitched up Lorena's horse and offered to drive Constance home, but Dorothea quickly said that she would do it. Her parents were reluctant to let her go lest she run into Cyrus Pearson or Mr. Liggett, but Dorothea told them she could not avoid them for long in a town the size of Creek's Crossing, and she refused to let them frighten her. Lorena had said that the town was evenly divided, so Cyrus and Mr. Liggett had to know they did not have everyone's support. They could not do as they pleased without fear of the consequences. Dorothea knew Cyrus well enough to be sure that he would not risk raising a public outcry by assaulting two unarmed women.

Dorothea and Constance rode to the ferry. The pilot's eyes widened at the sight of them, but he helped them aboard without referring to the events at Two Bears Farm. Dorothea was tempted to ask him for his version just to see how repeated tellings had embellished and warped the truth, but she said nothing. Ignoring a rumor starved it of its strength, hastening its demise. It would be better for their future passengers if rumors about the Wrights' and Grangers' involvement with runaways subsided quickly.

They reached the opposite shore and continued through the streets of Creek's Crossing. Cyrus and Mr. Liggett had apparently abandoned their blockade. Dorothea noticed a few curious glances as they made their way west along Water Street, but no one called out to them, either to praise or to censure.

They passed the site of the new library. To the sounds of hammer and saw, men pulled on ropes and raised the board frame of the eastern wall. A breeze carried the scent of sawdust and fresh pine. Dorothea breathed deeply and imagined bookshelves filled with enlightening biographies, inspiring poetry, entrancing novels.

Thanks to Mr. Nelson, the Authors' Album quilt would be on display, perhaps hanging on a wall like a great work of art in a museum. She hoped that curiosity would draw new readers to the writings of the authors whose names adorned the quilt, the men and women whose inclusion had sparked such controversy. In the troubled times that were sure to come, she could not allow Mrs. Engle's caustic letters to the editor of the *Creek's Crossing Informer* to be the only influence shaping the minds and hearts and opinions of the people of the Elm Creek Valley.

They turned down Creekside Road and spotted Miss Nadelfrau approaching on the opposite sidewalk, her head down and shoulders hunched over a basket she carried in both arms. She cringed like a dog that expected to be beaten, but she looked up at the sound of the wagon and brightened to see Dorothea and Constance. She called out to them and waved; Dorothea pulled the bay to a halt and waited as Miss Nadelfrau ran across the street to meet them.

"This town is all abuzz about the two of you," she said breathlessly. "Of course, one cannot believe half of what one hears; it's too fantastic. Is it true you shot a slavecatcher?"

"Good heavens, no," exclaimed Dorothea.

"Pity. Be that as it may, I wanted to invite you—" Miss Nadelfrau nodded to Constance. "*Both* of you to an organizational meeting at the schoolhouse tomorrow evening."

"What are you organizing?" asked Constance.

"The Creek's Crossing Abolitionist Society," said Miss Nadelfrau proudly. "I assumed you two would be interested in participating."

Dorothea and Constance exchanged a look of surprise. "We would indeed," said Dorothea. "I think my parents would like to join, too."

"Please tell them they will be welcome." Miss Nadelfrau gave them a cheery wave. "Don't forget. Six o'clock sharp!"

Dorothea assured her they would come and chirruped to the horses.

"I thought she was going to leave town since Mrs. Engle bought her shop," said Constance.

Dorothea shrugged. "I suppose she found reason to stay."

Her heart rose as they turned southwest out of town.

When they arrived at the Wright farm, Abel ran to meet them and climbed into the wagon to embrace his wife rather than wait for her to descend. He held her so long and so tightly that eventually Constance had to ask him to ease up a bit because she could only hold her breath so long. He chuckled and released her, but Dorothea spied tears in his eyes, and he took Constance's hand to help her down from the wagon and held fast to it long after they had entered the house.

They asked about Old Dan, but Abel could tell them nothing more than what he had already told Dorothea's parents. Constance asked about Mr. Nelson; Dorothea held her breath until assured that he was on the mend, being cared for by his housekeeper, who still blamed herself for being away at her sister's that fateful night. "She thinks if she had been there, those men would never have dared to cause so much trouble," said Abel, shaking his head. "Nelson says she's a force to be reckoned with when she has a rolling pin in hand and a noble cause."

They shared a laugh at the image, but their merriment was subdued.

"I am glad you were able to frighten them off in her absence," said Dorothea to Abel. "To think that such violent men would turn tail at a warning shot."

Abel Wright regarded her with surprise. "Is that what folks think? Is that what they say?"

After a moment, Dorothea understood. "You mean to say that you missed."

"Not by much. Cyrus Pearson was using his horsewhip on Old Dan at the time or maybe I would have just fired in the air to get their attention. Instead I nicked the top of Cyrus's ear. I guess with all the blood he thought he was hit worse than he was, 'cause he yelled for his friends to mount up and run for the forest. They did, too, as if I was the devil himself with an army behind me." He laughed again, shaking his head. "A warning shot. I guess I did give him a warning, all right."

"Good thing you aren't sweet on him no more," said Constance to Dorothea. "He won't be quite so handsome with a piece of his ear missing."

The Wrights laughed, but there was an edge to their mirth, and Dorothea found herself unable to join in.

THE WRIGHTS INVITED DOROTHEA to stay to supper, but she remained only long enough to feed and water the horse. She still had one call to make before returning home.

Two men she did not recognize were working in the fields with a team of horses when Dorothea arrived at Two Bears Farm. She climbed down from the wagon and, almost without realizing she did so, smoothed her skirt and tucked a stray lock of brown hair back into her bonnet. She climbed the porch stairs and knocked on the door.

A short, motherly woman in a floury apron opened the door.

"Good afternoon," said Dorothea, smiling. "I am Dorothea Granger. I came to see how Mr. Nelson is doing."

"Of course. You're the schoolteacher," said the housekeeper. She opened the door and welcomed Dorothea inside. Dorothea removed her bonnet and smoothed her hair. "Mr. Nelson is in the parlor. I will take you to him."

Dorothea thanked her and followed her to the room where only a few days before, Old Dan, Liza, and the girls had warmed themselves by the fire. Mr. Nelson sat in an armchair by the window, a quilt tucked over his legs, an open book resting face down on his lap. His eyes were closed, his glasses folded and lying on a table at his left hand. She thought he was asleep and was about to quietly leave the room when his eyes opened and fixed on hers.

"A Miss Granger here to see you," said the housekeeper. She gave Dorothea a stern look as if to warn her not to tire her patient and announced that she would be in the kitchen.

"Miss Granger," said Mr. Nelson. He made an effort to sit up straighter, and he gestured to a chair. "Please sit down."

She drew closer but remained standing, wishing she had not come. He seemed so pale and ill; she should not have disturbed him. "I stopped by to see how you are faring. I am exceedingly glad that you were not killed."

"A more unusual greeting from a lady I have never received." He allowed his head to rest against the high back of the armchair. "The woman and her daughters?"

"They are safe."

"Good." He coughed, winced, and involuntarily reached for his shoulder.

"Are you in much pain?" she asked, and immediately wished she had not.

"The wound troubles me very little, thank you." He looked away, and she knew he was concealing the truth. "At any rate, I am in far better condition than I imagine Old Dan is at this moment."

Dorothea felt heartsick at the thought of the courageous man, and she had to force herself not to think of him as tears sprang into her eyes. She inhaled deeply, the words she had planned to speak lost to her. "If not for you, the others would have met his same fate. I am grateful to you beyond my ability to describe it. I— I cannot—"

Then in a rush she said, "Oh, Mr. Nelson, what is to become of you?"

His eyebrows rose. "I must look far worse than I feel to inspire such alarm."

"I do not mean your wound. I mean—your probation. A runaway slave was discovered in your home. You concealed and defended him."

"Not terribly well, as it happens."

"You did, and it is against the law." She pressed a hand to her stomach in a vain attempt to settle its fluttering. "Will you be sent to prison?"

"Ah." He smiled, faintly. "No need to worry. Two of the witnesses who might accuse me have fled with their captive, and the other two are too busy denouncing each other to waste breath on me."

"What do you mean? Mr. Pearson and Mr. Liggett—"

"Have had a falling out, according to my housekeeper, who has an ear for the gossip of the town. Mr. Liggett is a grasping and greedy man who has learned there is little money to be gained in Mr. Pearson's employ, while Mr. Pearson does not wish to have his name embroiled in a scandal or associated with a man as disreputable and universally disliked as Mr. Liggett. I do not fear that they will conspire to have me arrested."

Dorothea felt a dark cloud lift from her thoughts. "That is good news." She had expected both men to boast of their adventure, but if they had turned on each other, perhaps they would admit little rather than acknowledge their former friendship.

"It is, since I could do runaways little good from inside a prison." He touched his shoulder and pulled a face. "Next time, however, I will endeavor not to be shot."

"There . . . will be a next time?"

"Not another confrontation with slavecatchers, with any luck, but Two Bears Farm will assist any fugitives in need of shelter as long as the need remains. It would be a pity to let the Carters' tunnel go to waste." He looked away. "Especially since Old Dan sacrificed his life to conceal its existence."

Dorothea's throat tightened. "If only we could discover where he has been taken. Perhaps we could buy his freedom."

"Even if Pearson or Liggett knows, I doubt they could be compelled to tell you. They would likely deny his existence just as they deny the rest of the truth."

Dorothea nodded, reluctant to release the fleeting hope that she and her friends might somehow rescue Old Dan. But of course, they could expect no help from Mr. Liggett or Cyrus, no matter how viciously they had turned against each other. "If they deny what really happened," she asked, "how do they account for Cyrus's injury?"

Mr. Nelson smiled in grim satisfaction. "Liggett tells of being ambushed by a band of murderous runaway slaves. It is quite a fanciful tale, with himself at the heroic center. I doubt anyone believes him."

"And Mr. Pearson? Has your housekeeper heard his version?"

Mr. Nelson's smile vanished and his gaze fell upon the book on his lap. "She has." He lifted the book, marked his place with a scrap of paper, and set it on the table beside his glasses. "She cannot trace the rumor directly back to him, but it seems he would have people believe I shot him."

"You?" exclaimed Dorothea. "Well, I suppose it makes perfect sense. You would have been defending your household."

"That would indeed have made sense, which is probably why Pearson did not think of it. Apparently we fought over a woman." He paused. "Over you."

Dorothea's breath caught in her throat. "Me?"

"Evidently I became enraged when my rival appeared and

declared his undying affection for you." He snorted. "Have you ever heard anything so ridiculous?"

"No," said Dorothea softly. "No one will believe it."

"Pearson's fiancée does, but she seems to be the only one. In any event, his engagement is off, and I understand he intends to find solace for his broken heart in another tour of Europe." He made a sudden, impatient gesture to a chair. "Would you please sit down? Shall I call for some tea? I apologize for being such a poor host. When I think of what I said about you upon the occasion of our first meeting, I cannot consider myself deserving of this visit."

Dorothea forced a shaky laugh as she seated herself. "So much has happened since then, I hardly remember what words we might have exchanged."

"I cannot forget them."

Dorothea flushed and bowed her head. "I have forgotten them, so you must do the same. If we are to keep teaching together, we must attempt to be civil."

"I do not think I will teach again."

"What? Why not?"

He indicated his shoulder wearily. "The term will be over before I am fit to stand all day in front of a classroom, and whatever version of recent events he chooses to believe, I doubt that the stepfather of Cyrus Pearson will be inclined to renew my contract."

"I expect the same for my own contract."

"They will have to allow you to finish out the school year. There is no one else." Mr. Nelson regarded her steadily. "You are a fine teacher, Miss Granger."

"And you are a fine man," said Dorothea. "When I think of all the trouble I have caused you, I regret coming to your door that night."

"Don't. Three people are closer to freedom because of it."

"I wonder why you did not hesitate to let us in, why you did not send us away."

"Do you?" He held her gaze, but his expression was unreadable. "Surely you know I could deny you nothing."

Dorothea did not know what to say.

He cleared his throat. "I am not the sort of man to make pretty speeches. I have always been straightforward with you, and I would ask the same in return."

She managed a nod. "Of course."

"You are too good to trifle with me. While I deserve nothing but your continued enmity—"

"That is not so," said Dorothea. "Where would I have gone that night if not for you? What would I have done?"

"It is only because you knew that you could come here that I speak of this at all. Your knock on the door, the trust you placed in me that night, gave me hope that perhaps you have forgiven me. Perhaps your opinion of me has changed."

"It has changed," said Dorothea fervently. "My opinion has changed—utterly."

"Then I am relieved that we may call ourselves friends." His head fell back against the chair again, and he regarded her in silence for a long moment. "I wonder if I might hope to someday make you love me."

His eyes, large and boyish without his glasses, were full of such affection and longing that she found herself unable to do anything but warm herself in his gaze.

Then she knelt on the floor beside him, brushed the hair from his forehead, and took his hand.

"I would not dream of discouraging such hopes," she said, and pressed his hand to her cheek.